The Martians

The Martians

KIM STANLEY ROBINSON

BANTAM BOOKS
New York • Toronto • London • Sydney • Auckland

THE MARTIANS

A Bantam Spectra Book / September 1999

SPECTRA and the portrayal of a boxed "s" are trademarks of Bantam Books, a division of Random House, Inc.

Book design by Casey Hampton.

ISBN 0-553-80117-1

Published simultaneously in the United States and Canada

Bantam Books are published by Bantam Books, a division of Random House, Inc. Its trademark, consisting of the words "Bantam Books" and the portrayal of a rooster, is Registered in U.S. Patent and Trademark Office and in other countries. Marca Registrada. Bantam Books, 1540 Broadway, New York, New York 10036.

PRINTED IN THE UNITED STATES OF AMERICA

Contents

The Martians

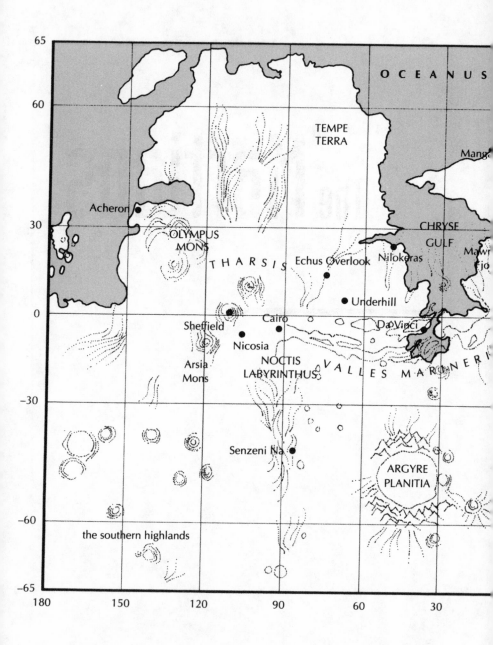

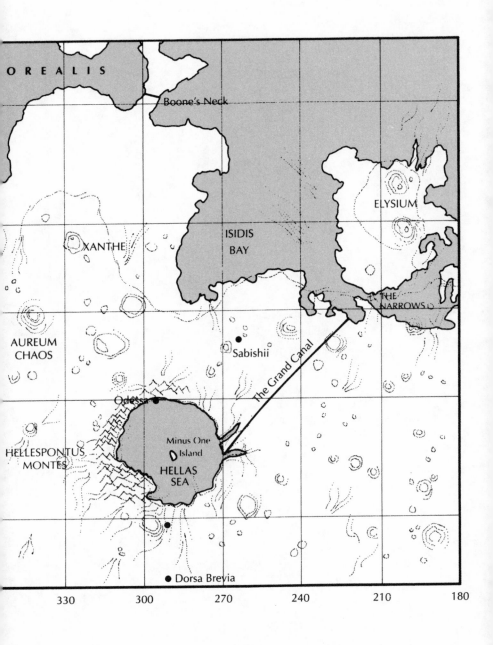

BOREALIS

Boone's Neck

ELYSIUM

XANTHE

ISIDIS BAY

THE NARROWS

AUREUM CHAOS

Sabishii

The Grand Canal

Odessa

HELLESPONTUS MONTES

Minus One Island

HELLAS SEA

Dorsa Brevia

330   300   270   240   210   180

Michel in Antarctica

At first it was fine. The people were nice. Wright Valley was awesome. Each day Michel woke in his cubicle and looked out his little window (everyone had one) at the frozen surface of Lake Vanda, a flat oval of cracked blue ice, flooding the bottom of the valley. The valley itself was brown and big and deep, its great rock sidewalls banded horizontally. Seeing it all, he felt a little thrill and the day began well.

There was always a lot to do. They had been dropped there in the largest of the Antarctic dry valleys with a load of disassembled huts and, for immediate occupancy, Scott tents. Their task through the perpetual day of the Antarctic summer was to build their winter home, which on assembly had turned out to be a fairly substantial and luxurious modular array of interconnected red boxes. In many ways it seemed analogous to what the voyagers would be doing when they arrived on Mars, and so of course to Michel it was all very interesting.

There were 158 people there, and only a hundred were going to be sent on the first trip out, to establish a permanent colony. This was the plan as designed by the Americans and Russians, who had then convened an international team to implement it. So this stay in Antarctica was a kind of test, or winnowing. But it seemed to Michel that everyone there assumed he or she would be among the chosen, so there was little of the tension one saw in people doing job interviews. As they said, when it was discussed at all—in other words when Michel asked about it—some candidates were going to drop out, others would be invalided out, and others placed on later trips to Mars, at worst. So there was no reason to worry. Most of the people there were not worriers anyway—they were capable, brilliant, assured, used to success. Michel worried about this.

They finished building their winter home by the fall equinox, March 21. After that the alternation of day and night was dramatic, the brilliant slanted light of the days ending with the sun sliding off to the north and over the Olympus Range, the long twilights leading to a black starry darkness that eventually would be complete, and last for months. At their latitude, perpetual night would begin a little after mid-April. The constellations as they revealed themselves were the stars of another sky, foreign and strange to a northerner like Michel, reminding him that the universe was a big place. Each day was shorter than the one before by a palpable degree, and the sun burned lower through the sky, its beams pouring down between the peaks of the Asgaard and Olympus Ranges like vibrant stagelights. People got to know each other.

When they were first introduced, Maya had said, "So you are to evaluate us!"—with a look that seemed to suggest this could be a process that went both ways. Michel had been impressed. Frank Chalmers, looking over Maya's shoulder at him, had seen this.

They were a mix of personality types, as one might expect. But they all had the basic social skillfulness that had allowed them to make it this far, so that whether outgoing or withdrawn in their basic nature, they could still all talk easily. They were interested in each other, naturally. Michel saw a lot of relationships beginning to bloom around him. Romances too. Of course.

To Michel all the women in camp were beautiful. He fell a little in love with a lot of them, as was his practice always. Men he loved as elder brothers, women as goddesses he could never quite court (fortunately). Yes: Every woman was beautiful, and all men were heroes. Unless of course they weren't. But most were; this was humanity's default state. So Michel felt; he always had. It was an emotional setting that cried out for psychoanalysis, and in fact he had undergone analysis, without changing this feeling a bit (fortunately). It was his take on people, as he had said to his therapists. Naive, credulous, obtusely optimistic—and yet it made him a good clinical psychologist. It was his gift.

Tatiana Durova, for instance, he thought as gorgeous as any movie star, with also that intelligence and individuality that derived from life lived in the real world of work and community. Michel loved Tatiana.

And he loved Hiroko Ai, a remote and charismatic human being, withdrawn into her own affairs, but kind. He loved Ann Clayborne, a Martian already. He loved Phyllis Boyle, sister to Machiavel. He loved Ursula Kohl like the sister he could always talk to. He loved Rya Jimenez for her black hair and bright smile, he loved Marina Tokareva for her tough logic, he loved Sasha Yefremova for her irony.

But most of all he loved Maya Toitovna, who was as exotic to him as Hiroko, but more extroverted. She was not as beautiful as Tatiana, but drew the eye. The natural leader of the Russian contingent, and a bit forbidding—dangerous somehow—watching everyone there in much the same way Michel was, though he was pretty sure she was a tougher judge of people. Most of the Russian men seemed to fear her, like mice under a hawk, or maybe it was that they feared falling hopelessly in love with her. If Michel were going to Mars (he was not), she was the one he would be most interested in.

Of course Michel, as one of the four psychologists there to help evaluate the candidates, could not act on any of these affections. That did not bother him; on the contrary he liked the constraint, which was the same he had with any of his clients. It allowed him to indulge his thoughts without having to consider acting on them. "If you don't act on it, it wasn't a true feeling"—maybe the old saying was right, but if you were forbidden to act for good reasons, then your feelings might not be false after all. So he could be both true and safe. Besides, the saying was wrong, love for one's fellow humans could be a matter of contemplation only. There was nothing wrong with it.

Maya was quite certain she was going to Mars. Michel therefore represented no threat to her, and she treated him like a perfect equal. Several others were like her in this respect—Vlad, Ursula, Arkady, Sax, Spencer, a few others. But Maya took matters beyond that; she was intimate from the very start. She would sit and talk to him about anything, including the selection process itself. They spoke English when they talked, their partial competence and strong accents making for a picturesque music.

"You must be using the objective criteria for selecting people, the psychological profiles and the like."

"Yes, of course. Tests of various kinds, as you know. Various indexes."

"But your own personal judgments must count too, right?"

"Yes. Of course."

"But it must be hard to separate out your personal feelings about people from your professional judgments, yes?"

"I suppose."

"How do you do it?"

"Well . . . I suppose you would say it is a habit of mind. I like people, or whatever, for different reasons to the reasons that might make someone good on a project like this."

"For what reasons do you like people?"

"Well, I try not to be too analytical about that! You know—it's a danger in my job, becoming too analytical. I try to let my own feelings alone, as long as they aren't bothering me somehow."

She nodded. "Very sensible, I'm sure. I don't know if I could manage that. I should try. It's all the same to me. That's not always good. Not appropriate." With a quick sidelong smile at him.

She would say anything to him. He thought about this, and decided that it was a matter of their respective situations: Since he was staying behind, and she was going (she seemed so sure), it didn't much matter what she said to him. It was as if he were dying to her, and she therefore giving herself to him, openly, as a farewell gift.

But he wanted her to care about what she said to him.

On April 18 the sun went away. In the morning it sparked in the east, shining directly up the valley for a minute or two, and then with a faint green flash it slipped behind Mount Newell. After that the dark days had midday twilights, shorter every day; then just night. Starry starry night. It was beyond Martian, this constant darkness—living by starlight with the aching cold outside, experiencing sensory deprivation in everything but one's sense of cold. Michel, a Provençal, found that he hated both the cold and the dark. So did many of the others. They had been living in an Antarctic summer, thinking life was good and that Mars would not be such a challenge after all, and then with winter they were suddenly getting a better idea of what Mars would be like—not exactly, but in the sense of experiencing a massive array of deprivations. It was sobering how hard it hit.

Of course some did better than others. Some seemed not even to notice. The Russians had experienced cold and dark almost like this before. Tolerance of confinement was also good among the senior scientists—Sax Russell, Vlad Taneev, Marina Tokareva, Ursula Kohl, Ann Clayborne—these and other dedicated scientists seemed to have the capacity to spend great amounts of their time reading, working at their computers, and talking. Presumably lives spent largely in labs had prepared them.

They also understood that this was the life Mars was waiting to give them. Something not that different from the lives they had always led. So that the best analogy to Mars, perhaps, was not Antarctica, but any intense scientific laboratory.

This led him to thoughts of the optimum life history when considering inclusion in the group: middle-aged lab scientist, dedicated, accomplished; childless; unmarried or divorced. Lots of applicants fit the criteria. In some ways you had to wonder. Though it wouldn't be fair; it was a life pattern with its own integrity, its own rewards. Michel himself fit the bill in every respect.

Naturally he had to divide his attention equally among all of the candidates, and he did. But one day he got to accompany Tatiana Durova alone, on a hike up the South Fork of Wright Valley. They hiked to the left of the flat-topped island ridge called the Dais that divided the valley lengthwise, and continued up the southern arm of Wright Valley to Don Juan Pond.

Don Juan Pond: What a name for this extraterrestrial desolation! The pond was so salty that it would not freeze until the air chilled to -54 C; then the ice coating the shallow saline pond, having been distilled by the freezing, would be freshwater ice, and so would not thaw again until the temperature rose above zero, usually in the following summer when trapped sunlight would greenhouse in the water under the ice and melt it from below. As Tatiana explained the process it hovered in Michel's mind as some kind of analogy to their own situation, hanging right on the edge of his understanding but never coming clear.

"Anyway," she was saying, "scientists can use the pond as a single-setting minimum-temperature thermometer. Come here in the spring and you know immediately if the previous winter has gotten below minus fifty-four."

As it had already, some cold night this fall; a layer of white ice sheeted the pond. Michel stood with Tatiana on the whitish, humped, salt-crusted shore. Over the Dais the noon sky was blue-black. Around them the steep valley walls fell to the floor of the canyon. Large dark boulders stuck out of the pond's ice sheet.

Tatiana walked out onto the white surface, plunging through it with every step, boots crackling, water splashing—liquid salt water, spilling over the fresh ice, dissolving it and sending up a thin frost smoke. A vision: the Lady of the Lake, become corporeal and thus too heavy to walk on water.

But the pond was only a few centimeters deep, it barely covered the tops of her thick boots. Tatiana reached down and touched the tip of one gloved finger into the water, pulled up her mask to taste the water with her impossibly beautiful mouth—which puckered to a tight square. Then she threw back her head and laughed. "My God! Come taste, Michel, but just a touch, I warn you. It's terrible!"

And so he clomped through the ice and over the wet sand floor of the pond, stepping awkwardly, a bull in a china shop.

"It's fifty times saltier than the sea, taste it."

Michel reached down, put his forefinger in the water; the cold was intense, it was amazing that it was liquid still, so cold it was. He raised it to his tongue, touched gingerly—cold fire. It burned like acid. "My God," he exclaimed, spitting out involuntarily. "Is it poison?" Some toxic alkali, or a lake of arsenic—

"No no." She laughed. "Salts only. A hundred twenty-six grams of salt per liter of water. As opposed to three point seven grams per liter, in seawater. Incredible." Tatiana was a geochemist, and so now shaking her head with amazement. This kind of thing was her work. Michel saw her beauty in a new way, masked but perfectly clear.

"Salt raised to a higher power," he said absently. A concentrated quality. So it might be in the Mars colony; and suddenly the idea he had felt hovering over him descended: The ordinary sea-salt of humanity would be concentrated by their isolation into a poisonous pond.

He shuddered and spat again, as if he could reject such a bad thought. But the taste remained.

As the perpetual darkness stretches on it becomes hard not to think it permanent, as if we are lingering on after the local star has burned out. People (some of them) are finally beginning to act as if they are being tested. As if the world has indeed ended, and we existing in some antechamber of the final judgment. Imagine a time of real religion, when everyone felt like this all the time.

Some of them avoided Michel, and Charles and Georgia and Pauline, the other psychologists. Others were too friendly. Mary Dunkel, Janet Blyleven, Frank Chalmers; Michel had to watch himself to avoid ending up alone with these three, or he would fall into a depression witnessing the spectacle of their great charm.

The best solution was to stay active. Remembering the pleasure of his hike with Tatiana, he went out as often as he could, accompanying the others as they performed various maintenance and scientific tasks. The days passed in their artificial rounds, everything measured out and lived just as if the sun were rising in the morning and setting in the evening. Wake, eat, work, eat, work, eat, relax, sleep. Just like home.

One day he went out with Frank on a hike up to an anenometer near the Labyrinth, to try to see if he could penetrate the man's pleasant surface. In the end it did not work; Frank was too cool, too professional, too friendly. Years of work in Washington, DC, had made him very smooth indeed. He had been involved in getting the first human expedition to Mars, a few years before; an old friend of John Boone, the first man to set foot on Mars. He was also said to be heavily involved in the planning for this expedition as well. He was certainly one of those who felt they were going to be among the hundred; extremely confident, in fact. He had a very American voice somehow, booming out to Michel's left as they hiked. "Check those glaciers, falling out of the passes and being blown away before they reach the valley floor. What an awesome place, really."

"Yes."

"These katabatic winds—falling off the polar cap—nothing can stop them. Cold as hell. I wonder if that little wind vane we set up here will even be there anymore."

It was. They pulled out its data cartridge, put in another one. Around them the huge expanse of brown rock bowled to the starry sky. They started back down.

"Why do you want to go to Mars, Frank?"

"What's this, we're still at work out here are we?"

"No no. I'm just curious."

"Sure. Well, I want to try it. I want to try living somewhere where you can actually try to do something new. Set up new systems, you know. I grew up in the South, like you did. Only the American South is a lot different than the French south. We were stuck in our history for a long, long time. Then things opened up, partly because it got so bad. Partly just a lot of hurricanes hitting the coast! And we had a chance to rebuild. And we did, but—not much changed. Not enough, Michel. So I have this desire to try it again. That's the truth." And he glanced over at Michel, as if to emphasize not only that it was the truth, but that it was a truth he seldom talked about. Michel liked him a bit better after that.

Another day (or, in another hour of their endless night) Michel went out with a group, to check on the climatology stations located around the lakeshore. They hauled banana sleds loaded with replacement batteries and tanks of compressed nitrogen and the like. Michel, Maya, Charles, Arkady, Iwao, Ben, and Elena.

They walked across Lake Vanda, Ben and Maya pulling the sleds. The valley seemed huge. The frozen surface of the lake gleamed and sparked blackly underfoot. To a Northerner the sky already seemed overstuffed with stars, and in the ice underfoot each star was shattered into many pricks of light. Next to him Maya shined her flashlight down, lighting a field of cracks and bubbles under her; it was like shining light into a glass floor that had no bottom. She turned the flashlight off and it suddenly looked to Michel like the stars of the other hemisphere were shining up through a clear world, an alien planet much closer to the center of its galaxy. Looking down into the black hole at the center of things, through burred starlight. Like the shattered bottomless pool of the self. Every step broke the sight into a different refraction, a kaleidoscope of white points in black. He could gaze down into Vanda for a long time.

They came to the far shore of the lake. Michel looked back: Their complex sparkled like a bright winter constellation coming up over the horizon. Inside those boxes their companions were working, talking, cooking, reading, resting. Tensions in there were subtle but high.

A door opened in the complex, a wedge of light was thrown onto rust-colored rock. It could have been Mars, sure; in a year or two it would be. Many of the current tensions would be resolved. But there would be no air. Outside they would go, yes, sometimes; but in space suits. Would that matter? The winter suit he was wearing at that moment was as much like a space suit as the designers could make it, and the frigid numbing downvalley breeze was like breathing purified oxygen just gasified from liquid stock, and insufficiently warmed. The sub-biological chill of Antarctica, of Mars; nothing much to choose between them. In that sense this year of training and testing had been a good idea. They were getting at least a taste of what it might be like.

Ben stepped down onto the uneven lower ice of the lake's summertime moat, slipped and went down in a flash. He cried out and the others rushed to him, Michel first because he had seen it happen. Ben groaned and writhed, the others crouched around him—

"Excuse me," Maya said, and ducked between Michel and Arkady to kneel at Ben's side.

"Is it your hip?"

"Ah—yeah—"

"Hold on. Hold steady." Ben clutched at her arm and she held him on his other side. "Here, let's get your harness unclipped from the sled. Okay, slip the sled under him. Move him gently! Okay. Hold still there, we'll get you back to the station. Can you stay steady or should we strap you down. Okay, let's go. Help stabilize the sled. Someone radio the station and tell them to get ready for us." She clipped her own harness onto the banana sled and started back across the lake, quickly but steadily, almost ice-skating on her boots, flashlight lit to show her the ice underfoot. The others followed beside Ben.

Across the Ross Sea, McMurdo Station had an extra complement of winter staff precisely to help support them out at Vanda, and so the winter helicopter came yammering down in a huge noise only an hour or so after their return to the station. By that time Ben was furious at himself for falling, more angry than hurt, though they found out later that his hip had been fractured. "He went down in a flash," Michel said to Maya afterward. "So fast he had no time to get a hand up. I'm not surprised it broke something."

"Too bad," Maya said.

"You were good out there," Michel said, surprising himself. "Very quick."

She blew this away with a sound and a wave of her hand. "How many times I've seen it. I spent my whole childhood on ice."

"Ah of course." Expertise. A fund of experience was the basis of all natural decision making. This was true of Maya in many different realms, he felt. Ergonomics, her specialty, was a matter of people getting along well with things. She was going to Mars. He was not. He loved her. Well, but he loved many women. That was just the way it was. But with her . . .

From Michel's personal notes, heavily encrypted:

Janet Blyleven: beautiful. Speaks rapidly, confidently. Friendly. Looks healthy. Nice breasts. Doggy friendship is no friendship at all.

Maya: very beautiful. A tiger slouches into the room, reeking of sex and murder. The alpha female before whom all submit. Quick in everything, including moods. I can talk to her. We have real conversations because she doesn't care what I'm here for. Can that be true?

Spencer Jackson: a power. A secret soul. Depths beyond all calculation, even for him. The Vanda inside us. His the mind into which the whole community falls, transmuted to art. Can sketch any face in a dozen strokes, and there they are pebble all bare. But I don't think he's happy.

Tatiana Durova: very beautiful. A goddess trapped in a motel. She's looking for a way out. She knows everyone thinks she is beautiful, and therefore trusts none of us. She needs to get back to Olympus, where her appearance would be taken for granted, and she able to get through to someone. To her peers. Perhaps she takes Mars to be Olympus.

Arkady Bogdanov is a power. A very steady reliable fellow, earnest almost to the point of dullness. One sees everything he's thinking: He doesn't bother to conceal it. What I am is enough to get me to Mars, he says in his manner. Don't you agree? And I do. An engineer, quick and ingenious, not interested in larger issues.

Marina Tokareva: a beauty. Very serious and intense, no small talk to her. One is forced to think about things. And she assumes you are as quick as she is. So it can be work to follow her. Narrow chiseled features, thick jet-black hair. Sometimes following her glances I think she is one of the homosexuals who must be among us; other times she seems fixated on Vlad Taneev, the oldest man here.

George Berkovic and Edvard Perrin are paired in their regard for Phyllis Boyle. Yet it is not a competition but a partnership. They both think they like Phyllis, but really what they like is the way the other one mirrors their affection. Phyllis likes this too.

Ivana is quite beautiful, despite a thin face and an overbite; a goofy smile lights up the face of the classic chemist nerd, and suddenly the goddess is revealed. Shared a Nobel Prize in chemistry, but one has to quash the thought that the smile is what won the prize. It makes one happy to see it. One would give her the Nobel Prize just to see that smile.

Simon Frazier: a very quiet power. English; public-school education from age nine. He listens very closely, speaks well, but he says about one-tenth as much as everyone else, which naturally gains him the reputation of a complete mute. He plays with this image, quietly. I

*think he likes Ann, who is like him in some ways, though not so ex-
treme; in other ways very unlike. Ann does not joke with her image
among the others, she is completely unaware of it—American lack of
self-consciousness, versus Simon's Brit irony.*

*Ann is a real beauty, though austere. Tall, angular, bony, strong; both
body and face. She draws the eye. She certainly does take Mars seriously. People see that in her and like her for it. Or not, as the case may
be. Her shadow is very distinct.*

*Alexander Zhalin is a power. He likes women with his eyes. Some of
them know it, some don't. Mary Dunkel and Janet Blyleven are both
with him a lot. He is an enthusiast. Whatever has taken his fancy becomes the horizon of all interest.*

*Nadia Cherneshevsky: At first you think she is plain, then you see she
is one of the most beautiful of all. It has to do with solidity—physical,
intellectual, and moral. The rock everyone rests on. Her physical
beauty is in her athleticism—short, round, tough, skillful, graceful,
strong—and in her eyes, as her irises are parti-colored, a dense stip-
pled carpet of color dots, bits of brown and green mostly, with some
blue and yellow, all flecked together in concentric rings of pattern, shot
by rays of a different pattern, merging in a casual glance to a color like
hazel. You could dive into those eyes and never come out. And she
looks back at you without fear.*

*Frank Chalmers: a power. I think. It's hard not to see him as an ad-
junct to John Boone. The sidekick, or enabler. On his own out here, not
so impressive. Diminished; less a historical character. He's elusive.
Big, bulky, dark-complexioned. He keeps a low profile. He is quite
friendly, but it doesn't seem to one that it is real friendliness. A political animal, like Phyllis; only they don't like each other. It's Maya he
likes. And Maya makes sure he feels part of her world. But what he
really wants is not clear. There's a person in there one does not know
at all.*

More formally, he administered the Revised Minnesota Multiphasic
Personality Inventory, giving the questionnaires in groups of ten.
Hundreds of questions, calibrated to give statistically significant personality profiles. Only one of several different tests he was giving over
the winter; testing was one of the main ways they passed the time.

They were taking this test in the Bright Room, which was lit by scores of high-wattage bulbs, until everything in it seemed incandescent, especially people's faces. Looking at them as they worked, Michel suddenly felt how absurd it was to be schoolmaster to this brilliant crowd. And he saw very clearly in their glowing faces that they were not answering the questions to tell him what they were like, but rather to say what they thought they should in order to get to go to Mars. Of course reading the answers with that in mind would reveal almost as much as if they were being sincere. Still it was a shock to see it so clearly right there on their faces.

He shouldn't have been surprised. Faces revealed mood and much else with extreme precision, in most people anyway. Perhaps all people; a poker face reveals someone who is feeling guarded. No, he thought while watching them, a whole language might be developed from this, if one paid proper attention. Blind people hear actors' voices as completely artificial and false, and in this world they were all blind to faces, but if they looked . . . it might yield a kind of phrenology of sight. He might become the one-eyed man in the kingdom of the blind.

So he watched their faces, fascinated. The Bright Room was very bright indeed; time spent in such spaces had been shown to ward off the worst of seasonal affective disorder. In this luminous glare each translucent face seemed not just to be speaking to him, but also to be a complete rebus of that person's character: variously strong, intelligent, humorous, guarded, whatever, but in any case the entire personality, all right there on the surface. There was Ursula, faintly amused, thinking this was just one of the many silly things psychologists did; she as a medical person recognized that it was both ludicrous and necessary, she knew all the medical sciences were as much art as science. Sax, on the other hand, was taking it all very seriously, as he seemed to take everything: This was a scientific experiment to him, and he trusted that scientists in other disciplines were honestly dealing with the methodological difficulties of that discipline. All right there on his face.

They were all experts. Michel had studied NDM, or Naturalistic Decision Making; he was an expert on the subject; and he knew that experts took the limited data available to them in any situation and compared it to their vast fund of experiences, then made quick decisions based on analogies to past experience. Thus now, in this situation, this group of experts were doing what they would do to win a grant, or to win over a committee judging a tenure-application package. Something like that. The fact that they had never faced a task quite like this one was problematic but not debilitating.

Unless they considered the situation to be unstable beyond the point of prediction. Some situations were like that; even the best meteorologists could not predict hailstorms well, even the best battlefield commanders could not predict the course of surprise attacks. For that matter some recent studies had shown that it was much the same with psychologists when they attempted to predict people's future mental diagnoses from their scores on standard psychological tests. In each case there weren't enough data. And so Michel stared intently at their faces, pink or brown summaries of their personalities, trying to read the whole in the part.

Except it was not really true. Faces could be deceptive, or uninformative; and personality theory was notoriously vexed by deep uncertainties of all kinds. The same events and environments produced radically different results in people, that was the plain fact. There were too many confounding factors to say much about any aspect of personality. All the models of personality itself—the many, many theories—came down to a matter of individual psychologists codifying their guesses. Perhaps all science had this aspect, but it was so obvious in personality theory, where new propositions were supported by reference to earlier theorists, who often supported their assertions by reference to even earlier theorists, in strings all the way back to Freud and Jung, if not Galen. The fascinating *Psychoanalytic Roots of Patriarchy* was a perfect example of this, as was Jones's classic *The New Psychology of Dreaming*. It was a standard technique: Citing a guess by a dead authority added weight to one's assertions. So that often the large statistical tests administered by contemporary psychologists were designed mostly to confirm or disconfirm preliminary intuitive stabs by near-Victorians like Freud, Jung, Adler, Sullivan, Fromm, Maslow, etc. You picked the earlier expert whose guesses seemed right to you, then tested these intuitions using current scientific techniques. If going back to the original either/or, Michel chose Jung over Freud; after that he was partial to the whole utopian self-definition crowd—Fromm, Erikson, Maslow—and the matching philosophers of freedom from the same era, people like Nietzsche and Sartre. And the latest in modern psychology, of course—tested, peer-reviewed, and published in the journals.

But all his ideas were elaborations of an original set of feelings about people. A matter of hunches. On that basis he was supposed to

evaluate who would or would not do well if removed to Mars. Predict-
ing hailstorms and surprise attacks. Interpreting personality tests designed according to the paradigms of alchemists. Even asking people
about their dreams, as if these were anything more than the detritus
of the sleeping brain! Dream interpretation: Once Jung dreamed
about killing a man named Siegfried, and he struggled mightily to figure out what the dream might have meant, never once wondering if
it had anything to do with his immense anger at his old friend Freud.
As Fromm noted later, "The slight change from *Sigmund* to *Siegfried*
was enough to enable a man whose greatest skill was the interpretation of dreams, to hide the real meaning of this dream from himself."
    It was a perfect image for the power of their methodology.

    Mary Dunkel sat beside him at lunch one day. Her leg pressed
against his. This was not an accident. Michel was surprised; it was a
tremendous risk on her part, after all. His leg responded with a matching pressure, before he had a chance to think things over. Mary was
beautiful. He loved Mary for her dark hair and brown eyes and the
turn of her hips as she went through doorways ahead of him, and
now for her boldness. Elena he loved for the kindness in her beautiful
pale eyes, and for her rangy shoulders, wide as any man's. Tatiana he
loved for being so gorgeous and self-contained.
    But it was Mary pressed against him. What did she mean by it? Did
she mean to influence his recommendation for or against her? But
surely she would know such behavior might very possibly be counted
against her. She had to know that. So knowing that and doing this
anyway meant that she must be doing it for other reasons, more important to her than going to Mars. Meant it personally, in other
words.
    How easy he was. A woman only had to look at him right and he was
hers forever. She could knock him down with the brush of a fingertip.
    Now his body began to fall over yet again, reflexively, like the jerk
of the lower leg when the knee is properly tapped. But part of his
mind's slow train of thought, trailing behind reality by a matter of
some minutes (sometimes it was hours, or days), began to worry. He
could not be sure what she meant. She could be a woman willing to
risk all on a single throw of the dice. Try sidling up to a man to get on
his good side. It often worked like a charm.
    He realized that to have power over another's destiny was intolera-
ble. It corrupted everything. He wanted to slip away to the nearest
bed with Mary, hers or his, to fall onto it and make love. But making

love could by definition only occur between two free human beings. And as he was warden, judge, and jury to this group . . .

He moaned at the thought, a little "uhnn" in his throat as the problem struck him in the solar plexus and forced air upward through his vocal cords. Mary gave him a glance, smiled. Across the table Maya picked this up and looked at them. Maya had perhaps heard him groan. Maya saw everything; and if she saw him wanting silly reckless Mary, when really he wanted Maya with all his heart, then it would be a double disaster. Michel loved Maya for her hawklike vision, her fierce sharp intelligence, now watching him casually but completely.

He got up and went to the counter for a piece of cheesecake, feeling his knees weakly buckling. He dared not look back at either of them.

Though it was possible the leg contact and all their looks had been in his mind only.

It was getting strange.

Two Russians, Sergei and Natasha, had started a relationship soon after their arrival at Lake Vanda. They did not try to hide it, like some other couples Michel knew about or suspected. If anything they were a bit too demonstrative, given the situation; it made some people uncomfortable how affectionate they were with each other. Ordinarily one could ignore strangers kissing in public, watch them or not as one chose. Here there were decisions to be made. Was it worse to be a voyeur or a prude? Did one apply to the program as an individual or as a part of a couple? Which gave one a better chance? What did Michel think?

Then during the winter solstice party, June 21, after everyone had drunk a glass of champagne and was feeling good about getting past that ebb tide in the psychological year, Arkady called them out to see the aurora australis, a filmy electric dance of colored veils and draperies, soft greens and blues and a pale pink flowing across the grain of their reality, shimmering through the black plenum in quick sine waves. And suddenly, in the midst of this magic, shouting erupted from inside the compound—muffled shrieks, bellows. Michel looked around and all the hooded ski-masked figures were looking at him, as if he should have known this was coming and forestalled it somehow, as if it were his fault—and he ran inside and there were Sergei and Natasha, literally at each other's throats. He tried to detach them and got hit in the side of the face for his trouble.

After that operatic debacle Sergei and Natasha were expelled to McMurdo—which itself took some doing, both getting the helicopter over during a week of stormy weather, and getting Sergei and Natasha to agree to leave. And after that people's trust in Michel was heavily damaged, if not shattered completely. Even the administrators of the program, back in the north, were faintly overinquisitive when they asked him about it. They noted that records showed he had had an interview with Natasha the day before the fight, and asked what they had talked about, and if he could please share his notes on the meeting, which he declined to do for reasons of professional confidentiality.

Natasha Romanova: very beautiful. Magnificent posture. The calmest Russian woman I have ever met. Biologist, working in hydroponic farming. Met Sergei Davydov and fell in love with him here in the camp. Very happy now.

But everyone knew he had been involved with the investigation of the incident, and naturally they must have discussed the fact that he was testing and judging them. And keeping records of course. Mary no longer pressed his leg with hers, if she ever had, nor even sat next to him. Maya watched him more closely than ever, without appearing to. Tatiana continued to seek her peers, speaking always to the person inside one, or behind one. Or inside her. And Michel wondered more and more, as the arbitrary divisions of time they called days passed in their cycles—sleep, hunger, work, Bright Room, tests, relaxation, sleep—whether they could hold it together, mentally or socially, when they got to Mars.

This of course had been his worry from the start, expressed to the others on the planning committee only partially, as a nervous joke: Since they're all going to go crazy anyway, why not send insane people in the first place, and save them the trouble?

Now, trying to shake the feeling of anxiety growing in him, in the Bright Rooms and out in the dark world, the joke got less and less funny. People were furtive. Relationships were forming, and Michel saw these relationships now by the absences created by their concealment. Like tracing footprints in air. People no longer caressed who had before; glances were exchanged, then avoided; some people never looked at each other anymore, and yet drew toward each other as they passed in the halls out of an internal magnetism too strong to tell the others about, but also too strong to conceal. There were trips out into the frigid starry night, often timed so that both parties were out there together, although they did not leave or return together, but with other parties. Lookout Point, a knob low on the Dais, could be observed through night IR goggles, and sometimes one saw two flowing green bodies delineated out there against the black phosphor background, the two figures overlapping in a slow dance, a beautiful mime. Michel hummed an old song in English as he watched, absorbed beyond shame: "I'm a spy, in the house of love—I know the things, that you're thinking of. . . ."

Some of these relationships might knit the community together, others might tear it apart. Maya was playing a very dangerous game with Frank Chalmers, for instance; she went out on walks with him, they talked late into the evenings; unself-consciously she would put a hand on his arm and laugh, head thrown back, in a way that she never had with Michel. A prelude to a later intensification, Michel judged, as the two were beginning to look like the natural leaders of the expedition. But at the same time she was always playing him off against the Russian men, with whom she would joke in Russian about the non-Russians, unaware perhaps that Frank spoke some Russian, as he did French (atrociously) and several other languages. Frank just watched her, a small inner smile playing over his lips, even when she joked about him and he could understand it. He would even glance at Michel, to see if he too caught what she was doing. As if they were complicit in their interest in Maya!

And of course she played Michel as well. He could see that. Perhaps just instinctively, as a matter of habit. Perhaps something more personal. He couldn't tell. He wanted her to care about him. . . .

Meanwhile, other small groups were withdrawing from the main one. Arkady had his admirers, Vlad his close group of intimates; they were harem keepers, perhaps. On the other hand, Hiroko Ai had her group, and Phyllis hers, each distinct; polyandry as well as polygamy, then, or at least it seemed possible to Michel. They all existed already— in potentiality or in his imagination, it was hard to tell. But it was impossible not to perceive at least part of what was going on among them as the group dynamics of a troop of primates, thrown together all unknown to each other, and therefore sorting things out, establishing consorts, dominance hierarchies, and so on. For they were primates: apes shut in cages; and even though they had chosen the cages themselves, still—there they were. In a situation. Like Sartre's *Huis Clos.* No exit. Social life. Lost in a prison of their own devise.

Even the stablest people were affected. Michel watched fascinated as the two most introverted personalities among them, Ann Clayborne and Sax Russell, became interested in each other. It was pure science for both of them, at first; they were very much alike in that, and also in that both were so straightforward and guileless that Michel was able to overhear many of their first conversations. They were all shoptalk; Martian geology, with Sax grilling her for the most part, learning from her as from a professor, but always able to contribute from the standpoint of a theoretical physicist, one of the leading lights a decade or two before, in his postgraduate years. Not that Ann seemed to care about that. She was a geologist, a planetologist who had studied Mars ever since grad school, until now in her forties she was one of the acknowledged authorities. A Martian ahead of the fact. So if Sax was interested, she could talk Mars for hours; and Sax was interested. So they talked on and on.

"It's a pure situation, you have to remember that. There might even be indigenous life, left there underground from the early warm wet period. So that we have to make a sterile landing and a sterile colony. Put a cordon sanitaire between us and Mars proper. Then a comprehensive search. If Terran life was allowed to invade the ground before we determined the presence or absence of life, it would be a disaster for science. And the contamination might work the other way too. You can't be too careful. No—if anyone tries to infect Mars, there will be opposition. Maybe even active resistance. Poison the poisoners. You can never tell what people will do."

Sax said little or nothing in reply to this.

Then one day it was those two, appearing as deadpan and phlegmatic as ever, who went out for night walks at the (carefully offset) same time, and, Michel saw through his goggles, made their way to Lookout Point. They might have been among those Michel had already seen out there. They sat there beside each other for some time.

But when they came back Sax's color was high, and he saw nothing of the world inside the compound. Autistic to all. And Ann's brow was furrowed, her eye distracted. And they did not talk to each other, or even look at each other, for many days after that. Something had happened out there!

But as Michel watched them, fascinated by this turn of events, he came to understand that he would never know what it had been. A wave of—what was it—grief? Or sorrow, at their distance from each other, their isolation—each in his or her own private world, sealed vessels jostling—cut off—the futility of his work—the deathly cold of the black night—the ache of living life so inescapably alone. He fled.

Because he was one of the evaluators, he could flee. He could leave Lake Vanda from time to time on the rare helicopter visits, and though he tried not to, to establish better solidarity with the group, still he had done it once before, in the darkest depth of winter before the solstice, after seeing Maya and Frank together. Now, though the midday twilights were returning, he took up an invitation from an acquaintance at McMurdo to visit the Scott and Shackleton huts, just north of McMurdo on Ross Island.

Maya met him in the lock as he left. "What—running away?"

"No no—no—I'm going to have a look at the Scott and Shackleton huts. A matter of research. I'll be right back."

Her look showed that she did not believe it. Also that she cared where he went.

But it was in the nature of research, after all. The little cabins left behind by the first explorers of Antarctica were the remains of some of the very few expeditions in human history that resembled in any way what they were proposing to do on Mars. Though of course all analogy was false and misleading, and dangerous—this was a new thing they were thinking, a new event in history, nothing like it before.

Still, the first decades of Antarctic exploration had been somewhat like their planned expedition, he had to admit as the helicopter landed on the black rock of Cape Evans, and he followed the other distinguished visitors to the small snow-slabbed wooden hut above the beach. This was the nineteenth-century equivalent of their settlement at Lake Vanda, though their compound was ever so much more luxurious. Here at Cape Evans they had had only the necessities, all the necessities except for some vitamins and the company of the opposite sex. How pale and odd they had become from those lacks, along with the lack of sunlight itself. Monastic malnourished troglodytes, suffering from seasonal affective disorder without knowing what a ferocious psychological problem it was (so that perhaps it hadn't been). Writing newspapers, acting out sketches, pumping music rolls through player pianos, reading books, doing research, and producing some food by fishing and killing seals. Yes—they had had their pleasures—deprived as they were, these men had still lived on Mother Earth, in contact with the cold fringe of her bounty. On Mars there would be none of those Inuit raptures to pass the time and ameliorate their confinement.

But the postmodern structure of feeling might already have made them used to disconnection from Earth. Everyone inhabiting their own personal spaceship, carrying it mobile with them like a hermit crab's shell, moving from one component of it to the next: home, office, car, plane, apartment, hotel room, mall. An indoor life, even a virtual life. How many hours a day did they spend in the wind? So that perhaps Mars would not feel very different.

As he considered these matters Michel wandered the big main room of Scott's hut, looking at all the artifacts in the gray light. Scott had erected a wall of boxes to separate the officers and scientists from the common seamen. So many different facets; Michel felt his thoughts ricocheting this way and that.

They flew up the coast to Cape Royds, where Shackleton's hut stood like a rebuke to Scott's—smaller, neater, more wind-sheltered. Everyone together. Shackleton and Scott had fallen out during the first expedition to Antarctica, in 1902. Similar disagreements were likely to occur in the Martian colony; but there would be no chance to build a new home elsewhere. At least not at first. And no going home. At least that was the plan. But was that wise? Here again the analogy to the first Antarcticans fell apart, for no matter how uncomfortable they had been in these huts (and Shackleton's looked quite homey, actually) they knew they were only going to be here for a year or three, and then out and back home to England. Almost anything could be endured if there was some release foreseeable at the end of it, coming closer every day. Without that it would be a life sentence—no exit indeed. Exile, to a surantarctic wasteland of frigid airless rock.

Surely it made better sense to cycle the scientists and technicians to Mars in a way similar to that of the early Antarcticans. Tours of duty at small scientific stations, the stations built and then manned continuously, but by rotating teams, with individuals out there for three years each. This would be more in keeping with recommended lifetime maximum radiation doses. Boone and the others on the first trip there and back, two years before, had taken about 35 rad. Subsequent visiting scientists could stick to something like that.

But the American and Russian space programs had decided otherwise. They wanted a permanent base, and they had invited scientists to move there for good. They wanted a commitment from people, no doubt hoping for a similar commitment of public interest back home—

interest in a permanent cast of characters that could be learned, their lives become a matter of drama for public consumption back on Earth, with its bottomless addiction to narrative—biography as spectacle. Part of the funding effort. It made sense in its way.

But who would want to do such a thing? This was a matter that troubled Michel greatly; it headed the long list of double binds he felt applicants were put in by the process of selection. In short, they had to be sane to be selected, but crazy to want to go.

Many other double binds accompanied that basic one. Applicants had to be extroverted enough to socialize, but introverted enough to have studied a discipline to the point of mastering it. They had to be old enough to have learned these primary, secondary, and sometime tertiary professions, and yet be young enough to withstand the rigors of the trip out and the work there. They had to do well in groups, but want to leave everyone they knew behind forever. They were being asked to tell the truth, but clearly had to lie to increase their chances of getting what they wanted. They had to be both ordinary and extraordinary.

Yes, the double binds were endless. Nevertheless this nearly final group had come from an initial pool of many thousands of applicants. Double binds? So what! Nothing new to fear there. Everyone on Earth was strung up in vast networks of double binds. Going to Mars might actually reduce their number, decrease their strain! Perhaps that was part of the appeal of going!

Perhaps that was why these men of the first Antarctic explorations had volunteered to come south. Still, looking around at the bare wooden room, it was amazing to Michel that those who had wintered down here had managed to stay sane. On the wall of Shackleton's hut there was a photo of them: three men, huddled before a black stove. Michel stared long at this evocative photo. The men were worn-looking, battered, dirty, frostnipped, tired. Also calm, even serene. They could sit and do nothing but watch fire burn in a stove, entirely satisfied. They looked cold but warm. The very structure of the brain had been different then, more inured to hardship and the long slow hours of sheer animal existence. Certainly the structure of feeling had changed; that was culturally determined; and thus the brain must necessarily have changed too. A century later their brains depended on great dollops of mediated stimulation, quick-cut inputs which had not even existed for earlier generations. So that reliance on inner resources was harder. Patience was harder. They were different animals than the people in this photo. The epigenetic interplay of DNA and culture was now changing people so fast that even a century was enough to make a measurable difference. Accelerated evolution. Or one of the punctuations in the long tale of punctuated evolution. And Mars would be more of the same. There was no telling what they would become.

Back to Lake Vanda, and the old huts quickly became like a dream interrupting the only reality, a reality so cold that space-time itself seemed to have frozen, leaving all of them living the same hour over and over. Dante's cold circle of hell, the worst of all, as he recalled.

The sensory deprivation was getting to them all. Every "morning" he found himself waking up in low spirits. It took hours after waking to work the weight out of his stomach and focus on the day. After he reached level neutrality, as it was beginning to turn blue twilight at the windows, he was able to ask to join whoever was going outside that day. Out there in the numbing gray or blue or purple twilight he hiked along, trailing the other thickly clad figures, who looked like pilgrims in a medieval winter, or prehistoric people struggling through the Ice Age. One slender bundle might be Tatiana, her beauty muffled but not entirely blanketed, for she moved like a dancer over the cracked mirror of the lake, under the high walls of the valley. Another might be Maya, focused on the others, though quite friendly and diplomatic to him too. It worried him. Beside her strode Frank, bulky and muffled.

Tatiana was easier to understand, and so attractive. Across the ice one day he followed her. On the far shore they stopped to inspect the dead body of a mummified seal. These disoriented Weddell seals were found far up all the Dry Valleys, dead for hundreds or thousands of years, frozen all that time, slowly frittered away by the winds, until the skeleton slowly emerged from the body like a soul taking off a fur coat, a soul white and wind-polished and articulated.

Tatiana grabbed his arm, exclaiming at the sight. She spoke French well, and had spent summers as a girl on the beaches of the Côte d'Azur; just the thought of that made him melt. Now they spoke, gloved hand in gloved hand, looking down through ski masks at the *memento mori* in the gray light. His heart beat hard at the thought of the beauty encased in the chrysalis parka beside him, saying, "It's such a shock to come on one of these poor creatures' vertebra, out on its own in all the rock, like someone's lost bracelet."

From across the lake Frank watched them.

.   .   .

And after that day Maya dropped Michel completely, with never a word nor any outward sign that things had changed, but only a single swift glance at Tatiana, in his presence, after which a purely formal politeness, no content whatsoever. And now Michel knew, very acutely, whose company in this group he craved the most; but would never have again.

Frank had done that.

And all around him it was happening: the pointless wars of the heart. It was all so small, petty, tawdry. Yet it mattered; it was their life. Sax and Ann had gone dead to each other, likewise Marina and Vlad, and Hiroko and Iwao. New cliques were forming around Hiroko and Vlad and Arkady and Phyllis, as they all spun out into their own separate orbits. No—this group would go dysfunctional. Was going dysfunctional, he could see it right before his eyes. It was too hard to live isolated in this sub-biological sensory deprivation; and this was paradise compared to Mars. There was no such thing as a good test. There was no such thing as a good analogy. There was only reality, unique and different in every moment, to be lived without rehearsal and without revision. Mars would not be like this cold continuous night on the bottom of their world; it would be worse. Worse than this! They would go mad. A hundred people confined in tanks and sent to a poisonous cold dead planet, a place to which winter in Antarctica was like paradise; a prison universe, like the inside of a head when your eyes are closed. They would all go mad.

In the first week of September the noonday twilight grew almost as bright as day, and they could see sunlight on the peaks of the Asgaard and Olympus Ranges, flanking the deep valley. Because the valley was such a narrow slot between such high ranges, it would be perhaps another ten days before the sun fell directly on the base, and Arkady organized a hike up the side of Mount Odin to catch an earlier glimpse of it. This turned into a general expedition, as almost everyone proved interested in seeing the sun again as soon as possible. So early on the morning of September 10, they stood nearly a thousand meters above Lake Vanda, on a shelf occupied by a small ice pond and tarn. It was windy, so the climb had not warmed them. The sky was a pale starless blue; the east sides of the peaks of both ranges were glazed gold with sunlight. Finally to the east, at the end of the valley, over the burnished plate of the frozen Ross Sea, the sun emerged over the horizon and burned like a flare. They cheered; their eyes ran with emotion, also an excess of new light and cold wind. People hugged each other, bundle after bundle. But Maya kept on the other side of the group from Michel, with Frank always between them. And it seemed to Michel that everyone's joy had a desperate edge to it, as of people who had just barely survived an extinction event.

Thus when the time came to make his report to the selection committees, Michel advised against the project as designed. "No group can stay functional under such conditions indefinitely," he wrote. In the meetings he made his case point by point. The long list of double binds was especially impressive.

This was in Houston. The heat and humidity were saunalike; Antarctica was already a nightmare memory, slipping quickly away.

"But this is just social life," Charles York pointed out, bemused. "All social existence is a set of double binds."

"No no," Michel said. "Social life is a set of contradictory demands. That's normal, agreed. But what we're talking about here are *requirements* to be two opposite things at once. Classic double binds. And they are already causing a lot of the classic responses. Hidden lives. Multiple personalities. Bad faith. Repression, then the return of the repressed. A close look at the results of the tests given down there will show it is not a viable project. I would advise starting with small scientific stations, with rotating crews. As Antarctica itself is operated now."

This caused a lot of discussion, even controversy. Charles remained for sending up a permanent colony, as proposed; but he had grown close to Mary. Georgia and Pauline tended to agree with Michel; though they too had had personal difficulties at Vanda.

Charles dropped by to see Michel in his borrowed office, shaking his head. He looked at Michel, serious but somehow still uninvolved, distanced. Professional. "Look, Michel," he said. "They want to go. They're capable of adapting. A lot of them did very well with that, so well that you couldn't pick them out of a crowd in any kind of blind test. And they want to go, it's clear. That's how we should choose who to send. We should give them their chance to do what they want. It's not really our business to decide for them."

"But it won't work. We saw that."

"I didn't see that. They didn't see that. What you saw is your concern, but they have the right to make their try at it. Anything could happen there, Michel. Anything. And this world is not so well arranged that we should deny people who want to take their chance to try something different. It could be good for us all." He stood abruptly to leave the office. "Think about it."

Michel thought about it. Charles was a sensible man, a wise man. What he had said had the ring of truth to it. And a sudden gust of fear blew through Michel, as cold as any katabatic downdraft in Wright Valley: he might, out of his own fear, be stopping something with greatness in it.

He changed his recommendation, describing all the reasons why. He explained his vote for the project to continue; he gave the committees his list of the best hundred candidates. But Georgia and Pauline continued to advise against the project as designed. And so an outside panel was convened to make an evaluation, a recommendation, a judgment. Near the end of the process Michel even found himself in his office with the American president, who sat down with him and told him he had probably been right the first time around, first impressions were usually that way, second-guessing was of little use. Michel could only nod. Later he sat in a meeting attended by both the American and Russian presidents; the stakes were that high. They both wanted a Martian base, for their own political purposes, Michel saw that clearly. But they also wanted a success, a project that worked. In that sense, the hundred permanent colonists as originally conceived was clearly the riskier of the options they had before them now. And neither president was a risk taker. Rotating crews were intrinsically less interesting, but if the crews were large enough, and the base large enough, then the political impact (the publicity) would be almost the same; the science would be the same; and everything would be that much safer, radiologically as well as psychologically.

So they canceled the project.

Exploring Fossil Canyon

Two hours before sunset their guide, Roger Clayborne, declared it was time to set camp, and the eight members of the tour trooped down from the ridges or up out of the side canyons they had been exploring that day as the group slowly progressed west, toward Olympus Mons. Eileen Monday, who had had her intercom switched off all day (the guide could override her deafness) turned to the common band and heard the voices of her companions, chattering. Dr. Mitsumu and Cheryl Martinez had pulled the equipment wagon all day, down a particularly narrow canyon bottom, and their vociferous complaints were making Mrs. Mitsumu laugh. John Nobleton was suggesting, as usual, that they camp farther down the ancient water-formed arroyo they were following; Eileen could not be sure which of the dusty-suited figures was him, but she guessed it was the one enthusiastically bounding up the wash, kicking up sand with every jump, and floating like an impala. Their guide, on the other hand, was unmistakable: tall even when sitting against a tall boulder, high on the spine flanking one side of the deep canyon. When the others spotted him, they groaned. The equipment wagon weighed less than seven hundred kilograms in Mars's gravity, but still it would take several of them to pull it up the slope to the spot Clayborne had in mind.

"Roger, why don't we just pull it down the road we've got here and camp around the corner?" John insisted.

"Well, we certainly could," Roger said—he spoke so quietly that the intercoms barely transmitted his dry voice—"but I haven't yet learned to sleep comfortably at a forty-five-degree angle."

Mrs. Mitsumu giggled. Eileen snicked in irritation, hoping Roger could identify the maker of the sound. His remark typified all she disliked about the guide; he was both taciturn and sarcastic, a combination Eileen did not like any more for considering it unusual. And his wide derisive grin was no help either.

"I found a good flat down there," John protested.

"I saw it. But I suspect our tent needs a little more room."

Eileen joined the crew hauling the wagon up the slope. "I suspect," she mimicked as she began to pant and sweat inside her suit.

"See?" came Roger's voice in her ear. "Ms. Monday agrees with me."

She snicked again, more annoyed than she cared to show. So far, in her opinion, this expedition was a flop. And their guide was a very significant factor in its failure, even if he was so quiet that she had barely noticed him for the first three or four days. But eventually his sharp tongue had caught her attention.

She slipped in some soft dirt and went to her knees; bounced back up and heaved again, but the contact reminded her that Mars itself shared the blame for her disappointment. She wasn't as willing to admit that as she was her dislike for Clayborne, but it was true, and it disturbed her. All through her many years at the University of Mars, Burroughs, she had studied the planet—first in literature (she had read every Martian tale ever written, she once boasted), then in areology, particularly seismology. But she had spent most of her twenty-four years in Burroughs itself, and the big city was not like the canyons. Her previous exposure to the Martian landscape consisted of visits to the magnificent domed section of Hephaestus Chasma called Lazuli Canyon, where icy water ran in rills and springs, in waterfalls and pools, and tundra grass grew on every wet red beach. Of course she knew that the virgin Martian landscape was not like Lazuli, but somewhere in her mind, when she had seen the advertisement for the hike—"Guaranteed to be terrain *never before trodden* by human feet"—she must have had an image of something similar to that green world. The thought made her curse herself for a fool. The slope they were struggling up at that very moment was a perfect representative sample of the untrodden terrain they had been hiking over for the past week: It was composed of dirt of every consistency and hue, so that it resembled an immense layered cake slowly melting, made of ingredients that looked like baking soda, sulfur, brick dust, curry powder, coal slag, and alum. And it was only one cake out of thousands of them, all stacked crazily for as far as the eye could see. Dirt piles.

Just short of Roger's flat campsite, they stopped to rest. Sweat was stinging in Eileen's left eye. "Let's get the wagon up here," Roger said, coming down to help. His clients stared at him mutinously, unmoving. The doctor leaned over to adjust his boot, and as he had been holding the wagon's handle, the others were caught off guard; a pebble gave way under the wagon's rear wheel, and suddenly it was out of their grasp and rolling down the slope—

In an explosion of dust Roger dived headfirst down the hill, chocking the rear wheel with a stone the size of a breadloaf. The wagon plowed the chock downhill a couple of meters and came to a halt. The group stood motionless, staring at the prone guide, Eileen as surprised as the rest of them; she had never seen him move so fast. He stood up at his usual lazy pace and started wiping dust from his faceplate. "Best to put the chock down before it starts rolling," he murmured, smiling to himself. They gathered to pull the wagon up the flat, chattering again. But Eileen considered it; if the wagon had careened all the way down to the canyon bottom, there would have been at least the possibility that it would have been damaged. And if it had been damaged badly enough, it could have killed them all. She pursed her lips and climbed up to the flat.

Roger and Ivan Corallton were pulling the base of the tent from the wagon. They stretched it out over the posts that kept it level and off the frozen soil; Ivan and Kevin Ottalini assembled the curved poles of the tension dome. The three of them and John carefully got the poles in place, and pulled the transparent tent material out of the base to stretch it under the framework. When they were done the others stood, a bit stiffly—they had traveled some twenty kilometers that day—and walked in through the flaccid airlock, hauling the wagon in behind them. Roger twisted valves on the side of the wagon, and compressed air pushed violently into their protective bag. Before it was full, Dr. Mitsumu and his wife were disengaging the bath and the latrine assemblies from the wagon. Roger switched on the heaters, and after a few minutes of gazing at the gauges, he nodded. "Home again home again," he said as always. Condensation was beading on the inside of their dome's clear skin. Eileen unclipped her helmet from her suit and pulled it off. "It's too hot." No one heard her. She walked to the wagon and turned down the heater, catching Roger's sardonic grin out of the corner of her eye; she always thought the tent's air was too hot. Dr. Mitsumu, regular as clockwork, ducked into the latrine as soon as his suit was off. The air was filled with the smells of sweat and urine, as everyone stripped their suits off and poured the contents of the runoffs into the water purifier on the wagon. Doran Stark got to the bath first as always—Eileen was amused by how quickly a group established its habits and customs—and stood in the ankle-deep water, sponging himself down and singing "I Met Her in a Phobos Restaurant." As she emptied her suit into the purifier Eileen found herself smiling at all their domestic routines, performed in a transparent bubble in the midst of an endless rust desolation.

She took her sponge bath last except for Roger. There was a shower curtain that could be pulled around the tiny tub at shoulder level, but nobody else used it, so Eileen didn't either, although she was made a bit uncomfortable by the surreptitious glances of John and the doctor. Nevertheless, she sponged down thoroughly, and in the constantly moving air her clean wet skin felt good. Besides it was rather a splendid sight, all the ruddy naked bodies standing about on the ledge of a spine extending thousands of meters above and below them, the convolutions of canyon after canyon scoring the tilted landscape, Olympus Mons bulging to the west, rising out of the atmosphere so that it appeared to puncture the dome of the sky, and the bloodred sun about to set behind it. Roger did know how to pick a campsite, Eileen admitted to herself (he somehow sponged down with his back always to her, shower curtain partly pulled out, and dressed while still wet, signaling the gradual rehabiliment of the others). It was truly a sublime sight, as all of their campsite prospects had been. Sublime: to have your senses telling you you are in danger, when you know you are not; that was Burke's definition of the sublime, more or less, and it fit practically every moment of these days, from dawn to dusk. But that in itself could get wearing. The sublime is not the beautiful, after all, and one cannot live comfortably in a perpetual sense of danger. But at sunset, in the tent, it was an apprehension that could be enjoyed: the monstrous bare landscape, her bare skin; the utter serenity of the slow movement of Beethoven's last string quartet, which Ivan played every day during the sun's dying moments.... "Listen to this," Cheryl said, and read from her constant companion, the volume *If Wang Wei Lived on Mars*:

> *Sitting out all night thinking.*
> *Sun half-born five miles to the east.*
> *Blood pulses through all this still air:*
> *The edge of a mountain, great distance away.*
> *Nothing moves but the sun,*
> *Blood to fire as it rises.*

How many, these dawns?
How far, our home?
Stars fade. Big rocks splinter
The mind's great fear:
Peace here. Peace, here.

It was a fine moment, Eileen thought, made so by what was specifically human in the landscape. She dressed with the rest of them, deliberately turning away from John Nobleton as she rooted around in her drawer of the wagon, and they fell to making dinner. For more than an hour after Olympus Mons blotted out the sun the sky stayed light; pink in the west, shading to brick-black in the east. They cooked and ate by this illumination. Their meal, planned by Roger, was a thick vegetable stew, seemingly fresh French bread, and coffee. Most of them kept off the common band during long stretches of the day, and now they discussed what they had seen, for they explored different side canyons as they went. The main canyon they were following was a dry outflow wash, formed by flash floods working down a small fault line in a large tilted plateau. It was relatively young, Roger said—meaning two billion years old, but younger than most of the water-carved canyons on Mars. Wind erosion and the marvelous erratics created by volcanic bombardment from Olympus Mons gave the expedition members a lot of features to discuss: beach terracing from long-lost lakes, meandering streambeds, lava bombs shaped like giant teardrops, or colored in a way that implied certain gases in copious quantities in the Hesperian atmosphere. . . . This last, plus the fact that these canyons had been carved by water, naturally provoked a lot of speculation about the possibilities of ancient Martian life. And the passing water, and the resiliencies of the rock, had created forms fantastical enough to seem the sculpture of some alien art. So they talked, with the enthusiasm and free speculation that only amateurs seem to bring to a subject: Sunday paper areologists, Eileen thought. There wasn't a proper scientist among them; she was the closest thing to it, and the only thing she knew was the rudiments of areology. Yet she listened to the talk with interest.

Roger, on the other hand, never contributed to these free-ranging discussions, and didn't even listen. At the moment he was engaged in setting up his cot and "bedroom" wall. There were panels provided so that each sleeper, or couple, could block off an area around their cot; no one took advantage of them but Roger, the rest preferring to lie out under the stars together. Roger set two panels against the sloping side of the dome, leaving just enough room for his cot under the clear low roof. It was yet another way that he set himself apart, and watching him, Eileen shook her head. Expedition guides were usually so amiable—how did he keep his job? Did he ever get repeat customers? She set out her cot, observing his particular preparations: He was one of the tall Martians, well over two meters (Lamarckism was back in vogue, as it appeared that the more generations of ancestors you had on Mars, the taller you grew; it was true for Eileen herself, who was fourth-generation, or *yonsei*)—long-faced, long-nosed, homely as English royalty . . . long feet that were clumsy once out of their boots. . . . He rejoined them, however, this evening, which was not always his custom, and they lit a lantern as the wine-dark sky turned black and filled with stars. Bedding arranged, they sat down on cots and the floor around the lantern's dim light and talked some more. Kevin and Doran began a chess game.

For the first time, they asked Eileen questions about her area of expertise. Was it true that the southern highlands now held the crust of both primeval hemispheres? Did the straight line of the three great Tharsis volcanoes indicate a hot spot in the mantle? Sunday paper areology again, but Eileen answered as best she could. Roger appeared to be listening.

"Do you think there'll ever be a marsquake we can actually feel?" he asked with a grin.

The others laughed, and Eileen felt herself blush. It was a common jest; sure enough, he followed it up: "You sure you seismologists aren't just inventing these marsquakes to keep yourselves in employment?"

"You're out here enough," she replied. "One of these days a fault will open up and swallow you."

"She hopes," Ivan said. The sniping between them had of course not gone unnoticed.

"So you think I might actually feel a quake someday," Roger said.

"Sure. There's thousands every day, you know."

"But that's because your seismographs register every footstep on the planet. I mean, a big one?"

"Of course. I can't think of anyone who deserves a shaking more."

"Might even have to use the Richter scale, eh?"

Now that was unfair, because the Harrow scale was necessary to make finer distinctions between low-intensity quakes. But later in the same conversation, she got hers back. Cheryl and Mrs. Mitsumu were asking Roger about where he had traveled before in his work, how many expeditions he had guided and the like. "I'm a canyon guide," he replied at one point.

"So when will you graduate to Marineris?" Eileen asked.

"Graduate?"

"Sure, isn't Marineris the ultimate goal of every canyon man?"

"Well, to a certain extent—"

"You'd better get assigned there in a hurry, hadn't you—I hear it takes a whole lifetime to learn those canyons." Roger looked to be about forty.

"Oh not for our Roger," Mrs. Mitsumu said, joining in the ribbing.

"No one ever learns Marineris," Roger protested. "It's eight thousand kilometers long, with hundreds of side canyons—"

"What about Gustafsen?" Eileen said. "I thought he and a couple others knew every inch of it."

"Well . . ."

"Better start working on that transfer."

"Well, I'm a Tharsis fan myself," he explained, in a tone so apologetic that the whole group burst out laughing. Eileen smiled at him and went to get some tea started.

After the tea was distributed, John and Ivan turned the conversation to another favorite topic, the terraforming of the canyons. "This system would be as beautiful as Lazuli," John said. "Can you imagine water running down the drops we took today? Tundra grass everywhere, finches in the air, little horned toads down in the cracks . . . alpine flowers to give it some color."

"Yes, it will be exquisite," Ivan agreed. With the same material that made their tent, several canyons and craters had been domed, and thin cold air pumped beneath, allowing arctic and alpine life to exist. Lazuli was the greatest of these terraria, but many more were springing up.

"Unnh," Roger muttered.

"You don't agree?" Ivan asked.

Roger shook his head. "The best you can do is make an imitation Earth. That's not what Mars is for. Since we're on Mars, we should adjust to what it is, and enjoy it for that."

"Oh but there will always be natural canyons and mountains," John said. "There's as much land surface on Mars as on Earth, right?"

"Just barely."

"So with all that land, it will take centuries for it all to be terraformed. In this gravity, maybe never. But centuries, at least."

"Yes, but that's the direction it's headed," Roger said. "If they start orbiting mirrors and blowing open volcanoes to provide gases, they'll change the whole surface."

"But wouldn't that be marvelous!" Ivan said.

"You don't seriously object to making life on the open surface possible, do you?" Mrs. Mitsumu asked.

Roger shrugged. "I like it the way it is."

John and the rest continued to discuss the considerable problems of terraforming, and after a bit Roger got up and went to bed. An hour later Eileen got up to do the same, and the others followed her, brushing teeth, visiting the latrine, talking more. . . . Long after the others had settled down, Eileen stood under one edge of the tent dome, looking up at the stars. There near Scorpio, as a high evening star, was the Earth, a distinctly bluish point, accompanied by its fainter companion the moon. A double planet of resonant beauty in the host of constellations. Tonight it gave her an inexplicable yearning to see it, to stand on it.

Suddenly John appeared at her side, standing too close to her, shoulder to shoulder, his arm rising, as if with a life of its own, to circle her waist. "Hike'll be over soon," he said. She didn't respond. He was a very handsome man; aquiline features, jet-black hair. He didn't know how tired Eileen was of handsome men. She had been as impetuous in her affairs as a pigeon in a park, and it had brought her a lot of grief. Her last three lovers had all been quite good-looking, and the last of them, Eric, had been rich as well. His house in Burroughs was made of rare stones, as all the rich new houses were: a veritable castle of dark purple chert, inlaid with chalcedony and jade, rose quartz and jasper, its floors intricately flagged patterns of polished yellow slate, coral, and bright turquoise. And the parties! Croquet picnics in the maze garden, dances in the ballroom, masques all about the extensive grounds. . . . But Eric himself, brilliant talker though he was, had turned out to be rather superficial, and promiscuous as well, a discovery that Eileen had been slow to make. It had hurt her feelings. And since that had been the third intimate relationship to go awry in four years, she felt tired and unsure of herself, unhappy, and particularly sick of that easy mutual attraction of the attractive which had gotten her into such painful trouble, and which was what John was relying on at that very moment.

Of course he knew nothing of all this, as his arm hugged her waist (he certainly didn't have Eric's way with words), but she wasn't inclined to excuse his ignorance. She mulled over methods of diplomatically slipping out of his grasp and back to a comfortable distance. This was certainly the most he had made so far in the way of a move. She decided on one of her feints—leaning into him to peck his cheek, then pulling away when his guard was down—and had started the maneuver, when with a bump one of Roger's panels knocked aside and Roger stumbled out, in his shorts, bleary-eyed. "Oh?" he said sleepily, as he noticed them; then saw who they were, and their position— "Ah," he said, and stumped away toward the latrine.

Eileen took advantage of the disturbance to slip away from John and go to bed, which was no-trespass territory, as John well knew. She lay down in some agitation. That smile, that "Ah"—the whole incident irritated her so much that she had trouble falling asleep. And the double star, one blue, one white, returned her stare all the while.

The next day it was Eileen and Roger's turn to pull the wagon. This was the first time they had pulled together, and while the rest ranged ahead or to the sides, they solved the many small problems presented by the task of getting the wagon down the canyon. An occasional drop-off was high enough to require winch, block, and tackle—sometimes even one or two of the other travelers—but mostly it was a matter of guiding the flexible little cart down the center of the wash. They agreed on band 33 for their private communication, but aside from the business at hand, they conversed very little. "Look out for that rock." "How nice, that triangle of shards." To Eileen it seemed clear that Roger had very little interest in her or her observations. Or else, it occurred to her, he thought the same of her.

At one point she asked, "What if we let the wagon slip right now?" It was poised over the edge of a six- or seven-meter drop, and they were winching it down.

"It would fall," his voice replied solemnly in her ear, and through his faceplate she could see him smiling.

She kicked pebbles at him. "Come on, would it break? Are we in danger of our lives most every minute?"

"No way. These things are practically indestructible. Otherwise, it would be too dangerous to use them. They've dropped them off four-hundred-meter cliffs—not sheer you understand, but steep—and it doesn't even dent them."

"I see. So when you saved the wagon from slipping down that slope yesterday, you weren't actually saving our lives."

"Oh no. Did you think that? I just didn't want to climb down that hill and recover it."

"Ah." She let the wagon thump down, and they descended to it. After that there were no exchanges between them for a long time. Eileen contemplated the fact that she would be back in Burroughs in three or four days, with nothing in her life resolved, nothing different about it.

Still, it would be good to get back to the open air, the illusion of open air. Running water. Plants.

Roger clicked his tongue in distress.

"What?" Eileen asked.

"Sandstorm coming." He switched to the common band, which Eileen could now hear. "Everyone get back to the main canyon, please, there's a sandstorm on the way."

There were groans over the common band. No one was actually in sight. Roger bounced down the canyon with impeccable balance, bounced back up. "No good campsites around," he complained. Eileen watched him; he noticed and pointed at the western horizon. "See that feathering in the sky?"

All Eileen could see was a patch where the sky's pink was perhaps a bit yellow, but she said, "Yes?"

"Dust storm. Coming our way too. I think I feel the wind already." He put a hand up. Eileen thought that feeling the wind through a suit when the atmospheric pressure was thirty millibars was strictly a myth, a guide's boast, but she stuck her hand up as well, and thought that there might be a faint fluctuating pressure on it.

Ivan, Kevin, and the Mitsumus appeared far down the canyon. "Any campsites down there?" Roger asked.

"No, the canyon gets even narrower."

Then the sandstorm was upon them, sudden as a flash flood. Eileen could see fifty meters at the most; they were in a shifting dome of flying sand, it seemed, and it was as dark as their long twilights, or darker.

Over band 33, in her left ear, Eileen heard a long sigh. Then in her right ear, over the common band, Roger's voice: "You all down the canyon there, stick together and come on up to us. Doran, Cheryl, John, let's hear from you—where are you?"

"Roger?" It was Cheryl on the common band, sounding frightened.

"Yes, Cheryl, where are you?"

A sharp thunder roll of static: "We're in a sandstorm, Roger! I can just barely hear you."

"Are you with Doran and John?"

"I'm with Doran, and he's just over this ridge, I can hear him, but he says he can't hear you."

"Get together with him and start back for the main canyon. What about John?"

"I don't know, I haven't seen him in over an hour."

"All right. Stay with Doran—"

"Roger?"

"Yes?"

"Doran's here now."

"I can hear you again," Doran's voice said. He sounded more scared than Cheryl. "Over that ridge there was too much interference."

"Yeah, that's what's happening with John I expect," Roger said.

Eileen watched the dim form of their guide move up the canyon's side slope in the wavering amber dusk of the storm. The "sand" in the thin air was mostly dust, or fines even smaller than dust particles, like smoke; but occasional larger grains made a light *tik tik tik* against her faceplate.

"Roger, we can't seem to find the main canyon," Doran declared, scratchy in the interference.

"What do you mean?"

"Well, we've gone up the canyon we descended, but we must have taken a different fork, because we've run into a box canyon."

Eileen shivered in her warm suit. Each canyon system lay like a lightning bolt on the tilted land, a pattern of ever-branching forks and tributaries; in the storm's gloom it would be very easy to get lost; and they still hadn't heard from John.

"Well, drop back to the last fork and try the next one to the south. As I recall, you're over in the next canyon north of us."

"Right," Doran said. "We'll try that."

The four who had been farther down the main canyon appeared like ghosts in mist. "Here we are," Ivan said with satisfaction.

"Nobleton! John! Do you read me?"

No answer.

"He must be off a ways," Roger said. He approached the wagon. "Help me pull this up the slope."

"Why?" Dr. Mitsumu asked.

"We're setting the tent up there. Sleep on an angle tonight, you bet."

"But why up there?" Dr. Mitsumu persisted. "Couldn't we set up the tent here in the wash?"

"It's the old arroyo problem," Roger replied absently. "If the storm keeps up the canyon could start spilling sand as if it were water. We don't want to be buried."

They pulled it up the slope with little difficulty, and secured it with chock rocks under the wheels. Roger set up the tent mostly by himself, working too quickly for the others to help.

"Okay, you four get inside and get everything going. Eileen—"

"Roger?" It was Doran.

"Yes."

"We're still having trouble finding the main canyon."

"We thought we were in it," Cheryl said, "but when we descended we came to a big drop-off!"

"Okay. Hold on a minute where you are. Eileen, I want you to come up the main canyon with me and serve as a radio relay. You'll stay in the wash, so you'll be able to walk right back down to the tent if we get separated."

"Sure," Eileen said. The others were carefully rolling the wagon into the lock. Roger paused to oversee that operation, and then he gestured at Eileen through the tawny murk and took off upcanyon. Eileen followed.

They made rapid time. On band 33 Eileen heard the guide say, in an unworried conversational tone, "I hate it when this happens." It was as if he were referring to a shoelace breaking.

"I bet you do!" Eileen replied. "How are we going to find John?"

"Go high. Always go high when lost. I believe I told John that with the rest of you."

"Yes." Eileen had forgotten, however, and she wondered if John had too.

"Even if he's forgotten," Roger said, "when we get high enough, the radios will be less obstructed and we'll be able to talk to him. Or at the worst, we can bounce our signals off a satellite and back down. But I doubt we'll have to do that. Hey, Doran!" he said over the common band.

"Yeah?" Doran sounded very worried.

"What can you see now?"

"Um—we're on a spine—it's all we can see. The canyon to the right—"

"South?"

"Yeah, the south, is the one we were in. We thought the one here to the north would be the main one, but it's too little, and there's a drop-off in it."

"Okay, well, my APS has you still north of us, so cross back to the opposite spine and we'll talk from there. Can you do that?"

"Sure," Doran said, affronted. "It'll take a while, maybe."

"That's all right, take your time." The lack of concern in Roger's voice was almost catching, but Eileen felt that John was in danger; the suits would keep one alive for forty-eight hours at least, but these sandstorms often lasted a week, or more.

"Let's keep moving up," Roger said on band 33. "I don't think we have to worry about those two."

They climbed up the canyon floor, which rose at an average angle of about thirty degrees. Eileen noticed all the dust sliding loosely downhill, sand grains rolling, dust wafting down; sometimes she couldn't see her feet, or make out the ground, so that she had to step by feeling.

"How are you doing back in camp?" Roger asked on the common band.

"Just fine," Dr. Mitsumu answered. "It's on too much of a tilt to stand, so we're just sitting around and listening to the developments up there."

"Still in your suits?"

"Yes."

"Good. One of you stay suited for sure."

"Whatever you say."

Roger stopped where the main canyon was joined by two large tributary canyons, branching in each direction. "Watch out, I'm going to turn up the gain on the radio," he warned Eileen and the others. She adjusted the controls on her wrist.

"JOHN! Hey, John! Oh, Jo-uhnnn! Come in, John! Respond on common band. Please."

The radio's static sounded like the hiss of flying sand grains. Nothing within it but crackling.

"Hmm," Roger said in Eileen's left ear.

"Hey Roger!"

"Cheryl! How are you doing?"

"Well, we're in what we think is the main canyon, but . . ."

Doran continued, embarrassed: "We really can't be sure, now. Everything looks the same."

"You're telling me," Roger replied. Eileen watched him bend over and, apparently, inspect his feet. He moved around some in this jack-knifed position. "Try going to the wash at the lowest point in the canyon you're in."

"We're there."

"Okay, lean down and see if you find any boot prints. Make sure they aren't yours. They'll be faint by now, but Eileen and I just went upcanyon, so there should still be—"

"Hey! Here's some," Cheryl said.

"Where?" said Doran.

"Over here, look."

Radio hiss.

"Yeah, Roger, we've found some going upcanyon and down."

"Good. Now start downcanyon. Dr. M, are you still in your suit?"

"Just as you said, Roger."

"Good. Why don't you get out of the tent and go down to the wash. Keep your bearing, count your steps and all. Wait for Cheryl and Doran. That way they'll be able to find the tent as they come down."

"Sounds good."

After some chatter: "You all down there switch to band 5 to talk on, and just listen to common. We need to hear up here." Then on band 33: "Let's go up some more. I believe I remember a gendarme on the ridge up here with a good vantage."

"Fine. Where do you think he could be?"

"You got me."

When Roger located the outcropping he had in mind, they called again, and again got no response. Eileen then installed herself on top of the rocky knob on the ridge: an eerie place with nothing to see but the fine sand whipped about her, in a ghost wind barely felt on her back, like the lightest puff of an air conditioner, despite the visual resemblance to some awful typhoon. She called for John from time to time. Roger ranged to north and south over difficult terrain, always staying within radio distance of Eileen, although once he had a hard time relocating her.

Three hours passed that way, and Roger's easygoing tone changed—not to worry, Eileen judged, but rather to boredom, and annoyance with John. Eileen herself was extremely concerned. If John had mistaken north for south, or fallen . . .

"I suppose we should go higher." Roger sighed. "Although I thought I saw him back when we brought the wagon down here, and I doubt he'd go back up."

Suddenly Eileen's earphones crackled. *"Pss ftunk bdzz,"* and it was clear again. *"Ckk ssss ger, lo! ckk."*

"Sounds like he may have indeed gone high," Roger said with satisfaction, and, Eileen noticed, just a touch of relief. "Hey, John! Nobleton! Do you read us?"

"*Ckk sssssssss* yeah, hey! *sssss kuh sssss.*"

"We read you badly, John! Keep moving, keep talking! Are you all—"

"Roger! *ckk.* Hey, Roger!"

"John! We read you, are you all right?"

". . . *sssss* not exactly sure where I am."

"Are you all right?"

"Yes! Just lost."

"Well not anymore, we hope. Tell us what you see."

"Nothing!"

So began the long process of locating him and bringing him back. Eileen ranged left and right on her own, helping to get a fix on John, who had been instructed to stay still and keep talking.

"You won't believe it." John's voice was entirely free of fear; in fact, he sounded elated. "You won't believe it, Eileen, Roger. *crk!* Just before the storm hit I was way off down a tributary to the south, and I found . . ."

"Found what?"

"Well . . . I've found some things I'm sure must be fossils. I swear! A whole rock formation of them!"

"Oh yeah?"

"No seriously, I've got some with me. Very small shells, like little sea snails, or crustacea. Miniature nautiloids, like. They just couldn't be anything else. I have a couple in my pocket, but there's a whole wall of them back there! I figure if I just left I wouldn't be able to find the same canyon ever again, what with this storm, so I built a duck trail on the way back over to the main canyon, if that's where I am. So it took me a while to get back in radio clear."

"What color are they?" Ivan asked from below.

"You down there, be quiet," Roger ordered. "We're still trying to find him."

"We'll be able to get back to the site. Eileen, can you believe it? We'll all be—*Hey!*"

"It's just me," Roger said.

"Ah! You gave me a start, there."

Eileen smiled as she imagined John startled by the ghostlike appearance of the lanky, suited Roger. Soon enough Roger had led John downcanyon to Eileen, and after John hugged her, they proceeded down the canyon to Dr. Mitsumu, who again led them up the slope to the tent, which rested at a sharper angle than Eileen had recalled.

Once inside, the reunited group chattered for an hour concerning their adventure, while Roger showered and got the wagon on an even keel, and John revealed the objects he had brought back with him:

Small shell-shaped rocks, some held in crusts of sandstone. Each shell had a spiral swirl on its inside surface, and they were mottled red and black. By and large they were black.

They were unlike any rocks Eileen had ever seen; they looked exactly like the few Terran shells she had seen in school. Seeing them there in John's hand, she caught her breath. Life on Mars; even if only fossil traces of it, *life on Mars*. She took one of the shells from John and stared and stared at it. It very well could be. . . .

They had to arrange their cots across the slope of the tent floor and prop them level with clothes and other domestic objects from the wagon. Long after they were settled they discussed John's discovery, and Eileen found herself more and more excited by the idea of it. The sand pelting the tent soundlessly only made its presence known by the complete absence of stars. She stared at the faint curved reflection of them all on the dome's surface, and thought of it. The Clayborne Expedition, in the history books. And Martian life. . . . The others talked and talked.

"So we'll go there tomorrow, right?" John asked Roger. The tilt of the tent made it impossible for Roger to set up his bedroom.

"Or as soon as the storm ends, sure." Roger had only glanced at the shells, shaking his head and muttering, "I don't know, don't get your hopes up too high." Eileen wondered about that. "We'll follow that duck trail of yours, if we can." Perhaps he was jealous of John now?

On and on they talked. Yet the hunt had taken it out of Eileen; to the sound of their voices she suddenly fell asleep.

She woke up when her cot gave way and spilled her down the floor; before she could stop herself, she had rolled over Mrs. Mitsumu and John. She got off John quickly and saw Roger over at the wagon, smiling down at the gauges. Her cot had been by the wagon; had he yanked out some crucial item of clothing? There was something of the prankster in the man. . . .

The commotion woke the rest of the sleepers. Immediately the conversation returned to the matter of John's discovery, and Roger agreed that their supplies were sufficient to allow a trip back up-canyon. And the storm had stopped; dust coated their dome, and was piled half a centimeter high on its uphill side, but they could see that the sky was clear. So after breakfast they suited up, more awkward than ever on the tilted floor, and emerged from their shelter.

The distance back up to where they had met John was much shorter than it had seemed to Eileen in the storm. All of their tracks had been covered, even the sometimes deep treadmarks of the wagon. John led the way, leaping upward in giant bounds that were almost out of his control.

"There's the gendarme where we found you," Roger said from below, pointing to the spine on their right for John's benefit. John waited for them, talking nervously all the while. "There's the first duck," he told them. "I see it way over there, but with all the sand, it looks almost like any other mound. This could be hard."

"We'll find them," Roger assured him.

When they had all joined John, they began to traverse the canyons to the south, each one a deep multifingered trench in the slope of Mars facing Olympus Mons. John had very little sense of where he had been, except that he had not gone much above or below the level they were on. Some of the ducks were hard to spot, but Roger had quite a facility for it, and the others spotted some as well. More than once none of them saw it, and they had to trek off in nine slightly different directions, casting about in hopes of running into it. Each time someone would cry, "Here it is," as if they were children hunting Easter eggs, and they would convene and search again. Only once were they unable to locate the next duck, and then Roger pumped John's memory of his hike; after all, as Ivan pointed out, it had been the full light of day when he walked to the site. A crestfallen John admitted that, each little red canyon looking so much like the next one, he couldn't really recall where he had gone from there.

"Well, but there's the next duck," Roger said with surprise, pointing at a little niche indicating a side ravine. And after they had reached the niche John cried, "This is it! Right down this ravine, in the wall itself. And some of them have fallen."

The common band was a babble of voices as they dropped into the steep-sided ravine one by one. Eileen stepped down through the narrow entrance and confronted the nearly vertical south wall. There, embedded in hard sandstone, were thousands of tiny black stone snail shells. The bottom of the ravine was covered with them; all of them were close to the same size, with holes that opened into the hollow interior of the shells. Many of them were broken, and inspecting some fragments, Eileen saw the spiral ribbing that so often characterized life. Her earphones rang with the excited voices of her companions. Roger had climbed the canyon wall and was inspecting a particular section, his faceplate only centimeters from stone. "See what I mean?" John was asking. "Martian snails! It's like those fossil bacterial mats they talk about, only further advanced. Back when Mars had surface water and an atmosphere, life *did* begin. It just didn't have time to get very far."

"Nobleton snails," Cheryl said, and they laughed. Eileen picked up fragment after fragment, her excitement growing. They were all very similar. She was taxing her suit's cooling system, starting to sweat. She examined a well-preserved specimen carefully, pulling it out of the rock to do so. The common band was distractingly noisy, and she was about to turn it off when Roger's voice said slowly, "Uh-ohh. . . . Hey, people. Hey."

When it was silent he said hesitantly, "I hate to spoil the party, but . . . these little things aren't fossils."

"What?"

"What do you mean?" John and Ivan challenged. "How do you know?"

"Well, there are a couple reasons," Roger said. Everyone was still now, and watching him. "First, I believe that fossils are created by a process that requires millions of years of water seepage, and Mars never had that."

"So we think now," Ivan objected. "But it may not be so, because it's certain that there was water on Mars all along. And after all, here are these things."

"Well . . ." Eileen could tell he was deciding to let that argument pass. "Maybe you're right, but a better reason is, I think I know what these are. They're lava pellets—bubble pellets, I've heard them called—although I've never seen ones this small. Little lava bombs from one of the Olympus Mons eruptions. A sort of spray."

Everyone stared at the objects in their hands.

"See, when lava pellets land hot in a certain sort of sand, they sink right through it and melt the sand fast, releasing gas that forms the bubble, and these glassy interiors. When the pellet is spinning, you get these spiral chambers. So I've heard, anyway. It must have happened on a flat plain long ago, and when the whole plain tilted and started falling down this slope, these layers broke up and were buried by later deposits."

"I don't believe that's necessarily so," John declared, while the others looked at the wall. But even he sounded pretty convinced to Eileen.

"Of course we'll have to take some back to be sure," Roger agreed in a soothing tone.

"Why didn't you tell us this last night?" Eileen asked.

"Well, I couldn't tell till I had seen the rock they were in. But this is lava-sprayed sandstone, they call it. That's why it's so hard in its upper layers. But you're an areologist, right?" He wasn't mocking. "Don't they look like they're made of lava?"

Eileen nodded, reluctantly. "Looks like it."

"Well, lava doesn't make fossils."

Half an hour later a dispirited group was stretched out over the duck trail, straggling along in silence. John and Ivan trailed far behind, weighted down by several kilos of lava pellets. Pseudofossils, as both areologists and geologists called them. Roger was ahead, talking with the Mitsumus, attempting to cheer them all up, Eileen guessed. She felt bad about not identifying the rock the previous night. She felt more depressed than she could easily account for, and it made her angry. Everything was so empty out here, so meaningless, so without form. . . .

"Once I thought I had found traces of aliens," Roger was saying. "I was off by myself around the other side of Olympus, hiking canyons as usual, except I was by myself. I was crossing really broken fretted terrain, when suddenly I came across a trail duck. Stones never stack up by themselves. Now the Explorer's Society keeps a record of every single hike and expedition, you know, and I had checked before and I knew I was in fresh territory, just like we are now. No humans had ever been in that part of the badlands, as far as the Society knew. Yet here was this duck. And I started finding other ones right away. Set not in a straight line, but zigzagging, tacking like. And little. Tiny piles of flat rock, four or five high. Like they were set up by little aliens who saw best out of the sides of their eyes."

"You must have been astounded," Mrs. Mitsumu said.

"Exactly. But, you know—there were three possibilities. It was a natural rock formation—extremely unlikely, but it could be that breadloaf formations had slid onto their sides and then been eroded into separate pieces, still stacked on each other. Or they were set up by aliens. Also unlikely, in my opinion. Or someone had hiked through there without reporting it, and had played a game, maybe, for someone later to find. To me, that was the most likely explanation. But for a while there . . ."

"You must have been disappointed," said Mrs. Mitsumu.

"Oh no," Roger replied easily. "More entertained than anything, I think."

Eileen stared at the form of their guide, far ahead with the others. He truly didn't care that John's discovery had not been the remnants of life, she judged. In that way he was different, unlike John or Ivan, unlike herself; for she felt his obviously correct explanation of the little shells as a loss larger than she ever would have guessed. She wanted life out there as badly as John or Ivan or any of the rest of them did, she realized. All those books she had read, when studying literature. . . . That was why she had not let herself remember that igneous rock would never be involved with fossilization. If only life had once existed here—snails, lichen, bacteria, anything—it would somehow take away some of this landscape's awful barrenness.

And if Mars itself could not provide, it became necessary to supply it—to do whatever was necessary to make life possible on its desolate surface, to transform it as soon as possible, to *give it life*. Now she understood the connection between the two main topics of evening conversation in their isolated camps: terraforming, and the discovery of extinct Martian life-forms; and the conversations took place all over the planet, less intently than out here in the canyons, perhaps, but still, all her life Eileen had been hoping for this discovery, had *believed* in it.

She pulled the half dozen lava pellets she had saved from one of her suit pockets and stared at them. Abruptly, bitterly, she tossed them aside, and they floated out into the rust waste. They would never find remnants of Martian life; no one ever would. She knew that was true in every cell of her. All the so-called discoveries, all the Martians in her books—they were all part of a simple case of projection, nothing more. Humans wanted Martians, that was all there was to it. But there were not, and never had been, any canal-builders; no lamppost creatures with heat-beam eyes, no brilliant lizards or grasshoppers, no manta ray intelligences, no angels and no devils; there were no four-armed races battling in blue jungles, no bigheaded skinny thirsty folk, no sloe-eyed dusky beauties dying for Terran sperm, no wise little Bleekmen wandering stunned in the desert, no golden-eyed golden-skinned telepaths, no doppelgänger race—not a fun-house mirror image of any kind; there weren't any ruined adobe palaces, no dried-oasis castles, no mysterious cliff dwellings packed like a museum, no hologrammatic towers waiting to drive humans mad, no intricate canal systems with their locks all filled with sand, no not a single canal; there were not even any mosses creeping down from the polar caps every summer, nor any rabbitlike animals living far underground; no plastic windmill-creatures, no lichen capable of casting dangerous electrical fields, no lichen of any kind; no algae in the hot springs, no microbes in the soil, no microbacteria in the regolith, no stromatolites, no nanobacteria in the deep bedrock . . . no primeval soup.

All so many dreams. Mars was a dead planet. Eileen scuffed the freeze-dried dirt and watched through damp eyes as the pinkish sand lofted away from her boot. All dead. That was her home: dead Mars. Not even dead, which implied a life and a dying. Just . . . nothing. A red void.

They turned down the main canyon. Far below was their tent, looking like it would slide down its slope any instant. Now there was a sign of life. Eileen grinned bleakly behind her faceplate. Outside her suit it was forty degrees below zero, and the air was not air.

Roger was hurrying down the canyon ahead of them, no doubt to turn on the air and heat in the tent, or pull the wagon out to move it all downcanyon. In the alien gravity she had lived in all her life, he dropped down the great trench as in a dream, not bounding gazelle-like in the manner of John or Doran, but just on the straightest line, the most efficient path, in a sort of boulder ballet all the more grace-ful for being so simple. Eileen liked that. Now there, she thought, is a man reconciled to the absolute deadness of Mars. It seemed his home, his landscape. An old line occurred to her: "We have met the enemy, and he is us." And then something from Bradbury: "The Martians were there . . . Timothy and Robert and Michael and Mom and Dad."

She pondered the idea as she followed Clayborne down their canyon, trying to imitate that stride.

"But there *was* life on Mars." That evening she watched him. Ivan and Doran talked to Cheryl; John sulked on his cot. Roger chatted with the Mitsumus, who liked him. At sunset when they showered (they had moved the tent to another fine flat site) he walked over to his paneled cubicle naked, and the flat onyx bracelet he wore around his left wrist suddenly seemed to Eileen the most beautiful ornamen-tation. She realized she was glancing at him in the same way John and the doctor looked at her—only differently—and she blushed.

After dinner the others were quiet, returning to their cots. Roger continued telling the Mitsumus and Eileen stories. She had never heard him talk so much. He was still sarcastic with her, but that wasn't what his smile was saying. She watched him move . . . and sighed, ex-asperated with herself; wasn't this just what she had come out here to get away from? Did she really need or want this feeling again, this quickening interest?

"They still can't decide if there's some ultrasmall nanobacteria down in the bedrock. The arguments go back and forth in the scientific journals all the time. Could be down there, so small we can't even see it. There's been reports of drilling contamination. . . . But I don't think so."

Yet he certainly was different from the men she had known in recent years. After everyone had gone to bed, she concentrated on that difference, that quality; he was . . . Martian. He was that alien life, and she wanted him in a way she had never wanted her other lovers. Mrs. Mitsumu had been smiling at them, as if she saw something going on, something she had seen developing long before, when the two of them were always at odds. . . . Earth girl lusts for virile Martian; she laughed at herself, but there it was. Still constructing stories to populate this planet, still falling in love, despite herself. And she wanted to do something about it. She had always lived by Eulert's saying: If you don't act on it, it wasn't a true feeling. It had gotten her in trouble too, but she was forgetting that. And tomorrow they would be at the little outpost that was their destination, and the chance would be gone. For an hour she thought about it, evaluating the looks he had given her that evening. How did you evaluate an alien's glances? Ah, but he was human—just adapted to Mars in a way she wished she could be—and there had been something in his eyes very human, very understandable. Around her the black hills loomed against the black sky, the double star hung overhead, that home she had never set foot on. It was a lonely place.

Well, she had never been particularly shy in these matters, but she had always favored a more inpulling approach, encouraging advances rather than making them (usually) so that when she quietly got off her cot and slipped into shorts and a shirt, her heart was knocking like a tympani roll. She tiptoed to the panels, thinking *Fortune favors the bold,* and slipped between them, went to his side.

He sat up; she put her hand to his mouth. She didn't know what to do next. Her heart was knocking harder than ever. That gave her an idea, and she leaned over and pulled his head around and placed it against her ribs, so he could hear her pulse. He looked up at her, pulled her down to the cot. They kissed. Some whispers. The cot was too narrow and creaky, and they moved to the floor, lay next to each other kissing. She could feel him, hard against her thigh; some sort of

Martian stone, she reckoned, like that flesh jade. . . . They whispered to each other, lips to each other's ears like headpiece intercoms. She found it difficult to stay so quiet making love, exploring that Martian rock, being explored by it. . . . She lost her mind for a while then, and when she came to she was quivering now and again; an occasional aftershock, she thought to herself. A seismology of sex. He appeared to read her mind, for he whispered happily in her ear, "Your seismographs are probably picking us up right now."

She laughed softly, then made the joke current among literature majors at the university: "Yes, very nice . . . the Earth moved."

After a second he got it and stifled a laugh. "Several thousand kilometers."

Laughter is harder to suppress than the sounds of love.

Of course it is impossible to conceal such activity in a group—not to mention a tent—of such small size, and the next morning Eileen got some pointed looks from John, some smiles from Mrs. M. It was a clear morning, and after they got the tent packed into the wagon and were on their way, Eileen hiked off whistling to herself. As they descended toward the broad plain at the bottom of the canyon mouth, she and Roger tuned in to their band 33 and talked.

"You really don't think this wash would look better with some cactus and sage in it, say? Or grasses?"

"Nope. I like it the way it is. See that pentagon of shards there?" He pointed. "How nice."

With the intercom they could wander far apart from each other and still converse, and no one could know they were talking, while each voice hung in the other's ear. So they talked and talked. Everyone has had conversations that have been crucial in their lives: clarity of expression, quickness of feeling, attentiveness to the other's words, a belief in the reality of the other's world—of these and other elements are such conversations made, and at the same time the words themselves can be concerned with the simplest, most ordinary things:

"Look at that rock."

"How nice that ridge is against the sky—it must be a hundred kilometers away, and it looks like you could touch it."

"Everything's so red."

"Yeah. Red Mars, I love it. I'm for red Mars."

She considered it. They hiked down the widening canyon ahead of the others, on opposite slopes. Soon they would be back in the world of cities, the big wide world. There were lots and lots of people out there, and anyone you met you might never see again. On the other hand . . . she looked across at the tall awkwardly proportioned man, striding with feline Martian grace over the dunes, in the dream gravity. Like a dancer.

"How old are you?" she asked.

"Twenty-six."

"My God!" He was already quite wrinkled. More sun than most.

"What?"

"I thought you were older."

"No."

"How long have you been doing this?"

"Hiking canyons?"

"Yes."

"Since I was six."

"Oh." That explained how he knew all this world so well.

She crossed the canyon to walk by his side; seeing her doing it, he descended his slope and they walked down the center of the wash.

"Can I come on another trip with you?"

He looked at her: behind the faceplate, a grin. "Oh yes. There are a lot of canyons to see."

The canyon opened up, then flattened out, and its walls melted into the broad boulder-studded plain on which the little outpost was set, some kilometers away. Eileen could just see it in the distance, like a castle made of glass: a tent like theirs, really, only much bigger. Behind it Olympus Mons rose straight up out of the sky.

The Archaea Plot

The little red people did not like terraforming. As far as they were concerned it wrecked everything, the way global warming wrecked things on Earth, only two magnitudes worse, as usual. Everything on Mars is two magnitudes more than it is on Earth—two magnitudes more or less.

Of course the relationship between the little red people and the introduced Terran organisms was already complex. To fully understand it you have to remember the little red people's even smaller cousins, the old ones. These were the Archaea, that third order of life along with bacteria and eucarya—and in this case, also citizens of the panspermic cloud which four billion years before fell on Mars from space, having flown many light-years from their point of spontaneous generation around an early second-generation star. Mostly *Thermoproteus* and *Methanospirillum*, it seems, with a few *Haloferax* thrown in as well. They were hyperthermophiles, so the early Mars of the heavy bombardment suited them just fine. But then some few of these travelers were blasted off the surface of Mars by a meteor strike, and crash-landed later on Earth, fructifying the third planet and sparking the long wild course of Terran evolution. Thus all Earthly life is Martian, in this limited sense, though in truth it is also far more ancient than that.

Then later Paul Bunyan, the distant descendant of these panspermic Archaea, came back to Mars to find it cold and ostensibly empty, though some of the old ones still persisted, golluming around in various submartian volcanic percolations. Paul and his big blue ox Babe were bested by Big Man, as you know, and inserted by him through the planetary interior, crust mantle, and core. From there Paul's inner bacterial family spread through all the regolith on the planet, and began the so-called cryptoendolithic great leap forward, that first submartian terraforming, which produced at the end of its evolution the little red people as we know them.

So the Martians had come home again, almost as small as the first time around—about two magnitudes bigger than the old ones left behind, that's right. But the relationship between the little red people and the Archaea was clearly not a simple one. Second cousins thrice removed? Something like that.

Despite this blood tie, the little red people discovered early on in their civilization that their ancestors the Archaea could be grown and harvested for food, also building material, cloth, and the like. Inventing this form of agriculture, or husbandry, or industry, allowed for a tremendous population explosion, as the little red people had just taken a step up the food chain, by exploiting the level of life just below theirs. Fine for them, and because they have helped us so much in their subtle way, fine for the humans on Mars as well; but the Archaea considered it barbarous. The little red people interpreted their sullen bovine glares as subservience only, but all the while the Archaea were looking at them thinking, You cannibals, we are going to get you someday.

And so they hatched a plot. They could see that the terraforming was just more of the aerobic same old same old; that the little red people would adapt to it, and become part of the new larger system, and move up onto the surface and take their little red place in the growing biosphere; and meanwhile the old ones would remain trapped in pitch-darkness, living off heat and water and the chemical reactions between hydrogen and carbon dioxide. It isn't fair, the Archaea said to each other. It won't do. It was our planet to begin with. We should take it back.

But how, some said. There's oxygen everywhere you go now, except down here. And they're making it worse every day.

We'll find a way, some of the others replied. We are *Thermoproteus*, we'll think of something. We'll infiltrate somehow. They've poisoned us; we'll poison them back. Just bide your time and keep in touch. The anaerobic revolt will have its day.

The Way the Land Spoke to Us

1. THE GREAT ESCARPMENT

You know that the origin of the big dichotomy between the northern lowlands and the southern cratered highlands is still a matter of dispute among areologists. It might be the result of the biggest impact of the early heavy bombardment, and the north therefore the biggest impact basin. Or it may be that tectonic forces were still roiling the early crust, and an early protocontinental craton, like Pangaea on Earth, had risen in the southern hemisphere and then hardened into place, as the smaller planet cooled faster than Earth, without any subsequent tectonic-plate breakup and drift. You would think these would be interpretations so diverse that areology would quickly devise questions that would make one or the other explanation either certain or impossible, but so far this is not the case; both explanations have attracted advocates making fully elaborated cases backing their views, and so the matter has shaped itself into one of the primary debates in areology. I myself have no opinion.

The question has ramifications for many other issues in areology, but it's worth remembering just what the big dichotomy means for people walking across the face of Mars. Hiking across Echus Chasma to its eastern cliffs gives one perhaps the most dramatic approach to the so-called Great Escarpment dividing the two.

The floor of Echus Chasma is chaos at its most chaotic, and for someone on foot, this means endless divagations and extravagances to make one's way forward. Nowadays one can follow the trail, and minimize the ups and downs, end runs, dead ends, and backtracking necessary to make one's way in any direction; and the Maze Trail is the very model of route-finding efficiency through such torn terrain; nevertheless, if one wanted to get a sense of what it was like in the early days, it is perhaps better to leave the trail, and strike out to forge a new and unrepeatable cross-country ramble through the waste.

If you do that, you will quickly find that your view of your surroundings is inadequate to plan a forward course very far. Often you can see across the land only a kilometer or less. Big blocks of chunky eroded basalt and andesite are the entirety of the landscape; it's as if one were crossing a talus whose particulates were two or three magnitudes larger than the talus one usually crushes underfoot. So that one threads through the terrain as an ant must make its way through talus. Small but unclimbable cliffs confront one everywhere one looks. The only way to make progress is to keep to ridgelines, skirting great hole after great hole, while hoping the ridgelines will connect to each other in ways that can be clambered over. It's like negotiating a hedge maze by staying on the hedge tops.

Chaotic terrain: The name is quite accurate. Here the surface of the world once lost its support, when the aquifer below it drained rapidly away, downhill and over the horizon in a great outflow flood—in this case, down Echus Chasma, round the big bend of Kasei Vallis, down Kasei's gorge canyon and out onto Chryse Planitia, some two thousand kilometers away. And when that happened the land came crashing down.

So you walk, or climb, or crawl, for day after day, across the tilted surfaces and broken edges of the great blocks of the fallen crust. You can see just what happened: The land dropped; it shattered; there was more of it than there was room for, and so it came to rest all atilt and acrackle. The violence of this ancient collapse has been scarcely masked by the three billion subsequent years of wind erosion and dustfall. It is an irony that such an unstable-looking landscape should actually be so ancient and unchanged.

So it is a matter of broken rock for as far as the eye can see. Which is not far, admittedly; even on the highest points along the way (the Maze Trail takes a line that runs from one of these to the next), the horizon is only three or four kilometers away. A very tight and jumbled wasteland of rust-tinted rock.

Then at the peak of one long roof beam of a ridge, you find yourself high enough that off to the east, a great distance away, just poking over the crackle, lie the tops of a mountain range, pale orange in the late-afternoon light. If you camp on this prominence, in the alpenglow the distant range looks like the side of a different world, rolling slowly up into the sky.

But the next morning you descend back into the maze of potholes and passlets, ridgelines and occasional flat block plateaus, like low rooftops in Manhattan. Crossing these terrains commands all your attention, and so you almost forget the sight of the distant mountain range, the problems are so great (it was in this region we found a providential crack in a thirty-meter cliff, which allowed us to climb down safely, lowering our packs on ropes)—until at the next prominence in your path through the chaos, it heaves back into view, closer now and seemingly taller, as one can see farther down its side. Not a mountain range, one now sees, but a cliff, extending north and south from horizon to horizon, etched in the usual spur-and-gully formation of cliffs everywhere, and somewhat saw-toothed at its top, but massively solid for all that—the etchings without any depth, like the brushing you see on certain metal surfaces.

And each day, when it stands over your horizon at all, it's closer. It tends to stay over the horizon longer; but never all the time, as very often you drop into the depths of the next sink in this sunken land. But eventually, continuing roughly eastward, every time you are not actually in the depths of a pothole, the cliff positively looms over the world to the east, towering over the horizon, which stubbornly remains no more than five kilometers away. So at that point you have two horizons, in effect; one near and low, the other far and high.

And eventually you get so close to it that the cliff simply fills the eastern sky. It rises astonishingly near the zenith; it's like running into the side of a bigger world. Like crawling over a dry cracked seabed to the side of a continental shelf. The gulleys and embayments in the cliff are whole landscapes in themselves now, canyon worlds of great depth and even greater steepness. Every spur between them is now seen to be a huge buttress, ribbing the side of a higher world. The occasional horizontal ledges marking the buttresses appear big enough to support complete island estates. But it's hard to tell from below.

And indeed, by the time you reach the point called Cliff Bottom View, where you stand on one of the last high points of the chaos, nearly as high as the narrow strip of hilly plateau between the chaos and the escarpment, and you can finally see all the land between where you are and the foot of the great cliff, you can no longer see the cliff's top. The mass of it blocks your view, and what you see rimming the sky, so far up toward the zenith, is not the true top, though it can seem so if you have not been paying attention, but is rather some prominence partway down its side.

Only by getting into a small blimp and taking off into the air, and flying up and away from the cliff, back out over the eastern part of the chaos, can you see the whole extent of it. If you keep sight of a reference mark, you can see that what down in the last camp you took for the top of the cliff was only about two-thirds of the way up it; the rest was blocked from view; and in any case the very strong optical effect of foreshortening had deceived you as to the true height of the thing. You keep floating up into the air, up and up and up, like a bird gyring on an updraft, and finally seeing all the cliff at once from this perspective, we just started to laugh, we couldn't help it—we were laughing or crying, or both at once, our mouths were hanging open to our chests, we positively *goggled* at it, and there was nothing really we could say, it was so big.

2. FLATNESS

There are places out in Argyre that are nothing but flat sand to the horizon in every direction.

Usually the sand is blown into dunes. Any kind of dune, from very fine ripples underfoot to truly gargantuan barchan dunes. But in some areas even that is missing, and it is simply a flat plane of sand or bedrock, with the sky arching over it.

They say that if you look at it closely, the sky forms the visual equivalent of a dome overhead. Not a true hemisphere, but flattened somewhat. This is a virtually universal human perception, the result of consistent overestimation of horizontal distance compared with vertical distance. On Earth the horizon seems to be two to four times farther off than the zenith overhead, and if you ask someone to divide the arc between the zenith and the horizon evenly, the point chosen averages well less than forty-five degrees; about twenty-two degrees by day, I have found, and thirty by night. Redness increases this effect. If you look at the sky through red glass it appears flatter; if through blue glass, taller.

On Mars the unobstructed horizon is only about half as far away as it is on Earth—about five kilometers—and sometimes this simply makes the zenith seem even lower—perhaps two kilometers high. It depends on the clarity of the air, which of course varies a great deal: Sometimes I have seen the dome of the sky appear ten kilometers high, or even transparent to infinity. Mostly lower than that. In fact the vault of the sky is a different shape every day, if you will take the time to look at it carefully.

But no matter the transparency of the sky, or the shape of the dome it makes overhead: The sand is always the same. Flat; reddish brown; redder out toward the horizon. The characteristic redness occurs if even one percent of the bedrock or the dust on the ground is made up of iron oxides such as magnetite. This condition obtains everywhere on Mars, except for the lava plains of Syrtis, which when blown free of dust are nearly black—one of my favorite places (also the first feature to be seen from Earth through telescopes, by Christiaan Huygens in 1654).

In any case: a perfect red plane in all directions, to the round horizon. Inside certain flat craters, you stand at the center and see a double horizon, in fact: the lower one five kilometers away, and perfectly straight; the higher one farther away, and usually less straight, even serrated. (This second horizon also considerably flattens the dome of the sky.)

But the completely flat areas are the purest view. Much of Vastitas Borealis is so flat that only millions of years of existence as the floor of an ocean can explain it. And parts of Argyre Planitia are equally flat. We cannot lose these places. In these regions one stands confronted by a radically simplified landscape. It is a surreal experience to look around oneself—surreal in the literal sense of the word, in that one seems to stand in a place "over-real," or "more than real"—a higher state than reality; or reality revealed in its barest, most heraldic simplicity. The world says then, This is what the cosmos consists of; rock, sky, sun, life (that's you). What a massive aesthetic impact is conveyed by this so-simplified landscape! It *forces* you to pay attention to it; it is so remarkable you keep looking at it, you cannot do or think anything else—as if living in a perpetual total eclipse, or within any other physical miracle. Which of course is always the case. Remember.

Maya and Desmond

1. FINDING HIM

After she saw the strange face through the bottle in the farm of the *Ares*, Maya couldn't stop thinking of it. It frightened her, but she was no coward. And that had been a stranger, not one of the hundred. There on her ship.

And then she told John about it, and he believed her. He believed in her; and so she was going to have to track that stranger down.

She began by calling up the plans for the ship and studying them like she had never studied them before. It surprised her to find how many spaces it contained, how large their total volume. She had known the areas the way one knows a hotel or a ship or a plane, or one's hometown for that matter—as a set of her life-routes, wound through the whole in an internal mental map, which itself could be called up sharply visible in her mind's eye; but the rest was only vagueness, deduced, if she ever thought about it, from the parts she knew; but deduced wrongly, as she now found out.

Still, there was only so much livable space in the thing. The axis cylinders were not livable, by and large, and the eight toruses were, for the most part; but they were also very heavily traveled. Hiding would not be easy.

She had seen him in the farm. It seemed possible, even perhaps likely, that the man had allies in the farm crew, helping him to hide. A lone stowaway, unknown to anyone aboard, was difficult for her to believe in.

So she began in the farm.

Each torus was octagonal, made of eight American shuttle fuel canisters that had been boosted into orbit and coupled together. More bundled canisters formed the long axis that speared down the centers of the torus octagons, and the octagons were connected to the central axis by narrow spokelike passage tubes. The entire spacecraft spun on the long axis as it moved forward toward Mars, spinning at a speed that created a centrifugal force the equivalent of Martian gravity, at least for people walking on the floors set against the outside of the torus rings. The Coriolis force meant that if you walked against the rotation of the ship you felt you were leaning forward a little. The opposite effect, walking in the other direction, was somehow not so noticeable. You had to lean into reality to make progress.

The farm chamber filled torus F, the well-lit rows of vegetable and cereal lined out in a circular infinity. Above the ceilings and under the floors the supplies were kept. A lot of spaces to hide, in other words, when you got right down to searching for someone. Especially if you were trying to search in secret, which Maya most definitely was. She did it at night, after people were asleep. Here they were in space and yet people were still incredibly diurnal, regular as clockwork; indeed only clockwork kept them to it, but it was the clockwork of their own biology; and indicative of just how much of their animal natures they were carrying with them. But it gave Maya her opportunity.

She started in the chamber where she had seen the face, and made sure that no one ever saw her at work. So already she was a kind of ally of the man. She worked her way forward through the farm, row by row, storage compartment by storage compartment, tank by tank. No one there. She moved down the ship one torus to the storage tanks, and did the same. Days were passing, and Mars was the size of a coin ahead of them.

As her search progressed she realized how much all the chambers looked the same, no matter how they had been customized for use. They were living inside tanks of metal, and each tank resembled the others, much like the years of a life. Much like city life everywhere, she saw one day: room after room after room. Occasionally the great bubble chamber that was the sky. Human life, a matter of boxes. The escape from freedom.

She searched all the toruses and didn't find him. She searched the axis tanks and didn't find him.

He could have been in someone's room, many of which were

locked, as in any hotel. He could be in a place she hadn't looked. He could be aware of her, and moving away from her as she searched.

She began again.

Time was running out. Mars was the size of an orange. A bruised and mottled orange. Soon they would arrive and go through aerobraking and orbit calming.

It was almost as if she were being watched. She had always felt observed somehow, as if she were living her life on an invisible stage, performing it for an invisible audience who followed her story with interest, and judged her. There had to be something that heard her endless train of thoughts, didn't there?

But this was more physical than that. She went through the crowded days prepping for arrival, slipping off to make love with John, fencing with Frank to avoid doing the same with him, and all the while feeling there was an eye on her, somewhere. She had learned that no matter where she was, she was in a tank filled with objects, and had trained herself to see the things filling the tank against the Platonic form of the tank itself, looking for discrepancies like false walls or floors, and finding some. Jumping around occasionally. But never catching that eye.

One night she came out of John's room and felt she was alone. Immediately she returned to the farm and went from its ceiling up to the axis tanks. Above the ceiling, under the low curve of the inner tank wall, was a storage chamber with a back wall that was too close to be the true end of the tank. She had seen that while eating breakfast one morning, without thinking about anything at all. Now she pulled away a stack of boxes set against this false wall, and saw the whole wall was a door, with a handle.

It was locked.

She leaned back, thought about it. She rapped lightly on the door, three times.

"Roko?" said a hoarse voice from within.

Maya said nothing. Her heart was beating hard and fast. The handle turned and she snatched it and yanked the door open, pulling out a thin brown arm. She let go of the door and grabbed the arm harder than the door; instantly she was yanked back into the tiny closet, and seized by hands with a talon grip.

"Stop it!" she cried, and as the man was trying to flee under her arm, she crashed down onto him, hitting boxes and insulation padding hard, but staying latched to a wrist. She sat on him with all her force, as if pinning an enraged child. "Stop it! *I know you're here.*"

He gave up trying to escape.

They both shifted to get more comfortable, and she lessened her grip on the man's arm, but still held on, not trusting him not to bolt. A small wiry black man, thin face bent or asymmetrical somehow, big brown eyes as frightened as a deer's. Thin wrist, but forearm muscles like rocks under the skin. He was quivering in her grip. Years later when she remembered their first meeting, what she remembered was his flesh trembling in her grip, trembling like a frightened fawn.

Fiercely she said, "What do you think I'm going to do? Do you think I'm going to tell everyone about you? Or send you home? Do you think I'm that kind of person?"

He shook his head, face averted, but glancing at her with a new surmise.

"No," he said, in almost a whisper. "I know you're not. But I been so afraid."

"Not necessary with me," she said. Impulsively she reached out with her free hand and touched the side of his head. He shivered like a horse. Body like a bantamweight wrestler. An animal, moving involuntarily at the touch of another animal. Starved for touch, perhaps. She moved back away from him, let go of his arm, sat with her back leaning against the padding on the wall, watching him. An odd face somehow, narrow and triangular, with that asymmetry. Like pictures in magazines of Rastafarians from Jamaica. From below wafted the smell of the farm. He had no smell as far as she could tell, or else just more of the farm.

"So who's helping you?" she said. "Hiroko?"

His eyebrows shot up. After a moment's hesitation: "Yeah. Of course. Hiroko Ai, God damn her. My boss."

"Your mistress."

"My owner."

"Your lover."

Disconcerted, he looked down at his hands, bigger than his body seemed to need. "Me and half the farm team," he said with a bitter little smile. "All of us wrapped around her little finger. And me living in a crawl space, for Christ's sake."

"To get to Mars."

"To get to Mars," he repeated bitterly. "To be with her, you mean. Crazy man that I am, damn fool idiot crazy man."

"Where are you from?"

"Tobago. Trinidad Tobago, do you know it?"

"Caribbean? I visited Barbados once."

"Like that, yeah."

"But now Mars."

"Someday."

"We're almost there," she said. "I was afraid we would get there before I found you."

"Hmph," he said, looking up at her briefly, thinking this over. "Well. Now I not in such a hurry to get there." He looked up again, with a shy smile.

She laughed.

She asked him more questions, and he replied, and asked more of his own. He was funny—like John in that—only sharper-edged than John. A bitterness there; and interesting, she suddenly realized, just as someone *new*, someone she didn't already know all too well. You got to watch out for Hiroko, he warned her at one point. "Hiroko, Phyllis, Arkady—they be trouble. Them and Frank, of course."

"Tell me about it."

"It's quite a crew you have," he replied slyly, observing her.

"Yes." She rolled her eyes; what could one say?

He grinned. "You won't tell them about me?"

"No."

"Thanks." Now it was him holding her by the wrist. "I'll help you, I swear. I'll be your friend." Staring her right in the eye, for the first time.

"And I'll be yours," she said, feeling touched, then suddenly happy. "I'll help you too."

"We'll help each other. There'll be the hundred and all their jostle, and then you and me, helping each other."

She nodded, liking the idea. "Friends."

She freed her arm, and with a brief squeeze of his shoulder got up to leave. He still trembled slightly under her hand.

"Wait—what's your name?"

"Desmond."

2. HELPING HIM

Thus in Underhill Maya always knew her stowaway Desmond was out there in the farm, getting by in circumstances almost as prisonlike as those he had suffered on the *Ares*. For days and months at a time she forgot this as she mangled her relationships with John and Frank, irritating Nadia and Michel, who were both nearly worthless to her, and irritating herself just as often or more—feeling incompetent and depressed, she didn't know why—having difficulty adjusting to life on Mars, no doubt. It was miserable in a lot of ways, to be cooped up in the trailers and then the quadrangle, with only each other. It wasn't that much different from the *Ares*, to tell the truth.

But every once in a while Maya would see a movement in the corner of her eye, and think of Desmond. His situation was worse than hers by far, and he never complained, did he? Not that she knew, anyway. She didn't want to bother him to find out. If he came to her, fine; if not, he would be observing from his hideaway, would see what he saw. He would know what kind of trouble she was facing, and if he cared to speak to her, he would come to her.

And he did. Every once in a while she would retire to her cubicle in the quadrangle of barrel vaults, or then to the larger one out in the arcade that Nadia built, and there would come that *scritch-tap-scritch* which was their private signal, somehow, and she would open the door and there he was, small and black and buzzing with energy and talk, always in an undertone. They would share their news. Out in the greenhouse it was getting strange, he said; Hiroko's polyandry was catching, and Elena and Rya were also enmeshed in multiple relationships, all of them becoming some kind of commune. Desmond obviously remained apart somehow, even though they were his only associates. He liked to come by and tell Maya all about them; and so when she saw them in the ordinary course of life, looking innocuous, it brought a smile to her face. It taught her that she was not the only one having trouble managing her affairs; that everyone was becoming strange. Everyone but Desmond and her, or so it felt as they sat there in her cubicle, on the floor, talking over every one of their colleagues as if numbering rosary beads. And each time as their talk wound down she would find some reason to reach out and touch him, hold his shoulder, and he would clasp her arm in his viselike grip, quivering with energy, as if his internal dynamo was spinning so fast he could barely hold himself together. And then he would be off. And the days after that would be easier. It was therapeutic, yes; it was what talks with Michel should have been but weren't, Michel being both too familiar and too strange. Lost in his own problems.

Or overwhelmed by everyone else's. One time, out walking with him to the salt pyramids they were constructing, he said something about the growing oddity of the farm team, and Maya pricked up her ears, thinking, If only you knew. But then he went on: "Frank is thinking they may have to be investigated by some kind of formal, I don't know, tribunal. Apparently material has gone missing, equipment, supplies, I don't know. They can't account for their hours properly to him, and people back in Houston are beginning to ask questions. Frank says some down there are even talking about sending up a ship to evacuate anyone who has been actively stealing things. I don't think that would do anyone any good, things are tenuous enough as it is. But Frank, well, you know Frank. He doesn't like it when there are things going on outside his control."

"Tell me about it," Maya muttered, pretending to worry only about Frank. And you could pretend anything with Michel, he was oblivious, more and more lost in his own world.

But afterward it was Desmond she worried about. The farm team she didn't care about at all, serve them right to be busted and sent home, Hiroko especially, but really all of them, they were so self-righteous and self-absorbed, a clique in a village too small to have cliques; but of course cliques only ever existed in contexts too small for them.

But if they did get rousted as they deserved, Desmond would be in trouble.

She did not know where he hid, or how to contact him. But from her conversations with Frank about Underhill affairs she judged that the problem of dealing with the farm team was going to develop slowly; so instead of searching for Desmond, as she had in the *Ares*, she merely walked around in the greenhouse late in the night, when she normally would not have, asking Iwao questions about things she would not usually show an interest in; and a few nights later she heard the *scritch-tap-scritch* at her door, and she rushed to let him in, realizing from his initial downcast glance that she was wearing only a shirt and underwear. But this had happened before; they were friends. She locked the door and sat down on the floor next to him, and told him what she had heard. "Are they really taking things?"

"Oh yeah, sure."

"But why?"

"Well, to have things that are their own. To be able to go out and explore different parts of Mars, and have things to keep their trips under the radar."

"Are they doing that?"

"Yeah. I've been out myself. You know, they say it's just a trip to

Hebes Chasma, and then they get over the horizon and set off to the east, mostly. Into the chaos. It's beautiful, Maya, really beautiful. I mean maybe it's just because I been cooped up so long, but I love being out there, I *love* it. It's what I came for, here at last. In my life. I have a hard time convincing myself to come back."

Maya looked at him closely, thinking it over. "Maybe that's what you all ought to do."

"What?"

"Take off."

"Where would I go?"

"Not just you—all of you. Hiroko's whole group. Take off and start your own colony. Go off where Frank and the rest of the police couldn't find you. Otherwise you may get busted and sent home." She told him what she had heard from Michel.

"Hmm."

"Could you do it, do you think? Hide them all, like you've hidden yourself?"

"Maybe. There's some cave systems in the chaoses east of here, you wouldn't believe what I've seen." He thought it over. "We'd need all the basics. And we'd have to disguise our thermal signal. Send it down into the permafrost, melt our water for us. Yeah, I suppose it could be worked out. Hiroko has been thinking about it already."

"You should tell her to hurry up then. Before she gets busted."

"Okay, I will. Thanks, Maya."

And the next time he dropped by in the middle of the night, it was to say good-bye. He hugged her and she held on to him, clutching. Then she pulled him onto her, and instantaneously, without any transition, they were getting their clothes off and making love. She rolled over onto him, shocked at how slight he was, and he flexed up to clasp her and they were off into that other world of sex, a wild pleasure. She did not have to play it safe with this man, who was the perfect outsider, an outlaw, her stowaway, and at this hard point in her life, one of her only real friends. Sex as an expression of friendship; it had happened to her before, a few times when she was young, but she had forgotten how much fun it could be, how friendly and pure, neither romantic nor anonymous.

Afterward she observed, "It's been a while."

He rolled his eyes, leaned up to gnaw on her collarbone. "Years since a time like that," he said happily. "Since I was about fifteen, I think."

She laughed and squished him under her. "Flatterer. I take it your Hiroko doesn't give you enough attention."

He made a disgusted noise. "We'll see how it goes in the outback."

That made her sad. "I'm going to miss you," she said. "Things won't be the same around here with you gone."

"I'll miss you too," he said intently, face nearly touching hers. "I love you, Maya. You've been a friend to me, a good friend when I didn't have any. When I really needed one. I'll never forget that. I'll come back and visit you whenever I can. I'm a very tenacious friend. You'll find out it's true."

"Good," she said, feeling better. Her stowaway came and went, it had always been that way; no different even if he left Underhill. Or so she could hope.

3. HELPING HER

So off the farm crew went, disappearing into the badlands of the backcountry. Good riddance, Maya thought, insulate smug mystics that they were—a cult, disfiguring the first town on Mars. In public she feigned surprise and indignation along with all the rest, her response unnoticed.

But she really was surprised, and indignant, to find that Michel had disappeared with them. Desmond had never mentioned him to her in any way that would indicate that Michel had been part of the farm's cult, and it seemed so unlike him that Maya could hardly believe it. But Michel was gone too. And with him gone, she had lost two of her best friends in the colony—even if Michel, always present, had been as unsatisfactory as Desmond in his occasional visits had been helpful; nevertheless she had felt close to Michel, as two maladjusted people in a community of the ordinary. As the melancholy client of the melancholy therapist. She missed him too, and was angry at him for leaving without a good-bye; she couldn't help but contrast that to Desmond. And as time passed she felt stronger than ever the afterglow of making love with a man who liked her but did not "love" her, i.e. want to possess her, in the way of Frank, or John.

So life went on, without friends. She broke up with Frank, then with John. Nadia despised her, which made Maya furious—to be dismissed by such a grub! And her sister at that. It was depressing. The whole damned situation was depressing; Tatiana killed by a fallen crane; everyone off in their own world.

And so no one welcomed the arrival of other colonists on Mars more than Maya. She was sick of the first hundred. Other settlements were established, and as soon as she could Maya left Underhill and struck out on her own, intending never to go back, any more than she would intentionally return to Russia. You can never go home, as the American saying had it. Which was true, though wrong as well.

She moved to Low Point, the deepest place on Mars, out near the middle of the Hellas Basin, which being the lowest would be the first place they would be able to breathe the new air generated by the ter-raforming effort. So they believed at the time, and believed them-selves very forward-thinking for it! Fools that they were. And she fell in love with an engineer named Oleg, and they moved in together, in a set of rooms at the end of one of the long worm-tube modules. And years passed while she worked like a dog to build a city that would end up at the bottom of a sea.

And fell out of love to boot, even though Oleg was a good man, ad-mirable in many ways, and he loved her like anything. It was her problem; but it was his heart that was going to get broken. So that for a long time she couldn't do it, and that made her angry, and so she fought with him, until they were as miserable as two people could make each other.

And still he clung to her, even as over time she made him come to hate her. Hated her but loved her; in love, frightened, scared to death that she would leave him; and Maya more and more disgusted at his cowardice and reliance on her. That he could love such a monster as she had become filled her with contempt and pity, and she would walk the crowded tubes home, slowing with every step, dreading the horrible evening and night that lay before her every day.

Then one day, out in a rover on the great flat plains of western Hel-las, a suited figure stepped from behind a boulder knot and waved her down. It was her Desmond. He got in her rover lock, vacuumed the outside of his suit free of dust, took off his helmet, came in the main compartment. "Hi!"

She almost crushed him with her hug. "What's up?"

"I wanted to say hi, that's all."

They sat in her rover and talked through the afternoon, holding hands or at least touching each other always, watching the shadow of the boulder knot lengthen over the empty ocher expanse.

"Are you this Coyote they talk about?"

"Yes." His crack-jawed grin. It was good to see him!

"I thought so, I was sure of it! So now you are a legend."

"No, I'm Desmond. But Coyote is a damn good legend, yes. Very helpful."

The lost colony was doing fine. Michel was prospering. They lived in shelters in the Aureum Chaos, for the most part, and made excursions in rovers disguised to look like boulders, completely insulated so that they had no heat signal. "The land is falling down so fast with this hydration, that a new boulder in a satellite photo is the most ordinary thing in the world. So I get around a lot now."

"And Hiroko?"

He shrugged. "I don't know." He stared out the window for a long time. "She's Hiroko, that's all. Making herself pregnant all the time, having kids. She's crazy. But, you know. I like being with her. We still get along. I still love her."

"And her?"

"Oh she loves everything."

They laughed.

"What about you?"

"Oh," Maya said, stomach falling. Then it was all pouring out, in a way she hadn't been able to say to anyone else: Oleg, his pitiful clinging, his noble suffering, how much she hated it, how she somehow could not make herself leave.

Sunset stretched over the land and their silence.

"That sounds bad," he said finally.

"Yes. I don't know what to do."

"Sounds to me like you do know what to do, but you aren't doing it."

"Well," she said, reluctant to say it out loud.

"Look," he said, "it's love that matters. You have to go for love, whatever it takes. Pity is useless. A very corrosive thing."

"False love."

"No not false, but a kind of replacement for love. Or when it is . . . I mean, love and pity together, that's compassion, I suppose. Something like Hiroko, and we need that. But pity without love, or instead of love, is a damn sorry thing. I been there and I know."

When darkness fell and the stars blazed in the black sky, he gave her a hug and a peck on the cheek, intending only to leave, but she grabbed him, and then they fell into it and made love so passionately, out there alone together in a rover, that she could hardly believe it; it was like waking up after many years of sleep. Just to be off in their solitude; she laughed, she cried, she whooped, she moaned loudly when she came. Rhythmic shouts of freedom.

"Drop by whenever you like," she joked when he was finally off. They laughed and then he was off into the night, not looking back.

She drove slowly back to Low Point, feeling warm. She had been visited by the Coyote, her stowaway, her friend.

That night, and for many nights after that, she sat in her little living room with Oleg, knowing she was going to leave him. They ate their dinner, and then she sat on the floor, leaning back against the wall, as she always did, while they watched the news on Mangalavid, drinking from little cups of ouzo or cognac. Huge cloudy feelings stuffed her chest—this was her life after all, these habitual evenings with Oleg, week after week the same, for year after year; and soon to end forever. Their relationship had gone bad but he was not a bad man, and after all, they had had their good times together—almost five years now, a whole life, all set in its shared ways. Soon to be smashed and gone. And she felt full of grief, for Oleg and for her too—for simply the passing of time, and the crash and dispersal of one life after another. Why, Underhill itself was gone forever! It was hard to believe. And sitting there in the little world she had made with Oleg, and was soon to unmake, she felt the stab of time like she never had before. Even if she didn't leave him, it would still go smash eventually—so that there was no evening ever when one should not feel this same melancholy, a kind of nostalgia for the present itself, slipping away like water down the drain.

For many years after she remembered so clearly that odd painful time, as one of those periods when she had in some way stepped out of herself and looked at her life from the outside. It was curious how terribly significant certain quiet moments could be, how she felt these charged moments, as in the eye of the storm, so much more than she did the events of the storm itself, when things happened so fast that she lived almost unconsciously.

So she and John got the treatment together, and renewed their partnership, better than ever. Then he was murdered, and the revolution came, and failed; and she flew through all of it as in a dream, in a nightmare in which one of the worst aspects was her inability in the rush of events to feel things properly. She did her best to join Frank and help stop the chaos from coming, and it came anyway. And Desmond appeared out of the smoke of battle and saved them from the fall of Cairo, and she was reunited with Michel and they made their desperate drive down Marineris, and Frank drowned, and they escaped to the ice refuge in the far south—all reeling by so fast that Maya scarcely comprehended it. Only afterward, in the long twilight of Hiroko's refuge, did it all fall on her—grief, rage—sorrow. Not only that all these disasters had happened, but that they too were now gone. Times she had been so alive she had not even known it!—but gone, and there only in memory. She felt things only afterward, when they could not do her any good.

Years of grieving passed in Zygote, like hibernation. Maya taught the kids and ignored Hiroko and the rest of the adults. Among them, Sax's flat manner was the least irritating to her. So she lived in a circular bamboo top room and taught the young brood of ectogenes with Sax, and kept to herself.

But the Coyote dropped by from time to time, and so she at least had someone to talk to. When he showed up she smiled, and some parts of her that were shut off turned on, and they took walks along the little lakeshore opposite Hiroko's grove, to the Rickover and back, crunching over the frosty dune grass. He told her stories from the rest of the underground, she told him about the kids, and the survivors of the First Hundred. It was their own private world. Mostly they did not sleep together, but once or twice they did—just following the flow of their feelings, their friendship, which mattered more than any physical coupling. Afterward he took off without good-byes to anyone else.

Once he shook his head. "You need more than this Maya, the big world is still out there. All of it waiting for you before it can make its next move, I judge."

"It can wait a while longer then."

Another time: "Why aren't you hooked up with a man."

"Who?"

"That's for you to say."

"Indeed."

He dropped the subject. He never intruded, that was part of the friendship.

Then Sax left for what Desmond called the demimonde, which made Maya restless, and unexpectedly sad. She had thought Sax enjoyed her company as the other main teacher of the kids. Though of course it was hard to tell with him. But to have his face surgically altered, in order to move out of Zygote to the north; it felt like a kind of rebuke. Not only to be such a small factor in his plans, but then to be staying behind herself, in their little refuge, when the world was still out there, changing every day. And then she missed him too, his flat affect and his peculiar thought, like that of a large brilliant toddler, or a member of some other primate species, cousin to theirs: *homo scientificus*. She missed him. And it began to feel like it was time for her to thaw, end her hibernation, and start another life.

Desmond helped with that. He came by after an unusually long time away, and asked Maya to go back out with him. "There's a man from Praxis here on planet I want to talk to. Nirgal thinks he's the something or other, the messenger, but I don't know."

"Sure," Maya said, pleased to be asked.

Half an hour's packing and she was ready to leave forever. She went to Nadia and told her to tell the others she was off, and Nadia nodded and said, "Good, good, you need to get out," always the critical sister.

"Yes yes," Maya said sharply, and she was off to the garage when she saw Michel going out to the dunes, and called to him. He had left Underhill without saying good-bye and it had bothered her ever since, and she wouldn't do the same to him. She walked out to the first ridge of dune sand.

"I'm going with Coyote."

"Not you too! Will you come back?"

"We'll see."

He regarded her face closely. "Well, good."

"You should get out too."

"Yes . . . perhaps now I will." He was serious, even grave, watching her so closely. Maybe it was Michel Desmond had been referring to, she thought. "Do you think it's time?" he asked.

"Time for?"

"For us? For us to be out there?"

"Yes," she ventured.

Then she was off, skulking north with the Coyote, to the equator west of Tharsis, following canyon walls and threading boulder plains. It was great to see the land again, but she didn't like the skulking. They ducked under the fallen elevator cable in a glaciated region midway up west Tharsis, and followed the cable downhill west for two days. They came on a giant moving building that was running over the cable, processing it for little cars running back up tracks to Sheffield, and Desmond said, "Look, he's out in a field car, let's follow." Maya watched as Coyote disabled the poor man's door to the building while he was out on a drive, and then stood by Coyote cautiously, ready for anything, as Coyote approached the man pounding fearfully on the door, and made his farcical greeting:

"Welcome to Mars!"

Indeed. One look at the man and Maya knew he knew just who they were, and had been sent out to contact them, and learn what he could and report back to his masters on Earth.

"He's a spy," she said to Desmond when they were alone.

"He's a messenger."

"You don't know that!"

"Okay, okay. But be careful with him. Don't be rude."

But then they heard that Sax had been captured. Caution was thrown to the winds—and did not come back, in Maya's life, for many years.

Desmond turned into a different version of himself, ferociously focused on rescuing Sax; this was the kind of friend he was, and he loved Sax as much as any of them. Maya watched him with something like fear. Then Michel and Nirgal joined them on their way to Kasei, and without a glance at her Desmond assigned her to Michel's car, in the western arm of their attack on the security compound. And she saw that she had been right; it was Michel whom Desmond had meant for her.

Which made her think. Indeed Michel was very close to her heart—her closest friend in some ways, from the days in Antarctica on. Someday she would have to forgive him for leaving Underhill without telling her. He was the man she trusted, after all. And loved—so much that Desmond had seen it. Of course what Michel thought was beyond her telling.

But she could find out. And did; and there in that boulder car, waiting for Desmond's windstorm, she held Michel in her arms and squeezed him so hard she worried for his ribs. "My friend."

"Yes."

"The one who understands me."

"Yes?"

Then the wind came down. They staggered into Kasei on their Ariadne thread, forced their way into the depths of the stronghold, and at every step of the way Maya became more frightened and angry—frightened for her life—angry that there was such a place on Mars, and such people to make it, disgusting despicable cowards and tyrants, who had killed John, killed Frank, killed Sasha in Cairo, in desperate circumstances very like these—she could be dead on the ground bleeding at the ears like Sasha at any moment, among these bastards who had killed all those innocents in '61, the forces of repression there and now here in the concrete walls, all in an ear-shattering boom and shriek that added to her fury—so that when she saw Sax wired onto the rack she tore him loose with a scream, and when she saw that Phyllis Boyle was there, as one of the torturers, she snapped and threw one of the explosive charges into the chamber; a murderous impulse, but never had she been so angry, it was like being outside oneself entirely. She wanted to kill somebody and Phyllis was the one.

Then afterward when they regained the cars, and met with the others south of Kasei, Spencer defended Phyllis and shouted at Maya, accused her of cold-blooded murder, and shocked by his assertion of Phyllis's innocence, she only had the instinct to shout back at him, to hide her shock and defend herself—but feeling like a murderer there in front of them all. "I killed Phyllis," she said to Desmond when he joined them, and they had all stared at her, all those men, as if she were a Medean horror—all but Desmond, who stepped to her side and kissed her cheek, something he had never before done in front of other people. "You did good," he declared, with a hand's electric touch to the arm. "You saved Sax."

Only Desmond. Though to be fair Michel had been stunned by a blow to the head, and was not himself. Later he too defended her action against Spencer's remonstrations. She nodded and huddled in his arms, frightened for him, vastly relieved when he returned to normal; holding him as he held her, with the clutch of people who had looked over the edge together. Her Michel.

So she and Michel became partners, their love, begun in the dark of Antarctica, forged in the crucible of that storm, in the rescue of Sax and her murder of Phyllis. They hid back in Zygote, now a terrible confinement to Maya. Michel helped Sax regain his speech, and Maya did what she could too. She worked on the idea of the revolution, with Nadia and Nirgal, Michel and even Hiroko. She lived her life; and from time to time they saw Desmond on one of his passthroughs. But of course it was not quite the same, even though she loved seeing him as much as ever. He watched her with Michel very fondly; a friendly look, exactly, like one who enjoyed seeing her happy at last. There was something in that she did not like; some smugness; the friend who knew better, perhaps.

. . .

In any case, things changed. They drifted apart. They were still friends, but it was a more distant thing. It was inevitable. So much of her life was caught up in Michel, and in the revolution.

Still, when the Coyote appeared out of nowhere, it made her smile. And when they heard of the attack on Sabishii, and the disappearance of the whole lost colony's membership, it had been a different kind of pleasure to see Desmond again, coming through and telling them what he had seen—relief; a negative pleasure; the removal of great fear. She had thought he too had been killed in the attack.

He was shaken, and needed her comfort—took it—was comforted—unlike Michel, who remained remote from her throughout this disaster, withdrawn into his own world of grief. Desmond was not like that; she could comfort him, wipe the tears from his narrow stubbly cheeks. Thus, by being comforted, by making it seem possible, he comforted her too. Looking at the two bereaved lovers of Hiroko, so different, she thought to herself, True friends can help each other when the time comes. And take help too. It's what friends are for.

And so Maya lived with Michel in Odessa, and they were partners—as married as anyone—for decade after decade of their unnaturally extended lives. But often it seemed to Maya that they were more friends than lovers, not "in love" in the way that she dimly remembered being with John, or Frank, or even Oleg. Or—when Coyote came through and she saw his face at the door—the memory sometimes came to her of that shocking encounter with her stowaway on the *Ares*, her discovery of him in the storage attic, their first conversation—making love before he took off with Hiroko's group, and the few times after that—yes, she had loved him too, no doubt about it. But now they were just friends, and he and Michel like brothers. It was good to have such a family of the remaining First Hundred, the first hundred and one, with all that had happened between them, twining together to make the familial bond. As the years passed it became more and more of a comfort to her. And as the second revolution approached, like a storm they could do nothing to avoid, she needed them more than ever.

Some nights, as the crises intensified and she had trouble sleeping, she read about Frank. There was a mystery at the center of him that resisted any final summation. In her mind he kept slipping away. For years she had been afraid to think about him, and then after Michel had advised her to face her fear, actually to research the matter, she had read as much about him as anyone could; and all it had done was confuse her memories with other people's speculations. Now she read in the hope of finding some account that would resemble what she ever less certainly remembered, to reinforce her own memory. It did not work, but it seemed as if it should, and so she went back to it from time to time, the way one will push a sore tooth with a tongue to confirm that it is still sore.

One night when Desmond was there staying with them, she had a dream about Frank, and then she got up and went out to read about him, feeling curious yet again. Desmond was asleep on a couch in the study. The book she was reading suddenly took up the matter of John's assassination, and she groaned at the memory of that awful night, reduced now in her mind to a few blurred images (standing under a streetlight with Frank, passing a body on the grass, holding John's head in her hands, sitting in a clinic) all now overlaid by the countless stories she had heard since.

Desmond, disturbed by dreams of his own, groaned and staggered out and passed her on the way to the bathroom. He too had been in Nicosia that night, she recalled suddenly. Or so one of the accounts had said. She looked in the book's index; no mention of him. But some accounts had him there that night, she was sure of it.

When he came back out, she steeled herself and asked him. "Desmond—were you in Nicosia the night John was killed?"

He stopped and looked down at her, his face a blank—an uncharacteristic, too-careful blank. He was thinking fast, she thought.

"Yes. I was." He shook his head, grimaced. "A bad night."

"What happened?" she said, sitting up straight, boring into him with her gaze. "What happened?" Then: "Did Frank do it, like they say he did?"

Again he looked at her, and again she thought she saw his mind racing, in there behind his eyes. What had he seen? What could he recall?

Slowly he said, "I don't think Frank did it." Then: "I saw him up in that triangular park, right around the time they must have attacked John."

"But Selim and he . . ."

He shook his head as if to clear it. "No one knows what went on between those two, Maya. That's all just talk. No one can ever know what other people really said to each other. They make that stuff up. And it doesn't matter what people say to each other either. Not compared to what they do. Even if Frank took this Arab and said, 'Kill John, I want you to do it, kill him kill him'—even if he said that, which I doubt very much, because Frank was never that straight-forward, you have to admit"—he waited for her to nod and force a smile—"even so, if this Selim then went off and killed John, got his friends to help him, then it was still their doing, you know? The people who do the deed are the ones responsible, if you ask me. All this stuff about following orders, or he made me do it or whatnot, all that is so much bullshit, it's just excuses."

"So if Hitler never killed anyone himself . . ."

"Then he's not as guilty as the guys in the camps, pulling the triggers and turning on the gas! That's right! He was just a crazy old fuck. But they were murderers. And there were a lot more of them than there were of him. Sad when you think of it that way."

"Yes." So sad it could hardly bear thinking about.

"But look, Nicosia was complicated. A lot of people were fighting that night. Arab factions were fighting each other, Arabs were fighting Swiss, construction crews were fighting other crews. People say, 'Oh that Frank Chalmers started it all, started the riots as a cover for his arranging the murder of John Boone'—give me a break! They just want to make it simple, they want a simple story, do you understand? They pin blame on a single person because then it makes a simple story. And they can only handle simple stories. Because then only one person has to be responsible, rather than all the people who were fighting that night."

She nodded, feeling heartened all of a sudden. "It's true. So—I mean—we were there too. So we were part of it too."

He nodded, grimacing again. He came over and sat on the couch beside her, put his head in his hands. "I think about that," he said, muffled at the floor, "sometimes. I was sneaking around town in my usual way, having a high old time. It was like carnival back home in Trinidad, I thought. Everyone dancing to the music and wearing masks. I had a red mask, a monster face, and I could go anywhere I wanted. I saw John, I saw Frank. I saw you talking to Frank, in that park—you were wearing a white mask, you looked beautiful. I saw Sax down in the medina. And John was partying as usual. I—if only I had known he was in trouble, ahhh. . . . I mean, I had no idea that anyone was out for him. If I had only guessed, I might have been able to pull him aside and tell him to get out of the way of it. I had introduced myself to him at that party up on Olympus, just a little before that. He was happy to see me. He had found out about Hiroko and Kasei, you know. He would have listened to me, I think. But I didn't know."

Maya laid her hand on his thigh. "None of us knew."

"No."

"Except," she said, "maybe Frank."

Desmond sighed. "Maybe. But maybe not. And if he did know, then that would be bad, sure. But if I know him, he would have paid for it later, in his mind. Because those two were close. It would be like killing your brother. People pay in their mind, I believe that. So . . ." He shook his head to get out of that train of thought, glanced at her. "No need to worry about it now, Maya. They're both gone now."

"Yes."

"They're gone and we're here." Gesturing around to include Michel, or all of them in Odessa. "It's the living who matter. It's life that matters."

"Yes. It's life that matters."

He staggered up, went back into the study. "G'night."

"Good night." And she put the book down on the floor and slept.

4. THE YEARS

In the years that followed she seldom thought of Frank again. He had been laid to rest, or else lost in the tumult of those times. The years flowed by like water downriver. Maya imagined Terran lives were like Terran rivers, fast and wild at their starts in the mountains, strong and full across the prairies, slow and meandering near the sea; while on Mars their lives resembled the abrupt jumbled paths of the streams they were only now creating—falling off scarps, disappearing in potholes, getting pumped up to unexpected new elevations great distances away.

Thus she rode out the tense approach to the second revolution, and took that drop with everyone else, then made the trip back to Earth. Thinking of her youth there was like trying to remember an earlier incarnation. She worked with Nirgal and the Terrans, visited Michel in Provence, and returned to Mars seeing both men better than she ever had before. She settled with Michel in Sabishii, and helped Nadia get the government going, when she could do it without Nadia seeing what she was doing. She knew the look she would get if she tried to intervene directly. So she stayed in Sabishii, and life quieted down a bit, or at least fell into a more predictable pattern: Michel had his practice and some work at the university, while Maya worked for the Tyrrhena Massif Water Project, and occasionally taught in the town's schools. She very seldom saw Desmond or thought of him much, and indeed she and Michel ran into the other old ones far less often than they ever had before. Their circle of acquaintances was largely that of their work places, and the neighborhood they lived in—new, like everything else in the second Sabishii. They lived in a third-floor apartment in a big hollow apartment block with a very nice park courtyard, and on evenings warm enough they often ate down at tables in the courtyard and talked with their neighbors, played games, read, did handwork. It was a real community, and sometimes Maya would look around her at the people in it and think that here was a historical reality that would not ever be recorded in any way: a good solid neighborhood, with everyone doing their work and having their families together as some kind of shared collective project, in which an individual family made sense as part of a larger whole that was not easy to characterize. Whole decades slipped by in this anonymous goodness, and very rarely did the ghosts of her previous incarnations come back to haunt her. Nor her old friends either.

5. HELPING HIM

Then many years after that, when Maya was beginning to have trouble with her extended déjà vus and other "mental events," as Michel called them, Desmond dropped by late at night, after the timeslip when no one else would have thought to visit.

Michel was already asleep, and Maya up reading. She gave Desmond a hug and brought him into the kitchen and sat him down while she got water on the stove for tea. He had been trembling when she hugged him. "What's wrong?" she asked.

He flinched. "Oh, Maya."

"What is it!"

He shrugged. "I visited Sax in Da Vinci, and Nirgal was there staying with him. His place up in the hills was covered by dust, did you hear?"

"Yes. Too bad."

"Yeah. But anyway they started talking about Hiroko. As if she was still alive. Sax even claimed to have seen her once, out in a storm. And I—I got so *angry*, Maya! I could have killed them!"

"Why?" she said.

"Because she's dead. Because she's dead and they refuse to face it. Just because they never saw the bodies, they make up all these stories."

"They're not the only ones."

"No. But they believe the stories, just because they want to. As if believing makes it true."

"And doesn't it?" she said, pouring out the water into cups.

"No. It doesn't. She's dead. The whole farm crew. All of them were killed." And he put his head down on the kitchen table and began to weep.

Surprised, Maya moved around to his side of the table, sat beside him. She put a hand on his back. Again he was trembling, but it wasn't the same. She reached out and pulled her teacup across the table, closer to her. She sipped from it. His spasming ribs calmed down.

"It's cruel," she said. "The, the disappearing. When you never see the bodies, you don't know what to think. You're stuck in limbo."

He straightened up, nodded. He sipped his tea.

"You never saw Frank's body," he said. "But you don't go around telling people you think he might still be alive."

"No," she said, and waved a hand. "But that flood . . ."

He nodded.

"The farm crew, though. You can see why people indulge themselves. They could have escaped, after all. Theoretically."

He nodded. "But they were behind me in the maze. I only just got out in time. And then I hung around for days, and they didn't come out. They didn't make it." He shuddered convulsively. A great deal of nervous energy, she thought, in that wiry little body. "No. They were caught and killed. If they had gotten out, I would have seen them. Or she would have contacted me. She was cruel, but not that cruel. She would have let me know by now." His face was twisted: grief, anger. He was still angry at her, she saw. It reminded her of Frank. She had been angry at him for years after his death. Wondering if he had killed John. Desmond had talked to her about that, many years before. She recalled: Desmond had been trying to figure out how to comfort her, that night. He had been lying, perhaps. If he knew a different truth, if he had seen Frank put a knife in John, would he have told her, that night? No.

Now she tried to figure out what would help him to think about Hiroko. She sipped her tea in the timeslip silence, and he did too.

"She loved you," she said.

He looked at her, surprised. Finally he nodded.

"She would have let you know if she was still around, like you say."

"I think so."

"So probably she is dead. But Nirgal and Sax—Michel too, for that matter—"

"Michel too?"

"Half the time, anyway. Half the time he thinks it is just compensation, a myth that helps them. The other half he's convinced they're out there. But if it helps them, you know . . ."

He sighed. "I suppose."

She thought some more. "You love her still."

"I do."

"Well. That's life too. Of a sort. Movement of, you know—Hiroko structures. In your mind. Quantum jumps, as Michel says. Which is all we ever are anyway. Right?"

Desmond regarded the scarred and wrinkled back of his hand. "I don't know. I think we are maybe more than that."

"Well. Whatever. It's life that matters, isn't that what you told me one time?"

"Did I?"

"I think so. It seems like you did. A good working principle, anyway, whoever said it."

He nodded. They sipped tea, their reflections transparent in the black windows. A bird in the sycamore outside broke the night silence.

"I worry that another bad time may be coming," Maya said, to change the subject. "I don't think Earth will let us get away with the immigration controls much longer. They'll break them and Free Mars will protest, and we'll be at war before you know it."

He shook his head. "I think we can avoid it."

"But how? Jackie would start a war just to keep her power."

"Don't worry so much about Jackie. She doesn't matter. The system is so much bigger than her—"

"But what if the systems collide? We're living on borrowed time. The two worlds have very different interests now, and diverging more all the time. And then the people at the top will matter."

He waggled a hand. "There are so many of them. We can tip the majority of them toward reasonable behavior."

"Can we? Tell me how."

"Well, we can always threaten them with the reds. There are still reds out there, plotting away. Trying to crash the terraforming any way they can. We can use that to our advantage."

And so they talked politics, until the sky in the windows went gray, and the scattered birdsong became a chirping chorus. Maya kept drawing him out. Desmond knew all the factions on Mars very well, and had some good ideas. She found it extremely interesting. They plotted strategy. By breakfast time they had worked out a kind of plan to try when the time came. Desmond smiled at this. "After all these years, we still think we can save the world."

"Well we can," Maya said. "Or we could, if only they would do what we told them to."

They woke Michel with the smell and crackle of frying bacon, and with Desmond singing some calypso tune into the bedroom. Maya felt warm, sleepy, hungry. Work would be hard that day but she didn't care.

6. LOSING HIM

Life went on. She lived with Michel, she worked, she loved, she coped with her health problems. Mostly she was content. But it was possible sometimes to regret that long-lost spark of true passion, unstable and wild though it had always been. Sometimes she knew she might have gotten more pure joy in life if John had lived, or Frank. Or if she had ever connected with Desmond as a partner—if, sometime when they were both free, they had committed to each other in some kind of intermittent monogamy, storklike, meeting after their travels and migrations year after year. A path not taken; and everything therefore different.

What happened instead was that life went on, and slowly, as the years passed, they drifted farther and farther apart; not because of any loss of feeling on either side, she felt, but just because they saw each other so seldom, and other people and other matters took up their thoughts. This was the way it happened; you lived and moved on, and the people closest to you did the same, and life drew you apart, somehow—jobs, partners, whatever—and after a while, when they were not there as part of daily life, as a physical presence, a body in the room, a voice saying new things, then it was possible to love them only as a certain kind of memory. It became the case that you used to love them, and only remembered that love, rather than felt it as you had when they were part of the texture of daily life. Only with your partner could you really keep on loving them, because it was only your partner you stayed with. And even with them it was possible to drift apart, into different sets of habits, different thoughts. If that was so with the person you slept with, how much more so with friends who had moved on too, and now lived on the other side of the world. So eventually you lost them, and there was no help for that. Only if you had been partnered with them. And you could only be partners with one person. If she and Desmond had ever joined each other in that way—who knew what would have happened. The banked coals of an old, distant friendship; when sparks might have flown forever, as from an open forge. She might have been able to make him quiver every time she touched him. She loved the memory of loving him so much that she sometimes thought it could have been that way.

And once in a very long while, she got inklings that Desmond felt somewhat the same; which was nice. One night, for instance, many years later, when Michel was out of town, Desmond came by in the early evening and rang the bell, and they went down together to the corniche and walked the seafront. It was lovely to be together again like that, Maya thought as they walked, alone and arm in arm, on the edge of her Hellas Sea, followed by dinner in a corner of one of the bistros, warming up and talking face-to-face over a table cluttered with glasses and plates. Such men she loved, such friends.

This time he was just passing through, and wanted to catch a sleeper train to Sabishii. So after dinner she walked with him up the staircase streets to the station, arm in arm, and as they approached the station he laughed and said, "I have to tell you my latest Maya dream."

"Maya dream?"

"Yes. I have them every year or so. I dream about all of us, really. But this one was funny. I dreamed I was going to Underhill to attend some conference, on gift economies or something, and I got there and lo and behold you were there too, attending a hydrological conference. A coincidence. And not only that, but we were staying at the same hotel—"

"A hotel in Underhill?"

"In my dream it was a city like any other, with skyscrapers and a lot of hotels. A conference center or something like that. So anyway, not only were we both staying at the same hotel, but they had made a mistake and booked us into the same room. We were happy to see each other in the lobby, because we hadn't known we were both going to be in town, but we didn't discover we were accidentally put in the same room until we were up there in the hall, looking at our key tabs. And so, being responsible people, we went back down to the desk to explain the error—"

Maya snorted at this, feeling her arm tighten reflexively on his, and he grinned and waved her off with his other hand—

"But then when we got to the desk, the night clerk gave us the same look you're giving me now, and he said, 'Listen you two, I am Cupid, the god of love, and I made that mistake on purpose, to give you two a chance to be together without having planned it, so get back up there and have fun, and don't try to cross me anymore!' "

Maya was laughing out loud, and Desmond laughed too.

"A great dream," Maya said, and stopped him and held his hands. "And then?"

"Ah, well, then I woke up! I was laughing too hard, just like now. I said, No, no, don't wake up yet! The good part is coming!"

She laughed and squeezed his hands. "No. The good part had already happened."

He nodded and they hugged each other. Then his train pulled in and he was off.

Four Teleological Trails

1. WRONG WAY

Dawn patrol up the west inner wall of Crommelin Crater. Tram at the Bubbles, climb one of the steepest trails in the crater, take the rim trail around to the pond at Featherbed, drop down a new trail, and walk the ring road back to the tram, just a couple of kilometers.

But that morning it was raining hard, and misty too, not much wind, and within a hundred meters of leaving the tram turnabout I was lost. I followed what I thought was the path and it petered out almost immediately, so it wasn't the trail; but rather than go back down I figured the trail was over to my right, and I angled up that way to run into it, but I never found it. But every route goes into Crommelin, you know, except for parts of Precipice Arc, so I decided to bushwhack on up with the hope of running into the trail eventually. I kept seeing what looked like an older version of the trail anyway—three or four stacked steps up a break in a wall; a long depression; some broken branches; and, most of all, rectangular gray paint marks on trees. They looked like the trail blazes you see on trees in the Cimmerian Forest. I was surprised anyone had chosen gray for the paint, and suspected it might be some kind of lichen, but it looked like paint no matter how close I got to it, even when I scraped it with my fingernail. Paint, I swear, and splashed on about chest or head high on trees, in a rough makable line up the slope. It was a broken ledgy crater wall, lots of trees, and then some worn old ramparts, and a few walls of bare rock that you had to get around or find cracks up. I figured anywhere trees grew I could scramble up, so I followed ramps of trees winding up through brecciated battlements, ducking under the branches. It was pouring down rain, so the showers I brought down on myself by moving the branches meant nothing to me. My real concern was my footing, because the leaf mats made lots of wet trap-doors in the basalt jumble of the ramps.

I kept slogging uphill, hoping of course that none of the battlements to left and right would extend unbroken across my path. And still wondering if I was on an old trail, drowned in leaves. Every time the gap between battlements became tight I would see rough stacks of stones helping me up, barely visible under the years of clutter. Then just as I was sure it was a trail it would all go away and I would be thrashing up through forest again. The question became the salient feature of the climb, absorbing all my thinking, all my rain-blurred inspection of the wall dripping around me, squishing and slipping underfoot—there, were those rocks stacked by hand to aid my way? Was that a gray trail blaze, on the tree right there in the middle of that tight little copse? But why put it there?

Up I fought, ducking to guard my face from scratchers, shouldering through larger branches. Always there was a way up and on, but no matter how hard I studied the landscape, I couldn't decide the question of the trail one way or another. It often looked like untraveled wild hillside. But then another little stair section would appear and help me up and through a tight spot.

The climb went on so long I began to wonder about it. The ascent was only four hundred meters—surely I had done that already? The rain cloud thinned and I had more light. Rain continued, however, and it got windy, in downgusts. The slope lay back and I came across a flat strip filled with trees, floored by an old rusty tram track. A little shock to see it. I recalled reading of an old cog tram to the peak, but that had been on the south wall of the crater. A little farther I came on West Apron Road, which takes the rim for its last up, and jogged along it for a few minutes before I came to the shop and cable-car facility on the rim. It was nice to have topped out and to know exactly where on the rim I was, but I had taken twice as long as expected, and used up three times the energy, and when I continued north on the rim trail, I lost it again! It was both raining and foggy, and the west rim is very broad, all open rock in broken terraces, with stone stacks marking the trail, and small head-high or waist-high forests here and there, all very tight and gnarly. A lot of trails ran into these trees and worked for a while and then petered off into a bramble. I got frustrated; also worried that I would be really late getting back to the house. On dawn patrols I try to get back while people are still getting up, or getting breakfast.

So I stopped and thought it over. My glasses were misted with rain, and the air was whipping by in a pure fog. I couldn't see more than twenty yards in any direction, and up here it wasn't enough.

I turned back and whacked along the rim to the road, deciding I would run down the wall road to the crater floor, then over to the Bubbles and the tram. All the distances in the crater are so small, I figured at most it would be 10 k, and downhill most of the way. Not so much fun as a rain scramble, but faster.

Before I took off I went into the shop and bought a soda. They had just opened up. I took it to the counter and two young women stared at me as I took my wallet out of my pocket, from under my rain pants you know. But the wallet was wet, and even my card inside the wallet was wet. I might as well have just dived into the lake. I decided to pass on explaining and drink the soda outside.

Running down the road was spacey. It switched back and forth, always in heavy mist and rain. I had no idea how high on the wall I was. I passed a bluff cut by the road, now a waterfall, very pretty. Got into the trees, then under them, a long green canopy tunnel floored by the road, and the rain still bombing down on us. Got back to the station and trammed home, but I missed breakfast that day.

And all the rest of the day—and ever since, really, but that day it really possessed me—I wondered whether I had been on an old trail or not.

2. MISTAKES CAN BE GOOD

I took my parents up Precipice Trail when they were in their mid-sixties, and to tell you the truth I had always run that trail before, pretty much, trying to do it quick and get back into town and do the family thing, so my memory of it was deficient. I realized that when I took them up it going slow. There's a hell of a lot of ladders on that trail. After the fairly acrobatic boulder traverse across the huge talus slide, it's nothing but ladder after ladder, with some exposed ledge traverses to get from the top of one ladder to the bottom of the next. On one of these ledges my mom said my name in that intonation of hers which means "you've got to be kidding," and my dad brought up the rear saying nothing—he maybe wasn't in as good a shape as my mom, and was wearing tight jeans. Later he said he thought I was getting back at them for all the things they might have ever done that I didn't like. But he was strong, and Mom too. We topped out and immediately descended, which was easier aerobically, but still pretty white-knuckle—worse, really. The ladders are just rungs of iron, drilled into sheer cliff as high as fifty feet. Looking down as you descend can be daunting. When we got back to the bottom I pointed up where we had gone—it looks like a pure cliff from below, and some climbers were there gearing up to do the face just to the left of the trail, so it was impressive. We got back to camp and they were high, they were high as kites. They couldn't believe they had done it. So even though it was a mistake I had done a good thing.

3. YOU CAN'T LOSE THE TRAIL

I had been hiking Crommelin Crater for years when a man published a history of the crater's trails and made it all new to me. I had seen but I hadn't understood. The trails had not been built by the co-op currently administering the crater, as I had assumed, but instead by a succession of inspired crazies, who had gotten into a kind of contest with each other to see who could build the most beautiful trails. The steep brecciated granite walls of the crater had become the canvases for their new art form, which they had pursued for some twenty or thirty years, back before the turn of the century. One had gotten his entire co-op into building trails, putting in several on the wall just above and behind the co-op's diskhouse.

But when the current administration took over, they closed down half the trails in the crater as being highly redundant, which they were. But they were works of art too, and being well built out of huge blocks of stone, a lot of them were still out there, but *not on the maps anymore*. And this man had published the old maps in his book and given directions for finding the old trailheads, which the current agency had allowed to become obscure. Finding the old trails—"trail phantoming" he called it—was a new art form, making use of and preserving the older one. I started doing it myself and loved it. It added route-finding, archaeology, and huge amounts of bushwhacking to the already beautiful experience of hiking the crater.

One day we took the kids and hunted for one of the old co-op's lost trails. First we found what must once have been a wide esplanade running along the foot of the wall, now all filled with birch. We crossed the northernmost trail still on the map and continued north on the overgrown esplanade, looking at the great wall for signs of a trail. There were a lot of possibilities, I thought—as usual. But then in all the leaves I spotted a big dressed stone, like someone's trunk, and we all ran over and there it was—a stone staircase, buried deep in dead leaves, leading up the wall. It was thrilling.

Off we went, kids first. We couldn't keep up with them. It was easy as could be to follow the trail, which was mostly a full staircase, set into the wall for flight after flight. But it was also obvious that it hadn't been walked on much in many years. One traverse section had lost its underpinnings and ten or twelve blocks had slid downslope, forming a loop of stone we had to negotiate. In another place a thick-trunked birch had fallen across the trail and we had to work around the roots. These digressions made us realize how hard the slope would have been without a trail. But with it: sidewalks and staircases.

And then, looking ahead, we saw the trail cutting up and across a big shadowed talus slope, under a curved section of the wall. All the great shatter of rock was light pink granite, and all the lichen growing on it was a pale green. Pale green circles mottling pale pink shatter—pale green carpet on pale pink stairs—it looked like something the Incas had built, or visitors from Atlantis. Even the kids stopped to look.

4. THE NATURAL GENIUS

Dorr obviously explored the eastern crater wall thoroughly, and then designed his trails to take advantage of features already there, leading travelers under overhangs, behind drop blocks, up cracks, and through tunnels. One section of the wall has a big steep concave bulge of granite, an exposed pluton, kind of unusual, with a vertical fissure running all the way up it, waist or chest deep all the way. Naturally Dorr put a trail right up that crack, filling its bottom with a steep narrow staircase, each granite block stacked on the back part of the one below it, in a flight that was hundreds of stones long.

I was hiking up this beautiful trail one dawn patrol in the rain, everything gray and misty so that I only saw a bit above and below me, and by the time I got to this section of the trail, the fissure had become a streambed. White water dropped down it step by step, as in fish ladders you see by dams. White water clattering stepwise down a granite slope, out of the mist—it was surreal.

To continue upward meant soaking my boots, as each step would submerge me in water to the ankle, if not the knee. Out in the back-country that would be a problem. But I knew I would be at the house twenty minutes after the end of my hike, and there take a shower, and put my boots by the fire. It wouldn't be that good for the boots, but so what. Worth it for the joy of hiking up that staircase waterfall. Step after step, splash, splash, white water, the noise of it, the rain and the wind. Every step placed securely, hands using the granite walls to both sides as railings. A beautiful ascent; something I never expect to see again.

Then at the top of the staircase, the trail stopped. For some reason Dorr never connected this trail to his others, and it ends on the top of that granite bulge, still only halfway up the crater wall. To get over to the nearest of Dorr's other staircase trails you have to traverse a broad tilted bench, thick with birch and dead logs. And currently soaked and obscured by mist.

I whacked on, enjoying the new nature of the problem. Here all the trail phantoms together make the trail, I thought, and looked for sign. I was not overly concerned when I didn't see any. Trail comes and goes depending on how much you need it. Where many ways will go, people disperse and take them all, and so the trail fades and disappears. You don't need it. When the way gets hard the trail becomes clear again—there are only a few ways to go, and people find those over and over. This happens everywhere, wherever people walk the land. Most trails were never planned, you see, but were made by a collective of people spread through time, all evaluating the slope on their own, and very often coming to the same conclusions. So when I lose the trail and then come back on it again I am always pleased to see that I have made the same judgment as others before me. I say, Hey, the natural genius here once again, inside all of us. How nice.

So I crashed across this wet bench, content to wander; it was fun. I would hit Dorr's next trail eventually.

Then I saw on a tree trunk ahead of me one of the rectangular gray paint spots I had seen on a previous rainy dawn patrol. Hey! I said, thinking I had confirmation. But then I noticed that there were more gray spots on the tree trunks around the first one, and in fact there were gray spots on every tree trunk I could see at that moment, in every direction. I realized that the rainy trail I had found on the other side of the crater must have been only a figment of my imagination, seeing something in the landscape that hadn't been there.

Only it had been there, I swear. *There is something out there.* This is why I don't think we can so easily dismiss some sort of teleology in history. The landscape itself seems to call forth the trail. It imposes on us the best way forward. And it could be that the human landscape, or even the continuum in which time unfolds, has invisible ramps and battlements that shape our course. Of course we still have choices, but there is a certain terrain to be crossed. So I suspect that seeing trails that are not there is actually an everyday activity of the human mind. When the going is hard people come together. And the trails appear out of nowhere.

Later I heard that there is indeed an engineered lichen called "gray paint patch lichen." I'm sure the designer thinks it's very funny.

That day in the rain it didn't matter. Soon enough I stumbled on Dorr's next masterpiece in stone, this one still on the maps, and so well used it was gleaming under its coat of water, which there, where the trail traversed the slope, was not deep.

But then it turned downhill again, back down toward town, and once again became a bounding waterfall. And I came to a section where the crater wall steepened and curved to a convex bowl, over-hanging a deep downward cut in the wall, next to a knob. There the trail dropped in big deep stairs, down a ravine between knob and wall. But now this ravine was a big violent waterfall, or rather several waterfalls, curtaining off the wall and then funneling down into a steep rapids, roaring between rocks that were ordinarily waist- or chest-high when you passed between them. To proceed I would have to descend this torrent.

I placed each boot carefully, holding on to rocks or branches on both sides of me. The water went knee deep, then thigh deep. I could feel it pushing at the backs of my legs.

Then a hard rain squall hit, and the crater wall became one great big waterfall. Then the rain turned to hail. Sheets of hail careened down on the rushing white water at me. I grabbed a rock beside the trail with both hands and ducked my head, watching the froth of floating hail rise up on my body, until I was chest deep in it as it poured by. For a second I feared the water would rise even farther and tear me away, or drown me right in place. Then the level of the flood dropped a bit, and I succeeded in fording the rapids and clambering down the opposite side of the ravine step by step, the water roaring everywhere around me. I got a good grip on a wet birch and laughed out loud. It was one of the most civilized moments of my life.

Coyote Makes Trouble

The city was beautiful at night. Tent invisible—it seemed they lived under the stars. And stars seemed to have fallen into the city as well, lining the sides of the nine mesas, so that walking the streets it appeared one sailed in a fleet of immense luxury liners, as during one well-remembered evening in his childhood, when suddenly four great white ships had appeared in Port of Spain's outer harbor, each an entire sparkling world. Like galaxies come down to anchor in their harbor.

Down by the canal the sidewalk cafés were open late; and rare was the night when the stars in the canal were not set awash by the plunge of some drunken reveler, or victimized passerby. Coyote spent many of his evenings on the grass fronting the Greek restaurant, at the end of the double row of Bareiss columns. When people were not splashing in the canal Coyote flicked pebbles into it, to make the stars dance under his boots. People came down and sat on the grass near him; made their reports; discussed plans; went on their way. Things were getting tighter these days. It was no longer such a simple thing to run a spy ring in the capital of the United Nations Transitional Authority. But there were still thousands of construction workers, rudimentarily documented, who were excavating the nine mesas and turning them into gargantuan buildings. As long as you had a work identity for the checkpoints, no one was bothering you yet. So Coyote worked by day (some days; he was not reliable) and caroused by night, like thousands of others; and gathered information for the underground, from a loose group of old friends and a few new ones.

The ring included Maya and Michel, who were holed up in an apartment above a dance studio, sharing information with Coyote and putting it to use, but staying out of sight and away from checkpoints, as they were on UNTA's growing wanted list. And after what had happened to Sax, and to Sabishii, it was clear that you didn't want to be found by them.

The current situation both frightened Coyote and made him very angry. Hiroko and her crowd, disappeared—killed, in other words (though he was not sure yet); Sax brain-damaged; Maya and Michel gone to ground; UNTA security police everywhere you looked. And checkpoints. And even his ring of spies; it was hard to be sure none of them had turned. One young woman, for instance—a clerk in the UNTA Burroughs headquarters, a very attractive Dravidian. She sat down on the grass beside him, telling him that Hastings was going to arrive by train from Sheffield the day after tomorrow. Hastings, Coyote's nemesis. But was it true? He thought that the good-looking young woman was brittle in a way she hadn't been before, friendly but glittery-eyed. His electronics said she was not wired. But turned and telling tales, or setting him up; who knew?

She was supposed to have been working on finding out what UNTA security had on the radical reds. Irritated, he asked her about it, but she nodded, and had a report there too. Apparently they knew quite a bit. He asked her question after question, getting more and more interested; she was telling him things about the reds he didn't know himself.

Finally he sent her on her way with a cheerful smile. He was always the same with everybody, all the time, and very much doubted that she would have seen any of his suspicions. He knocked back his glass of metaxa, left it on the grass, wandered down the Street of the Cypresses to the little dance studio. People behind plate glass were pirouetting. He slipped upstairs and scratched-tapped his knock. Maya let him in.

They discussed the latest news, went through their lists for each other. One of Maya's biggest current worries was that the radical reds would strike before the rest of the resistance was ready, and Coyote agreed it was a bad possibility, even though he liked the reds' attitude. But now he had news for her.

"Apparently they think they can bring the terraforming down," he told her. "Crash the system. UNTA has gotten a mole in somewhere, and this is what they're finding. There's a wing of the reds think they can do it biologically. Another faction wants to make something go wrong with the deep thermal bombs. Sabotage one of those nukes in such a way that the radiation reaches the surface, get the whole operation shut down."

Maya shook her head, disgusted. "Radiation on the surface. It's insane."

Coyote had to agree, though he liked their attitude anyhow. "I suppose we should hope that UNTA knocks out those groups before they act."

Maya grimaced. Misguided or not, the reds were their allies, UNTA their shared enemy. "No. We should warn them they are penetrated. Then get them to stop their crazies. Follow the general strategy."

"We might have to stop the crazies ourselves."

"No. I'll talk to Ann."

"Right." This in Coyote's opinion was a waste of time for anyone. But Maya looked determined.

Michel came in and they took a break for tea. Coyote sipped, shook his head. "Things are getting tight. We may be forced to make our move before we're ready."

"I want to wait for Sax," Maya said, as always.

When he was done with his tea Coyote got up to leave. "I want to do something in case Hastings comes here," he said.

Maya shook her head. It was no time to show their hand.

But Maya's whole project these days was to keep them all out of sight until the right moment came. Since she was in hiding she wanted the whole movement hidden. She was vehement on this point, and usually got her way with most of the movement. There'll be a trigger event, she would insist. I'll know it when I see it.

But Coyote, seeing her and Michel there in their little warren, was irritated. "Just a little sign," he said. "Nothing serious."

"No," she said.

"We'll see," he said.

He left their hideout and went back to the canal side. He had a couple more drinks, mulling things over. Irritated at the sight of Maya in such confinement. Well, she was a dangerous revolutionary. Precautions were necessary. Still, the whole situation was getting dangerous, and worse than that, tiresome. Something needed to be done.

Also he needed to know if that young woman had turned or not.

The next night, after the restaurant row had almost emptied out, and the waiters were turning chairs onto tabletops and cursing each other in dull tired voices, Coyote wandered in by way of the Niederdorf, checking to make sure he was not followed. His contacts were waiting at the last Bareiss column. Separately they walked up to the shops at the intersection of Great Escarpment Boulevard and the Street of the Cypresses. There between two cypresses they met: Coyote and two young women in black, including the one from headquarters.

"Such dryads in the night," he said.

The two women laughed nervously. "You have the banner?"

They nodded nervously, and one showed him a package that just filled her hand.

He led them through the night, uphill, until they looked down on the tips of the cypresses, swaying so slightly in the night air circulation. It was pleasantly cool at first, but began to seem warmer as they climbed.

Ellis Butte was steep, but he had long ago memorized the footpath beaten up a ravine cleaving the northern wall of the mesa. Burroughs's nine mesas had become stupendous buildings and in people's minds they were nothing more than that, like a convocation of massive cathedrals, so that climbing them now was like climbing the side of a building, and seldom done anymore. But every one of the mesas still had old footpaths draping its sides, if you knew where to find them. And Coyote had his routes, on every side of all nine of them.

The top of Ellis Butte was very expensive real estate, completely built over. But there was a ledge under the mesa proper, too narrow for anything but a trail, and he led the two young women along it, holding their hot hands in his. It seemed he could feel their heartbeats pulsing in their sweaty palms. Finally they came to an outcropping of the ancient basalt, ending the ledge and blocking their way. Leaning out they seemed to look directly down onto Great Escarpment Boulevard. The train station bulking against the tent wall was still lit, of course, but no night trains had arrived in the past hour, and all was quiet—so quiet they could hear voices above them, on some private terrace. Coyote gestured to his companions, and one of them got the package out of a pocket. The other touched a button on her wristpad.

"*Everyone freeze,*" said an amplified voice, and figures appeared behind them on the ledge. Coyote leaped up and grabbed the railing of the private terrace and did a John Carter up over the side. A mellow party barely registered his presence before he was through them and off into the picturesque Aegean alleys of the mesa top, very convenient for a man fleeing the cops. On the other side of the mesa there was a trail down that few knew about, and in the dark Coyote was able to get down it a good distance before the security people reached the railings overhead and shined lights down that side. He ducked and became a rock for the period of their search. When they moved on he continued his descent.

But at the bottom of the trail there were more security police. They were trying to cordon off the whole damned mesa. Coyote climbed back up to a bolt-hole that led him onto one of the mid-mesa internal floors. From there he took an elevator down to the subway system, and got on a subway and sat back unobtrusively catching his breath until they reached Hunt Mesa Station, where he got off.

Up and back onto Great Escarpment Boulevard, across from the commotion surrounding Ellis. Free to go his way in the dark night city. But he was mad. He had made a couple extra packages when they manufactured the first one, so he went back to his coffin room in the workers' section of Black Syrtis Mesa, and got one of them. He walked back down Thoth Boulevard, thinking things over. He had planned to hang the first banner between Ellis and Hunt, so that when people left the train station they would see it overhanging Great Escarpment Boulevard, greeting them. That no longer seemed a practical place to do it. But as they came down Great Escarpment they would reach Canal Park and be facing the great concourse where Thoth Boulevard intersected the park. So he could try hanging it between Table Mountain and Branch Mesa, and delay releasing the banner until they were down where they would see it.

Time to work fast, as the night was getting on, and this would have to be done very surreptitiously. In short, just the kind of job the Coyote liked. So, as sneaky as his namesake, he climbed Table Mountain and reached a boulder high on the east face of the mesa. He had to drill a ringbolt in place (he had prepared Ellis and Hunt ahead of time) but that was only a matter of laser work, all the while trying to muffle the noise. But a big city provides a high level of background noise at all hours, and it went well. He attached one end of the replacement banner to the ring and started back down the trail, trailing the banner's Ariadne thread, gossamer on the gentle night air circulation. Down to Thoth Boulevard, across it like any night-shift worker (a big city provided plenty of other night wanderers, as well), hurrying discreetly so that the exposure of the thread to passersby would be minimal. Then up another steep forgotten trail on the prow of Branch Mesa, until he was at an altitude level with the ringbolt on Table Mountain, some 250 meters above street level.

He drilled in another bolt. The commotion on Ellis was dying down. When the bolt was in far enough he pulled the Ariadne thread across the gulf of air, through the bolt over a kilometer away. Despite its gossamer fineness he had to pull the last part through hard, hand over hand, until the thicker line, like fishing line from his childhood but very much stronger, was all the way across. He tied a knot around the bolt, grinning as he pulled hard on the final loop. Later that morning, if Hastings did indeed emerge from the train station with his group of functionaries, Coyote would be able to activate the drop of the banner with a wave of a laser penlight, and it would drop and the visitors would be greeted by a banner hanging over Thoth Boulevard. The two young women had composed the message on the banner lost to their treachery on Ellis Butte, but Coyote had made a different banner for a backup. The young women's had read: "THE TRUE TRANSITION HAS NOT YET BEGUN," a telling reference no doubt to the United Nations *Transitional* Authority, very clever; but Coyote had revised the message somewhat, and his banner would read: "UNTA WE ARE GOING TO KICK YOUR ASS OFF MARS."

He laughed at the thought. It would be in the air less than ten minutes, he figured, but photos would be taken. Some would laugh, others scowl. Maya would be irritated with him, he knew. But it was a war of nerves at this point, and UNTA needed to know that the majority of the population was against them; this in Coyote's opinion was extremely important. Also important to have the laughter on your side. He would argue strategy with her if he had to.

We'll laugh them right off the planet, he said to her in his mind, angrily, and laughed at the thought. Dawn was lightening the sky to the east. Later that day he would have to get out of town. But first a good breakfast, maybe even a champagne breakfast, down by the canal before the train came in. It wasn't every day you got to announce a revolution.

Michel in Provence

Many years later Michel made it to Mars anyway.

There was a European Union base on the Argyre Planitia, at the foot of the Charitum Montes, and Michel flew up in one of the fast Lorenz rockets, so it only took six weeks to get there. Once there he settled in for a year and a half residency, the time it took for the planets to re-align properly for an inexpensive return. And though the Charitum Range was striking, like the baked ridges of the Atlas Mountains or the ranges in the Mojave, and the light very good (compared with night in Antarctica), he was never once outside, not really. Always indoors, even when out in a rover, or in the modified space suits, which were almost like divers' wetsuits, with helmets and backpacks, altogether very light in the magical gravity. Nevertheless, shut in. Contained; a sealed vessel. And Michel, like most of the others there, felt it more and more acutely as time passed. All the people at the eight scientific stations exhibited symptoms of claustrophobia, except a small minority who developed agoraphobia. Michel collected data on all of them, and recorded in particular some spectacular breakdowns and a few emergency medevacs. No—there was no doubt—he had been right. Mars was not habitable over the long haul. Terraforming, while theoretically possible, was thousands of years off. In the meantime it was a rock in space, in effect a giant asteroid. Like all the rest of his team, Michel was overjoyed when it was time to return to the warm blue world and the open air.

But had he really been right? Was Mars really any different than McMurdo, or even Las Vegas, a city located in an unlivable desert?

Might not a permanent Mars colony have given humanity a kind of purpose, a symbolic existence to guide it through the splendors and miseries of this dark century, this dangerous millennium? Here back on Earth miracles were being performed, the sciences changing everything on a daily basis, and particularly the medical sciences, where the antivirals and the anticancer treatments and the cell-rejuvenation treatments were all together adding up to some larger balking of death, mind-boggling in its implications. Decades were being tacked on to people's lives, to Michel's own life, which went far past the normal span, which went on and on, like many others. If they were lucky enough to have access to the care—if they could afford it, in other words—they would live for many extra decades. Decades! And given the vertiginous logarithmic expansions of scientific knowledge, perhaps that meant they would have the time to make decades into centuries. No one could say.

And yet at the same time no one knew what to do with the added years. An incomprehensible gift. It baffled one's sense of meaning, for the rest of the world's troubles did not go away. On the contrary, the immediate practical problems of the increased longevity were vicious—more people, more hunger, more jealousy, more war, more unnecessary premature death. The ingenuity of death seemed to be matching the life sciences stroke for stroke, as in some titanic hand-to-hand combat, so that it sometimes seemed to Michel, as he averted his eyes from the headlines, that they added years to their lives only to have more people to kill or render miserable. Famines were killing off millions in the "underdeveloped" world, while at the same time, on the same planet, near-immortals were sporting in their Xanadus.

Perhaps an international village on Mars could have made it clearer to all that they were a single culture on a single world. The sufferings of any individual Martian settler would have been inconsequential in comparison to the benefits of this great lesson. The project would have justified it. They would have been like cathedral builders, doing hard, life-eating, useless work, in order to make something beautiful that said, *We are all one.* And some of them certainly would have loved that work, and the life it brought, because of that very statement. That goal—the sheer act of sacrifice for others, of work for the good of later generations. So that people on Earth could look up at night and say, That too is what we are—not just the horrific headlines, but a living world in the sky. A project in history.

.   .   .

So Michel was uneasy when the red star shone in the sky, and his life in the decades after his return from Mars was troubled at best. He moved around Provence restlessly, and even around the rest of France and the Francophone world. Trying to catch hold somewhere, but always slipping off, and returning to Provence. That was home. But still he was not comfortable, there or anywhere.

He worked as a therapist, and felt like a fraud; the doctor was sick. But he knew no other trade. And so he talked to unhappy people, and kept them company, and that was how he made his living. And tried to avoid the headlines. And never looked up at night.

Then one year in the fall a big transnational meeting on space habitation took place in Nice, sponsored in part by the French space program, and as someone who had been there and studied the issues, Michel was invited to speak. As it was only a few kilometers from his apartment, and as something kept drawing him back to the idea, no matter how he resisted it—out of guilt, pride, compulsion, responsibility—who knew; who could know?—he agreed to attend. It was the centennial of their winter in Antarctica.

Then he ignored the thing, displeased with himself for agreeing to go, perhaps even somewhat afraid. And so ignored all the information that came in the mail about it. So that he drove down to the conference one morning, aware only that he would be speaking on a panel that afternoon—and there was Maya Toitovna, standing in the hall, talking to a circle of admirers.

She saw him and frowned slightly; then her eyebrows shot up, and with fingers splayed like wingtip feathers she touched the upper arm of the man next to her, excusing herself from the circle. And then she was standing before him, shaking his hand. "I am Toitovna, do you remember me?"

"Please, Maya," he said painfully.

She smiled briefly and gave him a hug. Held him at arm's distance. "You've aged well," she decided. "You look good."

"You too."

She waved him off, but it was true. She was silver-haired, her face harshly lined, big gray eyes as clear and intent as ever. A beauty, as always. Even with Tatiana around to obscure the matter, she had always been the most beautiful woman in his life, the most magnificent.

They talked standing there, looking at each other. They were old now, well into their second centuries. Michel had to work to remember his English, and to a lesser extent so did she; and he had to work to remember the tricks of her harsh accent. It turned out she too had been to Mars; she had spent six years there, during the worst of the troubles in the 2060s. She shrugged as she remembered: "It was hard to enjoy it with so much bad happening down here."

Heart beating hard, Michel suggested meeting for dinner. "Yes, good," she said.

The conference was transformed. Michel watched the people there freshly; most much younger than he and Maya, eager to get out into space, to live on the moon, on Mars, the Jovian moons—everywhere. Anywhere but Earth. The escapism inherent in their desire was obvious to Michel, but he ignored it, tried to see it their way, tried to temper his statements and responses to match their desire. Without desire who could live? Mars for these people was not a place, not even a destination, but a lens through which to focus their lives. That being the case he did not care to take his usual disparaging position on the issue, now in any case a century old, and perhaps inadequate to the new moment. The world was falling apart; Mars helped people see that. An escape, yes, perhaps; but also a lens. He could help, if he worked at it, to sharpen the focus that the lens gave, perhaps. Or point it at certain things.

So he paid attention, and tried to think about what he was saying. Maya, it turned out, was on the same afternoon panel as he. A bunch of Mars veterans on stage, speaking about their experiences, and what they thought ought to be done. Maya spoke of living on the edge, looking back; the perspective it gave one. How things appeared in their proper proportions, so that it was obvious that a stable permaculture was the most important thing society could work for now.

Someone from the audience asked if they thought the original Russian/American plan to send one hundred permanent colonists might have been, in retrospect, the best way to go.

From down the line of speakers Maya leaned forward to look at him. Apparently he was the obvious one to answer.

He leaned toward his mike.

"Anything can happen in any situation," he said, thinking hard. "A Mars colony in the 2020s might have become . . . all that we hoped for it. But . . ."

He shook his head, not knowing how to continue. *But I lost my nerve. I lost in love. I lost all hope.*

"But the odds were against it. Conditions would have been too hard to endure over the long haul. The hundred would have been condemned to . . ."

"Condemned to freedom," Maya said into her mike.

Michel looked down the line at her, shocked, feeling the desperation grow in him. "Freedom, yes, but in a box. Freedom in a jail. On a rock world, without an atmosphere. Physically it would have been too hard. Life in a box is life in a prison, even if it is a prison of one's own devise. No, we would have gone mad. Many who go there come back damaged for life. They exhibit symptoms of a kind of post-traumatic stress disorder."

"But you said anything could happen," said the person in the audience.

"Yes, it's true. It could have developed. But who can say. *What if* is never a question with an answer. Looking at the evidence, I said then that it was a project in big trouble. Now we should look at the current situation. We have moved incrementally on Mars, taken things in their proper sequence. The infrastructure is now there in place to start making it an easier place to live. Perhaps now is the time for permanent settlers."

And thankfully others took up this thread, and he was off the hook, released from their interrogation.

Except that night, over dinner, Maya watched him closely. And at one point the panel of the afternoon came up.

"I didn't know what to say," Michel confessed.

"The past," Maya said dismissively. She waved the whole idea of the past away with a single flick of the hand. A weight came off Michel's stomach. She did not appear to hold it against him.

They had a wonderful evening.

And the next day they walked the beaches near Nice, the little ones Michel knew from his youth, and on one Maya stripped to her underwear and ran out into the Mediterranean, an old woman with magnificent carriage, rangy shoulders, long legs—this was what science had done for them, giving them these extra years of health when by all rights they should be long dead. They should be dead and gone for decades and yet here they were, out in the sun, catching waves, vigorous and strong, not even bent by the years. In their bodies in any case. And as she staggered out of the surf, dripping, wet and sleek as a dolphin, Maya tilted back her head and laughed out loud. She made the brown young women sunning on the sand look like five-year-olds.

And that evening they ditched the conference, and Michel drove them to a restaurant he knew in Marseilles, overlooking the industrial harbor. They had a wonderful time. And arriving back at the conference hotel, late, Maya took him by the hand and pulled him along with her to her room, and they kissed like twenty-year-olds, blood turned to fire, and fell on her bed.

Michel woke just before dawn and looked at his lover's face. Sleep made even the old hawk girlish. A beauty. It was character that created beauty—intelligence, and nerve, and the power to feel deeply, to love. Courage was beauty, that was all there was to it. And so age only added to beauty in the end.

This made him happy—to see into the heart of things, to be so there, in reality, in such a gray dawn. But happier still was some feeling of relief he couldn't quite define. He considered it, watching her breathe. If she was in bed with him—had made love with him, passionately and with great good humor—then she must not bear him any grudge for advising against the Mars project, so many years before. Wasn't that right? At the time she had wanted to go, he knew that. So . . . So she must have forgiven him. The past, she had said, dismissing it all. The present was what counted to her, the moment we call now, in which anything could happen.

She woke and they got up, and went down to breakfast, and Michel felt a most curious sensation: It was as if he were walking in Martian g. His body was light, floating ever so slightly, feet just padding the floor. Walking on air! He laughed to feel such a cliché come true, right there in his own body, in this very moment. And he suddenly knew he would remember this moment for the rest of his life, no matter what happened, no matter if he lived a thousand years. Make this your last thought when you die, he told himself, and you'll be happy even then, to know that you once had such a moment. The balance will be even and more than even.

After breakfast they abandoned the conference entirely. Michel drove her around and showed her his Provence. He showed her Nîmes and Orange and Montpellier and Villefranche-sur-Mer, his old beach, where they swam again. And he showed her the Pont du Gard, where the Romans had made their most beautiful creation. "Nadia would like this." And he took her up to Les Baux, the hilltop village overlooking the Camargue and the Med, the peaks honeycombed with the ancient chambers of the hermitage, poor monks up there above the world and all its Saracens. And later that afternoon they sat in a sidewalk café in Avignon, down from the Pope's palace, under plane trees, and Michel sipped cassis and watched her relax into her metal chair like a cat. "This is nice," she said. "I like this." And again he felt himself floating in Martian g, and she laughed to see the idiot grin plastered across his face.

But the next day the conference was scheduled to end. And that night, in bed, after they had finished making love and were lying stretched against each other, sweaty and warm, he said impulsively, "Will you stay longer?"

"Ah no," she said. "No—I have to get back."

She got up abruptly to go to the bathroom. When she came back she saw the look on his face, and said immediately, "But I'll come back! I'll come back and visit."

"Yes?"

"Of course. What, did you think I wouldn't? What do you take me for? Did you think I was not here too?"

"No."

"Did you think I do this all the time?"

"No."

"I should hope not."

She returned to bed, pulled back to look at him. "I'm not the kind of person to pull back when the stakes get high."

"Me neither."

"Except in Antarctica, right? We could have been up there a century ago, had our own world to live in together." She jabbed him with a finger. "Right?"

"Ahh—"

"But you said no." Now the knives were showing. Nothing ever went away, not really. "You could have said yes and we would have been there a century ago, in 2026. We could have been a couple there, maybe. Eventually we might have gotten together. We could have been together for sixty or seventy years, who knows!"

"Oh come on," he said.

"We could have! I liked you, you liked me. It was a bit like this, even in Antarctica, admit it. But you said no. You lost your nerve."

He shook his head. "It wouldn't have been like this."

"You don't know! Anything could happen, you said so yourself on that panel the other day. You admitted it then, in front of everyone."

He felt himself getting heavy. Sinking down into the bed.

"Yes," he said. "Anything could have happened."

He had to admit it to her, admit it just to her, lying next to her naked in bed.

"It's true. And I said no. I was afraid. I'm sorry."

She nodded, severe as any hawk.

He rolled on his back and stared at the ceiling, unable to meet her gaze. A hotel ceiling. He was getting heavier by the moment. He had to exert himself, to swim back to the surface. "But," he said. He sighed. He looked at her. "Now it's now. And—here we are, right?"

"Please," she said. "You sound like John when he first landed there."

She and John Boone had been a celebrity couple for a few years, several decades ago; she had mentioned him briefly the day before. A shallow man, she had said. All he wants is to have fun.

"But it's true what he said," Michel said. "Here we are."

"Yes yes. And I'll come back too. I told you that. But I have business to attend to."

"But you'll come back?" he asked, clasping her arm. "Even though—even though I . . ."

"Yes yes," she said. She stopped, and looked like she was thinking something over. Then: "You admitted it. That's what I wanted to hear. That's where we are now. So I'll come back."

She kissed him; then rolled onto him. "When I can."

The next morning she left. Michel drove her to the airport, kissed her good-bye. Back at his car, looking at its shabby interior, he groaned; he wasn't sure she really would return.

But she had said she would. And here they were, on Earth, in the year 2126. What might have been was no more than a dream, forgotten on waking. They could only go on from the here and now. So he had to stop worrying about the past, and think about what he could do now. If Maya was going to return, it would not be to comfort a guilt-stricken unhappy old man, that was certain. Maya looked forward. She was ready to go on making her life, no matter what had happened in the past. That was one of the qualities that made him love her; she was alive to the present, living in it. And she would want a partner to be the same. So he would have to live up to that; he would have to construct a life here, now, in Provence, that was worthy of Maya's love, that would make her want to come back, again and again, perhaps to stay, at least to visit. Perhaps to invite him back with her to Russia. Perhaps to make a life together.

It was a project.

The question, then, was where to settle, where to make a home? He was a Provençal, therefore he would settle in Provence. But he had moved around so much over the years that no one place represented home above all the others. But now he wanted one. Now when Maya returned (if she did; on the phone it sounded like she had a lot to keep her there in Russia), he wanted to be able to show her a Michel centered in the moment, happy. At home, and by being at home, justifying after the fact his decision to say no to Mars, to opt instead for the Mediterranean, that cradle of civilization still rocking, the coast's sun-washed rocky headlands still glowing in the light. Seduce the Russian beauty with the warmth of Provence.

A sign appeared, in the form of a family event; Michel's great-uncle died, and left to Michel and his nephew Francis a house on the coast, east of Marseilles. Michel thought of Maya's love for the sea and went to see his nephew. Francis was deeply involved in Arlesian affairs, and was agreeable to selling his share of the house to Michel, trusting that he would remain welcome there, which he certainly would be— Michel's late brother's son was among the most cherished people in Michel's life, a rock of good humor and good sense. And now, bless him, perfectly amenable. He seemed to know what Michel intended.

So the place was Michel's. An unadorned old vacation house on the beach, at the back of a little inlet between Pointe du Déffend and Bandol. A very modest place, in keeping with his great-uncle's character, and with Michel's project; it looked very much like a place Maya would like, beautifully located under plane trees, on a low beach no more than three or four meters higher than the sea, behind a little creek-crossed beach wedged between two small rocky headlands. A line of cypress trees ran up the crease in the hills.

One evening after the place was established as his, after a day spent moving things into it, Michel stood on the sand with his feet in the water, looking in the open door of the old place, then out at the wide horizon of the sea. The Martian sense of lightness began to seep back into him. Oh Provence, oh Earth this most beautiful world, each beach a gift of time and space, pendant on the sea and sparkling in the sun. . . . He kicked at the spent wave washing up the strand, and the water jetted out from his foot, glazed bronze by the horizontal sunlight. The sky under the sun was a bright bar of pewter, on a blazing sea. He said to himself, Here is my home, Maya. Come back and live with me.

Green Mars

Olympus Mons is the tallest mountain in the solar system. It is a broad shield volcano, six hundred kilometers in diameter and twenty-seven kilometers high. Its average slope angles only five degrees above the horizontal, but the circumference of the lava shield is a nearly continuous escarpment, a roughly circular cliff that drops six kilometers to the surrounding forests. The tallest and steepest sections of this encircling escarpment stand near South Buttress, a massive prominence which juts out and divides the south and southeast curves of the cliff (on the map, it's at 15 degrees north, 132 degrees longitude). There, under the east flank of South Buttress, one can stand in the rocky upper edge of the Tharsis forest, and look up at a cliff that is twenty-two thousand feet tall.

Seven times taller than El Capitan, three times as tall as Everest's southwest face, twice as tall as Dhaulagiri wall: four miles of cliff, blocking out the western sky. Can you imagine it? (It's hard.)

"I can't get a sense of the scale!" the Terran Arthur Sternbach shouts, hopping up and down.

Dougal Burke, looking up through binoculars, says, "There's quite a bit of foreshortening from here."

"No no. That's not it."

The climbing party has arrived in a caravan of seven field cars. Big green bodies, clear bubbles covering the passenger compartments, fat field tires with their exaggerated treads, chewing dust into the wind: The cars' drivers have parked them in a rough circle, and they sit in the middle of a rocky meadow like a big necklace of paste emeralds.

This battered meadow, with its little stands of bristlecone pine and noctis juniper, is the traditional base camp for South Buttress climbs. Around the cars are treadmarks, wind-walls made of stacked rock, half-filled latrine trenches, cairn-covered trash dumps, and discarded equipment. As the members of the expedition wander around the camp, stretching and talking, they inspect some of these artifacts. Marie Whillans picks up two ultralight oxygen cylinders stamped with letters that identify them as part of an expedition she climbed with more than a century ago. Grinning, she holds them overhead and shakes them at the cliff, beats them together. "Home again!" *Ping! Ping! Ping!*

One last field car trundles into the meadow, and the expedition members already in the camp gather around it as it rolls to a halt. Two men get out of the car. They are greeted enthusiastically: "Stephan's here! Roger's here!"

But Roger Clayborne is in a bad mood. It has been a long trip for him. It began in Burroughs six days ago, when he left his offices at Government House for the last time. Twenty-seven years of work as Minister of the Interior came to an end as he walked out the tall doors of Government House, down the broad chert steps and onto the trolley that would take him to his flat. Riding along with his face in the warm wind, Roger looked out at the tree-filled capital city he had rarely left during his stint in the government, and it struck him that it had been twenty-seven years of continuous defeat. Too many opponents, too many compromises, until the last unacceptable compromise arrived, and he found himself riding out of the city with Stephan, into the countryside he had avoided for twenty-seven years, over rolling hills covered by grasses and studded by stands of walnut, aspen, oak, maple, eucalyptus, pine: every leaf and every blade of grass a sign of his defeat. And Stephan wasn't much help; though a conservationist like Roger, he has been a member of the Greens for years. "That's where the real work can be done," he insisted as he lectured Roger and neglected his driving. Roger, who liked Stephan well enough, pretended his agreement and stared out his window. He would have preferred Stephan's company in smaller doses—say a lunch, or a game of batball. But on they drove along the wide gravel highway, over the windblown steppes of the Tharsis Bulge, past the farms and towns in Noctis Labyrinthus, up into the krummholz forests of east Tharsis, until Roger fell prey to that feeling one gets near the end of a long journey, that all his life had been part of this trip, that the traveling would never end this side of the grave, that he was doomed to wander over the scenes of all his defeats and failures endlessly, and never come to anyplace that did not include them all, right in the rearview mirror. It was a long drive.

For—and this was the worst of it—he remembered everything.

Now he steps from the car door to the rocky soil of base camp. A late addition to the climb (Stephan invited him along when he learned of the resignation), he is introduced to the other climbers, and he musters the cordial persona built over many years in office. "Hans!" he says as he sees the familiar smiling face of the areologist Hans Boethe. "Good to see you. I didn't know you were a climber."

"Not one like you, Roger, but I've done my share in Marineris."

"So"—Roger gestures west—"are you going to find the explanation for the escarpment?"

"I already know it," Hans declares, and the others laugh. "But if we find any contributing evidence . . ."

A tall rangy woman with leathery cheeks and light brown eyes appears at the edge of the group. Stephan quickly introduces her. "Roger, this is our expedition leader, Eileen Monday."

"We've met before," she says as she shakes his hand. She looks down and smiles an embarrassed smile. "A long time ago, when you were a canyon guide."

The name, the voice; the past stirs, quick images appear in his mind's eye, and Roger's uncanny memory calls back a hike—(he once guided treks through the fossae to the north)—a *romance*, yes, with a leggy girl: Eileen Monday, standing now before him. They were lovers for quite some time, he recalls; she a student in Burroughs, a city girl, and he—off into the backcountry. It hadn't lasted. But that was over two hundred years ago! A spark of hope strikes in him—"You *remember*?" he says.

"I'm afraid not." Wrinkles fan away under her eyes as she squints, smiles the embarrassed smile. "But when Stephan told me you'd be joining us—well—you're known to have a complete memory, and I felt I should check. Maybe that means I did remember something. Because I went through my old journals and found references to you. I only started writing the journals in my eighties, so the references aren't very clear. But I know we met, even if I can't say I remember it." She looks up, shrugs.

It is a common enough situation for Roger. His "total recall" (it is nothing of the sort, of course) encompasses most of his three hundred years, and he is constantly meeting and remembering people who do not recall him. Most find it interesting, some unnerving; this Eileen's sun-chapped cheeks are a bit flushed; she seems both embarrassed and perhaps a bit amused. "You'll have to tell me about it," she says with a laugh.

Roger isn't in the mood to amuse people. "We were about twenty-five."

Her mouth forms a whistle. "You really do remember everything."

Roger shakes his head; the chill in the shadowed air fills him, the momentary thrill of recognition and recall dissipates. It's been a very long trip.

"And we were . . . ?" she prods.

"We were friends," Roger says, with just the twist on *friends* to leave her wondering. It is disheartening, this tendency of people to forget; his unusual facility makes him a bit of a freak, a voice from another time. Perhaps his conservation efforts grow out of this retention of the past; he still knows what the planet was like, back there in the beginning. When he's feeling low he tends to blame his generation's forgetfulness on their lack of vigilance, and he is often, as he is now, a bit lonely.

Eileen has her head crooked, wondering what he means.

"Come on, Mr. Memory," Stephan cries to him. "Let's eat! I'm starving, and it's freezing out here."

"It'll get colder up there," Roger says. He shrugs at Eileen, follows Stephan.

In the bright lamplight of the largest base-camp tent the chattering faces gleam. Roger sips at a bowl of hot stew. Quickly the remaining introductions are made. Stephan, Hans, and Eileen are familiar to him, as is Dr. Frances Fitzhugh. The lead climbers are Dougal Burke and Marie Whillans, current stars of New Scotland's climbing school; he's heard of both of them. They are surrounded in their corner by four younger colleagues of Eileen's, climbing guides hired by Stephan to be their porters: "We're the Sherpas," Ivan Vivanov says to Roger cheerfully, and introduces Ginger, Sheila, and Hannah. The young guides appear not to mind their supporting role in the expedition; in a party of this size there will be plenty of climbing for all. The group is rounded off by Arthur Sternbach, an American climber visiting Hans Boethe. When the introductions are done they all circle the room like people at any cocktail party anywhere. Roger works on his stew and regrets his decision to join the climb. He forgot (sort of) how intensely social big climbs must be. Too many years of solo bouldering, in the rock valleys north of Burroughs. That was what he had been looking for, he realizes: an endless solo rock climb, up and out of the world.

Stephan asks Eileen about the climb and she carefully includes Roger in her audience. "We're going to start up the Great Gully, which is the standard route for the first thousand meters of the face. Then, where the first ascent followed the Nansen Ridge up to the left of the Gully, we're planning to go right. Dougal and Marie have seen a line in the aerial photos that they think will go, and that will give us something new to try. So we'll have a new route most of the way. And we'll be the smallest party ever to climb the scarp in the South Buttress area."

"You're kidding!" Arthur Sternbach cries.

Eileen smiles briefly. "Because of the party size, we'll be carrying as little oxygen as possible, for use in the last few thousand meters."

"And if we climb it?" Roger asks.

"There's a cache for us when we top out—we'll change equipment there and stroll on up to the caldera rim. That part will be easy."

"I don't see why we even bother with that part," Marie interjects.

"It's the easiest way down. Besides, some of us want to see the top of Olympus Mons," Eileen replies mildly.

"It's just a big hill," says Marie.

Later Roger leaves the tent with Arthur and Hans, Dougal and Marie. Everyone will spend one last night of comfort in the cars. Roger trails the others, staring up at the escarpment. The sky above it is still a rich twilight purple. The huge bulk of the wall is scarred by the black line of the Great Gully, a deep vertical crack just visible in the gloomy air. Above it, a blank face. Trees rustle in the wind; the dark meadow looks wild.

"I can't believe how tall it is!" Arthur is exclaiming for the third time. He laughs out loud. "It's just unbelievable!"

"From this vantage," Hans says, "the top is over seventy degrees above our real horizon."

"You're kidding! I can't believe it!" And Arthur falls into a fit of helpless giggling. The Martians following Hans and his friend watch with amused reserve. Arthur is quite a bit shorter than the rest of them, and suddenly to Roger he seems like a child caught after breaking into the liquor cabinet. Roger pauses to allow the others to walk on.

The big tent glows like a dim lamp, luminous yellow in the dark. The cliff face is black and still. From the forest comes a weird yipping yodel. Some sort of mutant wolves, no doubt. Roger shakes his head. Long ago any landscape exhilarated him; he was in love with the planet. Now the immense cliff seems to hang over him like his life, his past, obliterating the sky, blocking off any progress westward. The depression he feels is so crushing that he almost sits on the meadow grass, to plunge his face in his hands; but others will be leaving the tent. Again, that mournful yowling: the planet, crying out Mars is gone! Mars is gone! Ow-ooooooooooo! Homeless, the old man goes to sleep in a car.

But as always, insomnia takes its share of the night. Roger lies in the narrow bed, his body relaxed, his consciousness bouncing help-lessly through scenes from his life. Insomnia, memory: Some of his doctors have told him there is a correlation between the two. Certainly for him the hours of insomniac awareness and half sleep are memory's playground, and no matter what he does to fill the time between lying down and falling asleep (like reading to exhaustion, or scratching notes), tyrannical memory will have its hour.

This night he remembers all the nights in Burroughs. All the opponents, all the compromises. The Chairman handing him the order to dam and flood Coprates Chasma, with his little smile and flourish, the touch of hidden sadism. The open dislike from Noyova, that evening years before, after the Chairman's appointments: "The reds are finished, Clayborne. You shouldn't be holding office—you are the leader of a dead party." Looking at the Chairman's dam-construction bill and thinking of Coprates the way it had been in the previous century, when he had explored it, it occurred to him that ninety percent of what he had done in office, he did to stay in a position to be able to do anything. That was what it meant to work in government. Or was it a higher percentage? What had he really done to preserve the planet? Certain bills balked before they began, certain development projects delayed; all he had done was resist the doings of others. Without much success. And it could even be said that walking out on the Chairman and his "coalition" cabinet was only another gesture, another defeat.

He recalls his first day in office. A morning on the polar plains. A day in Burroughs, in the park. In the Cabinet office, arguing with Noyova. And on it will go, for another hour or more, scene after scene until the memories become fragmented and dreamlike, spliced together surrealistically, stepping outside the realm of memory into sleep.

There are topographies of the spirit, and this is one of them.

Dawn on Mars. First the plum sky, punctuated by a diamond pattern of four dawn mirrors that orbit overhead and direct a little more of Sol's light to the planet. Flocks of black choughs caw sleepily as they flap and glide out over the talus slope to begin the day's hunt for food. Snow pigeons coo in the branches of a grove of tawny birch. Up in the talus, a clatter of rocks; three Dall sheep are looking surprised to see the base-camp meadow occupied. Sparrows flit overhead.

Roger, up early with a headache, observes all the stirring wildlife indifferently. He hikes up into the broken rock of the talus to get clear of it. The upper rim of the escarpment is struck by the light of the rising sun, and now there is a strip of ruddy gold overhead, bathing all the shadowed slope below in reflected sunlight. The dawn mirrors look dim in the clear violet sky. Colors appear in the tufts of flowers scattered through the rock, and the green juniper needles glow. The band of lit cliff quickly grows; even in full light the upper slopes look sheer and blank. But that is the effect of distance and foreshortening. Lower on the face, crack systems look like brown rain stains, and the wall is rough-looking, a good sign. The upper slopes, when they get high enough, will reveal their own irregularities.

Dougal hikes out of the rock field, ending some dawn trek of his own. He nods to Roger. "Not started yet, are we?" His English is accented with a distinctly Scottish intonation.

In fact they are. Eileen and Marie and Ivan have gotten the first packs out of the cars, and when Roger and Dougal return they are distributing them. The meadow becomes noisier as the long equipment sorting ends and they get ready to take off. The packs are heavy, and the Sherpas groan and joke when they lift theirs. Arthur can't help laughing at the sight of them. "On Earth you couldn't even move a pack that size," he exclaims, nudging one of the oversized bags with a foot. "How do you balance with one of these on?"

"You'll find out," Hans tells him cheerfully.

. . .

Arthur finds that balancing the mass of his pack in Martian gravity is difficult. The pack is almost perfectly cylindrical, a big green tube that extends from the bottom of his butt to just over his head; with it on his back he looks like a tall green snail. He exclaims at its lightness relative to its size, but as they hike through the talus its mass swings him around much more than he is prepared for. "Whoah! Look out there! Sorry!" Roger nods and wipes sweat from his eyes. He sees that the first day is one long lesson in balance for Arthur, as they wind their way up the irregular slope through the forest of house-sized boulders.

Previous parties have left a trail with rock ducks and blazes chopped onto boulder faces, and they follow it wherever they can find it. The ascent is tedious; although this is one of the smaller fans of broken rock at the bottom of the escarpment (in some areas mass wasting has collapsed the entire cliff), it will take them all of a very long day to wind their way through the giant rockpile to the bottom of the wall proper, some seven hundred meters above base camp.

At first Roger approves of the hike through the jumbled field of house-sized boulders. "The Khumbu Rockfall," Ivan calls out, getting into his Sherpa persona as they pass under a big stone serac. But unlike the Khumbu Icefall below the fabled Everest, this chaotic terrain is relatively stable; the overhangs won't fall on them, and there are few hidden crevasses to fall into. No, it is just a rock field, and Roger likes it. Still, on the way they pass little pockets of chir pine and juniper, and Hans apparently feels obliged to identify every flower to Arthur. "There's aconite, and those are anemones, and that's a kind of iris, and those are gentians, and those are primulas. . . ." Arthur stops to point. "What the hell is that!"

Staring down at them from a flat-topped boulder is a small furry mammal. "It's a dune dog," Hans says proudly. "They've clipped some marmot and Weddell seal genes onto what is basically a wolverine."

"You're kidding! It looks like a miniature polar bear."

Behind them Roger shakes his head, kicks idly at a stand of tundra cactus. It is flowering; the six-month Martian northern spring is beginning. Syrtis grass tufting in every wet sandy flat. Little biology experiments, everywhere you look; the whole planet one big laboratory. Roger sighs. Arthur tries to pick one of each variety of flower, making a bouquet suitable for a state funeral, but after too many falls he gives up, and lets the colorful bundle hang from his hand. Late in the day they reach the bottom of the wall. The whole world is in shadow, while the clear sky overhead is still a bright lavender. Looking up, they cannot see the top of the escarpment anymore; they will not see it again unless their climb succeeds.

Camp One is a broad flat circle of sand, surrounded by boulders that were once part of the face, and set under a slight overhang formed by the sheer rampart of basalt that stands to the right side of the Great Gully. Protected from rockfall, roomy and comfortable to lie on, Camp One is perfect for a big lower camp, and it has been used before; between the rocks they find pitons, oxygen cylinders, buried latrines overgrown with bright green moss.

The next day they wind their way back down through the talus to base camp—all but Dougal and Marie, who take the day to look at the routes leading out of Camp One. For the rest of them, it's off before dawn, and down through the talus at nearly a running pace; a quick reloading; and back up in a race to reach Camp One again before nightfall. Every one of the next four days will be spent in the same way, and the Sherpas will continue for three more days after that, threading the same trail through the boulders, until all the equipment has been lugged up to Camp One.

In the same way that a tongue will go to a sore tooth over and over, Roger finds himself following Hans and Arthur to hear the areologist's explanations. He has realized, to his chagrin, that he is nearly as ignorant about what lives on Mars as Arthur is.

"See the blood pheasant?"

"No."

"Over there. The head tuft is black. Pretty well camouflaged."

"You're kidding. Why there it is!"

"They like these rocks. Blood pheasants, redstarts, accentors—more of them than we ever see."

Later: "Look there!"

"Where?"

Roger finds himself peering in the direction Hans has pointed.

"On the tall rock, see? The killer rabbit, they call it. A joke."

"Oh, a joke," Arthur says. Roger makes a revision in his estimation of the Terran's subtlety. "A rabbit with fangs?"

"Not exactly. Actually there's very little hare in it—more lemming and pika, but with some important traits of the lynx added. A very successful creature. Some of Harry Whitebook's work. He's very good."

"So some of your biological designers become famous?"

"Oh yes. Very much so. Whitebook is one of the best of the mammal designers. And we seem to have a special love for mammals, don't we?"

"I know I do." Several puffing steps up waist-high blocks. "I just don't understand how they can survive the cold!"

"Well, it's not that cold down here, of course. This is the top of the alpine zone, in effect. The adaptations for cold are usually taken directly from arctic and antarctic creatures. Many seals can cut the circulation to their extremities when necessary to preserve heat. And they have a sort of antifreeze in their blood—a glycoprotein that binds to the surface of ice crystals and stops their growth—stops the accumulation of salts. Wonderful stuff. Some of these mammals can freeze limbs and thaw them without damage to the flesh."

"You're kidding," Roger whispers as he hikes.

"You're kidding!"

"And these adaptations are part of most Martian mammals. Look! There's a little foxbear. That's Whitebook again."

Roger stops following them. No more Mars.

Black night. The six big box tents of Camp One glow like a string of lamps at the foot of the cliff. Roger, out in the rubble relieving himself, looks back at them curiously. It is, he thinks, an odd group. People from all over Mars (and a Terran). Only climbing in common. The lead climbers are funny. Dougal sometimes seems a mute, always watching from a corner, never speaking. A self-enclosed system. Marie speaks for both of them, perhaps. Roger can hear her broad Midlands voice now, hoarse with drink, telling someone how to climb the face. She's happy to be here.

Inside Eileen's tent he finds a heated discussion in progress. Marie Whillans says, "Look, Dougal and I have already gone nearly a thousand meters up these so-called blank slabs. There are cracks all over the place."

"As far as you've gone there are," Eileen says. "But the true slabs are supposed to be above those first cracks. Four hundred meters of smooth rock. We could be stopped outright."

"So we could, but there's got to be *some* cracks. And we can bolt our way up any really blank sections if we have to. That way we'd have a completely new route."

Hans Boethe shakes his head. "Putting bolts in some of this basalt won't be any fun."

"I hate bolts anyway," Eileen says. "The point is, if we take the Gully up to the first amphitheater, we know we've got a good route to the top, and all the upper pitches will be new."

Stephan nods, Hans nods, Frances nods. Roger sips a cup of tea and watches with interest. Marie says, "The *point* is, what kind of climb do we want to have?"

"We want to get to the top," Eileen says, glancing at Stephan, who nods. Stephan has paid for most of this expedition, and so in a sense it's his choice.

"Wait a second," Marie says sharply, eyeing each of them in turn. "That's not what it's about. We're not here just to repeat the Gully route, are we?" Her voice is accusing and no one meets her eye. "That wasn't what I was told, anyway. I was told we were taking a new route, and that's why I'm here."

"It will inevitably be a new route," Eileen says. "You know that, Marie. We trend right at the top of the Gully and we're on new ground. We only avoid the blank slabs that flank the Gully to the right!"

"I think we should try those slabs," Marie says, "because Dougal and I have found they'll go." She argues for this route, and Eileen listens patiently. Stephan looks worried; Marie is persuasive, and it seems possible that her forceful personality will overwhelm Eileen's, leading them onto a route rumored to be impossible.

But Eileen says, "Climbing any route on this wall with only eleven people will be doing something. Look, we're only talking about the first twelve hundred meters of the climb. Above that we'll trend to the right whenever possible, and be on new ground above those slabs."

"I don't believe in the slabs," Marie says. And after a few more exchanges: "Well, that being the case, I don't see why you sent Dougal and me up the slabs these last few days."

"I didn't send you up," Eileen says, a bit exasperated. "You two choose the leads, you know that. But this is a fundamental choice, and I think the Gully is the opening pitch we came to make. We do want to make the top, you know. Not just of the wall, but the whole mountain."

After more discussion Marie shrugs. "Okay. You're the boss. But it makes me wonder. Why are we making this climb?"

On the way to his tent Roger remembers the question. Breathing the cold air, he looks around. In Camp One the world seems a place creased and folded: horizontal half stretching away into darkness—back down into the dead past; vertical half stretching up to the stars—into the unknown. Only two tents lit from within now, two soft blobs of yellow in the gloom. Roger stops outside his darkened tent to look at them, feeling they say something to him; the eyes of the mountain, looking. Why is he making this climb?

Up the Great Gully they go. Dougal and Marie lead pitch after pitch up the rough unstable rock, hammering in pitons and leaving fixed ropes behind. The ropes tend to stay in close to the right wall of the Gully, to avoid the falling rock that shoots down it all too frequently. The other climbers follow from pitch to pitch in teams of two and three. As they ascend they can see the four Sherpas, tiny animals winding their way down the talus again.

Roger has been teamed with Hans for the day. They clip themselves onto the fixed rope with jumars, metal clasps that will slide up the rope but not down. They are carrying heavy packs up to Camp Two, and even though the slope of the Gully is only fifty degrees here, and its dark rock knobby and easy to climb, they both find the work hard. The sun is hot and their faces are quickly bathed with sweat.

"I'm not in the best of shape for this," Hans puffs. "It may take me a few days to get my rhythm."

"Don't worry about me," Roger says. "We're going about as fast as I like."

"I wonder how far above Camp Two is?"

"Not too far. Too many carries to make, without the power reels."

"I look forward to the vertical pitches. If we're going to climb we might as well climb, eh?"

"Especially since the power reels will pull our stuff up."

"Yes." Breathless laugh.

Steep, deep ravine. Medium gray andesite, an igneous volcanic rock, speckled with crystals of dark minerals, knobbed with hard protrusions. Pitons hammered into small vertical cracks.

Midday they meet with Eileen, Arthur, and Frances, the team above, who are sitting on a narrow ledge in the wall of the Gully, jamming down a quick lunch. The sun is nearly overhead; in an hour they will lose it. Roger and Hans are happy to sit on the ledge. Lunch is lemonade and several handfuls of the trail mix Frances has made. The others discuss the Gully and the day's climb, and Roger eats and listens. He becomes aware of Eileen sitting on the ledge beside him. Her feet kick the wall casually, and the quadriceps on the tops of her thighs, big exaggerated muscles, bunch and relax, bunch and relax, stretching the fabric of her climbing pants. She is following Hans's description of the rock and appears not to notice Roger's discreet observation. Could she really not remember him? Roger breathes a soundless sigh. It's been a long life. And all his effort—

"Let's get up to Camp Two," Eileen says, looking at him curiously.

Early in the afternoon they find Marie and Dougal on a broad shelf sticking out of the steep slabs to the right of the Great Gully. Here they make Camp Two: four large box tents, made to withstand rockfalls of some severity.

Now the verticality of the escarpment becomes something immediate and tangible. They can only see the wall for a few hundred meters above them; beyond that it is hidden, except up the steep trough in the wall that is the Great Gully, etching the vertical face just next to their shelf. Looking up this giant couloir, they can see more of the endless cliff above them, dark and foreboding against the pink sky.

Roger spends an hour of the cold afternoon sitting at the Gully edge of their shelf, looking up. They have a long way to go; his hands in their thick pile mittens are sore, his shoulders and legs tired, his feet cold. He wishes more than anything that he could shake the depression that fills him; but thinking that only makes it worse.

Eileen Monday sits beside him. "So we were friends once, you say."

"Yeah." Roger looks her in the eye. "You don't remember at all?"

"It was a long time ago."

"Yes. I was twenty-six, you were about twenty-three."

"You really remember that long ago?"

"Some of it, yes."

Eileen shakes her head. She has good features, Roger thinks. Fine eyes. "I wish I did. But as I get older my memory gets even worse. Now I think for every year I live I lose at least that much in memories. It's sad. My whole life before I was seventy or eighty—all gone." She sighs. "I know most people are like that, though. You're an exception."

"Some things seem to be stuck in my mind for good," says Roger. He can't believe it isn't true of everyone! But that's what they all say. It makes him melancholy. Why live at all? "Have you hit your three hundredth yet?"

"In a few months. But—come on. Tell me about it."

"Well . . . you were a student. Or just finishing school, I can't remember." She smiles. "Anyway, I was guiding groups in hikes through the little canyons north of here, and you were part of a group. We started up a—a little affair, as I recall. And saw each other for a while after we got back. But you were in Burroughs, and I kept guiding tours, and—well, you know. It didn't last."

Eileen smiles again. "So I went on to become a mountain guide— which I've been for as long as I can remember—while you moved to the city and got into politics!" She laughs and Roger smiles wryly. "Obviously we must have impressed each other!"

"Oh yes, yes." Roger laughs shortly. "Searching for each other." He grins lopsidedly, feeling bitter. "Actually I only got into government about forty years ago. Too late, as it turned out."

Silence for a while. "So that's what's got you down," Eileen says.

"What?"

"The Red Mars party—out of favor."

"Out of existence, you mean."

She considers it. "I never could understand the Red point of view—"

"Few could, apparently."

"—until I read something in Heidegger, where he makes a distinction between *earth* and *world*. Do you know it?"

"No."

"*Earth* is that blank materiality of nature that exists before us and more or less sets the parameters on what we can do. Sartre called it facticity. *World* then is the human realm, the social and historical dimension that gives earth its meaning."

Roger nods his understanding.

"So—the Reds, as I understood it, were defending earth. Or planet, in this case. Trying to protect the primacy of planet over world—or at least to hold a balance between them."

"Yes," Roger says. "But the world inundated the planet."

"True. But when you look at it that way, you can see what you were trying to do was hopeless. A political party is inevitably part of the world, and everything it does will be worldly. And we only know the materiality of nature through our human senses—so really it is only world that we know directly."

"I'm not sure about that," Roger protests. "I mean, it's logical, and usually I'm sure it's true—but sometimes—" He smacks the rock of their shelf with his mittened hand. "You know?"

Eileen touches the mitten. "World."

Roger lifts his lip, irritated. He pulls the mitten off and hits the cold rock again. "Planet."

Eileen frowns thoughtfully. "Maybe."

And there was hope, Roger thought fiercely. We could have lived on this planet the way we found it, and confronted the materiality of earth every day of our lives. We could have.

Eileen is called away to help with the arrangement of the next day's loads. "We'll continue this later," she says, touching Roger lightly on the shoulder.

He is left alone over the Gully. Moss discolors the stone under him, and grows in the cracks in the couloir. Swallows shoot down the Gully like falling stones, hunting for cliff mice or warm-blooded lizards. To the east, beyond the great shadow of the volcano, dark forests mark the sunlit Tharsis Bulge like blobs of lichen. Nowhere can one see Mars, just Mars, the primal Mars. They forgot what it was like to walk out onto the empty face of old Mars.

Once he walked out onto the great northern desert of Vastitas Borealis. All of Mars's geographical features are immense by Terran scales, and just as the southern hemisphere is marked by huge canyons, basins, volcanoes, and craters, the northern hemisphere is strangely, hugely smooth; it had, in its highest latitudes, surrounding what at that time was the polar ice cap (it is now a small sea), a giant planet-ringing band of empty flat layered sand. Endless desert. And one morning before dawn Roger walked out of his campsite and hiked a few kilometers over the broad wavelike humps of the windswept sand, and sat down on the crest of one of the highest waves. There was no sound but his breath, his blood pounding in his ears, and the slight hiss of the oxygen regulator in his helmet. Light leaked over the horizon to the southeast and began to bring out the sand's dull ocher, flecked with dark red. When the sun cracked the horizon the light bounced off the short steep faces of the dunes and filled everything. He breathed the gold air, and something in him bloomed, he became a flower in a garden of rock, the sole consciousness of the desert, its focus, its soul. Nothing he had ever felt before came close to matching this exaltation, the awareness of brilliant light, of illimitable expanse, of the glossy, intense *presence* of material things. He returned to his camp late in the day, feeling that a moment had passed—or an age. He was nineteen years old, and his life was changed.

Just being able to remember that incident, after two hundred and eighty-odd years have passed, makes Roger a freak. Less than one percent of the population share this gift (or curse) of powerful, long-term recollection. These days Roger feels the ability like a weight—as if each year were a stone, so that now he carries the crushing burden of three hundred red stones everywhere he goes. He feels angry that others forget. Perhaps it is envious anger.

Thinking of that walk when he was nineteen reminds Roger of a time years later, when he read Herman Melville's novel *Moby Dick*. The little black cabin boy Pip (and Roger had always identified himself with Pip in *Great Expectations*), "the most insignificant of the *Pequod*'s crew," fell overboard while his whaleboat was being pulled by a harpooned whale. The boat flew onward, leaving Pip alone. "The intense concentration of self in the middle of such a heartless immensity, my God! who can tell it?" Abandoned on the ocean alone, Pip grew more and more terrified, until "By the merest chance the ship itself at last rescued him; but from that hour the little Negro went about the deck an idiot. . . . The sea had jeeringly kept his finite body up, but drowned the infinite of his soul."

Reading that made Roger feel strange. Someone had lived an hour very like his day on the polar desert, out in the infinite void of nature. And what had seemed to Roger rapture had driven Pip insane.

It occurred to him, as he stared at the thick book, that perhaps he had gone mad as well. Terror, rapture—these extremities of emotion circumnavigate the spirit and approach each other again, though departing from the origin of perception in opposite directions. Mad with solitude, ecstatic with Being—the two parts of the recognition of self sit oddly together. But Pip's insanity only shocked Roger into a sharper love for his own experience of the "heartless immensity." He *wanted* it; and suddenly all the farthest, most desolate reaches of Mars became his special joy. He woke at night and sat up to watch dawns, a flower in a garden of rock. And wandered days like John in the desert, seeing God in stones and frost and skies that arched like sheets of fire.

Now he sits on a ledge on a cliff on a planet no longer his, looking down on plains and canyons peppered with life, life *created by the human mind*. It is as if the mind has extruded itself into the landscape: each flower an idea, each lizard a thought. . . . There is no heartless immensity left, no mirror of the void for the self to see itself in. Only the self, everywhere, in everything, suffocating the planet, cloying all sensation, imprisoning every being.

Perhaps this perception itself was a sort of madness.

The sky itself, after all (he thought) provides a heartless immensity beyond the imagination's ability to comprehend, night after night.

Perhaps he needed an immensity he could imagine the extent of, to feel the perception of it as ecstasy rather than terror.

Roger sits remembering his life and thinking over these matters, as he tosses granules of rock—little pips—over the ledge into space.

To his surprise, Eileen rejoins him. She sits on her heels, recites quietly,

> *"I love all waste*
> *And solitary places, where we taste*
> *The pleasure of believing what we see*
> *Is boundless, as we wish our souls to be."*

"Who said that?" Roger asks, startled by the lines.

"Shelley," she replies. "In 'Julian and Maddalo.' "

"I like it."

"Me too." She tosses over a pip herself. "Come join us for dinner?"

"What? Oh sure, sure. I didn't know it was time."

That night, the sound of the tent scraping stone, as the wind shifts it and shifts it. The scritching of thought as world scrapes against planet.

Next day they start spreading out. Marie, Dougal, Hannah, and Ginger take off early up the Gully, around a rib and out of sight, leaving behind a trail of fixed rope. Occasionally those left below can hear their voices, or the ringing of a piton being hammered into the hard rock. Another party descends to Camp One, to begin dismantling it. When they have got everything up to Camp Two, the last group up will bring the fixed ropes up with them. Thus they will set rope above them and pull it out below them, all the way up the wall.

Late the next day Roger climbs up to carry more rope to Marie and Douglas and Hannah and Ginger. Frances goes with him.

The Great Gully is steeper above Camp Two, and after a few hours of slow progress Roger finds his pack growing very heavy. His hands hurt, the footholds grow smaller and smaller, and he finds he must stop after every five or ten steps. "I just don't have it today," he says as Frances takes over the lead.

"Me neither," she says, wheezing for air. "I think we'll have to start using oxygen during the climbing pretty soon."

But the lead climbers do not agree. Dougal is working his way up a constriction in the Gully, knocking ice out of a crack with his ice axe, then using his fists for chocks and his twisted shoe soles for a staircase, and stepping up the crack as fast as he can clear it. Marie is belaying him and it is left to Hannah and Ginger to greet Roger and Frances. "Great, we were just about to run out of rope."

Dougal stops and Marie takes the opportunity to point to the left wall of the Gully. "Look," she says, disgusted. Roger and Frances see a streak of light blue—a length of xylar climbing rope, hanging free from a rust-pitted piton. "That Terran expedition, I bet," Marie says. "They left ropes the entire way, I hear."

From above Dougal laughs.

Marie shakes her head. "I hate seeing stuff like that."

Frances says, "I think we'd better go onto oxygen pretty soon."

She gets some surprised stares. "Why?" asks Marie. "We've barely started."

"Well, we're at about four kilometers above the datum—"

"Exactly," Marie says. "I *live* higher than that."

"Yes, but we're working pretty hard here, and going up pretty fast. I don't want anyone to get edema."

"I don't feel a thing," Marie says, and Hannah and Ginger nod.

"I could use a bit of oxygen," Dougal says from above, grinning down at them briefly.

"You don't feel edema till you have it," Frances says stiffly.

"Edema," says Marie, as if she doesn't believe in it.

"Marie's immune," Dougal calls down. "Her head can't get more swollen than it already is."

Hannah and Ginger giggle at Marie's mock glare, her tug on the rope to Dougal.

"Down you come, boy."

"On your head."

"We'll see how the weather goes," Frances says. "But either way, if we make normal progress we'll be needing oxygen soon."

This is apparently too obvious to require comment. Dougal reaches the top of the crack, and hammers in a piton; the ringing strikes grow higher and higher in pitch as the piton sets home.

That afternoon Roger helps the leads set up a small wall tent. The wall tents are very narrow and have a stiff inflatable floor; they can be hung from a single piton if necessary, so that the inhabitants rest on an air-filled cushion hanging in space, like window washers. But more often they are placed on ledges or indentations in the cliff face, to give the floor some support. Today they have found that above the narrowing of the Great Gully is a flattish indentation protected by an overhang. The cracks above the indentation are poor, but with the addition of a couple of rock bolts the climbers look satisfied. They will be protected from rockfall, and tomorrow they can venture up to find a better spot for Camp Three without delay. As there is just barely room (and food) for two, Roger and Frances begin the descent to Camp Two.

During the descent Roger imagines the cliff face as flat ground, entertained by the new perspective this gives. Ravines cut into that flat land: Vertically these are called gullies, or couloirs, or chimneys, depending on their shape and tilt. Climbing in these gives the climber an easier slope and more protection. Flat land has hills, and ranges of hills: These vertically are knobs, or ridges, or shelves, or buttresses. Depending on their shape and tilt these can either be obstacles, or in the case of some ridges, easy routes up. Then walls become ledges, and creeks become cracks—although cracking takes its own path of least resistance, and seldom resembles water-carved paths.

As Roger belays Frances down one difficult pitch (they can see more clearly why their climb up was so tiring), he looks around at what little he can see: the gray-and-black walls of the Gully, some distance above and below him; the steep wall of the rampart to the left of the Gully. And that's all. A curious duality; because this topography stands near the vertical, in many ways he will never see it as well as he would an everyday horizontal hillside. But in other ways (looking right into the grain of the rock to see if one nearly detached knob will hold the weight of his entire body for a long step down, for instance) he sees it much more clearly, more *intensely* than he will ever see the safe world of flatness. This intensity of vision is something the climber treasures.

The next day Roger and Eileen team up, and as they ascend the Gully with another load of rope, a rock the size of a large person falls next to them, chattering over an outcropping and knocking smaller rocks down after it. Roger stops to watch it disappear below. The helmets they are wearing would have been no protection against a rock that size.

"Let's hope no one is following us up," Roger says.

"Not supposed to be."

"I guess getting out of this Gully won't be such a bad idea, eh?"

"Rockfall is almost as bad on the face. Last year Marie had a party on the face when a rock fell on a traverse rope and cut it. Client making the traverse was killed."

"A cheerful business."

"Rockfall is bad. I hate it."

Surprising emotion in her voice; perhaps some accident has occurred under her leadership as well? Roger looks at her curiously. Odd to be a climbing guide and not be more stoic about such dangers.

Then again, rockfall is the danger beyond expertise.

She looks up: distress. "You know."

He nods. "No precautions to take."

"Exactly. Well, there are some. But they aren't sufficient."

The lead climbers' camp is gone without a trace, and a new rope leads up the left wall of the Gully, through a groove in the overhang and out of sight above. They stop to eat and drink, then continue up. The difficulty of the next pitch impresses them; even with the rope it is hard going. They wedge into the moat between a column of ice and the left wall, and inch up painfully. "I wonder how long this lasts," Roger says, wishing they had their crampons with them. Above him, Eileen doesn't reply for over a minute. Then she says, "Three hundred more meters," as if out of the blue. Roger groans theatrically, client to guide.

Actually he is enjoying following Eileen up the difficult pitch. She has a quick rhythm of observation and movement that reminds him of Dougal, but her choice of holds is all her own—and closer to what Roger would choose. Her calm tone as they discuss the belays, her smooth pulls up the rock, the fine proportions of her long legs, reaching for the awkward foothold: a beautiful climber. And every once in a while there is a little jog at Roger's memory.

Three hundred meters above they find the lead climbers, out of the Gully and on a flat ledge that covers nearly a hectare, on the left side this time. From this vantage they can see parts of the cliff face to the right of the Gully, above them. "Nice campsite," Eileen remarks. Marie, Dougal, Hannah, and Ginger are sitting about, resting in the middle of setting up their little wall tents. "Looked like you had a hard day of it down there."

"Invigorating," Dougal says, eyebrows raised.

Eileen surveys them. "Looks like a little oxygen might be in order."

The lead group protests.

"I know, I know. Just a little. A cocktail."

"It only makes you crave it," Marie says.

"Maybe so. We can't use much down here, anyway."

In the midday radio call to the camps below, Eileen tells the others to pack up the tents from Camp One. "Bring those and the power reels up first. We should be able to use the reels between these camps."

They all give a small cheer. The sun disappears behind the cliff above, and they all groan. The leads stir themselves and continue setting up the tents. The air chills quickly.

Roger and Eileen descend through the afternoon shadows to Camp Two, as there is not enough equipment to accommodate more than the lead group at Camp Three. Descending is easy on the muscles compared with the ascent, but it requires just as much concentration as going up. By the time they reach Camp Two Roger is very tired, and the cold sunless face has left him depressed again. Up and down, up and down.

That night during the sunset radio conversation Eileen and Marie get into an argument when Eileen orders the leads down to do some portering. "Look, Marie, the rest of us haven't led a single pitch, have we? And we didn't come on this climb to ferry up goods for you, did we?" Eileen's voice has a very sharp, cutting edge to it when she is annoyed. Marie insists the first team is making good time, and is not tired yet. "That's not the point. Get back down to Camp One tomorrow, and finish bringing it up. The bottom team will move up and reel Camp Two up to Three, and those of us here at Two will carry one load up to Three and have a bash at the lead after that. That's the way it is, Marie—we leapfrog in my climbs, you know that."

Sounds behind the static from the radio, of Dougal talking to Marie. Finally Marie says, "Aye, well you'll need us more when the climbing gets harder anyway. But we can't afford to slow down much."

After the radio call Roger leaves the tents and sits on his ledge bench to watch the twilight. Far to the east the land is still sunlit, but as he watches the landscape darkens, turns dim purple under a blackberry sky. Mirror dusk. A few stars sprinkle the high dome above him. The air is cold but still, and he can hear Hans and Frances inside their tent, arguing about glacial polish. Frances is an areologist of some note, and apparently she disagrees with Hans about the origins of the escarpment; she spends some of her climbing time looking for evidence in the rock.

Eileen sits down beside him. "Mind?"

"No."

She says nothing, and it occurs to him she may be upset. He says, "I'm sorry Marie is being so hard to get along with."

She waves a mittened hand to dismiss it. "Marie is always like that. It doesn't mean anything. She just wants to climb." She laughs. "We go on like this every time we climb together, but I still like her."

"Hmph." Roger raises his eyebrows. "I wouldn't have guessed."

She does not reply. For a long time they sit there. Roger's thoughts return to the past, and helplessly his spirits plummet again.

"You seem . . . disturbed about something," Eileen ventures.

"Ehh," Roger says. "About everything, I suppose." And winces to be making such a confessional. But she appears to understand.

She says, "So you fought all the terraforming?"

"Most of it, yeah. First as head of a lobbying group. You must be part of it now—Martian Wilderness Explorers."

"I pay the dues."

"Then in the Red government. And in the Interior Ministry, after the Greens took over. But none of it did any good."

"And why, again?"

"*Because,*" he bursts out—stops—starts again; "Because I liked the planet the way it was when we found it. A lot of us did, back then. It was so beautiful . . . or not just that. It was more overwhelming than beautiful. The size of things, their shapes—the whole planet had been evolving, the landforms themselves I mean, for five billion years, and traces of all of that time were still on the surface to be seen and read, if you knew how to look. It was so wonderful to be out there."

"The sublime isn't always beautiful."

"True. It transcended beauty, it really did. One time I walked out onto the polar dunes, you know. . . ." But he doesn't know how to tell it. "And so, and so it seemed to me that we already had an Earth, you know? That we didn't need a Terra up here. And everything they did eroded the planet that we came to. They destroyed it! And now we've got—whatever. Some kind of park. A laboratory to test out new plants and animals and all. And everything I loved so much about those early years is gone. You can't find it anywhere anymore."

In the dark he can just see her nodding. "And so your life's work . . ."

"Wasted!" He can't keep the frustration out of his voice. Suddenly, he doesn't want to, he wants her to understand what he feels; he looks at her in the dark. "A three-hundred-year life, entirely wasted! I mean I might as well have just . . ." He doesn't know what.

Long pause.

"At least you can remember it," she says quietly.

"What good is that? I'd rather forget, I tell you."

"Ah. You don't know what that's like."

"Oh, the past. The God-damned past. It isn't so great. Just a dead thing."

She shakes her head. "Our past is never dead. Do you know Sartre's work?"

"No."

"A shame. He can be a big help to we who live so long. For instance, in several places he suggests that there are two ways of looking at the past. You can think of it as something dead and fixed forever; it's part of you, but you can't change it, and you can't change what it means. In that case your past limits or even controls what you can be. But Sartre doesn't agree with that way of looking at it. He says that the past is constantly altered by what we do in the present moment. The *meaning* of the past is as fluid as our freedom in the present, because every new act that we commit can revalue the entire thing!"

Roger humphs. "Existentialism."

"Well, whatever you want to call it. It's part of Sartre's philosophy of freedom, for sure. He says that the only way we can possess our past—whether we can remember it or not, I say—is to add new acts to it, which then give it a new value. He calls this 'assuming' our past."

"But sometimes that may not be possible."

"Not for Sartre. The past is always assumed, because we are *not* free to stop creating new values for it. It's just a question of what those values will be. For Sartre it's a question of *how* you will assume your past, not whether you will."

"And for you?"

"I'm with him on that. That's why I've been reading him these last several years. It helps me to understand things."

"Hmph." He thinks about it. "You were an English major in college, did you know that?"

She ignores the comment. "So—" She nudges him lightly, shoulder to shoulder. "You have to decide how you will assume this past of yours. Now that your Mars is gone."

He considers it.

She stands. "I have to plunge into the logistics for tomorrow."

"Okay. See you inside."

A bit disconcerted, he watches her leave. Dark tall shape against the sky. The woman he remembers was not like this. In the context of what she has just said, the thought almost makes him laugh.

For the next few days all the members of the team are hard at work ferrying equipment up to Camp Three, except for two a day who are sent above to find a route to the next camp. It turns out there is a feasible reeling route directly up the Gully, and most of the gear is reeled up to Camp Three once it is carried to Camp Two. Every evening there is a radio conversation, in which Eileen takes stock and juggles the logistics of the climb, and gives the next day's orders. From other camps Roger listens to her voice over the radio, interested in the relaxed tone, the method she has of making her decisions right in front of them all, and the easy way she shifts her manner to accommodate whomever she is speaking with. He decides she is very good at her job, and wonders if their conversations are simply a part of that. Somehow he thinks not.

Roger and Stephan are given the lead, and early one mirror dawn they hurry up the fixed ropes above Camp Three, turning on their helmet lamps to aid the mirrors. Roger feels strong in the early going. At the top of the pitch the fixed ropes are attached to a nest of pitons in a large, crumbling crack. The sun rises and suddenly bright light glares onto the face. Roger ropes up, confirms the signals for the belay, starts up the Gully.

The lead at last. Now there is no fixed rope above him determining his way; only the broad flat back and rough walls of the Gully, looking much more vertical than they have up to this point. Roger chooses the right wall and steps up onto a rounded knob. The wall is a crumbling, knobby andesite surface, black and a reddish gray in the harsh morning blast of light; the back wall of the gully is smoother, layered like a very thick-grained slate, and broken occasionally by horizontal cracks. Where the back wall meets the sidewall the cracks widen a bit, sometimes offering perfect footholds. Using them and the many knobs of the wall Roger is able to make his way upward. He pauses several meters above Stephan at a good-looking vertical crack to hammer in a piton. Getting a piton off the belt sling is awkward. When it is hammered in he pulls a rope through and jerks on it. It seems solid. He climbs above it. Now his feet are spread, one in a crack, one on a knob, as his fingers test the rock in a crack above his head; then up, and his feet are both on a knob in the intersection of the walls, his left hand far out on the back wall of the Gully to hold on to a little indentation. Breath rasps in his throat. His fingers get tired and cold. The Gully widens out and grows shallower, and the intersection of back wall and sidewall becomes a steep narrow ramp of its own. Fourth piton in, the ringing of the strikes filling the morning air. New problem: The degraded rock of this ramp offers no good cracks, and Roger has to do a tension traverse over to the middle of the Gully to find a better way up. Now if he falls he will swing back into the sidewall like a pendulum. And he's in the rockfall zone. Over to the left sidewall, quickly a piton in. Problem solved. He loves the immediacy of problem solving in climbing, though at this moment he is not aware of his pleasure. Quick look down: Stephan a good distance away, and below him! Back to concentrating on the task at hand. A good ledge, wide as his boot, offers a resting place. He stands, catches his breath. A tug on the line from Stephan; he has run out the rope. Good lead, he thinks, looking down the steep Gully at the trail left by the green rope, looping from piton to piton. Perhaps a better way to cross the Gully from right to left? Stephan's helmeted face calls something up. Roger hammers in three pitons and secures the line. "Come on up!" he cries. His fingers and calves are tired. There is just room to sit on his bootledge: immense world, out there under the bright pink morning sky! He sucks down the air and belays Stephan's ascent, pulling up the rope and looping it carefully. The next pitch will be Stephan's; Roger will have quite a bit of time to sit on this ledge and feel the intense solitude of his position in this vertical desolation. "Ah!" he says. Climbing up and out of the world. . . .

It is the strongest sort of duality: Facing the rock and climbing, his attention is tightly focused on the rock within a meter or two of his eyes, inspecting its every flaw and irregularity. It is not particularly good climbing rock, but the Gully slopes at about seventy degrees in this section, so the actual technical difficulty is not that great. The important thing is to understand the rock fully enough to find only good holds and good cracks—to recognize suspect holds and avoid them. A lot of weight will follow them up these fixed ropes, and although the ropes will probably be renailed, his piton placements will likely stand. One has to see the rock and the world beneath the rock.

And then he finds a ledge to sit and rest on, and turns around, and there is the great expanse of the Tharsis Bulge. Tharsis is a continent-sized bulge in the Martian surface; at its center it is eleven kilometers above the Martian datum, and the three prince volcanoes lie in a line, northeast to southwest, on the bulge's highest plateau. Olympus Mons is at the far northwestern edge of the bulge, almost on the great plain of Amazonis Planitia. Now, not even halfway up the great volcano's escarpment, Roger can just see the three prince volcanoes poking over the horizon to the southeast, demonstrating perfectly the size of the planet itself. He looks around one-eighteenth of Mars.

By midafternoon Roger and Stephan have run out their three hundred meters of rope, and they return to Camp Three pleased with themselves. The next morning they hurry up the fixed ropes in the mirror dawn, and begin again. At the end of Roger's third pitch in the lead he comes upon a good site for a camp: A sort of pillar bordering the Great Gully on its right side ends abruptly in a flat top that looks very promising. After negotiating a difficult short traverse to get onto the pillar top, they wait for the midday radio conference. Consultation with Eileen confirms that the pillar is about the right distance from Camp Three, and suddenly they are standing in Camp Four.

"The Gully ends pretty near to you anyway," Eileen says.

So Roger and Stephan have the day free to set up a wall tent and then explore. The climb is going well, Roger thinks: no major technical difficulties, a group that gets along fairly well together . . . perhaps the great South Buttress will not prove to be that difficult after all.

Stephan gets out a little sketchbook. Roger glances at the filled pages as Stephan flips through them. "What's that?"

"Chir pine, they call it. I saw some growing out of the rocks above Camp One. It's amazing what you find living on the side of this cliff."

"Yes," Roger says.

"Oh I know, I know. You don't like it. But I'm sure I don't know why." He has the blank sheet of the sketchbook up now. "Look in the cracks across the Gully. Lot of ice there, and then patches of moss. That's moss campion, with the lavender flowers on top of the moss cushion, see?"

He begins sketching and Roger watches, fascinated.

"That's a wonderful talent to have, drawing."

"Skill. Look, there's edelweiss and asters, growing almost together." He jerks, puts finger to lips, points. "Pika," he whispers.

Roger looks at the broken niches in the moat of the Gully opposite them. There is a movement and suddenly he sees them—two little gray furballs with bright black eyes—three—the last scampering up the rock fearlessly. They have a hole at the back of one niche for a

home. Stephan sketches rapidly, getting the outline of the three creatures, then filling them in. Bright Martian eyes.

And once, in the northern autumn in Burroughs, when the leaves
covered the ground and fell through the air, leaves the color of sand,
or the tan of antelopes, or the green of green apples, or the white of
cream, or the yellow of butter—he walked through the park. The
wind blew stiffly from the southwest out of the big funnel of the
delta, bringing clouds flying overhead swiftly, scattered and white
and sunbroken to the west, massed and dark dusky blue to the east;
and the evergreens waved their arms in every shade of dark green, before which the turning leaves of the hardwoods flared; and above the
trees to the east a white-walled church, with reddish arched roof tiles
and a white bell tower, glowed under the dark clouds. Kids playing on
the swings across the park, yellow-red aspens waving over the brick
city hall beyond them to the north—and Roger felt—wandering
among widely spaced white-trunked trees that thrust their white
limbs in every upward direction—he felt—feeling the wind loft the
gliding leaves over him—he felt what all the others must have felt
when they walked around, that Mars had become a place of exquisite
beauty. In such lit air he could see every branch, leaf, and needle waving under the tide of wind, crows flying home, lower clouds lofting
puffy and white under the taller black ones, and it all struck him all at
once: freshly colored, fully lit, spacious and alive in the wind—what a
world! What a world.

And then, back in his offices, he hadn't been able to tell anyone
about it. It wouldn't have been like him.

Remembering that, and remembering his recent talk with Eileen,
Roger feels uncomfortable. His past overwhelmed that day's walk
through the park: What kind of assumption was that?

Roger spends his afternoon free-climbing above Camp Four, looking around a bit and enjoying the exercise of his climbing skills.
They're coming back at last. But the rock is nearly crack-free once out
of the Gully, and he decides free-climbing is not a good idea. Besides,
he notices a curious thing: About fifty meters above Camp Four, the
Great Central Gully is gone. It ends in a set of overhangs like the ribs
under the protruding wall of a building. Definitely not the way up.
And yet the face to the right of the overhangs is not much better; it
too tilts out and out, until it is almost sheer. The few cracks breaking

this mass will not be easy to climb. In fact, Roger doubts he could climb them, and wonders if the leads are up to it. Well, sure, he thinks. They can climb anything. But it looks awful. Hans has talked about the volcano's "hard eon," when the lava pouring from the caldera was denser and more consistent than in the volcano's earlier years. The escarpment, being a sort of giant boring of the volcano's flow history, naturally reflects the changes in lava consistency in its many horizontal bands. So far they have been climbing on softer rock—now they have reached the bottom of a harder band. Back in Camp Four Roger looks up at what he can see of the cliff above, and wonders where they will go.

Another duality: the two halves of the day, forenoon and afternoon. Forenoon is sunny and therefore hot: a morning ice and rock shower in the Gully, and time to dry out sleeping bags and socks. Then noon passes and the sun disappears behind the cliff above. For an hour or so they have the weird half-light of the dusk mirrors; then they too disappear, and suddenly the air is biting, bare hands risk frostnip, and the lighting is indirect and eerie: a world in shadow. Water on the cliff face ices up, and rocks are pushed out—there is another period when rocks fall and go whizzing by. People bless their helmets and hunch their shoulders, and discuss again the possibility of shoulder pads. In the cold the cheery morning is forgotten, and it seems the whole climb takes place in shadow.

When Camp Four is established they try several reconnaissance climbs through what Hans calls the Jasper Band. "It looks like orbicular jasper, see?" He shows them a dull rock and after cutting away at it with a laser saw, shows them a smooth brown surface, speckled with little circles of yellow, green, red, white. "Looks like lichen," Roger says. "Fossilized lichen."

"Yes. This is orbicular jasper. For it to be trapped in this basalt implies a metamorphic slush—lava partially melting rock in the throat above the magma chamber, and then throwing it all up."

So it was the Jasper Band, and it was trouble. Too sheer—close to vertical, really, and without an obvious way up. "At least it's good hard rock," Dougal says cheerfully.

Then one day Arthur and Marie return from a long traverse out to the right, and then up. They hurry into camp grinning ear to ear.

"It's a ledge," Arthur says. "A perfect ledge. I can't believe it. It's about half a meter wide, and extends around this rampart for a couple hundred meters, just like a damn sidewalk! We just walked right around that corner! Completely vertical above and below—talk about a view!"

For once Roger finds Arthur's enthusiasm fully appropriate. The Thank God Ledge, as Arthur has named it ("There's one like this on Half Dome in Yosemite"), is a horizontal break in the cliff face, and a flat slab just wide enough to walk on is the result. Roger stops in the middle of the ledge to look around. Straight up: rock and sky. Straight down: the tiny tumble of the talus, appearing directly below them, as Roger is not inclined to lean out too far to see the rock in between. The exposure is astonishing. "You and Marie walked along this ledge without ropes?" Roger says.

"Oh, it's fairly wide," Arthur replies. "Don't you think? I ended up crawling there where it narrows just a bit. But mostly it was fine. Marie walked the whole way."

"I'm sure she did." Roger shakes his head, happy to be clipped on to the rope that has been fixed about chest high above the ledge. With its aid he can appreciate the strange ledge—perfect sidewalk in a completely vertical world: the wall hard, knobby, right next to his head—under him the smooth surface of the ledge, and then empty space.

Verticality. Consider it. A balcony high on a tall building will give a meager analogy: Experience it. On the side of this cliff, unlike the side of any building, there is no ground below. The world below is the world of belowness, the rush of air under your feet. The forbidding smooth wall of the cliff, black and upright beside you, halves the sky. Earth, air; the solid here and now, the airy infinite; the wall of basalt, the sea of gases. Another duality: To climb is to live on the most symbolic plane of existence and the most physical plane of existence *at the same time*. This too the climber treasures.

At the far end of the Thank God Ledge there is a crack system that breaks through the Jasper Band—it is like a narrow, miniature version of the Great Gully, filled with ice. Progress upward is renewed, and the cracks lead up to the base of an ice-filled half funnel that divides the Jasper Band even further. The bottom of the funnel is sloped just enough for Camp Five, which becomes by far the most cramped of the campsites. The Thank God Ledge traverse means that using the power reels is impossible between Camps Four and Five, however. Everyone makes ten or twelve carries between the two camps. Each time Roger walks the sidewalk through space, his amazement at it returns.

While the carries across the ledge are being made, and Camps Two and Three are being dismantled, Arthur and Marie have begun finding the route above. Roger goes up with Stephan to supply them with rope and oxygen. The climbing is "mixed," half on rock, half on black ice rimed with dirty hard snow. Awkward stuff. There are some pitches that make Roger and Hans gasp with effort, look at each other round-eyed. "Must have been Marie leading." "I don't know, that Arthur is pretty damn good." The rock is covered in many places by layers of black ice, hard and brittle: Years of summer rain followed by frost have caked the exposed surfaces at this height. Roger's boots slip over the slick ice repeatedly. "Need crampons up here."

"Except the ice is so thin, you'd be kicking rock."

"Mixed climbing."

"Fun, eh?"

Breath rasps over knocking heartbeats. Holes in the ice have been broken with ice axes; the rock below is good rock, lined with vertical fissures. A chunk of ice whizzes by, clatters on the face below.

"I wonder if that's Arthur and Marie's work."

Only the fixed rope makes it possible for Roger to ascend this pitch, it is so hard. Another chunk of ice flies by, and both of them curse.

Feet appear in the top of the open-book crack they are ascending.

"Hey! Watch out up there! You're dropping ice chunks on us!"

"Oh! Sorry, didn't know you were there." Arthur and Marie jumar down the rope to them. "Sorry," Marie says again. "Didn't know you'd come up so late. Have you got more rope?"

"Yeah."

The sun disappears behind the cliff, leaving only the streetlamp light of the dusk mirrors. Arthur peers at them as Marie stuffs their packs with new rope. "Beautiful," he exclaims. "They have parhelia on Earth too, you know—a natural effect of the light when there's ice crystals in the atmosphere. It's usually seen in Antarctica—big halos around the sun, and at two points of the halo these mock suns. But I don't think we ever had four mock suns per side. Beautiful!"

"Let's go," Marie says without looking up. "We'll see you two down at Camp Five tonight." And off they go, using the rope and both sides of the open-book crack to quickly lever their way up.

"Strange pair," Stephan says as they descend to Camp Five.

The next day they take more rope up. In the late afternoon, after a very long climb, they find Arthur and Marie sitting in a cave in the side of the cliff that is big enough to hold their entire base camp. "Can you believe this?" Arthur cries. "It's a damn hotel!"

The cave's entrance is a horizontal break in the cliff face, about four meters high and over fifteen from side to side. The floor of the cave is relatively flat, covered near the entrance with a thin sheet of ice, and littered with chunks of the roof, which is bumpy but solid. Roger picks up one of the rocks from the floor and moves it to the side of the cave, where floor and roof come together to form a narrow crack. Marie is trying to get somebody below on the radio, to tell them about the find. Roger goes to the back of the cave, some twenty meters in from the face, and ducks down to inspect the jumble of rocks in the long crack where floor and roof meet. "It's going to be nice to lie out flat for once," Stephan says. Looking out the cave's mouth, Roger sees a wide smile of lavender sky.

When Hans arrives he gets very excited. He bangs about in the gloom hitting things with his ice axe, pointing his flashlight into various nooks and crannies. "It's tuff, do you see?" he says, holding up a chunk for their inspection. "This is a shield volcano, meaning it ejected very little ash over the years, which is what gave it its flattened shape. But there must have been a few ash eruptions, and when the ash is compressed it becomes tuff—this rock here. Tuff is much softer than basalt and andesite, and over the years this exposed layer has eroded away, leaving us with our wonderful hotel."

"I love it," says Arthur.

The rest of the team joins them in the mirror dusk, but the cave is still uncrowded. Although they set up tents to sleep in, they place the lamps on the cave floor, and eat dinner in a large circle, around a collection of glowing little stoves. Eyes gleam with laughter as the climbers consume bowls of stew. There is something marvelous about this secure home, tucked in the face of the escarpment three thousand meters above the plain. It is an unexpected joy to loll about on flat ground, unharnessed. Hans has not stopped prowling the cave with his flashlight. Occasionally he whistles.

"Hans!" Arthur calls when the meal is over and the bowls and pots have been scraped clean. "Get over here, Hans. Have a seat. There you go. Sit down." Marie is passing around her flask of brandy. "All right, Hans, tell me something. Why is this cave here? And why, for that matter, is this escarpment here? Why is Olympus Mons the only volcano anywhere to have this encircling cliff?"

Frances says, "It's not the *only* volcano to have such a feature."

"Now, Frances," Hans says. "You know it's the only big shield volcano with a surrounding escarpment. The analogies from Iceland that you're referring to are just little vents of larger volcanoes."

Frances nods. "That's true. But the analogy may still hold."

"Perhaps." Hans explains to Arthur, "You see, there is still not a perfect agreement as to the cause of the scarp. But I think I can say that my theory is generally accepted—wouldn't you agree, Frances?"

"Yes. . . ."

Hans smiles genially and looks around at the group. "You see, Frances is one of those who believe that the volcano originally grew up through a glacial cap, and that the glacier made in effect a retaining wall, holding in the lava and creating this drop-off after the glacial cap disappeared."

"There are good analogies in Iceland for this particular shape for a volcano," Frances says. "And it's eruption under and through ice that explains it."

"Be that as it may," Hans says, "I am among those who feel that the *weight* of Olympus Mons is the cause of the scarp."

"You said that once before," Arthur says, "but I don't understand how that would work."

Stephan voices his agreement with this, and Hans sips from the flask with a happy look. He says, "The volcano is extremely old, you understand. Three billion years or so, on this same site, or close to it—very little tectonic drift, unlike on Earth. So magma upwells, lava spills out, over and over and over, and it is deposited over softer material—probably the gardened regolith that resulted from the intensive meteor bombardments of the planet's earliest years. A tremendous weight is deposited on the surface of the planet, you see, and this weight increases as the volcano grows. As we all know now, it is a very, very big volcano. And eventually the weight is so great that it squishes out the softer material beneath it. We find this material to the northeast, which is the downhill side of the Tharsis Bulge, and is naturally the side that the pressured rock would be pushed out to.

Have any of you visited the Olympus Mons aureole?" Several of them nod. "Fascinating region."

"Okay," Arthur says, "but why wouldn't that just sink the whole area? I would think that there would be a depression circling the edge of the volcano, rather than this cliff."

"Exactly!" Stephan cries.

But Hans is shaking his head, a smile on his face. He gestures for the brandy flask again. "The point is, the lava shield of Olympus Mons is a single unit of rock—layered, admittedly, but essentially one big cap of basalt, placed on a slightly soft surface. Now by far the greatest part of the weight of this cap is near the center—the volcano's peak, you know, still so far above us. So—the cap is a unit, a single piece of rock—and basalt has a certain flexibility to it, as all rock does. So the cap itself is somewhat flexible. Now the center of it sinks the farthest, being heaviest—and the outside edge of the shield, being part of a single flexible cap, bends upward."

"Up twenty thousand feet?" Arthur demands. "You're kidding!"

Hans shrugs. "You must remember that the volcano stands twenty-five kilometers above the surrounding plains. The volume of the volcano is one hundred times the volume of Earth's largest volcano, Mauna Loa, and for three billion years at least it has been pressing down on this spot."

"But it doesn't make sense that the scarp would be so symmetrical if that was what happened," Frances objected.

"On the contrary. In fact that is the really telling aspect of it. The outer edge of the lava shield is lifted up, okay? Higher and higher, until the flexibility of the basalt is *exceeded*. In other words, the shield is just so flexible and no more. At the point where the stress becomes too much, the rock sheers off, and the inner side of the break continues to rise, while what is beyond the break point subsides. So, the plains down below us are still part of the lava shield of Olympus Mons, but they are beyond the break point. And as the lava was everywhere approximately the same thickness, it gave way everywhere at about the same distance from the peak, giving us the roughly circular escarpment that we now climb!"

Hans waves a hand with an architect's pride. Frances sniffs. Arthur says, "It's hard to believe." He taps the floor. "So the other half of this cave is underneath the talus wash down there?"

"Exactly." Hans beams. "Though the other half was never a cave. This was probably a small, roughly circular layer of tuff, trapped in much harder basaltic lava. But when the shield broke and the escarpment was formed, the tuff deposit was cut in half, exposing its side to erosion. And a few eons later we have our cozy cave."

"Hard to believe," Arthur says again.

Roger sips from the flask and silently agrees with Arthur. It's remarkable how difficult it is to transfer the areologist's theories, in which mountains act like plastic or toothpaste, to the vast hard basalt reality underneath and above them. "It's the amount of time necessary for these transformations that's difficult to imagine," he says aloud. "It must take . . ." He waves a hand.

"Billions of years," Hans says. "We cannot properly imagine that amount of time. But we can see the sure signs of its passing."

And in three centuries we can destroy those signs, Roger says silently. Or most of them. And make a park instead.

Above the cave the cliff face lies back a bit, and the smoothness of the Jasper Band is replaced by a jumbled, complicated slope of ice gullies, buttresses, and shallow horizontal slits that mimic their cave below. These steps, as they call them, are to be avoided like crevasses on level ground, as the overhanging roof of each is a serious obstacle. The ice gullies provide the best routes up, and it becomes a matter of navigating up what appears to be a vertical delta, like the tracing of a lightning bolt burned into the face and then frozen. Every morning as the sun hits the face there is an hour or so of severe ice and rockfall, and in the afternoons in the hour after the sun leaves the face there is another period of rockfall. There are some close calls and one morning Hannah is hit by a chunk of ice in the chest, bruising her badly. "The trick is to stay in the moat between the ice in the gully and the rock wall," Marie says to Roger as they retreat down a dead-end couloir.

"Or to be where you want to be by the time the sun comes up," Dougal adds. And on his advice to Eileen, they begin rising long before dawn to make the exposed parts of the climb. In the frigid dark a wristwatch alarm beeps. Roger twists in his bag, trying to turn it off; but it is his tent mate's. With a groan he sits up, reaches over and switches on his stove. Soon the metal rings in the top of the cubical stove are glowing a friendly warm orange, heating the tent's air and giving a little bit of light to see by. Eileen and Stephan are sitting in their bags, beating sleep away. Their hair is tousled, their faces lined, puffy, tired. It is 3:00 A.M. Eileen puts a pot of ice on the stove, dimming their light. She turns on a lamp to its lowest illumination, which is still enough to make Stephan groan. Roger digs in a food pouch for tea and dried milk. Breakfast is wonderfully warming, but suddenly he has to visit the cave's convenient yet cold latrine. Boots on—the worst part of dressing. Like sticking one's feet into ice blocks. Then out of the warm tent into the intense cold of the cave's air. Through the dark to the latrine. The other tents glow dimly—time for another dawn assault on the upper slopes.

By the time Archimedes, the first dawn mirror, appears, they have been on the slopes above the cave for nearly an hour, climbing by the light of their helmet lamps. The mirror dawn is better; there is enough light to see well, and yet the rock and ice have not yet been warmed enough to start falls. Roger climbs the ice gullies using crampons; he enjoys using them, kicking into the plastic ice with the front points of the crampons, and adhering to the slopes as if glued to them. Below him Arthur keeps singing a song in tribute to his crampons: "Spider-man, Spiderman, Spiderman, Spidermannnnn." But once above the fixed ropes, there is no extra breath for singing; the lead climbing is extremely difficult. Roger finds himself spread-eagled on one pitch, right foot spiked into the icefall, left foot digging into a niche the size of his toenail; left hand holding the shaft of the ice axe, which is firmly planted in the icefall above, and right hand laboriously turning the handle of an ice screw, which will serve as piton in this little couloir: And for a moment he realizes he is ten meters above the nearest belay, hanging there by three tiny points. And gasping for breath.

At the top of that pitch there is a small outcropping to rest on, and when Eileen pulls herself up the fixed rope she finds Roger and Arthur laid out over the rock in the morning sunlight like fish set out to dry. She surveys them as she catches her wind, gasping herself. "Time for oxygen," she declares. In the midday radio call she tells the next teams up to bring oxygen bottles along with the tents and other equipment for the next camp.

With three camps established above the cave, which serves as a sort of base camp to return to from time to time, they are making fair progress. Each night only a few of them are in any given camp. They are forced to use oxygen for almost all of the climbing, and most of them sleep with a mask on, the regulator turned to its lowest setting. The work of setting up the high camps, which they try to do without oxygen, becomes exhausting and cold. When the camps are set and the day's climbing is done, they spend the shadowed afternoons wheezing around the camps, drinking hot fluids and stamping their feet to keep them warm, waiting for the sunset radio call and the next day's orders. At this point it's a pleasure to leave the thinking to Eileen.

. . .

One afternoon climbing above the highest camp with Eileen, Roger stands facing out as he belays Eileen's lead up a difficult pitch. Thunderheads like long-stemmed mushrooms march in lines blown to the northeast. Only the tops of the clouds are higher than they. It is late afternoon and the cliff face is a shadow. The cottony trunks of the thunderheads are dark, shadowed gray—then the thunderheads themselves bulge white and gleaming into the sunny sky above, actually casting some light back onto the cliff. Roger pulls the belay rope taut, looks up at Eileen. She is staring up her line of attack, which has become a crack in two walls meeting at ninety degrees. Her oxygen mask covers her mouth and nose. Roger tugs once—she looks down—he points out at the immense array of clouds. She nods, pulls her mask to one side. "Like ships!" she calls down. "Ships of the line!"

Roger pulls his mask over a cheek. "Do you think a storm might come?"

"I wouldn't be surprised. We've been lucky so far." She replaces her mask and begins a layback, shoving the fingers of both hands in the crack, putting the soles of both boots against the wall just below her hands, and pulling herself out to the side so that she can walk sideways up one of the walls. Roger keeps the belay taut.

Mars's prevailing westerlies strike Olympus Mons, and the air rises, but does not flow over the peak; the mountain is so tall it protrudes out of much of the atmosphere, and the winds are therefore pushed around each side. Compressed in that way, the air comes swirling off the eastern flank cold and dry, having dumped its moisture on the western flank, where glaciers form. That is the usual pattern, anyway; but when a cyclonic system sweeps out of the southwest, it strikes the volcano a glancing blow from the south, compresses, lashes the southeast quadrant of the shield, and rebounds to the east intensified.

"What's the barometer say, Hans?"

"Four hundred and ten millibars."

"You're kidding!"

"That's not too far below normal, actually."

"You're kidding."

"It is low, however. I believe we are being overtaken by a low-pressure system."

.   .   .

The storm begins as katabatic winds: cold air falling over the edge of the escarpment and dropping toward the plain. Sometimes the force of the west wind over the plateau of the shield blows the gusts out beyond the actual cliff face, which will then stand in perfect stillness. But the slight vacuum fills again with a quick downward blast, which makes the tents boom and stretch their frames. Roger grunts as one almost squashes the tent, shakes his head at Eileen. She says, "Get used to it—there are downdrafts hitting the upper face more often than not." *WHAM!* "Although this one does seem to be a bit stronger than usual. But it's not snowing, is it?"

Roger looks out the little tent-door window. "Nope."

"Good."

"Awful cold, though." He turns in his sleeping bag.

"That's okay. Snow would be a really bad sign." She gets on the radio and starts calling around. She and Roger are in Camp Eight (the cave is now called Camp Six); Dougal and Frances are in Camp Nine, the highest and most exposed of the new camps; Arthur, Hans, Hannah, and Ivan are in Camp Seven; and the rest are down in the cave. They are a little overextended, as Eileen has been loath to pull the last tents out of the cave. Now Roger begins to see why. "Everyone stay inside tomorrow morning until they hear from me at mirror dawn. We'll have another conference then."

The wind rises through the night, and Roger is awakened at 3:00 A.M. by a particularly hard blast to the tent. There is very little sound of the wind against the rock—then a *BANG* and suddenly the tent is whistling and straining like a tortured thing. It lets off and the rocks hoot softly. Settle down and listen to the airy breathing *WHAM*, the squealing tent is driven down into the niche they have set it in— then sucked back up. The comforting hiss of an oxygen mask, keeping his nose warm for once—*WHAM*. Eileen is apparently sleeping, her head buried in her sleeping bag; only her bunting cap and the oxygen hose emerge from the drawn-up opening at the top. Roger can't believe the gunshot slaps of the wind don't wake her. He checks his watch, decides it is futile to try falling back to sleep. New frost condensation on the inside of the tent falls on his face like snow, scaring him for a moment. But a flashlight gleam directed out the small clear panel in the tent door reveals there is no snow. By the dimmest light of the lamp Roger sets their pot of ice on the square bulk of the stove and turns it on. He puts his chilled hands back in the sleeping bag and watches the stove heat up. Quickly the rings under the pot are a bright orange, palpably radiating heat.

An hour later it is considerably warmer in the tent. Roger sips hot tea, tries to predict the wind's hammering. The melted water from the cave's ice apparently has some silt in it; Roger, along with three or four of the others, has had his digestion upset by the silt, and now he feels a touch of the glacial dysentery coming on. Uncomfortably he quells the urge. Some particularly sharp blows to the tent wake Eileen; she sticks her head out of her bag, looking befuddled.

"Wind's up," Roger says. "Want some tea?"

"Mmmph." She pulls away her oxygen mask. "Yeah." She takes a full cup and drinks. "Thirsty."

"Yeah. The masks seem to do that."

"What time is it?"

"Four."

"Ah. My alarm must have woken me. Almost time for the call."

Although it is cloudy to the east, they still get a distinct increase of light when Archimedes rises. Roger pulls on his cold boots and groans. "Gotta go," he says to Eileen, and unzips the tent just far enough to get out.

"Stay harnessed up!"

Outside, one of the katabatic blasts shoves him hard. It's very cold, perhaps twenty degrees below Celsius, so that the windchill factor when it is blowing hardest is extreme. Unfortunately, he does have a touch of the runs. Much relieved, and very chilled, he pulls his pants up and steps back into the tent. Eileen is on the radio. People are to stay inside until the winds abate a little, she says. Roger nods vigorously. When she is done she laughs at him. "You know what Dougal would say."

"Oh, it was very invigorating all right."

She laughs again.

Time passes. When he warms back up Roger dozes off. It's actually easier to sleep during the day, when the tent is warmer.

He is rudely awakened late in the morning by a shout from outside. Eileen jerks up in her bag and unzips the tent door. Dougal sticks his head in, pulls his oxygen mask onto his chest, frosts them with hard breathing. "Our tent has been smashed by a rock," he says, almost apologetically. "Frances has got her arm broken. I need some help getting her down."

"Down where?" Roger says involuntarily.

"Well, I thought to the cave, anyway. Or at least to here—our tent's crushed, she's pretty much out in the open right now—in her bag, you know, but the tent's not doing much."

Grimly Eileen and Roger begin to pull their climbing clothes on.

Outside the wind rips at them and Roger wonders if he can climb. They clip on to the rope and jumar up rapidly, moving at emergency speed. Sometimes the blasts of wind from above are so strong that they can only hang in against the rock and wait. During one blast Roger becomes frightened—it seems impossible that flesh and bone, harness, jumar, rope, piton, and rock will all hold under the immense pressure of the downdraft. But all he can do is huddle in the crack the fixed rope follows and hope, getting colder every second.

They enter a long snaking ice gully that protects them from the worst of the wind, and make better progress. Several times rocks or chunks of ice fall by them, dropping like bombs or giant hailstones. Dougal and Eileen are climbing so fast that it is difficult to keep up with them. Roger feels weak and cold; even though he is completely covered, his nose and fingers feel frozen. His intestines twist a little as he crawls over a boulder jammed in the gully, and he groans. Better to have stayed in the tent on this particular day.

Suddenly they are at Camp Nine—one big box tent, flattened at one end. It is flapping like a big flag in a gale, cracking and snapping again and again, nearly drowning out their voices. Frances is glad to see them; under her goggles her eyes are red-rimmed. "I think I can sit up in a sling and rappel down if you can help me," she says over the tent noise.

"How are you?" asks Eileen.

"The left arm's broken just above the elbow. I've made a bit of a splint for it. I'm awfully cold, but other than that I don't feel too bad. I've taken some painkillers, but not enough to make me sleepy."

They all crowd into what's left of the tent and Eileen turns on a stove. Dougal dashes about outside, vainly trying to secure the open end of the tent and end the flapping. They brew tea and sit in sleeping bags to drink it. "What time is it?" "Two." "We'd better be off then." "Yeah."

Getting Frances down to Camp Eight is slow, cold work. The exertion of climbing the fixed ropes at high speed was just enough to keep them warm on the climb up; now they have to hug the rock and hold on, or wait while Frances is belayed down one of the steeper sections. She uses her right arm and steps down everything she can, helping the process as much as possible.

She is stepping over the boulder that gave Roger such distress when a blast of wind hits her like a punch, and over the rock she tumbles, face against it. Roger leaps up from below and grabs her just as she is about to roll helplessly onto her left side. For a moment all he can do is hang there, holding her steady. Dougal and Eileen shout down from above. No room for them. Roger double-sets the jumar on the fixed rope above him, pulls up with one arm, the other around Frances's back. They eye each other through their goggles—she scrambles blindly for a foothold—finds something and takes some of her weight herself. Still, they are stuck there. Roger shows Frances his hand and points at it, trying to convey his plan. She nods. He unclips from the fixed rope, sets the jumar once again right below Frances, descends to a good foothold, and laces his hands together. He reaches up, guides Frances's free foot into his hands. She shifts her weight onto that foot and lowers herself until Roger keeps the hold in place. Then the other foot crosses to join Roger's two feet—a good bit of work by Frances, who is certainly hurting. Mid-move another gust almost wrecks their balance, but they lean into each other and hold. They are below the boulder, and Dougal and Eileen can now climb over it and belay Frances again.

They start down once more. But the exertion has triggered a reaction inside Roger, and suddenly peristalsis attacks him. He curses the cave silt and tries desperately to quell the urge, but it won't be denied. He signals his need to the others and jumars down the fixed rope away from them, to get out of the way of the descent and obtain a little privacy. Pulling his pants down while the wind drags him around the fixed rope is actually a technical problem, and he curses continuously as he relieves himself; it is without a doubt the coldest shit of his life. By the time the others get to him he is shivering so hard he can barely climb.

They barge into Camp Eight around sunset, and Eileen gets on the radio. The lower camps are informed of the situation and given their instructions. No one questions Eileen when her voice has that edge in it.

The problem is that their camp is low on food and oxygen. "I'll go down and get a load," Dougal says.

"But you've already been out a long time," Eileen says.

"No no. A hot meal and I'll be off again. You should stay here with Frances, and Roger's chilled down."

"We can get Arthur or Hans to come up."

"We don't want movement up, do we? They'd have to stay up here, and we're out of room as it is. Besides, I'm the most used to climbing in this wind in the dark."

Eileen nods. "Okay."

"You warm enough?" Dougal asks Roger.

Roger can only shiver. They help him into his bag and dose him with tea, but it is hard to drink. Long after Dougal has left he is still shivering.

"A good sign he's shivering," Frances says to Eileen. "But he's awfully cold. Maybe too hypothermic to warm up. I'm cold myself."

Eileen keeps the stove on high till there is a fug of warm air in the tent. She gets into Frances's bag with her, carefully avoiding her injured side. In the ruddy stove light their faces are pinched with discomfort.

"I'm okay," Frances mutters after a while. "Good'n warm. Get him now."

Roger is barely conscious as Eileen pushes into his bag with him. He is resentful that he must move. "Get your outers off," Eileen orders. They struggle around, half in the bag, to get Roger's climbing gear off. Lying together in their thermal underwear, Roger slowly warms up. "Man, you are cold," Eileen says.

" 'Preciate it," Roger mutters wearily. "Don't know what happened."

"We didn't work you hard enough on the descent. Plus you had to bare your butt to a windchill factor I wouldn't want to guess."

Body warmth, seeping into him. Long hard body pressed against him. She won't let him sleep. "Not yet. Turn around. Here. Drink this." Frances holds his eyelids up to check him. "Drink this!" He drinks. Finally they let him sleep.

Dougal wakes them, barging in with a full pack. He and the pack are crusted with snow. "Pretty desperate," he says with a peculiar smile. He hurries into a sleeping bag and drinks tea. Roger checks his watch—midnight. Dougal has been at it for almost twenty-four hours, and after wolfing down a pot of stew he puts on his mask, rolls to a corner of the tent, and falls into a deep sleep.

Next morning the storm is still battering the tent. The four of them get ready awkwardly—the tent is better for three, and they must be careful of Frances's arm. Eileen gets on the radio and orders those below to clear Camp Seven and retreat to the cave. Once climbing they find that Frances's whole side has stiffened up. Getting her down means they have to hammer in new pitons, set up rappelling ropes for her, lower her with one of them jumaring down the fixed rope beside her, while occasionally hunkering down to avoid hard gusts of wind. They stop in Camp Seven for an hour to rest and eat, then drop to the cave. It is dusk by the time they enter the dark refuge.

So they are all back in the cave. The wind swirls in it, and the others have spent the previous day piling rocks into the south side of the cave mouth, to build a protective wall. It helps a bit.

As the fourth day of the storm passes in the whistle and flat of wind, and an occasional flurry of snow, all the members of the climb crowd into one of the large box tents, sitting upright and bumping arms so they will all fit.

"Look, I don't want to go down just because one of us has a busted arm," Marie says.

"I can't climb," says Frances. It seems to Roger that she is holding up very well; her face is white and her eyes look drugged, but she is quite coherent and very calm.

"I know that," Marie says. "But we could split up. It'll only take a few people to get you back down to the cars. The rest of us can take the rest of the gear and carry on. If we get to the cache at the top of the scarp, we won't have to worry about supplies. If we don't, we'll just follow you down. But I don't fancy us giving up now—that's not what we came for, eh? Going down when we don't have to?"

Eileen looks at Ivan. "It'd be up to you to get Frances down."

Ivan grimaces, nods. "That's what Sherpas are for," he says gamely.

"Do you think four will be enough for it?"

"More would probably just get in the way."

There is a quick discussion of their supply situation. Hans is of the opinion that they are short enough on supplies to make splitting up dangerous. "It seems to me that our primary responsibility is to get Frances to the ground safely. The climb can be finished another time."

Marie argues with him, but Hans is supported by Stephan, and it seems neither side will convince the other. After an apprehensive silence, Eileen clears her throat.

"Marie's plan sounds good to me," she says. "We've got the supplies to go both ways, and the Sherpas can get Frances down by themselves."

"Neither group will have much margin for error," Hans says.

"We can leave the water for the group going down," Marie says. "There'll be ice and snow the rest of the way up."

"We'll have to be a bit more sparing with the oxygen," Hans says. "Frances should have enough to take her all the way down."

"Yes," Eileen says. "We'll have to get going again in the next day or two, no matter what the weather's like."

"Well?" says Marie. "We've proved we can get up and down the fixed ropes in any weather. We should get up and fix Camp Nine as soon as we can. Tomorrow, say."

"If there's a bit of a break."

"We've got to stock the higher camps—"

"Yeah. We'll do what we can, Marie. Don't fret."

While the storm continues they make preparations to split up. Roger, who wants to stay clear of all that, helps Arthur to build the wall at the cave's entrance. They have started at the southern end, filling up the initial crack of the cave completely. After that they must be satisfied with a two-meter-high wall, which they extend across the entrance until the boulders on the floor of the cave are used up. Then they sit against the wall and watch the division of the goods. Wind still whistles through the cave, but sitting at the bottom of the wall they can feel that they did some good.

The division of equipment is causing some problems. Marie is very possessive about the oxygen bottles. "Well, you'll be going down, right?" she demands of Ivan. "You don't need oxygen at all once you get a couple camps down."

"Frances will need it a lot longer than that," Ivan says. "And we can't be sure how long it'll take to get her down."

"Hell, you can reel her down once you get past the Thank God Ledge. Shouldn't take you any time at all—"

"Marie, get out of this," Eileen snaps. "We'll divide the supplies. There's no reason for you to bother with this."

Marie glares, stomps off to her tent.

Arthur and Roger give each other the eye. The division goes on. Rope will be the biggest problem, it appears. But everything will be tight.

At the first break in the winds the rescue party—Frances and the four Sherpas—take off. Roger descends with them to help them cross the Thank God Ledge, and to recover the fixed rope there. The wind still gusts, but with less violence. In the middle of the ledge crossing

Frances loses her balance and swings around; Roger reaches her (not noticing he ran) and holds her in. "We have to stop meeting like this," Frances says, voice muffled by her mask.

When they reach the Great Gully, Roger says his good-byes. The Sherpas are cheery enough, but Frances is white-faced and quiet. She has said hardly a word in the last couple of days, and Roger cannot tell what she is thinking. "Bad luck," he tells her. "You'll get another chance, though."

"Thanks for grabbing me during the drop from Camp Nine," she says just as he is about to leave. She looks upset. "You're awfully quick. That would have hurt like hell if I had rolled onto my left side."

"I'm glad I could help," Roger says. Then, as he leaves, "I like how tough you've been."

A grimace from Frances.

On the way back Roger must free the fixed rope to recover it for the climb above, so on the Thank God Ledge he is always belayed only to the piton ahead. If he were to fall he would drop—sometimes up to twenty-five meters—and swing like a pendulum over the rough basalt. The ledge becomes new again; he finds that the smooth surface of the sidewalk is indeed wide enough to walk on, but still—the wind pushes at his back—he is alone—the sky is low and dark, and threatens to snow—and all of a sudden the hair on his neck rises, the oxygen whistles in his mask as he sucks it down, the pitted rock face seems to glow with an internal light of its own, and all the world expands, expands ever outward, growing more immense with every pulse of his blood; and his lungs fill, and fill, and fill.

Back in the cave Roger says nothing about the eerie moment on the ledge. Only Eileen and Hans are still in the cave—the others have gone up to supply the higher camps, and Dougal and Marie have gone all the way up to Camp Nine. Eileen, Hans, and Roger load up their packs—very heavy loads, they find when they duck out the cave—and start up the fixed ropes. Jumaring up the somewhat icy rope is difficult, in places dangerous. The wind strikes from the left now rather than from above. By the time they reach Camp Seven it is nearly dark, and Stephan and Arthur already occupy the single tent. In the mirror dusk and the strong side wind, erecting another tent is no easy task. There is not another level spot to set it on either—they must place it on a slope, and tie it to pitons hammered into the cliff. By the time Eileen and Roger and Hans get into the new tent, Roger is freezing and starving and intensely thirsty. "Pretty bloody desperate," he says wearily, mimicking Marie and the Sherpas. They melt snow and cook up a pot of stew from their sleeping bags, and when they are done eating, Roger puts on his oxygen mask, sets the flow for sleep, and slumps off.

The moment on the Thank God Ledge jumps to mind and wakes him momentarily. Wind whips the taut walls of the tent, and Eileen, penciling logistic notes for the next day, slides down the slope under the tent until their two sleeping bags are one clumped mass. Roger looks at her: brief smile from that tired, puffy, frost-burned face. Great deltas of wrinkles under her eyes. His feet begin to warm up and he falls asleep to the popping of the tent, the hiss of oxygen, the scratching of a pencil.

That night the storm begins to pick up again.

The next morning they take down the tent in a strong wind—hard work—and start portering loads up to Camp Eight. Halfway between camps it begins to snow. Roger watches his feet through swirls of hard, dry granules. His gloved fingers twist around the frigid jumar, sliding it up the frosted rope, clicking it home, pulling himself up. It is a struggle to see footholds in the spindrift, which moves horizontally across the cliff face, from left to right as he looks at it. The whole face appears to be whitely streaming to the side, like a wave. He finds he must focus his attention entirely on his hands and feet. His fingers, nose, and toes are very cold. He rubs his nose through the mask, feels nothing. The wind pushes him hard, like a giant trying to make him fall. In the narrow gullies the wind is less strong, but they find themselves climbing up through waves of avalanching snow, drift after drift of it piling up between their bodies and the slope, burying them, sliding between their legs and away. One gully seems to last forever. Intermittently Roger is concerned about his nose, but mostly he worries about the immediate situation: moving up the rope, keeping a foothold. Visibility is down to about twenty meters—they are in a little white bubble flying to the left through white snow, or so it appears.

At one point Roger must wait for Eileen and Hans to get over the boulder that Frances had such trouble with. His mind wanders and it occurs to him that their chances of success have shifted radically—

and with them, the nature of the climb. Low on supplies, facing an unknown route in deteriorating weather—Roger wonders how Eileen will handle it. She has led expeditions before, but this kind only comes about by accident.

She passes him going strong, beats ice from the rope, sweeps spindrift from the top of the boulder. Pulls up and over it in one smooth motion. The wind cuts through Roger as he watches Hans repeat the operation: cuts through the laminated outer suit, the thick bunting inner suit, his skin. . . . He brushes spindrift from his goggles with a frigid hand and heaves up after them.

Though it is spring, the winterlike low-pressure system over Olympus Mons is in place, drawing the wet winds up from the south, creating stable storm conditions on the south and east arcs of the escarpment. The snow is irregular, the wind constant. For the better part of a week the seven climbers left on the face struggle in the miserable conditions. One night at sunset radio hour they hear from Frances and the Sherpas, down at base camp. There is a lot of sand in Martian snow, and their voices are garbled by static, but the message is clear: They are down, they are safe, they are leaving for Alexandria to get Frances's arm set. Roger catches on Eileen's averted face an expression of pure relief, and realizes that her silence in the past few days has been a manifestation of worry. Now, looking pleased, she gives the remaining climbers their instructions for the next day in a fresh determined tone.

Into camp at night, cold and almost too tired to walk. Big loaded packs onto the various ledges and niches that serve for this particular camp. Hands shaking with hunger. The camp—Thirteen, Roger believes—is on a saddle between two ridges overlooking a deep, twisted chimney. "Just like the Devil's Kitchen on Ben Nevis," Arthur remarks when they get inside the tent. He eats with gusto. Roger shivers and puts his hands two centimeters above the glowing stove ring. Transferring from climbing mode to tent mode is a tricky business, and tonight Roger hasn't done so well. At this altitude and in these winds, cold has become their most serious opponent. Overmitts off, and everything must be done immediately to get lightly gloved hands protected again as quickly as possible. Even if the rest of one's body is warmed by exertion, the fingertips will freeze if they have enough contact with cold things. And yet so many camp operations can be done more easily with hands out of mitts. Frostnip is the frequent result, leaving the fingers tender, so that pulling up a rock face, or even buttoning or zipping one's clothes, becomes a painful task. Frostnip blisters kill the skin, creating black patches that take a week or more to peel away. Now when they sit in the tents around the ruddy light of the stove, observing solemnly the progress of the cooking meal, they see across the pot faces splotched on cheek or nose: black skin peeling away to reveal bright pink new skin beneath.

They climb onto a band of rotten rock, a tuff-and-lava composite that sometimes breaks right off in their hands. It takes Marie and Dougal two full days to find decent belay points for the 150 meters of the band, and every morning the rockfall is frequent and frightening. "It's a bit like swimming up the thing, isn't it?" Dougal comments. When they make it to the hard rock above, Eileen orders Dougal and Marie to the bottom of their "ladder" to get some rest. Marie makes no complaint now; each day in the lead is an exhausting exercise, and Marie and Dougal are beat.

Every night Eileen works out plans for the following day, revising them as conditions and the climbers' strength and health change. The logistics are complicated, and each day the seven climbers shift partners and positions in the climb. Eileen scribbles in her notebook and jabbers on the radio every dusk, altering the schedules and changing her orders with almost every new bit of information she receives from the higher camps. Her method appears chaotic. Marie dubs her the "Mad Mahdi," and scoffs at the constant changes in plans; but she obeys them, and they work: Every night they are scattered in two or three camps up and down the cliff, with everything that they need to survive the night and get them higher the next day; and every new day they leapfrog up, pulling out the lowest camp, finding a place to establish a new high camp. The bitter winds continue. Everything is difficult. They lose track of camp numbers, and name them only high, middle, and low.

Naturally, three-quarters of everyone's work is portering. Roger begins to feel that he is surviving the rigors of the weather and altitude better than most of the rest; he can carry more faster, and even though most days end in that state where each step up is ten breaths' agony, he finds he can take on more the next day. His digestion returns to normal, which is a blessing—a great physical pleasure, in fact. Perhaps improvement in this area masks the effects of altitude, or perhaps the altitude isn't bothering Roger yet; it is certainly true that high altitude affects people differently, for reasons unconnected with basic strength—in fact, for reasons not yet fully understood.

So Roger becomes the chief porter; Dougal calls him Roger Sherpa, and Arthur calls him Tenzing. The day's challenge becomes to do all one's myriad activities as efficiently as possible, without frostnip, excessive discomfort, hunger, thirst, or exhaustion. He hums to himself little snatches of music. His favorite is the eight-note phrase repeated by the basses near the end of the first movement of Beethoven's Ninth: six notes down, two notes up, over and over and over. And each evening in the sleeping bag, warm, well fed, and prone, is a little victory.

One night he wakes up to darkness and silence, fully awake in an instant, heart pounding. Confused, he thinks he may have dreamed of the Thank God Ledge. But then he notices the silence again and realizes his oxygen bottle has run out. It happens every week or so. He uncouples the bottle from the regulator, finds another bottle in the dark, and clips it into place. When he tells Arthur about it next morning, Arthur laughs. "That happened to me a couple of nights ago. I don't think anybody could sleep through their oxygen bottle running out—I mean you wake up *very* awake, don't you?"

In the hard rock band Roger porters up a pitch that leaves him whistling into his mask: The gullies have disappeared, above is a nearly vertical black wall, and breaking it is one lightning-bolt crack, now marked by a fixed rope with slings attached, making it a sort of rope ladder. Fine for him, but the lead climb! "Must have been Dougal at it again."

And the next day he is out in the lead himself with Arthur, on a continuation of the same face. Leading is very unlike portering. Suddenly the dogged, repetitious, almost mindless work of carrying loads is replaced by the anxious attentiveness of the lead. Arthur takes the first pitch and finishes it bubbling over with enthusiasm. Only his oxygen mask keeps him from carrying on a long conversation as Roger takes over the lead. Then Roger is up there himself, above the last belay on empty rock, looking for the best way. The lure of the lead returns, the pleasure of the problem solved fills him with energy. Fully back in lead mode, he collaborates with Arthur—who turns out to be an ingenious and resourceful technical climber—on the best storm day yet: five hundred meters of fixed rope, their entire supply, nailed up in one day. They hurry back down to camp and find Eileen and Marie still there, dumping food for the next few days.

"By God we are a team!" Arthur cries as they describe the day's work. "Eileen, you should put us together more often. Don't you agree, Roger?"

Roger grins, nods at Eileen. "That was fun."

Marie and Eileen leave for the camp below, and Arthur and Roger cook a big pot of stew and trade climbing stories, scores of them: And every one ends, "but that was nothing compared to today."

Heavy snow returns and traps them in their tents, and it's all they can do to keep the high camp supplied. "Bloody desperate out!" Marie complains, as if she can't believe how bad it is. After one bad afternoon Stephan and Arthur are in the high camp, Eileen and Roger in the middle camp, and Hans, Marie, and Dougal in the low camp with all the supplies. The storm strikes Roger and Eileen's tent so hard they are considering bringing in some rocks to weight it down more. A buzz sounds from their radio and Eileen picks it up.

"Eileen, this is Arthur. I'm afraid Stephan has come up too fast."

Eileen scowls fearfully, swears under her breath. Stephan has gone from low camp to high in two days' hard climbing.

"He's very short of breath, and he's spitting up bloody spit. And talking like a madman."

"I'm okay!" Stephan shouts through the static. "I'm fine!"

"Shut up! You're not fine! Eileen, did you hear that? I'm afraid he's got edema."

"Yeah," Eileen says. "Has he got a headache?"

"No. It's just his lungs right now, I think. Shut up! I can hear his chest bubbling, you know."

"Yeah. Pulse up?"

"Pulse weak and rapid, yeah."

"Damn." Eileen looks at Roger. "Put him on max oxygen."

"I already have. Still . . ."

"I know. We've got to get him down."

"I'm okay!"

"Yeah," Arthur says. "He needs to come down, at least to your camp, maybe lower."

"Damn it," Eileen exclaims when off the radio. "I moved him up too fast."

An hour later—calls made below, the whole camp in action—Roger and Eileen are out in the storm again, in the dark, their helmet head-lights showing them only a portion of the snowfall. They cannot afford to wait until morning—pulmonary edema can be quickly fatal, and the best treatment by far is to get the victim lower, where his lungs can clear out the excess water. Even a small drop in altitude can make a dramatic difference. So off they go; Roger takes the lead and bashes ice from the rope, jumars up, scrabbles over the rock blindly with his crampon tips to get a purchase in the snow and ice. It is bitterly cold. They reach the bottom of the blank wall pitch that so impressed Roger, and the going is treacherous. He wonders how they will get Stephan down it. The fixed rope is the only thing making the ascent possible, but it does less and less to aid them as ice coats it and the rock face. Wind hammers them, and Roger has a sudden very acute sensation of the empty space behind them. The headlamps' beams reveal only swirling snow. Fear adds its own kind of chill to the mix.

By the time they reach high camp Stephan is quite ill. No more protests from him. "I don't know how we'll get him down," Arthur says anxiously. "I gave him a small shot of morphine to get the peripheral veins to start dilating."

"Good. We'll just have to truss him into a harness and lower him."

"Easier said than done, in this stuff."

Stephan is barely conscious, coughing and hacking with every breath. Pulmonary edema fills the lungs with water; unless the process is reversed, he will drown. Just getting him into the sling (another function of the little wall tents) is hard work. Then outside again—struck by the wind—and to the fixed ropes. Roger descends first, Eileen and Arthur lower Stephan using a power reel, and Roger collects him like a large bundle of laundry. After standing him upright and knocking the frozen spittle from the bottom of his mask, Roger waits for the other two, and when they arrive he starts down again. The descent seems endless, and everyone gets dangerously cold. Windblown snow, the rock face, omnipresent cold: nothing else in the world. At the end of one drop Roger cannot undo the knot at the end of his belay line, to send it back up for Stephan. For fifteen minutes he struggles with the frozen knot, which resembles a wet iron pretzel. Nothing to cut it off with either. For a while it seems they will all freeze to death because he can't untie a knot. Finally he takes his climbing gloves off and pulls at the thing with his bare fingers until it comes loose.

Eventually they arrive at the lower camp, where Hans and Dougal are waiting with a medical kit. Stephan is zipped into a sleeping bag, and given a diuretic and some more morphine. Rest and the drop in altitude should see him back to health, although at the moment his skin is blue and his breathing ragged: no guarantees. He could die—a man who might live a thousand years—and suddenly their whole enterprise seems crazy. His coughs sound weak behind the oxygen mask, which hisses madly on maximum flow.

"He should be okay," Hans pronounces. "Won't know for sure for several hours."

But there they are—seven people in two wall tents. "We'll go back up," Eileen says, looking to Roger. He nods.

And they go back out again. The swirl of white snow in their headlights, the cold, the buffets of wind . . . they are tired, and progress is slow. Roger slips once and the jumars don't catch on the icy rope for about three meters, where they suddenly grab hold and test his harness, and the piton above. A fall! The spurt of fear gives him a second wind. Stubbornly he decides that much of his difficulty is mental. It's dark and windy, but really the only difference between this and his daytime climbs during the last week is the cold, and the fact that he can't see much. But the helmet lamps do allow him to see—he is at the center of a shifting white sphere, and the rock he must work on is revealed. It is covered with a sheet of ice and impacted snow, and where the ice is clear it gleams in the light like glass laid over the black rock beneath. Crampons are great in this—the sharp front points stick in the snow and ice firmly, and the only problem is the brittle black glass that will break away from the points in big jagged sheets. Even black ice can be distinguished in the bright bluish gleam of the lights, so the work is quite possible. Look at it as just another climb, he urges himself, meanwhile kicking like a maniac with his left foot to spike clear a crack where he can nail in another piton to replace a bad hold. The dizzying freeness of a pull over an outcropping; the long reach up for a solid knob: He becomes aware of the work as a sort of game, a set of problems to be solved despite cold or thirst or fatigue (his hands are beginning to tire from the long night's hauling, so that each hold hurts). Seen that way, it all changes. Now the wind is an opponent to be beaten, but also to be respected. The same of course is true of the rock, his principal opponent—and it is a daunting one, an opponent to challenge him to his utmost performance. He kicks into a slope of hard snow and ascends rapidly.

He looks down as Eileen kicks up the slope: quick reminder of the stakes of this game. The light on the top of her helmet makes her look like a deep-sea fish. She reaches him quickly; one long-gloved hand over the wall's top, and she joins him with a smooth contraction of the biceps. Strong woman, Roger thinks, but decides to take another lead anyway. He is in a mood now where he doubts anyone but Dougal could lead as fast.

Up through the murk they climb.

An odd point is that the two climbers can scarcely communicate. Roger "hears" Eileen through varieties of tugging on the rope linking them. If he takes too long to study a difficult spot above, he feels a mild interrogatory tug on the rope. Two tugs when Roger is belaying means she's on her way up. Very taut belaying betrays her belief that he is in a difficult section. So communication by rope can be fairly complex and subtle. But aside from it, and the infrequent shout with the mask pulled up to one side (which includes the punishment of a face full of spindrift) they are isolated. Mute partners. The exchange of lead goes well—one passes the other with a wave—the belay is ready. Up Eileen goes. Roger watches and holds the belay taut. Little time for contemplating their situation, thankfully; but while taking a rest on crampon points in steps chopped out with his ice axe, Roger feels acutely the thereness of his position, cut off from past or future, irrevocably in this moment, on this cliff face that drops away bottomlessly, extends up forever. Unless he climbs well, there will never be any other reality.

Then they reach a pitch where the fixed rope has been cut in the middle. Falling rock or ice has shaved it off. A bad sign. Now Roger must climb a ropeless pitch, hammering in pitons on his way to protect himself. Every meter above the last belay is a two-meter fall. . . .

Roger never expected so hard a climb, and adrenaline banishes his exhaustion. He studies the first small section of a pitch that he knows is ten or twelve meters long, invisible in the dark snow flurries above. Probably Marie or Dougal climbed this crack the first time. He discovers that the crack just gives him room for his hands. Almost a vertical crack for a while, with steps cut into the ice. Up he creeps, crablike and surefooted. Now the crack widens and the ice is too far back in it to be of use—but the cramponed boots can be stuck in the crack and turned sideways, to stick tenuously into the thin ice coating the crack's interior. One creates one's own staircase, mostly using the tension of the twisted crampons. Now the crack abruptly closes and he has to look around, ah, there, a horizontal crack holding the empty piton. Very good—he hooks into it and is protected thus far. Perhaps the next piton is up the rampway to the right? Clawing to find the slight indentations that pass for handholds, crouching to lean up the ramp in a tricky walk—he wonders about the crampons here . . . ah. The next piton, right at eye level. Perfect. And then an area lined with horizontal strata about a meter in thickness, making a steep—a very steep—ladder.

And at the top of that pitch they find that the high-camp tent has been crushed under a load of snow. Avalanche. One corner of the tent flaps miserably.

Eileen comes up and surveys the damage in the double glare of their two headlamps. She points at the snow, makes a digging motion. The snow is so cold that it can't bind together—moving it is like kicking coarse sand. They get to work, having no other choice. Eventually the tent is free, and as an added benefit they are warmed as well, although Roger feels he can barely move. The tent's poles have been bent and some broken, and splints must be tied on before the tent can be redeployed. Roger kicks snow and ice chunks around the perimeter of the tent, until it is "certifiably bombproof," as the leads would say. Except if another avalanche hits it, something they can't afford to think about, as they can't move the camp anywhere else. They simply have to risk it. Inside, they drop their packs and start the stove and put a pot of ice on. Then crampons off, and into sleeping bags. With the bags around them up to the waist, they can start sorting out the mess. There is spindrift on everything, but unless it gets right next to the stove it will not melt. Digging in the jumbled piles of gear for a packet of stew, Roger feels again how tired his body is. Oxygen masks off, so they can drink. "That was quite an excursion." Raging thirst. They laugh with relief. He brushes an unused pot with his bare hand, guaranteeing a frostnip blister. Eileen calculates the chance of another avalanche without visible trepidation: ". . . so if the wind stays high enough we should be okay." They discuss Stephan, and sniff like hunting dogs at the first scent of the stew. Eileen digs out the radio and calls down to the low camp. Stephan is sleeping, apparently without discomfort. "Morphine will do that," Eileen says. They wolf down their meal in a few minutes.

The snow under the tent is torn up by boot prints, and Roger's sleeping surface is unbelievably lumpy. He rolls over until he is wedged against the length of Eileen's bag, coveting the warmth and hoping for a flatter surface. It is just as lumpy there. Eileen snuggles back into him and he can feel the potential for warmth; he can tell he will warm up. He wonders if getting into one bag would be worth the effort.

"Amazing what some people will do for fun," Eileen comments drowsily.

Short laugh. "This isn't the fun part."

"Isn't it? That climb . . ."

Big yawn. "That was some climb," he agrees. No denying it.

"That was a great climb."

"Especially since we didn't get killed."

"Yeah." She yawns too, and Roger can feel a big wave of sleep about to break over him and sweep him away. "I hope Stephan gets better. Otherwise, we'll have to take him down."

In the next few days everyone has to go out several times in the storm, to keep the high camp supplied and to keep the fixed ropes free of ice. The work is miserable when they can do it, and sometimes they can't: The wind on some days shuts down everything, and they can only huddle inside and hope the tents hold to the face. One dim day Roger is sitting with Stephan and Arthur in low camp. Stephan has recovered from the edema, and is anxious to climb again. "No hurry," Roger says. "No one's going anywhere anyway, and water in the lungs is serious business. You'll have to take it slow—"

The tent door is unzipped and a plume of snow enters, followed by Dougal. He grins hello. The silence seems to call for some comment. "Pretty invigorating out there," he says to fill it, and looks after a pot of tea. The shy moment having passed he chats cheerfully with Arthur about the weather. Tea done, he is off again; he is in a hurry to get a load up to the high camp. A quick grin and he is out the tent and gone. And it occurs to Roger that there are two types of climbers on their expedition (another duality): those who *endure* the bad weather and accidents and all the various difficulties of the face that are making this climb so uncomfortable, and those who, in some important peculiar way, *enjoy* all the trouble. In the former group are Eileen, who has the overriding responsibility for the climb—Marie, who is in such a hurry for the top—and Hans and Stephan, who are less experienced and would be just as happy to climb under sunny skies and with few serious difficulties. Each of these is steady and resolute, without a doubt; but they endure.

Dougal, on the other hand, Dougal and Arthur: Those two are quite clearly enjoying themselves, and the worse things get the more fun they seem to have. It is, Roger thinks, perverse. The reticent, solitary Dougal, seizing with quiet glee every possible chance to get out into the gale and climb. . . . "He certainly seems to be enjoying himself," Roger says out loud, and Arthur laughs.

"That Dougal!" he cries. "What a Brit he is. You know climbers are the same everywhere. I come all the way to Mars and find just the people you'd expect to find on Ben Nevis. 'Course it stands to reason, doesn't it? That New Scotland school and all."

It is true; from the very start of the colonization, British climbers have been coming to Mars in search of new climbs, and many of them have stayed.

"And I'll tell you," Arthur continues, "those guys are never happier than when it's blowing force ten and dumping snow by the dump truck. Or not snow, actually. More like sleet, that's what they want. One degree rain, or wet snow. Perfect. And you know why they want it? So they can come back in at the end of the day and say, 'Bloody desperate out today, eh mate?' They're all dying to be able to say that. 'Bluidy *das*perate, mite.' Ha! Do you know what I mean? It's like giving themselves a medal or something, I don't know."

Roger and Stephan, smiling, nod. "Very macho," Stephan says.

"But Dougal!" Arthur cries. "Dougal! He's too cool for that. He goes out there in the nastiest conditions he can possibly find—I mean look at him just now—he couldn't wait to get back out there! Didn't want to waste such a fine opportunity! And he climbs the hardest pitches he can find too. Have you seen him? You've seen the routes he leaves behind. Man, that guy could climb buttered glass in a hurricane. And what does he say about it? Does he say that was pretty bloody desperate? No! He says," and Roger and Stephan join in, like a chorus: "How invigorating!"

"Yeah." Stephan laughs. "Pretty invigorating out there all right."

"The Scots," Arthur says, giggling away. "Martian Scots, no less. I can't believe it."

"It's not just the Scots are strange," Roger points out. "What about you, Arthur? I notice you getting quite a giggle out of all this yourself, eh?"

"Oh yeah, yeah," Arthur says. "I'm having a good time. Aren't you? I'll tell you, once we got on the oxygen I started feeling great. Before that it wasn't so easy. The air seemed really thin, I mean *really* thin. Elevations here don't mean anything to me, I mean you haven't got a proper sea level so what does elevation really mean, right? But your air is like nothing, man. So when we got on the bottle I could really feel the difference. A lifesaver. And then there's the gravity! Now that's wonderful. What is it, two-fifths of a gee? Practically nothing! You might as well be on the moon! As soon as I learned to balance properly, I really started to have a good time. Felt like Superman. On this planet it just isn't that hard to go uphill, that's all." He laughs, toasts the other two with tea, "On Mars, I'm Superman."

High-altitude pulmonary edema works fast, and one either succumbs or recovers very quickly. When Stephan's lungs are completely clear Hans orders him to keep on maximum oxygen intake, and he is given a light load and ordered to take it slow and only move up from one low camp to the next. At this point, Roger thinks, it would be more difficult to get him back down the cliff than keep on going to the top—a common enough climbing situation, but one that no one talks about. Stephan complains about his reduced role, but agrees to go along with it. For his first few days back out Roger teams with him and keeps a sharp eye on him. But Stephan climbs fairly rapidly, and only complains about Roger's solicitousness, and at the cold winds. Roger concludes he is all right.

Back to portering. Hans and Arthur are out in the lead, having a terrible time with a broad, steep rampart that they are trying to force directly. For a couple of days they are all stalled as the camps are stocked, and the lead party cannot make more than fifty or seventy-five meters a day. One evening on the radio while Hans describes a difficult overhang, Marie gets on the horn and starts in. "Well, I don't know what's going on up there, but with Stephan sucking down the oxygen and you all making centimeters a day we're going to end up stuck on this damn cliff for good! What? I don't give a fuck *what* your troubles are, mate—if you can't make the lead you should bloody well get down and let somebody on there who can!"

"This is a big tuff band," Arthur says defensively. "Once we get above this it's more or less a straight shot to the top—"

"*If* you've got any bloody oxygen it is! Look what is this, a co-op? I didn't join a fucking co-op!"

Roger watches Eileen closely. She is listening carefully to the exchange, her finger on the intercom, a deep furrow between her eyes, as if she is concentrating. He is surprised she has not already intervened. But she lets Marie get off another couple of blasts, and only then does she cut in. "Marie! Marie! Eileen here—"

"I know that."

"Arthur and Hans are scheduled to come down soon. Meanwhile, shut up."

And the next day Arthur and Hans put up three hundred meters of fixed rope and top the tuff band. When Hans announces this on the sunset radio call (Roger can just hear Arthur in the background, saying in falsetto, "So there! So there!"), a little smile twitches Eileen's mouth before she congratulates them and gets on to the orders for the next day. Roger nods thoughtfully.

After they get above Hans and Arthur's band, the slope lies back a bit and progress is more rapid, even in the continuous winds. The cliff is like a wall of immense irregular bricks which have been shoved back, so that each brick is set a bit behind the one below it. This great jumble of blocks and ledges and ramps makes for easy zigzag climbing, and good campsites. One day, Roger stops for a break and looks around. He is portering a load from middle camp to high camp, and has gotten ahead of Eileen. No one in sight. There is a cloud layer far below them, a gray rumpled blanket covering the whole world. Then there is the vertical realm of the cliff face, a crazed jumble of a block wall, which extends up to a very smooth, almost featureless cloud layer above them. Only the finest ripples, like waves, mar this gray ceiling. Floor and ceiling of cloud, wall of rock: It seems for a moment that this climb will go on eternally; it is a whole world, an infinite wall that they will climb forever. When has it been any different? Sandwiched like this, between cloud and cloud, it is easy not to believe in the past; perhaps the planet is a cliff, endlessly varied, endlessly challenging.

Then in the corner of Roger's eye, a flash of color. He looks at the deep crack between the ledge he is standing on and the next vertical block. In the twisted ice nestles a patch of moss campion. Cushion of black-green moss, a circle of perhaps a hundred tiny dark pink flowers on it. After three weeks of almost unrelieved black and white, the color seems to burst out of the flowers and explode in his eyes. Such a dark, intense pink! Roger crouches to inspect them. The moss is very finely textured, and appears to be growing directly out of the rock, although no doubt there is some sand back in the crack. A seed or a scrap of moss must have been blown off the shield plateau and down the cliff, to take root here.

Roger stands, looks around again. Eileen has joined him, and she observes him sharply. He pulls his mask to the side. "Look at that," he says. "You can't get away from it anywhere."

She shakes her head. Pulls her mask down. "It's not the new landscape you hate so much," she says. "I saw the way you were looking at that plant. And it's just a plant after all, doing its best to live. No, I think you've made a displacement. You use topography as a symbol. It's not the landscape, it's the people. It's the history we've made that you dislike. The terraforming is just part of it—the visible sign of a history of exploitation."

Roger considers it. "We're just another Terran colony, you mean. Colonialism—"

"Yes. That's what you hate, see? Not topography, but history. Because the terraforming, so far, is a waste. It's not being done for any good purpose."

Uneasily Roger shakes his head. He has not thought of it like that, and isn't sure he agrees: It's the land that has suffered the most, after all. Although—

Eileen continues, "There's some good in that, if you think about it. Because the landscape isn't going to change back, ever. But history—history must change, by definition."

And she takes the lead, leaving Roger to stare up after her.

The winds die in the middle of the night. The cessation of tent noise wakes Roger up. It is bitterly cold, even in his bag. It takes him a while to figure out what woke him; his oxygen is still hissing softly in his face. When he figures out what did it, he smiles. Checking his watch, he finds it is almost time for the mirror dawn. He sits up and turns on the stove for tea. Eileen stirs in her sleeping bag, opens one eye. Roger likes watching her wake; even behind the mask, the shift from vulnerable girl to expedition leader is easy to see. It's like ontogeny recapitulating phylogeny: Coming to consciousness in the morning recapitulates maturation in life. Now all he needs is the Greek terminology, and he will have a scientific truth. Eileen pulls off her oxygen mask and rolls onto one elbow.

"Want some tea?" he says.

"Yeah."

"It'll be a moment."

"Hold the stove steady—I've got to pee." She stands in the tent doorway, sticks a plastic urine scoop into the open fly of her pants, urinates out the door. "Wow! Sure is cold out. And clear! I can see stars."

"Great. The wind's died too, see?"

Eileen crawls back into her bag. They brew their tea with great seriousness, as if mixing delicate elixirs. Roger watches her drink.

"Do you really not remember us from before?" he asks.

"Nooo. . . ." she says slowly. "We were in our twenties, right? No, the first years I really remember are from my fifties, when I was training up in the caldera. Wall climbs, kind of like this, actually." She sips. "But tell me about us."

Roger shrugs. "It doesn't matter."

"It must be odd. To remember when the rest don't."

"Yes, it is."

"I was probably awful at that age."

"No no. You were an English major. You were fine."

She laughs. "Hard to believe. Unless I've gone downhill since."

"No, not at all. You sure couldn't have done all this back then."

"I believe that. Getting half an expedition strung out all over a cliff, people sick—"

"No no. You're doing fine."

She shakes her head. "You can't pretend this climb has gone well. I remember that much."

"What hasn't gone well hasn't been your fault, as you must admit. In fact, given what has happened, we're doing very well, I think. And that's mostly your doing. Not easy with Frances and Stephan, and the storm, and Marie."

"Marie!"

They laugh. "And this storm," Roger says. "That night climb we did, getting Stephan down!" He sips his tea.

"That was a wild one," Eileen agrees.

Roger nods. They have that. He gets up to pee, letting in a blast of intensely cold air. "My God that's cold! What's the temperature?"

"Sixty below, outside."

"Oh. No wonder. I guess that cloud cover was doing us *some* good." Outside it is still dark, and the ice-bearded cliff face gleams whitely under the stars.

"I like the way you lead us," Roger says. "It's a very light touch, but you still have things under control." He zips the tent door closed and hustles back into his bag.

"More tea?"

"Definitely."

"Here—roll back here, you'll warm up faster, and I could use the insulation myself."

Roger nods, shivering, and rolls his bag into the back side of hers, so they are both on one elbow, spooned together.

They sip tea and talk. Roger warms up, stops shivering. Pleasure of empty bladder, of contact with her. They finish the tea and doze for a bit in the warmth. Keeping the oxygen masks off prevents them from falling into a deep sleep. "Mirrors'll be up soon." "Yeah." "Here— move over a bit." Roger remembers when they were lovers, so long ago. Previous lifetime. She was the city dweller then, he the canyon crawler. Now . . . now all the comfort, warmth, and contact have given him an erection. He wonders if she can feel it through the two bags. Probably not. Hmmm. He remembers suddenly—the first time they made love was in a tent. He went to bed, and she came right into his little cubicle of the communal tent and jumped him! Remembering it does nothing to make his erection go away. He wonders if he can get away with a similar sort of act here. They are definitely pressed together hard. All that climbing together: Eileen pairs the climbing teams, so she must have enjoyed it too. And climbing together has that sort of dancelike teamwork—boulder ballet; and the constant kinetic juxtaposition, the felt relationship of the rope, has a certain sensuousness to it. It is a physical partnership, without a doubt. Of course all that can be true and climbing remain a profoundly nonsexual relationship—there are certainly other things to think about. But now . . .

Now she is dozing again. He thinks about her climbing, her leadership. The things she said to him back down in the first camps, when he was so depressed. A sort of teacher, really.

Thoughts of that lead him to memories of his past, of the failed work. For the first time in many days his memory presents him with the usual parade of the past, the theater of ghosts. How can he ever assume such a long and fruitless history? Is it even possible?

Mercifully the tea's warmth, and the mere fact of lying prone, have their way with him, and he dozes off.

The day dawns. Sky like a sheet of old paper, the sun a big bronze coin below them to the east. The sun! Wonderful to see sunlight, shadows. In the light the cliff face looks sloped back an extra few degrees, and it seems there is an end to it up there. Eileen and Roger are in the middle camp, and after ferrying a load to the high camp they follow the rope's zigzag course up the narrow ledges. The fine, easy face, the sunlight, the dawn's talk, the plains of Tharsis *so* far below: All conspire to please Roger. He is climbing more strongly than ever, hopping up the ledges, enjoying the variety of forms exhibited by the rock. Such a beauty to rough plated angular broken rock.

The face continues to lie back, and at the top of one ledge ramp they find themselves at the bottom of a giant amphitheater filled with snow. And the top of this white half bowl is . . . sky. The top of the escarpment, apparently. Certainly nothing but sky above it. Dougal and Marie are about to start up it, and Roger joins them. Eileen stays behind to collect the others.

The technically difficult sections of the climb are done. The upper edge of the immense cliff has been rounded off by wind erosion, broken into alternating ridges and ravines. There they stand at the bottom of a big bowl broken in half; at bottom the slope is about forty degrees, and it curves up to a final wall that is perhaps sixty degrees. But the bottom of the bowl is filled with deep drifts of light, dry, granular snow, sheeted with a hard layer of windslab. Crossing the stuff is hard work, and they trade the lead often. The leader crashes through the windslab and sinks to his or her knees, or even to the waist, and thereafter has to lift a foot over the windslab above, crash through again, and in that way struggle uphill through the snow. They secure the rope with deadmen—empty oxygen tanks in this case, buried deep in the snow. Roger takes his lead, and quickly begins to sweat under the glare of the sun. Each step is an effort, worse than the step before because of the increasing angle of the slope. After ten minutes he gives the lead back to Marie. Twenty minutes later it is his turn again—the other two can endure it no longer than he can. The steepness of the final wall is actually a relief, as there is less snow.

They stop to strap crampons on their boots. Starting again, they fall into a slow steady rhythm. Kick, step, kick, step, kick, step. Glare of light breaking on snow. The taste of sweat.

When Roger's tenth turn in the lead comes, he sees that he is within striking distance of the top of the wall, and he resolves not to give up the lead again. The snow is soft under windslab, and he must lean up, dig away a bit with his ice axe, swim up to the new foothold, dig away some more—on and on, gasping into the oxygen mask, sweating profusely in the suddenly overwarm clothing. But he's getting closer. Dougal is behind him. He finds the pace again and sticks to it. Nothing but the pace. Twenty steps, rest. Again. Again. Again. Sweat trickles down his spine, even his feet might warm up. Sun glaring off the steep snow.

He stumbles onto flatness. It feels like some terrible error, like he might fall over the other side. But he is on the edge of a giant plateau, which swoops up in a broad conical shape, too big to be believed. He sees a flat boulder almost clear of snow and staggers over to it. Dougal is beside him, pulling his oxygen mask to one side of his face: "Looks like we've topped the wall!" Dougal says, looking surprised. Gasping, Roger laughs.

As with all cliff climbs, topping out is a strange experience. After a month of vertical reality, the huge flatness seems all wrong—especially this snowy flatness that extends like a broad fan to each side. The snow ends at the broken edge of the cliff behind them, extends high up the gentle slope of the conical immensity before them. It is easy to believe they stand on the flank of the biggest volcano in the solar system.

"I guess the hard part is over," Dougal says matter-of-factly.

"Just when I was getting in shape," says Roger, and they both laugh.

A snowy plateau, studded with black rocks, and some big mesas. To the east, empty air: far below, the forests of Tharsis. To the northwest, a hill sloping up forever.

Marie arrives and dances a little jig on the boulder. Dougal hikes back to the wall and drops into the amphitheater again, to carry up another load. Not much left to bring; they are almost out of food. Eileen arrives, and Roger shakes her hand. She drops her pack and gives him a hug. They pull some food from the packs and eat a cold lunch while watching Hans, Arthur, and Stephan start up the bottom of the bowl. Dougal is already almost down to them.

When they all reach the top, in a little string led by Dougal, the celebrating really begins. They drop their packs, they hug, they shout, Arthur whirls in circles to try to see it all at once, until he makes himself dizzy. Roger cannot remember feeling exactly like this before.

"Our cache is a few kilometers south of here," Eileen says after consulting her maps. "If we get there tonight we can break out the champagne."

They hike over the snow in a line, trading the lead to break a path. It is a pleasure to walk over flat ground, and spirits are so light that they make good time. Late in the day—a full day's sunshine, their first since before base camp—they reach their cache, a strange camp full of tarped-down, snowdrifted piles, marked by a lava causeway that ends a kilometer or so above the escarpment.

Among the new equipment is a big mushroom tent. They inflate it and climb in through the lock and up onto the tent floor for the night's party. Suddenly they are inside a giant transparent mushroom, bouncing over the soft clear raised floor like children on a feather bed; the luxury is excessive, ludicrous, inebriating. Champagne corks pop and fly into the transparent dome of the tent roof, and in the warm air they quickly get drunk, and tell each other how marvelous the climb was, how much they enjoyed it—the discomfort, exhaustion, cold, misery, danger, and fear already dissipating in their minds, already turning into something else.

The next day Marie is not at all enthusiastic about the remainder of their climb. "It's a walk up a bloody hill! And a long walk at that!"

"How else are you going to get down?" Eileen asks acerbically. "Jump?"

It's true; the arrangement they have made forces them to climb the cone of the volcano. There is a railway that descends from the north rim of the caldera to Tharsis and civilization; it uses for a rampway one of the great lava spills that erase the escarpment to the north. But first they have to get to the railway, and climbing the cone is probably the fastest, and certainly the most interesting, way to do that.

"You could climb down the cliff alone," Eileen adds sarcastically. "First solo descent . . ."

Marie, apparently feeling the effects of last night's champagne, merely snarls and stalks off to snap herself into one of the cart harnesses. Their new collection of equipment fits into a wheeled cart, which they must pull up the slope. For convenience they are already wearing the space suits that they will depend on higher up; during this ascent they will climb right out of most of Mars's new atmosphere. They look funny in their silvery green suits and clear helmets, Roger thinks; it reminds him of his days as a canyon guide, when such suits were necessary all over Mars. The common band of the helmet radios makes this a more social event than the cliff climb, as does the fact that all seven of them are together, four hauling the cart, three walking freely ahead or behind. From climb to hike: The first day is a bit anticlimactic.

．　．　．

On the snowy southern flank of the volcano, signs of life appear everywhere. Goraks circle them by day, on the lookout for a bit of refuse; at dusk ball owls dip around the tent like bats. On the ground Roger sees marmots on the boulders and volcanic knobs, and in the system of ravines cut into the plateau they find twisted stands of Hokkaido pine, chir pine, and noctis juniper. Arthur chases a pair of Dall sheep with their curved horns, and they see prints in the snow that look like bear tracks. "Yeti," Dougal says. One mirror dusk they catch sight of a pack of snow wolves, strung out over the slope to the west. Stephan spends his spare time at the edges of the new ravines, sketching and peering through binoculars. "Come on, Roger," he says. "Let me show you those otterines I saw yesterday."

"Bunch of mutants," Roger grumbles, mostly to give Stephan a hard time. But Eileen is watching him to see his response, and dubiously he nods. What can he say? He goes with Stephan to the ravine to look for wildlife. Eileen laughs at him, eyes only, affectionately.

Onward, up the great hill. It's a six-percent grade, very regular, and smooth except for the ravines and the occasional small crater or lava knob. Below them, where the plateau breaks to become the cliff, the shield is marked by some sizable mesas—features, Hans says, of the stress that broke off the shield. Above them, the conical shape of the huge volcano is clearly visible; the endless hill they climb slopes away to each side equally, and far away and above they see the broad flat peak. They've got a long way to go. Wending between the ravines is easy, and the esthetic of the climb, its only point of technical interest, becomes how far they can hike every day. It's 250 kilometers from the escarpment up to the crater rim; they try for twenty-five a day, and sometimes make thirty. It feels odd to be so warm; after the intense cold of the cliff climb, the space suits and the mushroom tent create a distinct disconnection from the surroundings.

Hiking as a group is also odd. The common band is a continuous conversation, that one can switch on or off at will. Even when not in a mood to talk, Roger finds it entertaining to listen. Hans talks about the areology of the volcano, and he and Stephan discuss the genetic engineering that makes the wildlife around them possible. Arthur points out features that the others might take for granted. Marie complains of boredom. Eileen and Roger laugh and add a comment once in a while. Even Dougal clicks into the band around midafternoon, and displays a quick wit, spurring Arthur toward one amazing discovery after another. "Look at that, Arthur, it's a yeti."

"What! You're kidding! Where?"

"Over there, behind that rock."

Behind the rock is Stephan, relieving himself. "Don't come over here!"

"You liar," Arthur says.

"It must have slipped off. I think a Weddell fox was chasing it."

"You're kidding!"

"Yes."

Eileen: "Let's switch to a private band. I can't hear you over all the rest."

Roger: "Okay. Band 33."

"Why that one?"

"Ah—" It *was* a long time ago, but this is the kind of weird fact his memory will pop up with. "It may be our private band from our first hike together."

She laughs. They spend the afternoon behind the others, talking.

One morning Roger wakes early, just after mirror dawn. The dull horizontal rays of the quartet of parhelia light their tent. Roger turns his head, looks past his pillow, through the tent's clear floor. Thin soil over rock, a couple of meters below. He sits up; the floor gives a little, like a gel bed. He walks over the soft plastic slowly so that he will not bounce any of the others, who are sleeping out where the cap of the roof meets the gills of the floor. The tent really does resemble a big clear mushroom; Roger descends clear steps in the side of the stalk to get to the lavatory, located down in what would be the mushroom's volva. Emerging he finds a sleepy Eileen sponging down in the little bath next to the air compressor and regulator. "Good morning," she says. "Here, will you get my back?"

She hands him the sponge, turns around. Vigorously he rubs down the hard muscles of her back, feeling a thrill of sensual interest. That slope, where back becomes bottom: beautiful.

She looks over her shoulder: "I think I'm probably clean now."

"Ah." He grins. "Maybe so." He gives her the sponge. "I'm going for a walk before breakfast."

"Okay. Thanks."

Roger dresses, goes through the lock, walks over to the head of the meadow they are camped by: a surarctic meadow, covered with moss and lichen, and dotted with mutated edelweiss and saxifrage. A light frost coats everything in a sparkling blanket of white, and Roger feels his boots crunch as he walks.

Movement catches his eye and he stops to observe a white-furred mouse hare, dragging a loose root back to its hole. There is a flash and flutter, and a snow finch lands in the hole's entrance. The tiny hare looks up from its work, chatters at the finch, nudges past it with its load. The finch does its bird thing, head shifting instantaneously from one position to the next and then freezing in place. It follows the hare into the hole. Roger has heard of this, but he has never seen it. The hare scampers out, looking for more food. The finch appears, its head snaps from one position to the next. An instant swivel and it is staring at Roger. It flies over to the scampering hare, dive-bombs it, flies off. The hare has disappeared down another hole.

Roger crosses the ice stream in the meadow, crunches up the bank. There beside a waist-high rock is an odd pure white mass, with a white sphere at the center of it. He leans over to inspect it. Slides a gloved finger over it. Some kind of ice, apparently. Unusual-looking.

The sun rises and a flood of yellow light washes over the land. The yellowish white half globe of ice at his feet looks slick. It quivers; Roger steps back. The ice is shaking free of the rock wall. The middle of the bulge cracks. A beak stabs out of the globe, breaks it open. Busy little head in there. Blue feathers, long crooked black beak, beady little black eyes. "An egg?" Roger says. But the pieces are definitely ice— he can make them melt between his gloved fingers, and feel their coldness. The bird (though its legs and breast seem to be furred, and its wings stubby, and its beak sort of fanged) staggers out of the white bubble and shakes itself like a dog throwing off water, although it looks dry. Apparently the ice is some sort of insulation—a home for the night, or no—for the winter, no doubt. Yes. Formed of spittle or something, walling off the mouth of a shallow cave. Roger has never heard of such a thing, and he watches openmouthed as the bird-thing takes a few running steps and glides away.

A new creature steps on the face of green Mars.

That afternoon they hike out of the realm even of the surarctic meadow. No more ground cover, no more flowers, no more small animals. Nothing now but cracks filled with struggling moss, and great mats of otoo lichen. Sometimes it is as if they walk on a thin carpet of yellow, green, red, black—splotches of color like those seen in the orbicular jasper, spread out as far as they can see in every direction, a carpet crunchy with frost in the mornings, a bit damp in the midday sun, a carpet crazed and parti-colored. "Amazing stuff," Hans mutters, poking at it with a finger. "Half our oxygen is being made by this wonderful symbiosis. . . ."

Late that afternoon, after they have stopped and set up the tent and tied it down to several rocks, Hans leaps through the lock waving his atmosphere kit and hopping up and down. "Listen," he says, "I just radioed the summit station for confirmation of this. There's a high-pressure system over us right now. We're at fourteen thousand meters above the datum, but the barometric pressure is up to three hundred fifty millibars because there's a big cell of air moving over the flank of the volcano this week." The others stare. Hans says, "Do you see what I mean?"

"No," exclaim three voices at once.

"High-pressure zone," Roger says unhelpfully.

"Well," Hans says, standing at attention, "it's enough to breathe! Just enough, but enough, I say. And of course no one's ever done it before—done it this high before, I mean. Breathed free Martian air."

"You're kidding!"

"So we can establish the height record right here and now! I propose to do it, and I invite whoever wants to to join me."

"Now wait a minute," Eileen says.

But everyone wants to do it.

"Wait a minute," Eileen says. "I don't want everyone taking off their helmets and keeling over dead up here, for God's sake. They'll revoke my license. We have to do this in an orderly fashion. And you—" She points at Stephan. "You can't do this. I forbid it."

Stephan protests loudly and for a long time, but Eileen is adamant, and Hans agrees. "The shock could start your edema again, for sure. None of us should do it for long. But for a few minutes, it will go. Just breathe through the mesh face masks, to warm the air."

"You can watch and save us if we keel over," Roger tells Stephan.

"Shit," Stephan says. "All right. Do it."

They gather just out from under the cap of the tent, where Stephan can, theoretically, drag them back through the lock if he has to. Hans checks his barometer one last time, nods at them. They stand in a rough circle, facing in. Everyone begins to unclip helmet latches.

Roger gets his unclipped first—the years as canyon guide have left their mark on him, in little ways like this—and he lifts the helmet up. As he places it on the ground the cold strikes his head and makes it throb. He sucks down a breath: dry ice. He refuses the urge to hyperventilate, fearful he will chill his lungs too fast and damage them. Regular breathing, he thinks, in and out. In and out. Though Dougal's mouth is covered by a mesh mask, Roger can tell he is grinning widely. Funny how the upper face reveals that. Roger's eyes sting, his chest is frozen inside, he sucks down the frigid air and every sense quickens, breath by breath. The edges of pebbles a kilometer away are sharp and clear. Thousands of edges. "Like breathing nitrous oxide!" Arthur cries in a lilting high voice. He whoops like a little kid and the sound is odd, distant. Roger walks in a circle, on a quilt of rust lava and gaily colored patches of lichen. Intense awareness of the process of breathing seems to connect his consciousness to everything he can see; he feels like a strangely shaped lichen, struggling for air like all the rest. Jumble of rock, gleaming in the sunlight. "Let's build a cairn," he says to Dougal, and can hear his voice is wrong somehow. Slowly they step from rock to rock, picking them up and putting them in a pile. The interior of his chest is perfectly defined by each intoxicating breath. Others watch bright-eyed, sniffing, involved in their own perceptions. Roger sees his hands blur through space, sees the flesh of Dougal's face pulsing pinkly, like the flowers of moss campion. Each rock is a piece of Mars, he seems to float as he walks, the size of the volcano gets bigger, bigger, bigger; finally he is seeing it at true size. Stephan strides among them grinning through his helmet, holding up both hands. It's been ten minutes. The cairn is not yet done, but they can finish it tomorrow. "I'll make a messenger canister for it tonight!" Dougal wheezes happily. "We can all sign it." Stephan begins to round them all up. "Incredibly cold!" Roger says, still looking around as if he has never seen any of it before—any of anything.

Dougal and he are the last two into the lock; they shake hands. "Invigorating, eh?" Roger nods. "Very fine air."

But the air is just part of all the rest of it—part of the world, not of the planet. Right? "That's right," Roger says, staring through the tent wall down the endless slope of the mountain.

That night they celebrate with champagne again, and the party gets wild as they become sillier and sillier. Marie tries to climb the inner wall of the tent by grabbing the soft material in her hands, and falls to the floor repeatedly; Dougal juggles boots; Arthur challenges all comers to arm wrestle, and wins so quickly they decide he is using "a trick," and disallow his victories; Roger tells government jokes ("How many ministers does it take to pour a cup of coffee?"), and institutes a long and lively game of spoons. He and Eileen play next to each other and in the dive for spoons they land on each other. Afterward, sitting around the heater singing songs, she sits at his side and their legs and shoulders press together. Kid stuff, familiar and comfortable, even to those who can't remember their own childhoods.

So that, that night, after everyone has gone out to the little sleeping nooks at the perimeter of the tent's circular floor, Roger's mind is full of Eileen. He remembers sponging her down that morning. Her playfulness this evening. Climbing in the storm. The long nights together in wall tents. And once again the distant past returns—his stupid, uncontrollable memory provides images from a time so far gone that it shouldn't matter anymore . . . but it does. It was near the end of that trip too. She sneaked into his little cubicle and jumped him! Even though the thin panels they used to create sleeping rooms were actually much less private than what they have here; this tent is big, the air regulator is loud, the seven beds are well spaced and separated from each other by ribbing—clear ribbing, it is true, but now the tent is dark. The cushioned floor under him (so comfortable that Marie calls it uncomfortable) gives as he moves, without even trembling a few feet away, and it never makes a sound. In short, he could crawl silently over to her bed, and join her as she once joined him, and it would be entirely discreet. Turnabout is fair play, isn't it? Even three hundred years later? There isn't much time left on this climb, and as they say, fortune favors the bold. . . .

He is about to move when suddenly Eileen is at his side, shaking his arm. In his ear she says, "I have an idea."

And afterward, teasing: "Maybe I *do* remember you."

They trek higher still, into the zone of rock. No animals, plants, insects; no lichen; no snow. They are above it all, so high on the volcano's cone that it is getting difficult to see where their escarpment drops to the forests; two hundred kilometers away and fifteen kilometers below, the scarp's edge can only be distinguished because that's where the broad ring of snow ends. They wake up one morning and find a cloud layer a few k's downslope, obscuring the planet below.

They stand on the side of an immense conical island in an even greater sea of cloud: the clouds a white wave-furrowed ocean, the volcano a great rust rock, the sky a low dark violet dome, all on a scale the mind can barely encompass. To the east, poking out of the cloud sea, three broad peaks—an archipelago—the three Tharsis volcanoes in their well-spaced line, princes to the king Olympus. Those volcanoes, fifteen hundred kilometers away, give them a little understanding of the vastness visible. . . .

The rock up here is smoothly marbled, like a plain of petrified muscles. Individual pebbles and boulders take on an eerie presence, as if they are debris scattered by Olympian gods. Hans's progress is greatly slowed by his inspection of these rocks. One day, they find a mound that snakes up the mountain like an esker or a Roman road; Hans explains it was a river of lava harder than the surrounding basalt, which has eroded away to reveal it. They use it as an elevated road and hike on it for all of one long day.

Roger picks up his pace, leaves the cart and the others behind. In a suit and helmet, on the lifeless face of Mars: Centuries of memory flood him, he finds his breathing clotted and uneven. This is my country, he thinks. This is the transcendent landscape of my youth. It's still here. It can't be destroyed. It will always be here. He finds that he has almost forgotten, not what it looks like, but what it *feels* like to be in such wilderness. That thought is the thorn in the exhilaration that mounts with every step. Stephan and Eileen, the other two out of harness this day, are following him up. Roger notices them and frowns. I don't want to talk about it, he thinks. I want to be alone in it.

But Stephan hikes right by him, looking overwhelmed by the desolate rock expanse, the world of rock and sky. Roger can't help but grin. And Eileen is content just to walk with him.

Next day, however, in the harness of the cart, Stephan plods beside him and says, "Okay, Roger, I can see why you love this. It is sublime, truly. And in just the way we want the sublime—it's a pure landscape, a pure place. But . . ." He plods on several more steps, and Roger and Eileen wait for him to continue, pulling in step together. "But there *is* life on Mars. And it seems to me that you don't need the whole planet this way. This will always be here. The atmosphere will never rise this high, so you'll always have this. And the world down below, with all that life growing everywhere—it's beautiful." The beautiful and the sublime, Roger thinks. Another duality. "And maybe we need the beautiful more than the sublime?"

They haul on. Eileen looks at the mute Roger. He cannot think what to say. She smiles. "If Mars can change, so can you."

"The intense concentration of self in the middle of such a heartless immensity, my God! who can tell it?"

That night Roger seeks out Eileen, and makes love to her with a peculiar urgency; and when they are done he finds himself crying a bit, he doesn't know why; and she holds his head against her breast, until he shifts, and turns, and falls asleep.

And the following afternoon, after climbing all day up a hill that grows ever gentler, that always looks as if it will peak out just over the horizon above them, they reach flattened ground. An hour's hike, and they reach the caldera wall. They have climbed Olympus Mons.

They look down into the caldera. It is a gigantic brown plain, ringed by the round cliffs of the caldera wall. Smaller ringed cliffs inside the caldera drop to collapse craters, then terrace the round plain with round depressions, which overlap each other. The sky overhead is almost black; they can see stars, and Jupiter. Perhaps the high evening star is Earth. The thick blue rind of the atmosphere actually starts below them, so that they stand on a broad island in the middle of a round blue band, capped by a dome of black sky. Sky, caldera, ringed stone desolation. A million shades of brown, tan, red, rust. The planet Mars.

Along the rim a short distance stands the ruins of a Tibetan Buddhist lamasery. When Roger sees it his jaw drops. It is brown, and the main structure appears to have been a squarish boulder the size of a large house, carved and excavated until it is more air than stone. While it was occupied it must have been hermetically sealed, with airlocks in the doorways and windows fixed in place; now the windows are gone, and side buildings leaning against the main structure are broken-walled, roofless, open to the black sky. A chest-high wall of stone extends away from the outbuildings and along the rim; colored prayer wheels and prayer flags stick up from it on thin poles. Under the light touch of the stratosphere the wheels spin slowly, the flags flap limply.

. . .

"The caldera is as big as Luxembourg."

"You're kidding."

"No."

Finally even Marie is impressed. She walks to the prayer wall, touches a prayer wheel with one hand; looks out at the caldera, and from time to time spins the wheel, absently.

"Invigorating view, eh?"

It will take a few days to hike around the caldera to the railway station, so they set up camp next to the abandoned lamasery, and the heap of brown stone is joined by a big mushroom of clear plastic, filled with colorful gear.

The climbers wander in the later afternoon, chatting quietly over rocks, or the view into the shadowed caldera. Several sections of the ringed inner cliffs look like good climbing.

The sun is about to descend behind the rim to the west, and great shafts of light spear the indigo sky below them, giving the mountaintop an eerie indirect illumination. The voices on the common band are rapt and quiet, fading away to silence.

Roger gives Eileen a squeeze of the hand and wanders off by himself. The ground is black, the rock cracked in a million pieces, as if the gods have been sledgehammering it for eons. Nothing but rock. He clicks off the common band. It is nearly sunset. Great lavender shafts of light spear the purple murk to the sides, and overhead, stars shine in the blackness. All the shadows stretch off to infinity. The bright bronze coin of the sun grows big and oblate, slows in its descent. Roger circles the lamasery. Its western walls catch the last of the sun and cast a warm orange glaze over the ground and the ruined outbuildings. Roger kicks around the low prayer wall, replaces a fallen stone. The prayer wheels still spin—some sort of light wood, he thinks, cylinders carved with big black eyes and cursive lettering, and white paint, red paint, yellow paint, all chipped away. Roger stares into a pair of stoic Asian eyes, gives the wheel a slow spin, feels a little bit of vertigo. World everywhere. Even here. The flattened sun lands on the rim, across the caldera to the west. A faint gust of wind lofts a long banner out, ripples it slowly in dark orange air—"All right!"

Roger says aloud, and gives the wheel a final hard spin and steps away, circles dizzily, tries to take in everything at once. "All right! All right. I give in. I accept."

He wipes red dust from the glass of his faceplate and recalls the little bird-thing, pecking free of clouded ice. A new creature steps on the face of green Mars.

Arthur Sternbach Brings the Curveball to Mars

He was a tall skinny Martian kid, shy and stooping. Gangly as a puppy. Why they had him playing third base I have no idea. Then again they had me playing shortstop and I'm left-handed. And can't field grounders. But I'm American so there I was. That's what learning a sport by video will do. Some things are so obvious people never think to mention them. Like never put a lefty at shortstop. But on Mars they were making it all new. Some people there had fallen in love with baseball, and ordered the equipment and rolled some fields, and off they went.

So there we were, me and this kid Gregor, butchering the left side of the infield. He looked so young I asked him how old he was, and he said eight and I thought, Jeez you're not *that* young, but realized he meant Martian years of course, so he was about sixteen or seventeen, but he seemed younger. He had recently moved to Argyre from somewhere else, and was staying at the local house of his co-op with relatives or friends, I never got that straight, but he seemed pretty lonely to me. He never missed practice even though he was the worst of a terrible team, and clearly he got frustrated at all his errors and strikeouts. I used to wonder why he came out at all. And so shy; and that stoop; and the acne; and the tripping over his own feet, the blushing, the mumbling—he was a classic.

English wasn't his first language either. It was Armenian, or Moravian, something like that. Something no one else spoke, anyway, except for an elderly couple in his co-op. So he mumbled what passes for English on Mars, and sometimes even used a translation box, but basically tried never to be in a situation where he had to speak. And made error after error. We must have made quite a sight—me about waist-high to him, and both of us letting grounders pass through us like we were a magic show. Or else knocking them down and chasing them around, then winging them past the first baseman. We very seldom made an out. It would have been conspicuous except everyone else was the same way. Baseball on Mars was a high-scoring game.

But beautiful anyway. It was like a dream, really. First of all the horizon, when you're on a flat plain like Argyre, is only three miles away rather than six. It's very noticeable to a Terran eye. Then their diamonds have just over normal-sized infields, but the outfields have to be huge. At my team's ballpark it was nine hundred feet to dead center, seven hundred down the lines. Standing at the plate the outfield fence was like a little green line off in the distance, under a purple sky, pretty near the horizon itself—what I'm telling you is that the baseball diamond about covered *the entire visible world*. It was so great.

They played with four outfielders, like in softball, and still the alleys between fielders were wide. And the air was about as thin as at Everest base camp, and the gravity itself only bats .380, so to speak. So when you hit the ball solid it flies like a golf ball hit by a big driver. Even as big as the fields were, there were still a number of home runs every game. Not many shutouts on Mars. Not till I got there anyway.

I went there after I climbed Olympus Mons, to help them establish a new soil-sciences institute. They had the sense not to try that by video. At first I climbed in the Charitums in my time off, but after I got hooked into baseball it took up most of my spare time. Fine, I'll play, I said when they asked me. But I won't coach. I don't like telling people what to do.

So I'd go out and start by doing soccer exercises with the rest of them, warming up all the muscles we would never use. Then Werner would start hitting infield practice, and Gregor and I would start flailing. We were like matadors. Occasionally we'd snag one and whale it over to first, and occasionally the first baseman, who was well over two meters tall and built like a tank, would catch our throws, and we'd slap our gloves together. Doing this day after day Gregor got a little less shy with me, though not much. And I saw that he threw the ball pretty damned hard. His arm was as long as my whole body, and boneless it seemed, like something pulled off a squid, so loose-wristed that he got some real pop on the ball. Of course sometimes it would still be rising when it passed ten meters over the first baseman's head, but it was moving, no doubt about it. I began to see that maybe the reason he came out to play, beyond just being around people he didn't have to talk to, was the chance to throw things really hard. I saw too that he wasn't so much shy as he was surly. Or both.

Anyway our fielding was a joke. Hitting went a bit better. Gregor learned to chop down on the ball and hit grounders up the middle; it was pretty effective. And I began to get my timing together. Coming to it from years of slow-pitch softball, I had started by swinging at everything a week late, and between that and my shortstopping I'm sure my teammates figured they had gotten a defective American. And since they had a rule limiting each team to only two Terrans, no doubt they were disappointed by that. But slowly I adjusted my timing, and after that I hit pretty well. The thing was their pitchers had no breaking stuff. These big guys would rear back and throw as hard as they could, like Gregor, but it took everything in their power just to throw strikes. It was a little scary because they often threw right at you by accident. But if they got it down the pipe then all you had to do was time it. And if you hit one, how the ball flew! Every time I connected it was like a miracle. It felt like you could put one into orbit if you hit it right, in fact that was one of their nicknames for a home run, Oh that's orbital they would say, watching one leave the park headed for the horizon. They had a little bell, like a ship's bell, attached to the backstop, and every time someone hit one out they would ring that bell while the batter rounded the bases. A very nice local custom.

So I enjoyed it. It's a beautiful game even when you're butchering it. My sorest muscles after practice were in my stomach from laughing so hard. I even began to have some success at short. When I caught balls going to my right I twirled around backward to throw to first or second. People were impressed though of course it was ridiculous. It was a case of the one-eyed man in the country of the blind. Not that they weren't good athletes, you understand, but none of them had played as kids, and so they had no baseball instincts. They just liked to play. And I could see why—out there on a green field as big as the world, under a purple sky, with the yellow-green balls flying around— it was beautiful. We had a good time.

I started to give a few tips to Gregor too, though I had sworn to myself not to get into coaching. I don't like trying to tell people what to do. The game's too hard for that. But I'd be hitting flies to the outfielders, and it was hard not to tell them to watch the ball and run under it and then put the glove up and catch it, rather than run all the way with their arms stuck up like the Statue of Liberty's. Or when they took turns hitting flies (it's harder than it looks) giving them batting tips. And Gregor and I played catch all the time during warm-ups, so just watching me—and trying to throw to such a short target—he got better. He definitely threw hard. And I saw there was a whole lot of movement in his throws. They'd come tailing in to me every which way, no surprise given how loose-wristed he was. I had to look sharp or I'd miss. He was out of control, but he had potential.

And the truth was, our pitchers were bad. I loved the guys, but they couldn't throw strikes if you paid them. They'd regularly walk ten or twenty batters every game, and these were five-inning games. Werner would watch Thomas walk ten, then he'd take over in relief and walk ten more himself. Sometimes they'd go through this twice. Gregor and I would stand there while the other team's runners walked by as in a parade, or a line at the grocery store. When Werner went to the mound I'd stand by Gregor and say, You know Gregor you could pitch better than these guys. You've got a good arm. And he would look at me horrified, muttering, No no no no, not possible.

But then one time warming up he broke off a really mean curve and I caught it on my wrist. While I was rubbing it down I walked over to him. Did you see the way that ball curved? I said.

Yes, he said, looking away. I'm sorry.

Don't be sorry. That's called a curveball, Gregor. It can be a useful throw. You twisted your hand at the last moment and the ball came over the top of it, like this, see? Here, try it again.

So we slowly got into it. I was all-state in Connecticut my senior year in high school, and it was all from throwing junk—curve, slider, split-finger, change. I could see Gregor throwing most of those just by accident, but to keep from confusing him I just worked on a straight curve. I told him, Just throw it to me like you did that first time.

I thought you weren't to coach us, he said.

I'm not coaching you! Just throw it like that. Then in the games throw it straight. As straight as possible.

He mumbled a bit at me in Moravian, and didn't look me in the eye. But he did it. And after a while he worked up a good curve. Of course the thinner air on Mars meant there was little for the balls to bite on. But I noticed that the blue-dot balls they played with had higher stitching than the red-dot balls. They played with both of them as if there was no difference, but there was. So I filed that away and kept working with Gregor.

We practiced a lot. I showed him how to throw from the stretch, figuring that a windup from Gregor was likely to end up in knots.

And by mid-season he threw a mean curve from the stretch. We had not mentioned it to anyone else. He was wild with it, but it hooked hard; I had to be really sharp to catch some of them. It made me better at shortstop too. Although finally in one game, behind 20–0 as usual, a batter hit a towering pop fly and I took off running back on it, and the wind kept carrying it and I kept following it, until when I got it I was out there sprawled between our startled center fielders.

Maybe you should play outfield, Werner said.

I said, Thank God.

So after that I played left-center or right-center, and I spent the games chasing line drives to the fence and throwing them back in to the cutoff man. Or more likely, standing there and watching the other team take their walks. I called in my usual chatter, and only then did I notice that no one on Mars ever yelled anything at these games. It was like playing in a league of deaf-mutes. I had to provide the chatter for the whole team from two hundred yards away in center field, including of course criticism of the plate umpire's calls. My view of the plate was miniaturized but I still did a better job than they did, and they knew it too. It was fun. People would walk by and say, Hey there must be an American out there.

One day after one of our home losses, 28–12 I think it was, everyone went to get something to eat, and Gregor was just standing there looking off into the distance. You want to come along? I asked him, gesturing after the others, but he shook his head. He had to get back home and work. I was going back to work myself, so I walked with him into town, a place like you'd see in the Texas panhandle. I stopped outside his co-op, which was a big house or little apartment complex, I could never tell which was which on Mars. There he stood like a lamppost, and I was about to leave when an old woman came out and invited me in. Gregor had told her about me, she said in stiff English. So I was introduced to the people in the kitchen there, most of them incredibly tall. Gregor seemed really embarrassed, he didn't want me to be there, so I left as soon as I could get away. The old woman had a husband, and they seemed like Gregor's grandparents. There was a young girl there too, about his age, looking at both of us like a hawk. Gregor never met her eye.

Next time at practice, I said, Gregor, were those your grandparents?

Like my grandparents.

And that girl, who was she?

No answer.

Like a cousin or something?

Yes.

Gregor, what about your parents? Where are they?

He just shrugged and started throwing me the ball.

I got the impression they lived in another branch of his co-op somewhere else, but I never found out for sure. A lot of what I saw on Mars I liked—the way they run their businesses together in co-ops takes a lot of pressure off them, and they live pretty relaxed lives compared to us on Earth. But some of their parenting systems—kids brought up by groups, or by one parent, or whatever—I wasn't so sure about those. It makes for problems if you ask me. Bunch of teenage boys ready to slug somebody. Maybe that happens no matter what you do.

Anyway we finally got to the end of the season, and I was going to go back to Earth after it. Our team's record was three and fifteen, and we came in in last place in the regular-season standings. But they held a final weekend tournament for all the teams in the Argyre Basin, a bunch of three-inning games, as there were a lot to get through. Immediately we lost the first game and were in the loser's bracket. Then we were losing the next one too, and all because of walks, mostly. Werner relieved Thomas for a time, then when that didn't work out Thomas went back to the mound to rerelieve Werner. When that happened I ran all the way in from center to join them on the mound. I said, Look you guys, let Gregor pitch.

Gregor! they both said. No way!

He'll be even worse than us, Werner said.

How could he be? I said. You guys just walked eleven batters in a row. Night will fall before Gregor could do that.

So they agreed to it. They were both discouraged at that point, as you might expect. So I went over to Gregor and said, Okay, Gregor, you give it a try now.

Oh no, no no no no no no no. He was pretty set against it. He glanced up into the stands where we had a couple hundred spectators, mostly friends and family and some curious passersby, and I saw then that his like-grandparents and his girl something-or-other were up there watching. Gregor was getting more hangdog and sullen every second.

Come on Gregor, I said, putting the ball in his glove. Tell you what, I'll catch you. It'll be just like warming up. Just keep throwing your curveball. And I dragged him over to the mound.

So Werner warmed him up while I went over and got on the catcher's gear, moving a box of blue-dot balls to the front of the ump's supply area while I was at it. I could see Gregor was nervous, and so was I. I had never caught before, and he had never pitched, and bases were loaded and no one was out. It was an unusual baseball moment.

Finally I was geared up and I clanked on out to him. Don't worry about throwing too hard, I said. Just put the curveball right in my glove. Ignore the batter. I'll give you the sign before every pitch; two fingers for curve, one for fastball.

Fastball? he says.

That's where you throw the ball fast. Don't worry about that. We're just going to throw curves anyway.

And you said you weren't to coach, he said bitterly.

I'm not coaching, I said, I'm catching.

So I went back and got set behind the plate. Be looking for curveballs, I said to the ump. Curveball? he said.

So we started up. Gregor stood crouched on the mound like a big praying mantis, red-faced and grim. He threw the first pitch right over our heads to the backstop. Two guys scored while I retrieved it, but I threw out the runner going from first to third. I went out to Gregor. Okay, I said, the bases are cleared and we got an out. Let's just throw now. Right into the glove. Just like last time, but lower.

So he did. He threw the ball at the batter, and the batter bailed, and the ball cut right down into my glove. The umpire was speechless. I turned around and showed him the ball in my glove. That was a strike, I told him.

Strike! he hollered. He grinned at me. That was a curveball, wasn't it.

Damn right it was.

Hey, the batter said. What was that?

We'll show you again, I said.

And after that Gregor began to mow them down. I kept putting down two fingers, and he kept throwing curveballs. By no means were they all strikes, but enough were to keep him from walking too many batters. All the balls were blue-dot. The ump began to get into it.

And between two batters I looked behind me and saw that the entire crowd of spectators, and all the teams not playing at that moment, had congregated behind the backstop to watch Gregor pitch. No one on Mars had ever seen a curveball before, and now they were crammed back there to get the best view of it, gasping and chattering at every hook. The batter would bail or take a weak swing and then look back at the crowd with a big grin, as if to say, Did you see that? That was a curveball!

So we came back and won that game, and we kept Gregor pitching, and we won the next three games as well. The third game he threw exactly twenty-seven pitches, striking out all nine batters with three pitches each. Walter Johnson once struck out all twenty-seven batters in a high-school game; it was like that.

The crowd was loving it. Gregor's face was less red. He was standing straighter in the box. He still refused to look anywhere but at my glove, but his look of grim terror had shifted to one of ferocious concentration. He may have been skinny, but he was tall. Out there on the mound he began to look pretty damned formidable.

So we climbed back up into the winner's bracket, then into a semifinal. Crowds of people were coming up to Gregor between games to get him to sign their baseballs. Mostly he looked dazed, but at one point I saw him glance up at his co-op family in the stands and wave at them, with a brief smile.

How's your arm holding out? I asked him.

What do you mean? he said.

Okay, I said. Now look, I want to play outfield again this game. Can you pitch to Werner? Because there were a couple of Americans on the team we played next, Ernie and Caesar, who I suspected could hit a curve. I just had a hunch.

Gregor nodded, and I could see that as long as there was a glove to throw at, nothing else mattered. So I arranged it with Werner, and in the semifinals I was back out in right-center field. We were playing under the lights by this time, the field like green velvet under a purple twilight sky. Looking in from center field it was all tiny, like something in a dream.

And it must have been a good hunch I had, because I made one catch charging in on a liner from Ernie, sliding to snag it, and then another running across the middle for what seemed like thirty seconds, before I got under a towering Texas leaguer from Caesar. Gregor even came up and congratulated me between innings.

And you know that old thing about how a good play in the field leads to a good at bat. Already in the day's games I had hit well, but now in this semifinal I came up and hit a high fastball so solid it felt like I didn't hit it at all, and off it flew. Home run over the center-field fence, out into the dusk. I lost sight of it before it came down.

Then in the finals I did it again in the first inning, back-to-back with Thomas—his to left, mine again to center. That was two in a row for me, and we were winning, and Gregor was mowing them down. So when I came up again the next inning I was feeling good, and people were calling out for another homer, and the other team's pitcher had a real determined look. He was a really big guy, as tall as Gregor but massive-chested as so many Martians are, and he reared back and threw the first one right at my head. Not on purpose, he was out of control. Then I barely fouled several pitches off, swinging very late, and dodging his inside heat, until it was a full count, and I was thinking to myself, Well heck, it doesn't really matter if you strike out here, at least you hit two in a row.

Then I heard Gregor shouting, Come on, coach, you can do it! Hang in there! Keep your focus! All doing a passable imitation of me, I guess, as the rest of the team was laughing their heads off. I suppose I had said all those things to them before, though of course it was just the stuff you always say automatically at a ball game, I never meant anything by it, I didn't even know people heard me. But I definitely heard Gregor, needling me, and I stepped back into the box thinking, Look I don't even like to coach, I played ten games at shortstop trying not to coach you guys, and I was so irritated I was barely aware of the pitch, but hammered it anyway out over the right-field fence, higher and deeper even than my first two. Knee-high fastball, inside. As Ernie said to me afterward, You *drove* that baby. My teammates rang the little ship's bell all the way around the bases, and I slapped hands with every one of them on the way from third to home, feeling the grin on my face. Afterward I sat on the bench and felt the hit in my hands. I can still see it flying out.

So we were ahead 4–0 in the final inning, and the other team came up determined to catch us. Gregor was tiring at last, and he walked a couple, then hung a curve and their big pitcher got into it and clocked it far over my head. Now I do okay charging liners, but the minute a ball is hit over me I'm totally lost. So I turned my back on this one and ran for the fence, figuring either it goes out or I collect it against the fence, but that I'd never see it again in the air. But running on Mars is so weird. You get going too fast and then you're pinwheeling along trying to keep from doing a faceplant. That's what I was doing when I saw the warning track, and looked back up and spotted the ball coming down, so I jumped, trying to jump straight up, you know, but I had a lot of momentum, and had completely forgotten about the gravity, so I shot up and caught the ball, amazing, but found myself *flying right over the fence.*

I came down and rolled in the dust and sand, and the ball stayed stuck in my glove. I hopped back over the fence holding the ball up to show everyone I had it. But they gave the other pitcher a home run anyway, because you have to stay inside the park when you catch one, it's a local rule. I didn't care. The whole point of playing games is to make you do things like that anyway. And it was good that that pitcher got one too.

So we started up again and Gregor struck out the side, and we won the tournament. We were mobbed, Gregor especially. He was the hero of the hour. Everyone wanted him to sign something. He didn't say much, but he wasn't stooping either. He looked surprised. Afterward Werner took two balls and everyone signed them, to make kind-of trophies for Gregor and me. Later I saw half the names on my trophy were jokes, "Mickey Mantel" and other names like that. Gregor had written on it "Hi Coach Arthur, Regards Greg." I have the ball still, on my desk at home.

Salt and Fresh

At first the water in the new streams was always silty, like liquid brick running down creases in the land. So many salts dissolved out of the dirt that the water became almost viscous, and the stream banks were often coated with fantastic strips of white crystals. In certain watersheds it looked like streams of blood were running through banks of rock candy. And there was more truth to that than people suspected.

You see, after the little red people became the nineteenth reincarnation of the Dalai Lama, they became enlightened, and were faced with a dilemma. Before, the humans and all their claptrap on the surface had served as high entertainment; now they were the little red people's problem, or at least a matter of great concern. The little red people needed to save Mars from humans in a way that would not harm these charming bunglers, but help them.

At the same time, they saw immediately what the resentful looks coming from their archaea crops had meant—it was obvious on the face of it. Just as the Dalai Lama would not eat cows on Earth, the little red people should not eat archaea on Mars.

This created an instantaneous famine situation for the little red people. For the most part they considered it a fortunate rise in consciousness, though there was some dismay as they changed to a vegan diet which took no lives at all, based on seeds and bacterial fruit, milk, and honey equivalents. They went hungry for a long time setting up these new agricultures, foraging also up on the surface when they had to, in the scraps of the humans, to make ends meet. But humans tended to react to these kinds of activities with pesticides, so they were only pursued in desperation; dangerous times call for dangerous measures.

Meanwhile, just as the humans were coming down on them from above, the ungrateful archaea were biting them from below. Many of the old ones were not appeased by their liberation; they wanted compensation, they wanted revenge, some of them were calling for a return to their original dominion over the Martian surface. It is an unfortunate fact that if you give archaea an inch they will take a mile; all the corners of my kitchen prove this. So cadres of disaffected archaea were plotting revolution from below, and though they were a minority at first, these malcontents managed to poison the minds of many other archaea, threatening to create results that would cascade upward through the larger levels of the planetary ecosystem.

So the little red people were caught in the middle, as moderates so often are. We need a lot more compassion to appear very quickly, they said to each other, on all levels of the ecosphere. But though they were telepathic, and now united by a single spirit of bodhisattva grace, they found themselves divided on the question of policy in the face of this crisis. Some thought they should focus on the archaea, others on the humans; some on both, others on neither. More compassion, sure—but how?

Finally the current stage of the terraforming, sometimes called the Great Rehydration, gave a group of them the idea that they could solve both problems at once.

They would never be able to influence humans directly, this group of little red scientists argued. Setting up towns in the porches of their ears and singing a continuo of common sense had only put them at terrible risk in the offices of ear nose and throat specialists. At the same time, the archaea could no longer be confined against their will in the cryptoendolithic world. So what did they have to work with? They had lots of water, lots of salt, lots of archaea, and lots of humans. The proposal involved mixing them all.

The evaporite salts on the surface were being dissolved back into the new hydrosphere. Carbonates, sulfates, and nitrates had all been left behind by the slow evaporation of the ancient Martian seas; there were huge deposits of them, now mixing with the water as it ran across the surface. The mechanics of saltification were still very poorly understood, but clearly the surface water on Mars was going to pick up salt for a long time to come. The archaea, meanwhile, were already hardy halophiles; one species, *Haloferax*, could live directly on and inside salt crystals. Human beings were not as salt tolerant as that, but their blood was about as salty as Earth's ocean water, and many of them heavily oversalted most of their food. So an opportunity might exist. Salt was common ground.

A group of little red scientists advocated a subtle double intervention. Archaea would be released onto the surface, in salt containers that would look to them like ocean liners. These would get into the water, and would slip easily into the bloodstream when introduced into human hosts. Here even smaller vessels would carry some of these archaea across the blood-brain barrier—special varieties, genetically engineered by the little red scientists to create certain electrical fields, triggering the excretion of beneficial hormones and other brain chemicals.

Some of the little red people decried this as no more than drug therapy. The group of little red scientists defended it as such. State of mind was in great part chemical condition, as all admitted. Chemical intervention could be defended on that score. This was an emergency; very possibly humans were in the process of overrunning Mars, devastating the planet for all its unseen indigenous life. Meanwhile the archaea were experiencing a population explosion, and spoiling for a fight. A solution that neutralized both sides would be very welcome. The archaea would see it as the freedom of the surface; the little people would see it as drug therapy; the humans would see it as a deliberate mutation in their values. If no one ever suspected otherwise, where was the harm? Why not let them think so?

So all over Mars streams ran red with silt and salt, across the rain-soaked land. Eventually some of these streams combined to become rivers, and ran out estuaries into the burgeoning new ocean. Since the northern sea had been pumped up out of deep permafrost aquifers, its water at this point was still extremely pure. It was in effect an ocean of distilled water, while the streams and rivers were salty. Humans never failed to comment that this was the reverse of the situation on Earth.

A fair number of the new streams fell off cliffs right into the sea; in these places it looked like someone was pouring red paint into a clear pristine pond, where it spread out on rings and dabs of foam. That looks awful, the humans said to each other, though they didn't know the half of it. Then they would take a swim in the ocean nearby, and get out and eat their lunches, and on their way home feel funny and resolve to be nicer to people that week.

The Constitution of Mars

We the people of Mars have gathered here on Pavonis Mons in the year 2128 to write a constitution which will serve as a legal framework for an independent planetary government. We intend this constitution to be a flexible document subject to change over time in the light of experience and changing historical conditions, but assert here that we hope to establish a government that will forever uphold the following principles: the rule of law; the equality of all before the law; individual freedom of movement, association, and expression; freedom from political or economic tyranny; control of one's work life and the value thereof; communal stewardship of the planet's natural resources; and respect for the planet's primal heritage.

ARTICLE 1. LEGISLATIVE DEPARTMENT

Section 1. The Legislative Bodies

1. The legislative body for Martian global issues will be a two-house *congress*, consisting of a *duma* and a *senate*.
2. The duma will be composed of five hundred members, selected every m-year by a lottery drawn from a list of all Martian residents over ten m-years old. It will meet on Ls=0 and Ls=180, every m-year, and stay in session for as long as necessary to complete its business.
3. The senate will be composed of one senator from each town or

settlement on Mars with a population larger than five hundred people (changed by Amendment 22 to three thousand people), elected every two m-years, using an Australian ballot system. The senate will remain permanently in session, aside from breaks of no more than a month out of every twelve.

Section 2. Powers Granted to the Congress

1. The duma will elect the executive council's seven members, using an Australian ballot system.
2. The senate will elect one-third of the members of the global environmental court, and one-half of the members of the constitutional court, using an Australian ballot system.
3. The congress will pass laws enabling it: to lay and collect taxes equitably from the towns and settlements represented in the senate; to provide for the common defense of Mars; to regulate commerce on Mars, and with other worlds; to regulate immigration to Mars; to print money and regulate its value; to form a criminal court system; and to form a standing police and security group to enforce the laws and defend the commonwealth.
4. All laws passed by the congress shall be subject to review by the executive council; if the executive council vetoes a proposed law, the congress can override the veto with a two-thirds vote.
5. All laws passed by the congress shall also be subject to review by the constitutional and environmental courts, and a veto by these courts cannot be overridden, but shall be grounds for rewriting the law if the congress sees fit, after which the process of passing the law shall begin again.

ARTICLE 2. EXECUTIVE DEPARTMENT

Section 1. The Executive Council

1. The *executive council* shall be formed of seven members, elected by the duma every two m-years. Executive council members must be Martian residents at the time of their election, and at least ten m-years old.
2. The executive council shall elect one of its members as council president, using an Australian ballot system. It shall also elect or appoint a reasonable number of officers needed to help perform its various functions.

Section 2. Powers of the Executive Council

1. The executive council shall command the global police and security force in the defense of Mars, and in the upholding and enforcement of the constitution on Mars.
2. The executive council shall have the power, subject to the review and approval of the congress, to make treaties with Terran political and economic bodies (and the other political entities in the solar system, as stated in Amendment 15).
3. The executive council will elect or appoint one-third of the members of the environmental court, and one-half of the members of the constitutional court.

ARTICLE 3. JUDICIAL DEPARTMENT

Section 1. The Global Courts

1. There shall be two global courts, the *environmental court* and the *constitutional court.*
2. The environmental court shall consist of sixty-six members, one-third elected by the senate, one-third elected or appointed by the executive council, and one-third elected by the vote of all Martian residents over ten m-years old. Individuals elected or appointed to the court shall hold their office for ten m-years.
3. The constitutional court shall consist of twelve members, half elected by the senate, half elected or appointed by the executive council. Court members shall hold their office for ten m-years.

Section 2. Powers Granted the Environmental Court

1. The environmental court shall have the power to review all laws passed by the congress for their impact on the Martian environment, and have the right to veto such laws without appeal if their environmental impact is judged unconstitutional; to appoint regional land commissions to monitor the activities of all Martian towns and settlements for their environmental impact; to make judgments in disputes between towns or settlements concerning environmental matters; and to regulate all land and water stewardship and tenure rights, which are to be written in conjunction with the congress, to replace or adapt Terran concepts of property for the Martian commonality.
2. The environmental court shall rule on all cases brought before it in accordance with concepts ensuring a slow, stable, gradualist ter-

raforming process, which terraforming will have among its goals a maximum air pressure of 350 millibars at six kilometers above the datum in the equatorial latitudes, this figure to be reviewed for revision every five m-years.

Section 3. Powers Granted the Constitutional Court

1. The constitutional court shall review all laws passed by the congress for their adherence to this constitution, and judge all local and regional cases submitted to it that it determines to concern significant global constitutional issues, or to impinge on the individual rights established in this constitution. Congressional and local laws it judges unconstitutional can be revised, and resubmitted to the court by the relevant legislative bodies.

2. The constitutional court shall oversee an economic commission of fifty members. The court shall appoint twenty members, all Martian residents of at least ten m-years of age, to terms of five m-years. The other thirty members shall be appointed or elected by guild cooperatives representing the various professions and trades practiced on Mars (provisional list appended). The economic commission shall submit for legislative approval a body of economic law and practices which will combine publicly owned not-for-profit basic services, and privately owned taxed for-profit enterprises; specify what the public services shall be and how they will be regulated; set legal size limits on all private enterprises; establish legal guidelines for private enterprises which ensure that employees own their enterprises and the capital and profits associated with them; and oversee the welfare of a participatory, democratic economy.

Section 4. Reconciliation of the Two Courts

1. The executive council shall elect a reconciliation board, composed of five members of the environmental court and five members of the constitutional court, which shall mediate, arbitrate, and reconcile any disputes, discrepancies, or other conflicts between the judgments of the two global courts.

ARTICLE 4. THE GLOBAL GOVERNMENT AND THE TOWNS AND SETTLEMENTS

1. The towns, tented canyons, tented craters, and smaller settlements on Mars shall be semiautonomous in relation to the global state and to each other.

2. Towns and settlements are free to establish their own local laws, political systems, and cultural practices, except where these laws, systems, or practices would abrogate the individual rights guaranteed by this global constitution.
3. Citizens of each town and settlement shall be entitled to all the rights guaranteed in this constitution, and to all the rights of all the other towns and settlements.
4. Towns and settlements shall not form regional political alliances that would function as the equivalent of nation-states. Regional interests must be pursued and defended by occasional and temporary coordinated activities between towns and settlements.
5. No town or settlement shall practice physical or economic aggression on any other town or settlement. Disagreements between any two or several towns or settlements are to be resolved by arbitration or judicial ruling by the appropriate court.
6. The physical extent of local law established by any town or settlement shall be set by the land commission, in consultation with the towns and settlements affected by the judgment. Tented craters and canyons, and freestanding tent towns, have obvious physical boundaries that can function as the equivalent of "city limits," but these towns, as well as diffuse open-air settlements, have legitimate "spheres of influence" that will often overlap the spheres of influence of neighboring towns and settlements. The land inside these spheres of influence is not to be construed as "territory" owned by the towns and settlements, in keeping with the general withdrawal from Terran notions of sovereignty and property as such. Nevertheless, all towns and settlements will have the legal right to consideration concerning all land-use issues, including water rights, within their sphere of influence as established by the land commission.

ARTICLE 5. INDIVIDUAL RIGHTS AND OBLIGATIONS

Section 1. Individual Rights
1. Freedom of movement and assembly.
2. Religious freedom.
3. Freedom of speech.
4. Right to vote in global elections not to be abridged.
5. Right to legal counsel, timely trial, and habeas corpus.
6. Freedom from unreasonable search or seizure, double jeopardy, or

involuntary self-incrimination.

7. Freedom from cruel or unusual punishments.
8. Right to choice of employment.
9. Right to the majority of the economic benefits of one's own labor, as calculated by formulas to be approved by the economic commission, but never less than 50 percent in any case.
10. Right to a meaningful part in the management of one's work.
11. Right to a minimum living wage for life.
12. Right to proper health care, including the body of practices known collectively as the "longevity treatment."

Section 2. Individual Obligations

1. The citizens of Mars shall, over the course of their lives, give one m-year of work to global service and the public good, such work to be defined by the economic commission, but never to be military or police work.
2. The right to own or bear lethal weapons is expressly denied to everyone on Mars, including police or riot control officers.

ARTICLE 6. THE LAND

Section 1. Terraforming Goals and Limits

1. The primal state of Mars shall have legal consideration, and shall not be altered except as part of a terraforming program dedicated to making the surface of the planet survivable by humans up to the six-kilometer altitude contour. Above the six-kilometer elevation the goal shall be to keep the surface as close to its primal condition as possible.
2. The air pressure of the atmosphere shall not exceed 350 millibars at six kilometers above the datum, in the equatorial latitudes (30 degrees north to 30 degrees south).
3. The amount of carbon dioxide in the atmosphere shall not exceed ten millibars.
4. The sea level of Oceanus Borealis (the northern sea) shall not exceed the -1 kilometer contour.
5. The sea level of the Hellas Basin sea shall not exceed the datum.
6. Argyre Basin is to remain a dry basin.
7. Deliberate introduction of any and all species, natural or engineered, is to be approved by the environmental court's agencies, after review for environmental impacts on already existing biomes and ecologies.

8. No terraforming methods will be employed that release radiation to the land, groundwater, or air of Mars.
9. No terraforming methods will be employed which are unstable and prone to rapid collapse, or that do violent damage to the Martian landscape, as determined by the environmental court.

ARTICLE 7. AMENDMENTS TO THIS CONSTITUTION

Whenever two-thirds of the members of both houses of the legislature, or a majority of the voters in a majority of the towns and settlements of Mars, shall propose amendments to this constitution, the proposed amendment shall be put to a general global vote during the next scheduled global election, and shall require a supermajority of two-thirds to pass.

ARTICLE 8. RATIFICATION OF THE CONSTITUTION

After approval of the text of this constitution, point by point, by a majority vote of the representatives of the constitutional convention, the constitution as a whole shall be presented to all the people of Mars over five m-years old, for a vote of approval or disapproval, and if it receive a supermajority of two-thirds in approval, shall become the supreme law of the planet.

Some Worknotes and Commentary on the Constitution, by Charlotte Dorsa Brevia

PREAMBLE Though the very idea of a constitution was opposed by some, the notion of a constitution as a "structure for debate" carried the day, and the process proceeded.

1.1.2 The idea of government as jury duty has rarely been enacted, but the theoretical arguments for the idea were interesting enough to inspire the framers to try it. The possibility that any citizen can become a lawmaker has had profoundly positive psychological and social impacts, even though the actual duma in practice has not usually been the driving force in legislative matters—and, yes, sometimes has been a circus, and always has a (refreshing) feel of unprofessionalism. But combined with the economic autonomy enjoyed by the ordinary person, this tangible sensation of self-government has raised the concept of citizenship to new heights of responsibility, and given people a stronger sense of the collective that has always existed.

2.1.1 A seven-member executive council is derived from the Swiss system. The aim is to depersonalize the executive functions of government, without rendering them inoperative by giving them over to an entire congressional-sized body. Though political fighting among the council membership is inevitable, votes quickly decide arguments and then the executive branch has decided on a course of action. This is not much different than a council of advisers influencing a single executive. But it does remove the tendency to personalize politics, to demonize or valorize individuals when really, in this particular realm of social life, it is policy that matters. The method has worked well in Switzerland, where many well-educated citizens do not know who their president is, but know where they stand on all issues current in the Swiss polity. And the same has proved to be true on Mars.

2.1.2 The Australian ballot system is required so often in the constitution because the framers became convinced that it encourages "reaching to the Other" by candidates. Voters vote for at least three candidates, placing them first second third and so on, and their first choice gets more points in a weighted system. Candidates are thus encouraged to seek second- and third-place votes from voters outside their own constituency, whatever it might be. On Earth this has worked very well in fractured electorates, healing some profound divisions over time, and given the polyglot nature of Martian society, the framers decided it was appropriate for Mars as well.

3.1.3 The splitting of the global judiciary into two branches was questioned at the constitutional congress, but in the end it was decided that so many questions of environmental law lay at the heart of the Martian experience, that it deserved a special body devoted specifically to regulating that function. People at the time argued that the constitutional court was vestigial and redundant, which has not really proven to be true, as its caseload is always filled with significant problems for Martian society. People also argued that the environmental court would, because of the artificial nature of the Martian biosphere itself, become the most powerful political body on Mars. This has indeed been a much more accurate prediction, and it could be argued that Martian history since the constitution has been the story of how the environmental court has integrated its tremendous power into the rest of social life. But this is not necessarily a bad kind of history to have.

3.2.2 Legislating atmospheric pressure has made the Martian constitution the butt of many jokes, but the Grand Gesture, as it was called, to red considerations, is what allowed the constitution to be completed in the first place. And it does no harm to remind people that the environment on Mars is to a certain extent a matter of human choice. This has been true on Earth as well for almost two centuries, but only since the Great Flood has it been a truth generally acknowledged.

3.3.1 This provision attempts to chart the difficult course between local autonomy and global justice. It is the paradox of a free and tolerant society that in order for it to work, intolerance cannot be tolerated. The two injunctions "people can govern themselves" and "no one can oppress another person" must exist as a living contradiction or dynamic tension.

In practice, local laws that violate the Martian spirit of justice (as detailed in the constitution) have stuck out like sore thumbs.

3.3.2 The idea that the constitution should mandate certain kinds of economies was controversial and hotly debated at the constitutional congress, but the argument that prevailed was unassailable: Economics is politics, and a just political existence, a just life, depends on a just economic system. This being the case, the framers were not free to ignore this issue, or all their efforts would have been rendered a kind of huge gesture or joke in the face of history.

As it turns out, the establishment of a democratic participatory economy has been complicated and fraught with problems and argument, but not vicious or even particularly divisive. The old argument that "human nature" could never behave in anything but a feudal economic hierarchal manner disappeared like a mist the moment people were enfranchised in their work, and the capital created by generations of labor turned over to the ownership of the collective, and run by the people who operate it. Hierarchies still exist within each social structure, but in a context of general equality they are seen as the result of work, experience, and age rather than unearned privilege, and so they do not engender the same resentments. In other words, people are still people; argue, resent, hate, are selfish, will share only with kin or those they know, if that is what you mean by "human nature"; but are now in an economic framework where they are roughly equal to those they despise, and cannot grossly oppress or be oppressed by them, financially. This takes the sting out of anger at others, believe me. But you have to have lived under the old regime fully to feel the difference.

3.4.1 This provision provoked much hilarity during the constitutional convention, as being an afterthought body "papering over" profound contradictions in the judiciary and government as designed; it was even predicted that the whole government would eventually be run by this tacked-on reconciliation board.

Indeed this has sometimes proved to be the case. What has to be remembered is that this is not necessarily a bad thing. The fulcrum of government should be in the courts, rather than in, say, army head-quarters. I have never found the debates before the reconciliation board to be anything less than fascinating: the whole philosophy of government and human nature, squabbled over in every nit-picking bureaucratic detail. Of course you may say, But this is your job, Charlotte, you like this kind of thing. But I would reply by pointing out how many people are like me, nowadays, and very much enjoy their work; which is no longer time that you give to others to earn the money to do what you want, but actually something you have chosen because you find it interesting (if you are sensible), because you are fully involved in the results of the work, and are recompensed for it in much the same ways and to the same degree as everyone else in the world, with sufficiency at least, and usually much more: This is the situation that the society based on this constitution has managed to achieve. That's what I find so interesting about it, you see.

4.2 Again, the great paradox: intolerance of intolerance. But how else can justice be achieved?

4.4 This clause was clearly included to try to drive Martian politics down to the local and up to the global, effectively abolishing anything like the nation-states of Earth. Whether the nation-state was actually the source of Earth's terrible problems is arguable, but no one could see why there should be any nations on Mars, and so the clause passed. No one has missed the nation-state here, and indeed when you look at the word *patriotism* you can see that it is not a concept Mars need concern itself with.

4.5 Making war unconstitutional; this too was laughed at by many at the convention, but passed nevertheless. Perhaps you can't mandate goodness, but it may be worth trying anyway.

5.1.9 While controversial, this clause alone has been a major force in the struggle for equality and justice on Mars.

5.2.1 This practice was also taken from the Swiss, modified to demilitarize it and make it a matter of public work for the collective well-being of Martian society. The usual pattern has become six months after secondary education, three three-month sessions in the four years immediately after that, and nine more months on an occasional basis in the years after that. Thus the bulk of public service is done by the young and is part of their education. One study showed that over thirty percent of Martian couples met their partners during their public-service time, so if nothing else it works as mixer and matchmaker.

5.2.2 This clause encountered surprisingly little resistance at the convention. A no-brainer, Art called it.

6 Treatment of the land is fundamental to any government concerned with permaculture, that is, with stewardship of the biosphere for the good of future generations. Society is "a partnership not only between those who are living, but between those who are living, those who are dead, and those who are to be born." (Edmund Burke.) And so we must care for the land.

7 There have been fourteen amendments passed in the twenty m-years the constitution has been law. Most reconcile contradictions embedded in the constitution, or in the local/global or tolerance situations, or refine the terraforming laws to meet current conditions.

8 Passed October 11, m-year 52, by 78% to 22%. Now operating successfully for twenty-one m-years.

At this point I believe the constitution can be judged a success. Those who argued at the time that a constitution was itself anachronistic and unnecessary did not understand its function: not to be a static "final law" wherein all social contradiction was resolved forever, but rather to be a template to structure argument, and a spur to justice. Despite the difficulties encountered since with enacting the vaguer or more radical sections of the document, I believe it has, like its great American and Swiss predecessors, succeeded in this sense.

The form of government mandated by this constitution can be called polyarchy; power is distributed out through a great number of institutions and individuals, in a web of checks and balances that reduces any possibilities of oppressive hierarchy. The goals of the constitution, listed in the preamble, come down to justice and peaceful dissent. Where those have been created, all else will follow.

Of course the constitution has somewhat receded into the background now, as huge masses of legislation and informal practice have accreted around it, regulating the day-to-day activities of most Martians. But that was its function to begin with and not to be lamented.

The constitution was, to my mind, written to give people a sense that their management of their affairs was in no way "natural" or written in stone; laws and governments have always been artificial inventions, practices, and habits. They can change, they have changed, they will change again. That being the case, there is no reason not to try to change them for the better. And that is what we did. What the result will be in the long run no one can say. But I think it has been a good beginning.

Jackie on Zo

It didn't seem that bad to me but I had an epidural so what do I know. It was like an extremely arduous athletic effort that I couldn't choose not to do. I've seen people's scornful looks when I mention the epidural, but I say we're Terran animals and if we're going to give birth on another planet we deserve a little medical intervention. To insist on a natural childbirth on Mars is a kind of machismo I'm not interested in.

She was hard from the start. She was pulled out of me and put on my chest and I saw this little red face looking me right in the eye and yelling in protest. She was pissed off, you could read that on her face just as clear as on anyone older than her. I doubt not that we're conscious in the womb, for at least the last part of the confinement, lost in thought without language, like music or meditation. And so we come out with our character already in place, intact and complete. Nothing afterward changes it. And in fact she was pissed off like that for years to come.

She sucked voraciously, cried inconsolably, slept fitfully, shrieked in her sleep as if fully awake—then woke up terrified by her own noise and cried some more. I often wondered what she dreamed about to scare her so. For thousands of years they've called it colic and no one knows what it is. Some say it's the slow adjustment of the digestive system to the barrage of new chemicals. From the writhing of her torso I judge there is some truth to that. But I also think she was still pissed off about being ejected from the womb. Rage at the unfair loss of that narcissistic oceanic bliss. She remembered the womb. Even later when she forgot she remembered, and did everything she could to get back to that place. That's Zo's whole story really.

The colic drove me crazy. I couldn't comfort her and couldn't get her to stop crying. Nothing worked, and believe me I tried everything I could think of, because it exasperated me no end. Sometimes she cried ten hours straight. That's a long time when a baby's crying. The only thing that worked even a little was to hold her in my hands, one under her butt and one behind her head and neck, and raise her up and down rapidly, as if she were in a swing. This boggled her into silence and she even seemed to like it, or at least be interested. In any case she would stop crying. But one time when I was doing it an Arab woman came up to me and put her hand out and said, "Please, you should not do that, you might hurt the baby."

"I've got her head supported," I told her, and showed her.

"Still, their necks are so weak." She was nervous, even scared, but persisting.

"She likes it. I know what I'm doing."

But I never did it again. And I thought later about the kind of courage it takes to remonstrate with a stranger about his or her parenting.

If Michel's belief in the theory of the four temperaments is correct, which I doubt, then she was choleric. Moody—like Maya, yes, she was. This similarity didn't bother me as much as people might think. I liked Maya a lot more than she liked me—who wouldn't, she's like something out of Sophocles—but she wanted to fight, and I wasn't going to back down. It was the same with Zo. It's all a matter of one's biochemistry—one's moods I mean. That's what Michel was saying too really, with all his biological correlations. The four temperaments, sure, except there are forty, or forty thousand. Grouped perhaps loosely in his four, who knows. Anyway Zo was a choleric's choleric, the pure product.

She was extremely frustrated throughout her first year, when she couldn't talk or walk. She could see all the rest of us doing those things and she wanted to too. She tipped over a million times, like a top-heavy doll. I kept a supply of butterfly Band-Aids on hand, in fact a complete little medical kit. She babbled authoritatively at everyone, but when they failed to understand her she got furious. She grabbed things out of your hand. She threw her cups and spoons and dishes at you, or on the floor. She would take big swings at you, and was so fast that some of them landed. She would head-butt you with the back of her head—she split my lip twice, but after that my face got faster than her head. Which made her furious. She would throw herself headlong on the floor and beat the ground with fists and feet, and howl. It was hard not to laugh at such histrionics, but I usually avoided letting her see me laugh, as it drove her berserk and her face would go an alarming purple color. So I tried to be noncommittal. It got easy to ignore. "Oh that's just Zo doing her thing," I would say. "It's like an electrical storm going through her nervous system. There's nothing you can do except let it run its course."

When she learned to walk she got less cranky. She learned to feed herself too, very quickly. She refused high chairs or boosters or any baby utensils as affronts to her dignity. Once she could get around she was a danger to herself even more than before. She would eat anything. Changing her diapers, I found sand, dirt, pebbles, roots, twigs, small toys, little household objects—it was a real mess. And she would fight like crazy while you tried to change her. Not always, but about half the time. It was like that with all the daily routine—changing clothes, brushing teeth, getting in the bath, getting out of the bath— half the time she would cooperate, half she would object and fight you all the way. And if you let her win it only got worse next time. Give a centimeter and she would go for the kilometer.

I suppose eating dirt might have been how she got sick. She got some variant of the Guillain-Barré virus, but we didn't know that at the time, we only saw the forty-degree temperature and then she was paralyzed completely, for six days. I couldn't believe it. I was still in the full shock of it happening when she came out of it and started to move again—first twitches, then everything. It was an amazing relief. But I have to admit that after that she was worse than ever. Her tantrums would last an hour, and if you put her in a room by herself she would do her best to destroy it. She broke bones in both hands. So you had to stay in the room to watch her. I seriously considered making it a padded room.

She was also terrible to other kids. She would walk right up to them and knock them down, almost as if experimentally. It was impersonal, and she didn't seem malicious—more like deranged. And indeed later we figured out that she had a perceptual problem after her illness, and thought she was farther away from things than she really was. So when she got interested in another person, bam, over they went. She was a cheery little anarchist in her day care, so high-maintenance I was embarrassed to inflict her on the place. But I needed to work and I needed time away from her, so I did it anyway. They didn't complain, not directly.

The more she learned to talk the more she challenged the rules. NO was her first word and her favorite for years. She said it with immense conviction. The trick questions got the biggest NOs of all. Will you get out of the bath? No. Don't you want to get to read a book? No. Don't you want to have dessert? No. Do you like to say no? NO.

She picked up language so fast I couldn't really remember how it happened. For a few months it was just a few words, then all of a sudden she could say whatever she wanted. That made her more relaxed in some ways. Her good moods were really good, and lasted longer. She was so cute you could hardly stand it. It has to be some kind of evolutionary mechanism to keep you from killing them. She was always on the move, jumping around, looking to do something or go somewhere. She developed a passion for trams and trucks, and would cry out, "Tram!" or "Truck!" Once I was out by myself and I saw a truck and said, "Oooh, big truck," and the people sitting around me on the tram looked at me.

But she still had a hell of a temper. And now when she got mad she would chew you out as well as hit you and throw things at you. You had to laugh at how basic she was. She said the meanest things she could think of. "Go 'way!" "I don't like you!" "You're not my friend!" "You're not my mom!" "You're nothing!" "I don't love you anymore!" "I hate you!" "You're dead!" "Go 'way!"

In public this could be embarrassing. Often when I took her out she would look at someone nearby and announce loudly, "I don't like that guy." And sometimes add, "Go 'way!"

"Be polite Zo," I would say, with an apologetic look, trying to convey that she did this to everyone. "That's not nice."

After that infancy when she hit the so-called terrible twos it was kind of hard to tell the difference. Though it did get worse in some ways. At times it was almost impossible to deal with her. It was like living with a psychotic. Every day was a complete roller coaster, with several great highs and just as many shrieking tantrums. Everything you told her to do she would stop and decide whether she wanted to obey or not, and usually the very idea of being told what to do would offend her, and she would opt for defiance just on principle. Often she would do the opposite of what she was told to do. I had to be ready for that or it was trouble. I had to decide whether it was worth it to tell her not to do something—if it really mattered. If it did then I had to be prepared for the whole melodrama. Once I said, "Zo, don't bang that mug on the table," and she slammed it down before I could get to her and it broke the mug and the tabletop, which was glass. She was round-eyed but unrepentant. Angry at me, as if I had tricked her. She also wanted to break a few more to see how it worked.

All these intensities were constant and across the board, and so she could be a joy when she was in a good mood. We explored Mars like John in the beginning. I never felt more strongly that I was in the presence of mental brilliance than when I was with her, out walking together on the moors or in the streets of a town, when she was about three—not even with Sax or Vlad or Bao Shuyo. The sense that here was someone intently observing the world and then putting things together faster than I could ever dream of doing. She laughed at things all the time, often for reasons I couldn't see, and when she laughed she was so beautiful. At all times she was an exceptionally good-looking child, but when she laughed there was a physical beauty that along with the innocence was heart-stopping to see. How we manage to ruin that quality is humanity's great crime, repeated over and over.

Anyway, that beauty and laughter made all the temper tantrums a lot easier for me, sure. You couldn't help but love her, she was so passionate. When she blew up and hit the deck screaming and pounding and thrashing on the floor I would think, Oh well, that's just Zo. No need to take it personally. Not even the I hate you Moms—they weren't personal either, not really. It was just she was passionate. I loved her so much.

Which only made it worse seeing Nirgal. What a contrast—week after week taking care of Zo, exhausted a lot of the time, and then he would drop by, just as airy and vague and agreeable as ever—everyone's friend, mild and somewhat removed. Like Hiroko a bit. And yes he was Zo's father, I admit it now, but who could imagine that she had anything to do with him, so blithe and smooth he was, all his life. He may be the Great Martian, everyone seems to think so, but he was nothing to her I tell you. One time he came by and everyone was fawning over him as usual, drawn to him as if to some kind of magic mirror, and Zo took one look at him and turned to me and said, "I don't like that guy."

"Zo."

A daring glance at him: "Go 'way!"

"Zo! Be nice!" I looked at him. "She does this with everybody."

Immediately she ran to Charlotte and hugged her legs, glancing at me. Everyone laughed and she glowered, not expecting that.

"Okay," I said, "she does it with fifty percent of everybody, and hugs the other half. But which half you're in keeps changing."

Nirgal nodded and smiled at her, but he still looked startled when she loudly insisted, "I don't like that guy!"

"Zo, stop it! Be polite."

And eventually, I mean over years, she did get a bit more polite. Eventually the world wears you down, you get a veneer of civilization over your real self. But how I loved her when she was a little animal and you saw just what she was really like. How I loved her. These days we get together for lunch and she is the most arrogant supercilious young woman you can imagine, completely full of herself, condescending to me from an enormous height, and I just look at her and laugh, thinking, You think you're so tough—you should have seen yourself when you were two.

Keeping the Flame

Once during one of his long runs across the land, after he had given up looking for Hiroko but before he had stopped the movement of the search, Nirgal crossed the great dark forest of Cimmeria, south of Elysium. In the forest it was slow going. The trees were tall fir and linden trees, with a dense understory of Hokkaido pine and birch. The sun lanced through the thick roof of the canopy in bright pencils of light, which struck pads of dark moss, curled ferns, wild onions, and mats of electric green lichen. In those shadows and through the myriad parallel shafts of buttery light he ran slowly for day after day, lost but unconcerned, as a general western push would eventually lead him out of the forest to some point on the Great Canal. The forest silence was broken only by the chirps of birds, the deep soughing chorus of wind in the pine needles above, and twice the distant yodeling of coyotes, or wolves. Once something big that he never saw crashed away through brush. He had been running for sixty days straight.

Low crater rings were the only relief, all softened and buried under trees, leaf mats, humus, and rocky carpets of moss. Most of the craters were rimless, so that jogging along he would come on the arc of a sunken round room, and through branches spy a little round meadow, or a shallow round lake, infilling with meadow from the sides. Usually he circled them and continued on his way. But in one little sunken meadow there stood the ruins of a white-stone temple.

He dropped down the gentle slope of the depression, approached at a walk, feeling hesitant. The stone of the temple was alabaster, and very white. It reminded him of the white-stone village in Medusa Fossa. It looked Greek, though it was round. Twelve slender white Ionic pillars, made of stacked drums of stone, set around the flat base like the points of a clock. No roof, which made it look even more like a Greek ruin, or a British henge. Lichen was growing in the cracks of its base.

Nirgal walked around and through it, suddenly aware of the silence. There was no wind, no sound of bird or beast. All was in shadow; the world had stopped. Apollo might step out of the gloom. Something reminded him of Zygote; perhaps simply the white of the columns, somewhat like Zygote's dome, back there in his past which now seemed to him like a fairy tale from another age, a tale with a child hero and an animal mother. The notion that that fairy tale and the moment he lived in were parts of the same life—his life—it took a leap of faith that he was incapable of making. Hard to imagine how it would feel a century or two on, in other words what it felt like now for Nadia and Maya and the rest of the issei. . . .

Something moved and he jumped. But it was nothing. He shook his head, touched the smooth cool surface of a column. A human mark in the forest. Human marks, both temple and forest. In this ancient eroded crater.

Two old people appeared across the clearing, walking to the temple, unaware of Nirgal. His heart leaped in him like a child trying to escape—

But they were strangers. He had never seen them before. Old men; Caucasian; bald; wrinkled; one short, the other shorter.

Both now looking at him suspiciously.

"Hello!" he said.

They approached, one pointing a dart gun at the ground.

He said, "What is this place?"

One stopped, held the other back by the arm. "Aren't you Nirgal?"

Nirgal nodded.

They glanced at each other.

"Come back to our place," the same one said. "We'll tell you there."

They hiked up through the woods covering the old crater wall, to the edge of the crater, where stood a little cottage, constructed of logs, roofed by dark red slates. The men led Nirgal into this home of theirs, Nirgal ducking under the lintel.

It was dim inside. One window overlooked the crater. The tops of the monument's pillars were visible in the treetops.

They served Nirgal an odd herb tea, made from a kind of pond weed. They were issei, they said—not only issei, but members of the First Hundred. Edvard Perrin and George Berkovic. Edvard did most of the talking. Friends, they were. And colleagues of Phyllis Boyle. The monument in the crater was a memorial to her. The three of them had built a similar structure long ago, out of ice drums, for fun. On the first trip to the North Pole, with Nadia and Ann, in m-year 2.

"In the beginning," George added with a flinty smile.

They told him their story, and he saw it had once been oft-repeated. Edvard told most of it, with George adding comments, or finishing some of Edvard's trailing sentences.

"We were there when it all came down. There wasn't any reason for it. They screwed it up when it all could have been so easy. I'm not saying we're bitter, but we are. 2061 wasn't *necessary*."

"It could have been avoided, if they had listened to Phyllis. It was all Arkady's fault."

"Bogdanov's stupid confidence. Whereas Phyllis had a plan that would have worked fine, without all the destruction and death."

"Without the war."

"She saved us all when we were marooned on Clarke. After saving everyone on Mars before that."

They glowed dimly as they remembered her. Happy to have their tale to tell. They had survived '61, they had worked for peace in the years between revolutions, helping UNTA in Burroughs to coordinate mining efforts in Vastitas, sequencing them so that sites in danger of inundation by the north sea were strip-mined with enormous speed before the ice and water buried them. Those were the glory years, a moment in history when the tremendous power of technology could be wielded on the landscape without consequences—no environmental impact statements, no scars that would last . . . billions of dollars of metals extracted before the ice overwhelmed the sites.

"That was when we found this place," George said.

"Amazonia was full of metals," Edvard added. "No way we got it all out."

"And now, of course," Edvard said, and sipped his tea.

Silence fell. George poured more tea, and Edvard began again.

"We were in Burroughs when the second revolution began, working for UNTA. Phyllis was dead at that point. Killed by red terrorists."

"In Kasei."

Nirgal kept his face still.

They watched him.

"Maya, in fact. Maya killed Phyllis. So we have heard."

Nirgal stared back at them, sipping his tea.

They gave up the gambit. "Well, it's well-known. She was certainly capable of it. She would be the one to do it. Murderous. I'm still sick about it. Sick."

"I can't believe it happened."

"I sometimes wonder if it did. If maybe Phyllis got away and disappeared, like Hiroko is supposed to have. They never did find her body. I never saw it. We opposed Free Mars, we opposed you." Glancing defiantly at him as he said it.

"We despised the red guerrillas. At least until—"

"But our special hatred is reserved for our crèchemates, isn't it."

"It's always that way."

"Nadia, Sax, Maya—death and mass destruction. That's all they brought us with their so-called ideals. Death and mass destruction."

"Not your fault," George told Nirgal.

"But if Phyllis had lived . . . We were in Burroughs during the protests. The standoff with UNTA. The flooding of the city—the deliberate flooding of the greatest city on Mars! Phyllis would never have let that happen."

"We were on the planes that evacuated."

"Five planes, five giant planes. We flew to Sheffield. So we were there for that one too. Death and destruction. We tried to mediate. We tried to do what Phyllis would have done."

"Tried to mediate."

"Yes, to mediate, between UNTA and the reds. It was impossible, but we did it. We did it. The cable would have gone twice if it weren't for us. It's a monument to Phyllis just as much as our little gazebo down there. She was the first advocate of the elevator. A visionary. So we did what we could."

"After the truce we went east."

"By piste where it was still possible. In rovers where it wasn't. We separated at Underhill, didn't we."

"And met again on Elysium. But only after the most amazing adventures I've ever heard of."

"Crossing the north sea ice."

"Slipping across the bridge over La Manche."

"Walking all the way across the Hump. Finally we reunited, here, and helped to build Cimmeria Harbor. Lobbying all the while for the name Boyle Harbor, to match Boone Harbor in Tempe."

"And all the places named Bogdanov."

"But no such luck. She's a forgotten hero. But someday justice will be done. History will judge. Meanwhile we're helping to establish Cimmeria, and doing some prospecting in the forest."

Nirgal said, "Ever hear anything of Hiroko?"

They looked at each other. Nirgal had no idea what their glances meant, but there was quite a silent conversation going on between them.

"No. Hiroko . . . she disappeared so long ago. We never heard from her again. But she's your mother, no?"

"Yes."

"You don't hear from her?"

"No. She disappeared in Sabishii. When UNTA burned it down." Reminding them. "Some say she was killed then. Others say that she got away with Iwao and Gene and Rya and the rest of them. Lately I heard they may have come to Elysium. Or to somewhere near here."

They frowned. "I've never heard that, have you?"

"No. But they wouldn't have told us, would they."

"No."

"But you've seen nothing out here," Nirgal said. "No settlements or camps?"

"No. Well . . ."

"There are settlements all over. But they all come into town. They're all natives like you. A few Kurds."

"No one unusual."

"And so all the settlements are accounted for, you think?"

"I think so."

"I think so."

Nirgal considered it. These were two of only a few, maybe a half dozen, of the First Hundred who had sided with the UNTA all the way. Would Hiroko reveal herself to them? Would she try to hide from them? If they knew of her presence, would they tell him?

But they didn't know. He sat there in the big comfortable armchair, falling asleep. There was nothing to know.

Around him the two wizened old men moved quietly about the dim room. Old turtleheads, deep in their dark cave. But they had loved Phyllis. Both of them. As friends. Or maybe it hadn't been like that. Maybe it hadn't been that simple. However it had happened, they were the partners now. Maybe they had always been the partners. In the First Hundred that might have been a difficulty. Phyllis of course seemed an unlikely refuge. All the better perhaps. Who knew what had happened in the beginning. The past was a mystery. Even to those who had been there and lived it. And of course even at the time none of it had made sense, not the kind of sense people talked about afterward. Now they puttered about in the dusk. He felt the exhaustion of his long run take hold of him.

Let him sleep.

We should tell him.

No.

Why not?

There's no need. Everyone will find out soon enough.

When things start dying. Phyllis wouldn't have wanted that.

But they killed her. So they don't have her here to save them.

So they get what they deserve? Everything dying?

Everything won't die.

It will if it works the way they want. She wouldn't have wanted that.

We had no choice. You know that. They would have killed us.

Would they? I'm not so sure. I think you wanted it. They kill Phyllis, and so we—

We had no choice I say! Come on. They could have gotten the locations from the records. And who's to say they aren't right anyway.

Revenge.

Okay, revenge. Say it was. Serves them right. This was never their planet.

Much later Nirgal found himself suddenly awake, and cold. Neck sore from being bent in the big armchair. The old men were slumped at the kitchen table over books, as still as wax figurines. One of them was asleep, dreaming the other's dream. The other watched it in the air. Their fire had banked to gray coals. Nirgal whispered that he had to leave. He got up and walked out into a frigid predawn, walked for a while and then ran again through the dark trees, running as if to escape something.

Saving Noctis Dam

The Noctis Dam was not a good idea in any case, and then unfortunately they botched the engineering as well. They placed the dam in the mouth of the southernmost Noctis canyon, where the rim is a basalt cap resting on old sandstone. Naturally as soon as the reservoir filled the sandstone began to saturate, which weakened the dam foundations. Then the only emergency runoff as designed was a big glory hole that ran water down through a tunnel in the rock on the side, letting it out into the headwaters of the Ius River below. They lined the tunnel with concrete, of course, but it was sandstone behind that. Thus when the weather became more violent and we saw the first superstorms, the dam was not designed to handle such runoffs. The reservoir level would rise very fast. One of the very first times that happened I was there to see it, and it was a daunting thing to witness. We opened the glory hole the moment rain was forecast, but it seemed to make little difference. And this time the rock behind the concrete was so weakened by seepage that the cavitation ripped the concrete right out of there, apparently. All the instrument readings for the tunnel went dead, and then we saw the concrete being shot out of the hole at the bottom into the shallows of the headwaters; sometimes after a minute or two of complete blockage, so that house-sized chunks of concrete went flying hundreds of meters, as out of a cannon. A very disturbing sight for all of us.

Of course the water going down the tunnel would immediately begin to rip the sandstone out of the hole, and soon enough there would be no rim underneath us left to hold up the south side of the dam.

Thus we had no choice but to close the glory hole from the top; indeed we were happy that the option still existed. But after that we had no other way to release water from the reservoir. And it was still raining harder than we had ever seen, as if the clouds had been seeded; and Noctis Labyrinthus is an extremely big watershed, even just the southernmost quadrant of it, which was what drained into the reservoir.

So the reservoir level rose, two meters in an hour, then three. At that rate we had only a few more hours before it reached the top of the dam and started pouring over, and then inevitably the top would tear somewhere, and without further ado the entire dam, all 330 vertical meters of it, would peel down, probably in a single collapse. The rim walls just behind the dam were very likely to go as well. More importantly, the resulting flood would certainly sweep away all the canyon-floor settlements in Oudemans Crater and upper Marineris, perhaps all the way down to Melas Chasma.

For some time after we closed the glory hole we were at a loss concerning what next to do. Mary of course called emergency services in Cairo, and told them to warn the people down in Oudemans and in Ius Chasma to get out of the crater and canyon, or at least as high on their walls as they could, as there was no quick way for great numbers of people to get out of that deep crater and gorge. But beyond that it was not clear what we could do. We hastened back and forth between the command center and the dam, looking at the water rising, then walking back up to the command center to check the weather reports, all the while in a terrific downpour. The reports gave us reason to hope that the rain might soon stop—it already had upstream in the watershed, and farther west. And the last squall had consisted mostly of hail—hail the size of oranges, which drove us to the shelter of the center, but had the advantage of staying where it was on the ground upstream, at least until it melted. So that too gave us some hope.

Nevertheless, the upstream flow readings coming in to the center made it clear that the lake was going to rise higher than the dam, by what the AI said would be two or three meters. Some rough calculations led me to the conclusion that the overflow would probably be more than the lip of the dam could tolerate. I informed the others of this unhappy conclusion.

"Three meters!" Mary said at last, and expressed the wish that the dam were just four meters higher. Certainly that would have helped.

Without really considering it, I said, "Perhaps we can make it four meters higher."

They said, "How is that?"

"Well," I said, "the pressure up top will not be *that* bad. Even just a plywood barrier might do the trick."

This they found amusing, nevertheless we got in the truck and drove wildly to Cairo Lumber over a road sheeted with big hail balls, and we bought their entire stock of plywood sheets. We were too nervous to tell them what we wanted it for.

Back at the dam we set up the plywood sheets against the railing, nail-gunning them to the plastic footing of the rail just to keep the wind from blowing them away before the water trapped them against the railing. It started to rain again while we did this. We worked at the highest speed we could manage, I assure you—never have I worked with such a sense of haste. Even so, by the time we finished our work, the water had lipped over the concrete, and we had to run back along the road on the top of the dam splashing ankle deep through the water—an awful experience.

Once off the dam and up the road toward the command center, we stopped to look back. If the plywood did not hold and the dam gave way, the rim there would very likely go too, and we would all be killed; nevertheless, we stopped to look back. We could not help it.

The last squall had passed while we labored, and the sky had gone wild over our heads: dark orange to the east, then both to north and south an intense turquoise, like no sky color we had ever seen. It was still black to the west, but the sun was peeping under a distant cloud, illuminating the scene in brassy horizontal light. Below us we saw that the lake was continuing to rise, up the sides of the plywood. Finally, as dusk fell, it was quite a bit more than halfway up the plywood sheets. When we couldn't see it very well anymore—and I didn't want to see it either, I confess, it looked so flimsy—we walked back to the command center.

Up there we waited. Very possibly the whole structure would go very quickly; we would see this on the instrumentation, then perhaps be taken along with it, swept down with the rim walls. So all night we watched the readouts on the computers. Meanwhile we told people over the phone what we had done. My throat stayed dry no matter how hard I swallowed. We occupied ourselves telling jokes—a specialty of mine, but never had people laughed so hard at my jokes before. After one Mary hugged me, and I felt she was shaking; and I saw my hands too were shaking.

In the morning the water was still flush against the plywood, but it did not seem so high. It seemed it was going to hold. It remained a frightening sight, however; the lake surface was simply too high, as in some optical illusion; yet undeniably there below us, spread vast and colorful in the morning light.

So the dam held. But our celebration, after pumps arrived and we slowly lowered the water level back below the top of the dam, was muted, almost stunned. We too were drained, so to speak. Looking at the wet curve of plywood sheets topping the dam, Mary said, "By God, Stephan, we did a Nadia on that dam!"

Later of course they took it out. I cannot say I regret it.

Big Man in Love

When Big Man fell in love with a human woman, it was big trouble.

Her name was Zoya. Yes, she had the same first name as Zo Boone—she was a clone of Zo's, in fact, cloned by Zo's friends after Zo's fatal accident. So genetically Zoya was another daughter of Jackie's, therefore granddaughter of Kasei, and great-granddaughter of John Boone himself. That wasn't all; because Zo's body had floated for a while in the north sea, she had been slightly salted, and thereby became inadvertently related to the resurgent archaea. And in that salty fizzing primeval soup of a sea it seems she also picked up traits of kelp and limpet, dolphin and sea otter, and who knows what else. So she was a lot of things—big like Paul Bunyan, wild like Zo, rebellious like the archaea, happy like John, and as stormy and tempestuous as the northern sea. That was Zoya; Zoya was everything. She swam through icebergs, and flew in the jet stream, and ran the round-the-worlder for an afternoon jog. She drank and she smoked and she took strange drugs, she had casual sex with strangers and even with friends, and she skipped work anytime the waves were big. In short, she was a thrill seeker; she was a disgrace to propriety and morality; she mocked all principles of human progress. She could kill with a glance or a palm punch to the nose. Her motto was "Fun at all costs."

Thus when Big Man dropped by Mars one day, and saw Zoya out surfing the hundred-meter waves of the Polar Peninsula, it was love at first sight. This was his kind of woman!

And Zoya proved agreeable. She liked big men, and Big Man was a big man. So they played around Mars together, Big Man stepping carefully in his old footsteps to avoid wreaking any new havoc, and trying hard not to get tangled in things. But he couldn't help it. They gamboled along the Ius Ridge Trail, and his tiptoeing is what brought down all those cliffs ten years ago. He went swimming with Zoya and that's what flooded Boone's Neck peninsula, even though he only went in knee deep. He flew in the jet stream with her and his shadow caused the first year without a summer. They didn't notice any of that; they were having too much fun together.

They even tried to have sex together. Zoya would climb into Big Man's ears and fool around, and afterward he would hold her in the palm of his hand and moan like King Kong with Fay Wray, you know, Come on, baby, please let's make love, make love with me, and she would just laugh and point down at his erection and say, Sorry, Big Man. I'd like to but you won't fit. Why it'd take me all day just to climb that willful tower, it'd be as hard as climbing Dishes in the Sink or the Other Old Man of Hoy. And to show him she even tried a little of that too, free-climbing to the overhang and massaging what she could reach. But to Big Man it felt like he was being pinched by an ant.

Too bad, she would say, going for a swim. Best I can do.

But I gotta, moaned Big Man, I wanna, I hafta, I needta, the usual line, familiar to guys and gals everywhere. But this time there was nothing to be done. Sorry, Zoya would say. No can do. If only you were smaller.

Then one time, looking a bit flushed and frustrated herself, she said, Look, it's a matter of will. If only you were smaller we'd be fine! I'd ride you all night. Maybe you should look into getting yourself a smaller cock.

What? Big Man cried. What do you mean?

I mean a smaller cock. You know, get a transplant. Have that one cut off and a smaller one sewn on in its place.

A *smaller* one? Cut *off*?

That's what the situation calls for, big guy. That's what will have to happen for us to work out.

What? What?

Transplant! Transplant! You can get one wherever you get organ transplants. Hospitals, right?

No way, said Big Man. For one thing—and there's a lot more than one here—transplanted organs come from cadavers.

You could get your own cultured and grown to a smaller size. They do stuff like that now.

Oh please, Big Man said. It makes me queasy just *talking* about this stuff.

Not my fault, Zoya said. Where there's a will there's a way. And she went out flying by herself.

Well, you know. Life was no fun anymore. Eventually Big Man got desperate. He got so desperate that he very surreptitiously began looking into the matter, going to a clinic and telling the people there a clever story about a friend of his who had a very small fiancée. And he found out that the latest in what people called starfish biotechnology was indeed up to the task as described. He could have his private parts surgically removed and replaced by a cultured replacement grown from cells of the original. Cells from its most sensitive part, one doctor assured him. A two-magnitude reduction done twice would make him about right for Zoya.

Peace of mind left Big Man. He was cast on the horns of a dilemma, one big one small. This is horrible! he said. This is ridiculous! I will not do this. I will forget her. He left the cosmetic urology clinic and did not return.

But the fact of the matter is that Big Man was in love, and Big Man's love was a big love. And love is a big thing; a very willful thing. And a life without love is a sad thing. And a life without Zoya was dull beyond belief.

So finally one day Big Man said, All right all right all right, and dragged back to the clinic to let them take some cells from the most sensitive spot. It hurt a lot.

After that he went out to the Oort cloud to commune with himself. We'll draw a curtain on that scene and let him have some private time, and only say that when he came back, looking tired and apprehensive, he declared himself ready. And Zoya held his hand while they administered several liters of general anesthetic to him, and performed the operation, and when he came to he had private parts twice two magnitudes smaller than before.

Ridiculous, he said.

As a tribute to his courage Zoya had his old organ chemically petrified and airlifted out to the Hellespontus, where it was placed next to the rock tower called Dishes in the Sink. It has since become a popular climbing tower, as you know, sporting scores of routes up it.

And after all the stitches had dissolved and Big Man was physically healed, Zoya took him up to the shores of Chryse Gulf, in midsummer, to a favorite beach of hers, an empty strand on a lost bay.

Will you love me now? Big Man asked her.

I will, Zoya said.

Here again we will draw a curtain and give them some privacy. Suffice it to say that when they came back south, Big Man was light on his feet for the first time; he was walking ten meters off the ground. He hadn't known it could be so good.

Later on Zoya left him and broke his heart, unfortunately, and he had to get used to that, as well as to his organ being just a sweet little thing between his legs. It was kind of strange, but not really bad. It meant that when he met other human women he liked, he was sometimes able to form quite satisfactory relationships with them. And occasionally he would run into Zoya, and sometimes they would renew their old affair, with considerable passion. So that all in all, in the long run, looking at everything that had happened since and putting it all in the balance, he judged that it had been worth it. And the climbers on Mars continue to appreciate the decision as well.

An Argument for the Deployment of All Safe Terraforming Technologies

The Oxia River runs heavy with silt after storms on Margaritifer Terra, and the muddy water pours through the sandbars at the river's mouth and stains Chryse Gulf as red as blood, in a bloom extending three or four kilometers out toward the archipelago on the horizon. When the flow recedes, and the silt settles to the bottom, the river's channel is almost always changed. The mouth might have moved all the way to the other end of the beach. The old channel then silts up, its underwater banks continuing to serve as point breaks for incoming waves, until the waves wear them down. It's all new, week by week, storm by storm—except for the elements involved, of course: sun, sea, sky; the bluffs nosing out into the sea, the river canyon between them; the river's final beach-dammed lagoon, the dunes, the river water rippling out the break and over the tide bars to slide under the waves of the shorebreak. These are always there.

"Always" in the relative sense, of course. I mean that for years it had been this way. But on Mars the landscape is a matter of perpetual change. Punctuated equilibrium, as Sax once said, without the equilibrium. And the cooling of the 2210s, the years without summer, was such that if something were not done, this river-mouth scene would not exist like this for many more years.

But the methods that seemed to contain any hope of stopping the trend sounded drastic indeed. For someone who loves the land, the idea of a million thermonuclear explosions in the deep regolith is a shocking thing, an ugly thing. You can make all the arguments you like about the containment of radiation, about the essential heat from below, even about the disposal of old Terran weapons, and still it doesn't seem like something an environmentalist should approve.

And it didn't help that there were advocates using the stupidest language possible to argue for the various heavy-industrial methods being proposed. These were people who did not understand the power of language. They would speak casually of a "manifest destiny" for Mars, as if this phrase did not come from a determinate moment in American history, a moment inextricably tied to imperialist wars of conquest, to idiot yahoo patriotism, and to a genocide that most Americans still did not like to admit had occurred. So that to use that horrible old phrase to describe the rescue of the Martian biosphere was insane; but some people did it anyway.

And other people, like Irishka, were extremely put off by it. And all because of words. I sat through the whole of that session of the global environmental court, listening to the arguments pro and con, and though my work is in words I thought to myself, This is absurd, this is horrible. Language is nothing but a huge set of false analogies. There has to be a better way to make one's point.

So when the session was over I got Irishka and her partner Freya to come with me, and we took the equatorial piste west to Ares Fjord, then drove northwest up the shore of Chryse Gulf to the gravel road that went out to Soochow Point, above the Oxia River's broad beach of a mouth. Early one summer morning we drove around a turn in the sea-cliff road, and all was clear. The horizon was a clean line between sea and sky. Both were blue: the sky a very dark blue with purplish tinges, as if there were a red shell above the blue one; the sea a blue almost black, its water on this day transparent to a great depth. The land was the usual red rock, though here tinted blackish, as it tended to be through the region, darkening as you move east toward black Syrtis. There was no wind, and the stillness of the water was such that the waves broke as in a wave tank in a physics class, peeling cleanly across their breaks, purring in, leaving white tapestries fizzing behind them, until the shorebreak foamed up the wet red strand.

I saw right away that the bottom had changed again in the most recent storm. There was a new point break off to the far left side of the beach. And this offshore sandbar was angled perfectly to the morning's incoming swell, which was fairly big. Probably there was a hard wind blowing down Kasei's great canyon and fjord on the other side of Chryse Gulf, creating these waves some thirteen hundred kilometers away. We could see the swells right out to the horizon, crests perfectly spaced and slightly bowed toward us, like arcs of a circle bigger than the Chryse Gulf itself, sweeping in to curl around Soochow Point and onto our beach, one after the next, all pitching over first at the new point break, then breaking in a continuous clean line all the way across the beach to the new river mouth, far to the right. The break was swift but not too swift, and each was slightly different, of course, shallow bowls giving way to quick walls, or long tubular sections purling over in perfect clear waterfalls. Conditions could never be more perfect. "Oh my God," Irishka said. "Heaven has come."

We parked on the bluff just above the beach, got out of the car and put on our wetsuits, then walked down the path and across the beach with flippers in hand. The shorebreak foam ran over our booties and we hooted at the cold water seeping into our wetsuits at the calves—it was about eight or ten degrees, but quickly warmed up. We walked out to where it was waist-deep, then put on fins and pulled up our wetsuit hoods, and dived under the next breaker. Though only our faces were exposed, that was enough to have us all screaming at the shock of the cold, standing again chest deep. We breasted out, still on foot, turning our backs when the waves crashed into us, then dived under a tall white wall of broken water and started swimming.

It was hard work getting outside. The waves always look smaller from the beach, and smaller still from up on a bluff, especially when there's no one riding them to give you a sense of scale. Now we saw firsthand that the broken waves were walls between two and three meters overhead, and getting under one of those can be a workout if you don't do it right. And no matter how good wetsuits have gotten, it still feels cold in them at first.

I dived deep just before a wall hit me and relaxed, letting the bottom of the wave's underwater revolution shove me back. A bit of turbulence shook me like a flag in a wind, then pushed me up hard, out of the break. I hit the surface swimming head-up freestyle as hard as I could, through the hissing wrack to the next boiling wall, where I dived under again. If you time it right, so that you use the waves' underwater action to help you, it makes getting out much easier than if you fight the break directly. Irishka is a real master at this, and on this day as always she was already far ahead of us.

Six times under for me, and then I saw that I might make it over or through the next wave just before it broke, so I sprinted hard, kicking my long fins and feeling the backwash sucking me out as well, and flew up the face of the next wave and smashed through the clear upper section, then fell down the back of it and swam on to get free of the turbulence. Outside!

And the next wave was just a lift into the air, giving me a brief view around. I was floating just down the line from the point break, and I could see Irishka and Freya already out there ahead of me. Irishka swam out to a wave, then turned and was swimming backstroke hard when the wave picked her up—a big mass of water, a mound swelling into a wall as if by magic, carrying Irishka higher and higher on it.

Then she spun onto her chest and fell down the face of the wave. She extended her webbed gloves down and before her, making a little planing surface, then twisted and made a sharp bottom turn, throwing a white wing of water out away from her cut. Wetsuits these days are much like birdsuits, in that they stiffen in reaction to the stress on them, and the knees will lock together, allowing Irishka to hydroplane over the water's surface, touching it only with her hands, lower legs, and fins.

She skidded like that out onto the broad shoulder of the wave, which was breaking left at a steady majestic pace, not fast except in occasional bowl sections, which she fired across; but usually she had time enough to carve lines up and down the face, slipping up near the crest and then shooting down and dangerously far out in front of the break, where in effect she had to catch the wave all over again, but with much more momentum this time, so she could rise back up the steepening face toward the waterfall that was pitching out over the flat water below. A tube, yes! There was a fast section mid-beach, it appeared, where the wave went tubular for long stretches, so that Irishka disappeared from my sight for seconds, then shot out of the tube high onto the shoulder, cutting down again to stay in the wave.

Yow! I cried, and swam hard for the point break. Freya took off on one just as I arrived, and disappeared past me with a whoop. Now I had the break entirely to myself, and the very next wave looked just as good as all the previous ones, even a bit better. I swam for the steepest part of it, and saw I had gotten to its takeoff zone in time, and so turned and swam hard for shore. The wave picked me up and I began falling down its face, and knew I had caught it. After a big turn at the bottom I barreled out onto the shoulder of the wave, studying the wave rising up under me to my left, but aware also of the rivermouth canyon standing to my right, and the sky. I was riding the wave as if it were a toboggan ride, down a shifting hill perpetually swinging up into reality before me.

The experience of riding a wave is so strange it is hard to describe. During the ride time changes, or I should say consciousness of time changes—if these are not the same statement. The moment balloons.

You seem to notice ten or a hundred times as many things as you could in any ordinary second. Yet at the same time, or in a paradoxical oscillation, everything seems to rush by in a moment. Each ride seems to be a timeless little eternity, jammed into a few seconds. Often the rides really are only a few seconds long, but they feel that way at their ends even if they have lasted a minute or more. Maybe it's just that at the end you always feel it wasn't long enough!

However one experiences these knots in time, afterward one can scarcely remember the details of what has been a day of perpetual activity, on the part of both you and the world. Something impedes the memory; there aren't the words for it, perhaps. One ride merges with the next, and at the end of the day, back on the beach in ordinary reality, if you struggle to remember, only certain peak moments come to mind, moments of vision where an image or a movement branded itself in the brain for good, to come back in unexpected moments and unremembered dreams.

So of any particular ride that day I can say little, although the first of the day (like most firsts) stuck better than most. It was a long and eventful ride, like all the rest that followed. I planed across the shoulder, roller-coastering up and down as the wave bulged beneath me, feeling the way my body was both still and moving rapidly, shifting my angles to stay in the right spot. I saw the fast section coming, and stalled back into a tube that lasted for some time; then I saw the tube was collapsing, and shot out of its last little oval gate, skidding back out high on the shoulder and almost off the back side of the swell, so that I did a 360 spinner to fall back into the wave, and nailed a bottom turn to fly on again. The ride went on like that for the whole length of the beach, lasting almost two minutes.

And all the rides were like that. When they ended we found it easier to roll like grunion onto the shore, spent, and walk back down the beach and swim out at the point, than it would have been to swim out and back south the length of the beach. So we all three got rides and then walked back together, kicking the shallows into fans of spray ahead of us, exclaiming over the rides, and looking around at the sun-drenched day. Then back out for another strenuous fight to get outside, and another wild ride.

The waves got bigger as morning gave way to afternoon, and a wind finally disturbed the glassy surface of the water. It was an offshore wind, however, the surfer's friend; it held the waves up for us by swooshing downcanyon into the afternoon sun, stalling the breaks and whipping spray off their tops, spray that fell like heavy rain onto the back side of the waves. Looking down the line as we bobbed over the crests, we saw some of those brief rainbows in the blown spray that the Hawaiians call *ehukai*. And late in the day I took off and saw Irishka dropping in ahead of me on the shoulder of the same wave, and after a timeless time I was streaking along deep in the tube behind her, both of us as still as statues and yet flying through a great rolling tube of water swirling up on our left and out over our heads. And I saw the tube close-out begin ahead of Irishka, and both of us turned up and burst back out into the air at the same time, inside the spray flung back by the wind, and I looked over and saw her suspended in the *ehukai* with her arms outstretched, like a mermaid trying to fly up a rainbow.

Selected Abstracts from The Journal of Areological Studies

"A Possible Indigenous Nano-organism Found in the Ceraunius Tholus Region." Vol. 56, 2 November m61. By Forbes, G.N., and Taneev, V.L. et al., Department of Microbiology, Acheron Institute for Areological Studies.

SNC Crater, at the foot of the north flank of Ceraunius Tholus, is well supported as the source of the SNC meteorites found on Earth (cf. Clayborne and Frazier, m4d). Drillings were made to a depth of 1 km under the north flank of Ceraunius Tholus, in locations where the ground was 10–50 microkelvins warmer than the flank median. Most drill sites were within 4 kms of the prominent lava channel running from the Ceraunius caldera down into SNC Crater. Five drill shafts on the west side of the laval channel (see map 1) encountered the collapsed remains of a thermal spring, which contained ice and pockets of liquid water in the ml. range. The walls of these fractures exhibited ovoid forms, all under 20 nanometers long, resembling the structures found in SNC meteorite ALH 84001. No metabolic activity was detected in the Ceraunius forms, but electron microscopy reveals what appear to be cell walls, and RNA protein fragments within the forms. PCR was performed on the samples using primers specific for ribosomal RNA, and the products were sequenced, revealing a magnetotactic sequence similar to Terran marine methanogens. Some silicates in the collapsed thermal vent near the recovered material also exhibit stratified spongiform structures highly stromatolitic in appearance, the strata two magnitudes finer than that observed in Terran samples. It is suggested that these are stromatolites, and that the ovoid forms are archaea or nanobacteria, either dormant or slowed metabolically in response to a long-failing environment.

"Terran Origins Possible in the Ceraunius Basement Samples." Vol. 57, 1 January m62. By Claparede, R., and Borazjani, H.X. et al., Department of Ecology, University of Mars, Burroughs.

We examined the nanobacteria-like structures discovered in drill samples on the north flank of Ceraunius Tholus (cf. Forbes and Taneev, m61a). They exhibit the carbonates, magnetites, and PAHs seen in ALH 84001, but no movement or metabolic action. As in the case of ALH 84001 in Antarctica, recent contamination of the rock is a possibility, in this case anthropogenic contamination; hydration of the fault in question may have occurred when the lava tunnel on Ceraunius Tholus was used as a streambed, from m15 to m38. Also, while the samples do contain magnetites, we question whether any indigenous archaea or nanobacteria would evolve to produce magnetites when Mars has a magnetic field so slight that it could not be registered for biological use.

"Ancient Areomagnetosphere Substantially Stronger in the Noachian Epoch Than at Present." Vol. 57, 2 April m62. By Kim, C.H., Institute of Areophysics, Senzeni Na; and Forbes, G.N., Department of Microbiology, Acheron Institute for Areological Studies.

Paleomagnetic studies in the southern half of the crustal dichotomy demonstrate that the paleointensity of the Martian magnetic field was as high as 250 to 1000 nT as recently as 1.3 Gyr ago, probably because of the presence of an active dynamo in the core. This suggests that Mars generated a magnetic moment greater than 10^{13} T-m^3 (compared with Earth's moment of 8 x 10^{15} T-m^3) throughout the Noachian, from approximately 4.1 Gyr to 1.3 Gyr (cf. Russell et al., m6j). Development of biomagnetism in any early indigenous life would therefore be unsurprising.

"Paleomagnetosphere Not Yet Determined." Vol. 57, 2 August m62. By Russell, S., Da Vinci Co-op Laboratories.

A survey of recent studies indicates the Martian magnetosphere was probably negligible after approximately 3.5 Gyr.

"Similarities between Indigenous Archaea Found under Ceraunius Tholus and the Columbia Basement Archaea

Methanospirillum jacobii." Vol. 58, 1 August m63. By Forbes, G.N., Department of Microbiology, University of Mars, Cairo; Taneev, V.L., Acheron Institute for Areological Studies; and Allan, P.F., Department of Microbiology, University of Mars, Cairo.

The archaealike organisms found in Ceraunius, and what appear to be nanofossils of these organisms, resemble in many physical and chemical respects the *Methanospirillum jacobii* found in the Columbia River basement rock (see Figure 1.2). Nitrogen in the Martian samples all exhibit the isotropically heavy nitrogen that distinguishes the atmosphere of Mars from virtually all other volatile reservoirs in the solar system, which eliminates contamination as a possible origin. Partial genomic analysis of RNA fragments in the Ceraunius organisms shows a 44.6% match with DNA from the Columbia basement archaea *Methanospirillum jacobii*. Such a match cannot be explained by independent origin. Seeding of life from one planet to the other is suggested as the most plausible explanation. Lewontin-Thierry mutation-rate analysis gives a tentative date for division of the two species at approximately 3.9 Gyr, near the end of the heavy bombardment.

"Preponderance of Left-Handedness Found in Ceraunius Archaeac Organisms' Amino Acids." Vol. 58, 2 October m63. By Forbes, G.N., Allan, P.F., and Wang, W.W., Department of Microbiology, University of Mars, Cairo; and Taneev, V.L., Acheron Institute for Areological Studies.

Left-handedness in amino acids found in *Archaea ceraunii* from Ceraunius Tholus is shown to predominate in proportion similar to the handedness of the Columbia basement *Methanospirillum jacobii* (cf. Ellsworth, N.W., 2067a). Organisms dead longer than 1 Myr would have yielded roughly the same amount of left- and right-handed amino acids in the sample, so the high incidence in the Ceraunius samples indicates some specimens must either still be alive, or have been alive in the last Myr. It is now well established (cf. Nabdullah, 2054) that extremophiles under worsening conditions react to the stress by slowing metabolisms to rates in which cell divisions occur less than once a century. With biologic functions temporarily suspended or greatly slowed, indications of life are clearest in biochemical states such as handedness.

"Genomic Analysis of Ceraunius and Columbia Nanobacteria Reveal Recent Division of Populations." Vol. 59, 1 February

m64. By Claparede, R. and Borazjani, H.X., Department of Ecology; and Olson, G.B., and Thresh, J.J. et al., Department of Microbiology, University of Mars, Burroughs.

We determined that, while there appear to be nanobacteria under the north flank of Ceraunius, genomic analysis of DNA fragments from both populations reveals they share 85.4% of their DNA. Mutation rates as recalibrated by Nguyen and McGonklin gave results indicating the two organisms underwent species division within the last 5000 generations. This suggests the rocks of Ceraunius Tholus were contaminated with Terran nanobacteria some 20 m-years ago, which is within the period when the lava tunnel on the north flank of the volcano was used as a streambed. This practice was discontinued by order of the global environmental court (cf. *GEC Proceedings*, m46, pp. 3245–47) because the floor of the tunnel was found to be too porous, and in the words of the report, "risk of contaminating the deep regolith is considerable."

"Stromatolitic Formations under Ceraunius Tholus Match Structure and Chemical Composition of Hydatogenic Geyserite Discovered under Tharsis Tholus." Vol. 60, 1 May m65. By Borazjani, H.X., Department of Ecology; Robertson, L.D., Wulf, V.W., and Flores, N., Department of Areology, University of Mars, Burroughs.

A siliceous deposit composed of nearly pure opaline silica was discovered during drilling in Tharsis Tholus. The thermal spring on the west flank, 4.2 kms below the surface, was still active, and the resulting geyserite formation was clearly abiologic in origin. No microbacteria, nanobacteria, archaea, or nanofossils were found in any retrieved rock, all of which was retrieved and handled using GEC-mandated sterilization techniques.

"Mitochondrial Analysis of *Archaea ceraunii* and Columbia *Methanospirillum jacobii* Indicate the Ceraunius Population Is the Older of the Two." Vol. 60, 2 May m65. By Forbes, G.N., Department of Microbiology, and Pieron, I.I., Department of Genetics, University of Mars, Cairo; and Kim, C.H., Institute of Areophysics, Senzeni Na.

Though abiologic processes account for geyserite formations in Ceraunius Tholus, imbibition rates for basaltic lava as calculated by Russell et al., m12t, indicate that the archaea coating the fractures in the basalt cannot have penetrated quickly enough into the rock to be anthropogenic in origin. Mitochondrial analysis clearly shows that the fossil *Archaea ceraunii* found on site along with living specimens are older than any dated Columbia basement *Methanospirillum*. Mitochondrial analysis also suggests that the descendant Terran species split from its ancestor about 180 Myr, the time when SNC Crater was formed, and the SNC meteorites thereby cast into space (cf. Matheson, N., 1997b). This indicates that the Terran archaea may have arrived on Earth in the SNC meteorites.

"SNC Crater Not Necessarily the Source of SNC Meteorites."
Vol. 60, 1 December m65. By Claparede, R., Department of
Ecology; Xthosa, N., Institute of Areophysics, Senzeni Na; and
Taneev, V.L., Acheron Institute for Areological Studies.
Spectrographic analyses of the Shergotty and Zagami meteorites show that both diabase stones consist mainly of the pyroxenes pigeonite and augite, and of maskelynite, a shocked plagioclase glass. The maskelynite is zoned, with accessory phases of titanomagnetite, ilmenite, pyrrhotite, fayalite, tridymite, whitlockite, chlorapatite, and baddeleyite. In situ investigation of the brecciated diabase in SNC Crater and surrounding region reveal that ilmenite and whitlockite are missing from this inventory. Studies at another oval crater about the same age and size on the Elysium Massif, Crater Tf, show that it has the same brecciated diabase, with the same phase accessories, as SNC Crater and environs. The Crater Tf diabase also exhibits a poikilitic texture like that seen in the Chassigny meteorite (Banin, Clark, and Wänke, 1992). Either crater could have been the origin for the SNC meteorites so far found on Earth.

"Exotic Features in *Archaea ceraunii* Confirm Indigenous
Origin." Vol. 64, 1 April m69. By Forbes, G.N., Department of
Biology, Sabishii College.
Proportions of isotropically heavy nitrogen unique to Mars are present in the archaea found 2.3 kms beneath the surface of Ceraunius Tholus, in ancient thermal springs. Mitochondrial analysis using the revised Thurmond equations confirms that *Archaea ceraunii* and the Columbia basement nanobacteria *Methanospirillum jacobii* split from a common ancestor from 6000 to 15,000 generations ago. Rates of mutation in extremophiles that have radically slowed their metabolisms are not yet certain, but there are strong indications that they may be well over a magnitude slower than described by earlier estimates (cf. Whitebook, H., m33f). This means the Ceraunius and Columbia

nanobacteria could have split into separate species over 1.8 Gyr. Imbibition rates in basalt are <1 cm/Myr (cf. Russell et al., m12t), and not all of the *Archaea ceraunii* were found on the surfaces of cracked rocks in the thermal vent; some were recovered as much as a meter deep inside unbroken samples. These and other considerations show that *Archaea ceraunii* cannot have been placed in situ by anthropogenic action; there has not been enough time for them to get there. Indigenous origin is the only good explanation of all the data.

Keyword Search

In-*The Journal of Areological Studies*, vols. 65–75

Keyword-*Archaea ceraunii*

No match found.

Odessa

Oh in those days we were so happy. In love, sure. Just the two of us;
no kids; interesting work; lots of free time; all Mars there to be explored together. We would go out into the backcountry on long
walkabouts, wandering and talking. Out under the stars at night. For
several years we spent the fall in Odessa, where we had work in the
vineyards and wineries. We rented a little house in the beach village
a few kilometers west of Odessa, at the end of the tram line. A hillside village, looking down on a crook of a beach, buildings clustered
at the bottom, scattered among the trees higher up. Our house was
pretty high on the hill, with a view down over treetops and tile
roofs, and the broad blue plate of the Hellas Sea. Little patio out
back, a table and two chairs. A lot of flowering vines, a little lemon
tree in a tub. Almost all the summer visitors would be gone by then,
so that only one restaurant stayed open, down behind the beach.
The cats were friendly and looked sleek and well fed, though no one
owned them. In the restaurant one jumped right into my lap and
purred. I remember the first time we stood on the patio, looking
down, then back at the house—whitewash, vines, the bedroom balcony with an iron railing, the brown hills above and behind, the sea
and the sky. We laughed at how perfect it was. Most mornings we
trammed into town to work, then came back in the afternoons and
went to the beach. Or vice versa. Sunset on the patio with a glass of
wine. Dinners in our little kitchen, or down at the restaurant, where
a guitar and mandolin duo played on Fridays. Then nights in bed in

a house all to ourselves. Sometimes I woke before dawn and went down to start coffee and go out on the patio. One of those mornings the sky was plastered with a herringbone cloud that turned pink, then gold.

Sexual Dimorphism

The potential for hallucination in paleogenomics was high. There was not only the omnipresent role of instrumentation in the envisioning of the ultramicroscopic fossil material, but also the metamorphosis over time of the material itself, both the DNA and its matrices, so that the data were invariably incomplete, and often shattered. Thus the possibility of psychological projection of patterns onto the *rorschacherie* of what in the end might be purely mineral processes had to be admitted.

Dr. Andrew Smith was as aware of these possibilities as anyone. Indeed it constituted one of the central problems of his field—convincingly to sort the traces of DNA in the fossil record, distinguishing them from an array of possible pseudofossils. Pseudofossils littered the history of the discipline, from the earliest false nautiloids to the famous Martian pseudonanobacteria. Nothing progressed in paleogenomics unless you could show that you really were talking about what you said you were talking about. So Dr. Smith did not get too excited, at first, about what he was finding in the junk DNA of an early dolphin fossil.

In any case there were quite a few distractions to his work at that time. He was living on the south shore of the Amazonian Sea, that deep southerly bay of the world-ringing ocean, east of Elysium, near the equator. In the summers, even the cool summers they had been having lately, the extensive inshore shallows of the sea grew as warm as blood, and dolphins—adapted from Terran river dolphins like the baiji from China, or the boto from the Amazon, or the susu from the

Ganges, or the bhulan from the Indus—sported just off the beach. Morning sunlight lanced through the waves and picked out their flashing silhouettes, sometimes groups of eight or ten of them, all playing in the same wave.

The marine laboratory he worked at, located on the seafront of the harbor town Eumenides Point, was associated with the Acheron labs, farther up the coast to the west. The work at Eumenides had mostly to do with the shifting ecologies of a sea that was getting saltier. Dr. Smith's current project dealing with this issue involved investigating the various adaptations of extinct cetaceans who had lived when the Earth's sea had exhibited different levels of salt. He had in his lab some fossil material, sent to the lab from Earth for study, as well as the voluminous literature on the subject, including the full genomes of all the living descendants of these creatures. The transfer of fossils from Earth introduced the matter of cosmic-ray contamination to all the other problems involved in the study of ancient DNA, but most people dismissed these effects as minor and inconsequential, which was why fossils were shipped across at all. And of course with the recent deployment of fusion-powered rapid vehicles, the amount of exposure to cosmic rays had been markedly reduced. Smith was therefore able to do that research on mammal salt tolerance both ancient and modern, thus helping to illuminate the current situation on Mars, also joining the ongoing debates concerning the paleohalocycles of the two planets, now one of the hot research areas in comparative planetology and bioengineering.

Nevertheless, it was a field of research so arcane that if you were not involved in it, you tended not to believe in it. It was an offshoot, a mix of two difficult fields, its ultimate usefulness a long shot, especially compared to most of the inquiries being conducted at the Eumenides Point Labs. Smith found himself fighting a feeling of marginalization in the various lab meetings and informal gatherings, in coffee lounges, cocktail parties, beach luncheons, boating excursions. At all of these he was the odd man out, with only his colleague Frank Drumm, who worked on reproduction in the dolphins currently living offshore, expressing any great interest in his work and its applications. Worse yet, his work appeared to be becoming less and less important to his adviser and employer, Vlad Taneev, who as one of the First Hundred, and the cofounder of the Acheron labs, was ostensibly the most powerful scientific mentor one could have on Mars; but who in practice turned out to be nearly impossible to access, and rumored to be in failing health, so that it was like having no boss at all, and therefore no access to the lab's technical staff and so forth. A bitter disappointment.

And then of course there was Selena—his partner, roommate, girl-friend, significant other, lover—there were many words for their rela-tionship, though none was quite right. The woman with whom he lived, with whom he had gone through graduate school and two postdocs, with whom he had moved to Eumenides Point, taking a small apartment near the beach, near the terminus of the coastal tram, where when one looked back east the point itself just heaved over the horizon, like a dorsal fin seen far out to sea. Selena was making great progress in her own field, genetically engineering salt grasses; a subject of great importance there, where they were trying to stabilize a thousand-kilometer coastline of low dunes and quicksand swamps. Scientific and bioengineering progress; important achievements, relevant to the situation; all things were coming to her professionally, including of course offers to team up in any number of exciting public/co-op collaborations.

And all things were coming to her privately as well. Smith had al-ways thought her beautiful, and now he saw that with her success, other men were coming to the same realization. It took only a little attention to see it; an ability to look past shabby lab coats and a gen-erally unkempt style to the sleekly curving body and the intense, al-most ferocious intelligence. No—his Selena looked much like all the rest of the lab rats when in the lab, but in the summers when the group went down in the evening to the warm tawny beach to swim, she walked out the long expanse of the shallows like a goddess in a bathing suit, like Venus returning to the sea. Everyone in these parties pretended not to notice, but they couldn't help it.

All very well; except that she was losing interest in him. This was a process that Smith feared was irreversible; or, to be more precise, that if it had gotten to the point where he could notice it, it was too late to stop it. So now he watched her, furtive and helpless, as they went through their domestic routines; there was a goddess in his bath-room, showering, drying off, dressing, each moment like a dance.

But she didn't chat anymore. She was absorbed in her thoughts, and tended to keep her back to him. No—it was all going away.

They had met in an adult swim club in Mangala, while they were both grad students at the university there. Now, as if to reinvoke that time, Smith took up Frank's suggestion and joined him at an equiva-lent club in Eumenides Point, and began to swim regularly again. He went from the tram or the lab down to the big fifty-meter pool, set on a terrace overlooking the ocean, and swam so hard in the mornings that the whole rest of the day he buzzed along in a flow of beta-endorphins, scarcely aware of his work problems or the situation at home. After work he took the tram home feeling his appetite kick in, and banged around the kitchen throwing together a meal and eating much of it as he cooked it, irritated (if she was there at all) with Selena's poor cooking and her cheery talk about her work, irritated also probably just from hunger, and dread at the situation hanging over them; at this pretense that they were still in a normal life. But if he snapped at her during this fragile hour she would go silent the whole rest of the evening; it happened fairly often; so he tried to contain his temper and make the meal and quickly eat his part of it, to get his blood-sugar level back up.

Either way she fell asleep abruptly around nine, and he was left to read into the timeslip, or even slip out and take a walk on the night beach a few hundred yards away from their apartment. One night, walking west, he saw Pseudophobos pop up into the sky like a distress flare down the coast, and when he came back into the apartment Selena was awake and talking happily on the phone; she was startled to see him, and cut the call short, thinking about what to say, and then said, "That was Mark, we've gotten tamarisk three fifty-nine to take repetitions of the third salt flusher gene!"

"That's good," he said, moving into the dark kitchen so she wouldn't see his face.

That annoyed her. "You really don't care how my work goes, do you."

"Of course I do. That's good, I said."

She dismissed that with a noise.

Then one day he got home and Mark was there with her, in the living room, and at a single glance he could see they had been laughing about something; had been sitting closer together than when he started opening the door. He ignored that and was as pleasant as he could be.

The next day as he swam at the morning workout, he watched the women swimming with him in his lane. All three of them had swum all their lives, their freestyle stroke perfected beyond the perfection of any dance move ever made on land, the millions of repetitions making their movement as unconscious as that of the fish in the sea. Under the surface he saw their bodies flowing forward, revealing their sleek lines—classic swimmer lines, like Selena's—rangy shoulders tucking up against their ears one after the next, rib cages smoothed over by powerful lats, breasts flatly merged into big pecs or else bobbing left then right, as the case might be; bellies meeting high hipbones accentuated by the high cut of their swimsuits, backs curving up to bottoms rounded and compact, curving to powerful thighs then long calves, and feet outstretched like ballerinas'. Dance was a weak analogy for such beautiful movement. And it all went on for stroke after stroke, lap after lap, until he was mesmerized beyond further thought or observation; it was just one aspect of a sensually saturated environment.

Their current lane leader was pregnant, yet swimming stronger than any of the rest of them, not even huffing and puffing during their rest intervals, when Smith often had to suck air—instead she laughed and shook her head, exclaiming, "Every time I do a flip turn he keeps kicking me!" She was seven months along, round in the middle like a little whale, but still she fired down the pool at a rate none of the other three in the lane could match. The strongest swimmers in the club were simply amazing. Soon after getting into the sport, Smith had worked hard to swim a hundred-meter freestyle in less than a minute, a goal appropriate to him, and finally he had done it once at a meet and been pleased; then later he heard about the local college women's team's workout, which consisted of a hundred hundred-meter freestyle swims *all on a minute interval*. He understood then that although all humans looked roughly the same, some were stupendously stronger than others. Their pregnant leader was in the lower echelon of these strong swimmers, and regarded the swim she was making today as a light stretching-out, though it was beyond anything her lane mates could do with their best efforts. You couldn't help watching her when passing by in the other direction, because despite her speed she was supremely smooth and effortless—she took fewer strokes per lap than the rest of them, and yet still made substantially better time. It was like magic. And that sweet blue curve of the new child inside.

Back at home things continued to degenerate. Selena often worked late, and talked to him less than ever.

"I love you," he said. "Selena, I love you."

"I know."

He tried to throw himself into his work. They were at the same lab, they could go home late together. Talk like they used to about their work, which though not the same, was still genomics in both cases;

how much closer could two sciences be? Surely it would help to bring them back together.

But genomics was a very big field. It was possible to occupy different parts of it, no doubt about that. They were proving it. Smith persevered, however, using a new and more powerful electron microscope, and he began to make some headway in unraveling the patterns in his fossilized DNA.

It looked like what had been preserved in the samples he had been given was almost entirely what used to be called the junk DNA of the creature. In times past this would have been bad luck, but the Kohl labs in Acheron had recently been making great strides in unraveling the various purposes of junk DNA, which proved not to be useless after all, as might have been guessed, evolution being as parsimonious as it was. Their breakthrough consisted in characterizing very short and scrambled repetitive sequences within junk DNA that could be shown to code instructions for higher hierarchical operations than they were used to seeing at the gene level—cell differentiation, information order sequencing, apoptosis and the like.

Using this new understanding to unravel any clues in partially degraded fossil junk DNA would be hard, of course. But the nucleotide sequences were there in his EM images—or, to be more precise, the characteristic mineral replacements for the adenine-thymine and cytosine-guanine couplets, replacements well established in the literature, were there to be clearly identified. Nanofossils, in effect; but legible to those who could read them. And once read, it was then possible to brew identical sequences of living nucleotides, matching the originals of the fossil creature. In theory one could re-create the creature itself, though in practice nothing like the entire genome was ever there, making it impossible. Not that there weren't people trying anyway with simpler fossil organisms, either going for the whole thing or using hybrid DNA techniques to graft expressions they could decipher onto living templates, mostly descendants of the earlier creature.

With this particular ancient dolphin, almost certainly a freshwater dolphin (though most of these were fairly salt tolerant, living in river mouths as they did), complete resuscitation would be impossible. It wasn't what Smith was trying to do anyway. What would be interesting would be to find fragments that did not seem to have a match in the living descendants' genome, then hopefully synthesize living in vitro fragments, clip them into contemporary strands, and see how these experimental animals did in hybridization tests and in various environments. Look for differences in function.

He was also doing mitochondrial tests when he could, which if successful would permit tighter dating for the species' divergence from precursor species. He might be able to give it a specific slot on the marine mammal family tree, which during the early Pliocene was very complicated.

Both avenues of investigation were labor-intensive, time-consuming, almost thoughtless work—perfect, in other words. He worked for hours and hours every day, for weeks, then months. Sometimes he managed to go home on the tram with Selena; more often he didn't. She was writing up her latest results with her collaborators, mostly with Mark. Her hours were irregular. When he was working he didn't have to think about that; so he worked all the time. It was not a solution, not even a very good strategy—it even seemed to be making things worse—and he had to attempt it against an ever-growing sense of despair and loss; but he did it nevertheless.

"What do you think of this Acheron work?" he asked Frank one day at work, pointing to the latest printout from the Kohl lab, lying heavily annotated on his desk.

"It's very interesting! It makes it look like we're finally getting past the genes to the whole instruction manual."

"If there is such a thing."

"Has to be, right? Though I'm not sure the Kohl lab's values for the rate adaptive mutants will be fixed are high enough. Ohta and Kimura suggested ten percent as the upper limit, and that fits with what I've seen."

Smith nodded, pleased. "They're probably just being conservative."

"No doubt, but you have to go with the data."

"So—in that context—you think it makes sense for me to pursue this fossil junk DNA?"

"Well, sure. What do you mean? It's sure to tell us interesting things."

"It's incredibly slow."

"Why don't you read off a long sequence, brew it up and venter it, and see what you get?"

Smith shrugged. Whole-genome shotgun sequencing struck him as slipshod, but it was certainly faster. Reading small bits of single-stranded DNA, called expressed sequence tags, had quickly identified most of the genes on the human genome; but it had missed some, and it ignored even the regulatory DNA sequences controlling the protein-coding portion of the genes, not to mention the so-called junk DNA itself, filling long stretches between the more clearly mean-ingful sequences.

Smith expressed his doubts to Frank, who nodded, but said, "It isn't the same now that the mapping is so complete. You've got so many reference points you can't get confused where your bits are on the big sequence. Just plug what you've got into the Lander-Waterman, then do the finishing with the Kohl variations, and even if there are massive repetitions, you'll still be okay. And with the bits you've got, well they're almost like ests anyway, they're so degraded. So you might as well give it a try."

Smith nodded.

That night he and Selena trammed home together. "What do you think of the possibility of shotgun sequencing in vitro copies of what I've got?" he asked her shyly.

"Sloppy," she said. "Double jeopardy."

A new schedule evolved. He worked, swam, took the tram home. Usually Selena wasn't there. Often their answering machine held messages for her from Mark, talking about their work. Or messages from her to Smith, telling him that she would be home late. As it was happening so often, he sometimes went out for dinner with Frank and other lane mates, after the evening workouts. One time at a beach restaurant they ordered several pitchers of beer, and then went out for a walk on the beach, and ended up running out into the shallows of the bay and swimming around in the warm dark water, so different from their pool, splashing each other and laughing hard. It was a good time.

But when he got home that night, there was another message on the answering machine from Selena, saying that she and Mark were working on their paper after getting a bite to eat, and that she would be home extra late.

She wasn't kidding; at two o'clock in the morning she was still out. In the long minutes following the timeslip Smith realized that no one stayed out so late working on a paper without calling home. This was therefore a message of a different kind.

Pain and anger swept through him, first one then the other. The indirection of it struck him as cowardly. He deserved at least a revelation—a confession—a scene. As the long minutes passed he got angrier and angrier; then frightened for a moment, that she might have been hurt or something. But she hadn't. She was out there somewhere fooling around. Suddenly he was furious.

He pulled cardboard boxes out of their closet and yanked open her drawers, and threw all her clothes in heaps into the boxes, crushing them in so they would all fit. But they gave off their characteristic scent of laundry soap and her, and smelling it he groaned and sat down on the bed, knees weak. If he carried through with this he would never again see her putting on and taking off these clothes, and just as an animal he groaned at the thought.

But men are not animals. He finished throwing her things into boxes, took them outside the front door, and dropped them there.

She came back at three. He heard her kick into the boxes and make some muffled exclamation.

He hurled open the door and stepped out.

"What's this?" She had been startled out of whatever scenario she had planned, and now was getting angry. Her, angry! It made him furious all over again.

"You know what it is."

"What!"

"You and Mark."

She eyed him.

"Now you notice," she said at last. "A year after it started. And this is your first response." Gesturing down at the boxes.

He hit her in the face.

Immediately he crouched at her side and helped her sit up, saying, "Oh God Selena I'm sorry, I'm sorry, I didn't mean to," he had only thought to slap her for her contempt, contempt that he had not noticed her betrayal earlier, "I can't believe I—"

"Get away"—striking him off with wild blows, crying and shouting, "Get away, get away"—frightened—"you bastard, you miserable bastard, what do you, don't you *dare* hit me!" in a near shriek, though she kept her voice down too, aware still of the apartment complex around them. Hands held to her face.

"I'm sorry, Selena. I'm very very sorry, I was angry at what you said but I know that isn't, that doesn't . . . I'm sorry." By now he was as angry at himself as he had been at her—what could he have been thinking, why had he given her the moral high ground like this, it was she who had broken their bond, it was she who should be in the wrong! She who was now sobbing—turning away—suddenly walking off into the night. Lights went on in a couple of windows nearby.

Smith stood staring down at the boxes of her lovely clothes, his right knuckles throbbing.

That life was over. He lived on alone in the apartment by the beach, and kept going in to work, but he was shunned there by the others, who all knew what had happened. Selena did not come in to work again until the bruises were gone, and after that she did not press charges, or speak to him about that night, but she did move in with Mark, and avoided Smith at work when she could. As who wouldn't. Occasionally she dropped by his nook to ask in a neutral voice about some logistical aspect of their breakup. He could not meet her eye. Nor could he meet the eye of anyone else at work, not properly. It was strange how one could have a conversation with people and appear to be meeting their gaze during it, when all the time they were not really quite looking at you and you were not really quite looking at them. Primate subtleties, honed over millions of years on the savannah.

He lost appetite, lost energy. In the morning he would wake up and wonder why he should get out of bed. Then looking at the blank walls of the bedroom, where Selena's prints had hung, he would sometimes get so angry at her that his pulse hammered uncomfortably in his neck and forehead. That got him out of bed, but then there was nowhere to go, except work. And there everyone knew he was a wife beater, a domestic abuser, an asshole. Martian society did not tolerate such people.

Shame or anger; anger or shame. Grief or humiliation. Resentment or regret. Lost love. Omnidirectional rage.

Mostly he didn't swim anymore. The sight of the swimmer women was too painful now, though they were as friendly as always; they knew nothing of the lab except him and Frank, and Frank had not said anything to them about what had happened. It made no difference. He was cut off from them. He knew he ought to swim more, and he swam less. Whenever he resolved to turn things around he would swim two or three days in a row, then let it fall away again.

Once at the end of an early-evening workout he had forced himself to attend—and now he felt better, as usual—while they were standing in the lane steaming, his three most constant lane mates made quick plans to go to a nearby trattoria after showering. One looked at him. "Pizza at Rico's?"

He shook his head. "Hamburger at home," he said sadly.

They laughed at this. "Ah come on. It'll keep another night."

"Come on, Andy," Frank said from the next lane. "I'll go too, if that's okay."

"Sure," the women said. Frank often swam in their lane too.

"Well . . ." Smith roused himself. "Okay."

He sat with them and listened to their chatter around the restaurant table. They still seemed to be slightly steaming, their hair wet and wisping away from their foreheads. The three women were young. It was interesting; away from the pool they looked ordinary and undistinguished: skinny, mousy, plump, maladroit, whatever. With their clothes on you could not guess at their fantastically powerful shoulders and lats, their compact smooth musculatures. Like seals dressed up in clown suits, waddling around a stage.

"Are you okay?" one asked him when he had been silent too long.

"Oh yeah, yeah." He hesitated, glanced at Frank. "Broke up with my girlfriend."

"Ah-ha! I *knew* it was something!" Hand to his arm (they all bumped into each other all the time in the pool): "You haven't been your usual self lately."

"No." He smiled ruefully. "It's been hard."

He could never tell them about what had happened. And Frank wouldn't either. But without that none of the rest of his story made any sense. So he couldn't talk about any of it.

They sensed this and shifted in their seats, preparatory to changing the topic. "Oh well," Frank said, helping them. "Lots more fish in the sea."

"In the pool," one of the women joked, elbowing him.

He nodded, tried to smile.

They looked at each other. One asked the waiter for the check, and another said to Smith and Frank, "Come with us over to my place, we're going to get in the hot tub and soak our aches away."

She rented a room in a little house with an enclosed courtyard, and all the rest of the residents were away. They followed her through the dark house into the courtyard, and took the cover off the hot tub and turned it on, then took their clothes off and got in the steaming water. Smith joined them, feeling shy. People on the beaches of Mars sunbathed without clothes all the time, it was no big deal really. Frank seemed not to notice, he was perfectly relaxed. But they didn't swim at the pool like this.

They all sighed at the water's heat. The woman from the house went inside and brought out some beer and cups. Light from the kitchen fell on her as she put down the dumpie and passed out the cups. Smith already knew her body perfectly well from their many hours together in the pool; nevertheless he was shocked seeing the whole of her. Frank ignored the sight, filling the cups from the dumpie.

They drank beer, talked small talk. Two were vets; their lane leader, the one who had been pregnant, was a bit older, a chemist in a pharmaceutical lab near the pool. Her baby was being watched by her co-op that night. They all looked up to her, Smith saw, even here. These days she brought the baby to the pool and swam just as powerfully as ever, parking the baby-carrier just beyond the splash line. Smith's muscles melted in the hot water, he sipped his beer while listening to them.

One of the women looked down at her breasts in the water and laughed. "They float like pull buoys."

Smith had already noticed that.

"No wonder women swim better than men."

"As long as they aren't so big they interfere with the hydrodynamics."

Their leader looked down through her fogged glasses, pink-faced, hair tied up, misted, demure. "I wonder if mine float less because I'm nursing."

"But all that milk."

"Yes but the water in the milk is neutral density, it's the fat that floats. It could be that empty breasts float even more than full ones."

"Whichever has more fat, yuck."

"I could run an experiment, nurse him from just one side and then get in and see—" But they were laughing too hard for her to complete this scenario. "It would work! Why are you laughing!"

They only laughed more. Frank was cracking up, looking blissed, blessed. These women friends trusted them. But Smith still felt set apart. He looked at their lane leader: a pink bespectacled goddess, serenely vague and unaware; the scientist as heroine; the first full human being.

But later when he tried to explain this feeling to Frank, or even just to describe it, Frank shook his head. "It's a bad mistake to worship women," he warned. "A category error. Women and men are so much the same it isn't worth discussing the difference. The genes are identical almost entirely, you know that. A couple hormonal expressions and that's it. So they're just like you and me."

"More than a couple."

"Not much more. We all start out female, right? So you're better off thinking that nothing major ever really changes that. Penis just an oversize clitoris. Men are women. Women are men. Two parts of a reproductive system, completely equivalent."

Smith stared at him. "You're kidding."

"What do you mean?"

"Well—I've never seen a man swell up and give birth to a new human being, let me put it that way."

"So what? It happens, it's a specialized function. You never see women ejaculating either. But we all go back to being the same afterward. Details of reproduction only matter a tiny fraction of the time. No, we're all the same. We're all in it together. There are no differences."

Smith shook his head. It would be comforting to think so. But the data did not support the hypothesis. Ninety-five percent of all the murders in history had been committed by men. This was a difference.

He said as much, but Frank was not impressed. The murder ratio was becoming more nearly equal on Mars, he replied, and much less frequent for everybody, thus demonstrating very nicely that the matter was culturally conditioned, an artifact of Terran patriarchy no longer relevant on Mars. Nurture rather than nature. Although it was a false dichotomy. Nature could prove anything you wanted, Frank insisted. Female hyenas were vicious killers, male bonobos and muriquis were gentle cooperators. It meant nothing, Frank said. It told them nothing.

But Frank had not hit a woman in the face without ever planning to.

Patterns in the fossil *Inia* data sets became clearer and clearer. Stochastic-resonance programs highlighted what had been preserved.

"Look here," Smith said to Frank one afternoon when Frank leaned in to say good-bye for the day. He pointed at his computer screen. "Here's a sequence from my boto, part of the GX three-oh-four, near the juncture, see?"

"You've got a female then?"

"I don't know. I think this here means I do. But look, see how it matches with this part of the human genome. It's in Hillis eighty-fifty. . . ."

Frank came into his nook and stared at the screen. "Comparing junk to junk . . . I don't know. . . ."

"But it's a match for more than a hundred units in a row, see? Leading right into the gene for progesterone initiation."

Frank squinted at the screen. "Um, well." He glanced quickly at Smith.

Smith said, "I'm wondering if there's some really long-term persistence in junk DNA, all the way back to earlier mammal precursors to both these."

"But dolphins are not our ancestors," Frank said.

"There's a common ancestor back there somewhere."

"Is there?" Frank straightened up. "Well, whatever. I'm not so sure about the pattern congruence itself. It's sort of similar, but, you know."

"What do you mean, don't you see that? Look right there!"

Frank glanced down at him, startled, then noncommittal. Seeing this Smith became inexplicably frightened.

"Sort of," Frank said. "Sort of. You should run hybridization tests, maybe, see how good the fit really is. Or check with Acheron about repeats in nongene DNA."

"But the congruence is perfect! It goes on for hundreds of pairs, how could that be a coincidence?"

Frank looked even more noncommittal than before. He glanced out the door of the nook. Finally he said, "I don't see it that congruent. Sorry, I just don't see it. Look, Andy. You've been working awfully hard for a long time. And you've been depressed too, right? Since Selena left?"

Smith nodded, feeling his stomach tighten. He had admitted as much a few months before. Frank was one of the very few people these days who would look him in the eye.

"Well, you know. Depression has chemical impacts in the brain, you know that. Sometimes it means you begin seeing patterns that others can't see as well. It doesn't mean they aren't there, no doubt they are there. But whether they mean anything significant, whether they're more than just a kind of analogy, or similarity—" He looked down at Smith and stopped. "Look, it's not my field. You should show this to Amos, or go up to Acheron and talk to the old man."

"Uh-huh. Thanks, Frank."

"Oh no, no, no need. Sorry, Andy. I probably shouldn't have said anything. It's just, you know. You've been spending a hell of a lot of time here."

"Yeah."

Frank left.

. . .

Sometimes he fell asleep at his desk. He got some of his work done in dreams. Sometimes he found he could sleep down on the beach, wrapped in a greatcoat on the fine sand, lulled by the sound of the waves rolling in. At work he stared at the lined dots and letters on the screens, constructing the schematics of the sequences, nucleotide by nucleotide. Most were completely unambiguous. The correlation between the two main schematics was excellent, far beyond the possibility of chance. X chromosomes in humans clearly exhibited nongene DNA traces of a distant aquatic ancestor, a kind of dolphin. Y chromosomes in humans lacked these passages, and they also matched with chimpanzees more completely than X chromosomes did. Frank had appeared not to believe it, but there it was, right on the screen. But how could it be? What did it mean? Where did any of them get what they were? They had natures from birth. Just under five million years ago, chimps and humans separated out as two different species from a common ancestor, a woodland ape. The *Inis geoffrensis* fossil Smith was working on had been precisely dated to about 5.1 million years old. About half of all orangutan sexual encounters are rape.

One night after quitting work alone in the lab, he took a tram in the wrong direction, downtown, without ever admitting to himself what he was doing, until he was standing outside Mark's apartment complex, under the steep rise of the dorsum ridge. Walking up a staircased alleyway ascending the ridge gave him a view right into Mark's windows. And there was Selena, washing dishes at the kitchen window and looking back over her shoulder to talk with someone. The tendon in her neck stood out in the light. She laughed.

Smith walked home. It took an hour. Many trams passed him.

He couldn't sleep that night. He went down to the beach and lay rolled in his greatcoat. Finally he fell asleep.

He had a dream. A small hairy bipedal primate, chimp-faced, walked like a hunchback down a beach in east Africa, in the late-afternoon sun. The warm water of the shallows lay greenish and translucent. Dolphins rode inside the waves. The ape waded out into the shallows. Long powerful arms, evolved for hitting; a quick grab and he had one by the tail, by the dorsal fin. Surely it could escape, but it didn't try. Female; the ape turned her over, mated with her, released her. He left and came back to find the dolphin in the shallows, giving birth to twins, one male one female. The ape's troop swarmed into the shallows, killed and ate them both. Farther offshore the dolphin birthed two more.

The dawn woke Smith. He stood and walked out into the shallows. He saw dolphins inside the transparent indigo waves. He waded out into the surf. The water was only a little colder than the workout pool. The dawn sun was low. The dolphins were only a little longer than he was, small and lithe. He bodysurfed with them. They were faster than he in the waves, but flowed around him when they had to. One leaped over him and splashed back into the curl of the wave ahead of him. Then one flashed under him, and on an impulse he grabbed at its dorsal fin and caught it, and was suddenly moving faster in the wave, as it rose with both of them inside it—by far the greatest bodysurfing ride of his life. He held on. The dolphin and all the rest of its pod turned and swam out to sea, and still he held on. This is it, he thought. Then he remembered that they were air-breathers too. It was going to be all right.

Enough Is As Good As a Feast

We built our house on the apron of Jones Crater, latitude 19 degrees south, longitude 20 degrees. The apron was pretty well populated, some two thousand farms like ours scattered around it, but we could not see any other homesteads from ours, even though we built most of it on the top of a broad-backed low ridge raying down the southwest flank of the crater. We could see the vineyards of the Namibians' village to the north of us, and the tops of the line of cypresses that bordered their pond. And down the apron the bare rock in our prospect was patched with light green squares, marking young orchards like ours.

Craters turned out to be one of the places that people homed in on when they moved out into the backcountry, especially in the southern highlands. For one thing there were a million of them, so it was easy to find empty ones. At first people sheltered inside them, in the early years often doming the craters over and establishing little central crater lakes. By the time the ambient air had become livable, people had learned that settling inside a crater is like moving into a hole. Short days, no view, problems with flooding, and so on. So the new open-air settlements moved out over the rims onto the aprons, to have a look around. The interiors became full crater lakes, or lakes and rice terraces, depending on their climate, water allotment, pan integrity, and the like. Meanwhile the aprons were developed into crops, orchards, and pasturage, wherever there were the right conditions for soil creation. Fissures raying down the aprons served as the streambeds for rapid tumultuous creeks, the water pumped to their tops, or drawn down from rim water tanks that were pump-filled. Irrigation systems were always elaborate. Meanwhile the rims themselves tended to turn into the downtowns, as they had the longest views, and access both back in to the old towns in the crater interiors, and out to the many new settlements stretching down the apron. Rim roads called High Street became common, with fully developed urbanization all the way around. For small craters, the thousands that are around one kilometer in diameter, the densely populated rim was like a large village, very homey and comfortable; everyone known by sight, that kind of thing. Perhaps a thousand people; then the apron would typically have a population of half that, or less. With bigger craters the rim towns got bigger, of course, and a town of fifty thousand people on the rim of a ten-kilometer crater was a common sight, something like the hilltop city-states of the Italian Renaissance, or American Midwestern college towns, in their characters—and there were hundreds of them. Some prospered and became bustling little cities, spilling down into their interiors, which were like central parks, with round lakes or sculptured wetlands. The aprons almost always stayed agricultural, often supplying most of the food for the city up top. All these aspects of crater culture grew up spontaneously as the pattern language of the landscape, so to speak, combined with the emerging co-op culture, and, most simply, the needs of the people in the region being met in a rational way. Of course there was some planning. People would arrive at an unoccupied crater (among the some twenty thousand still listed by the environmental court for the southern highlands alone) with permits and programs, and set to work, and the first decade's economic activity in the town was primarily the building of it, often by people who had an idea what they wanted; sometimes with people holding tattered copies of *A Pattern Language* or some other design primer in their hands, or surfing the Web for things they liked. But soon enough every crater had people moving in who were out of the original group's control, and then it was a matter of spontaneous group self-organization, a process which works extremely well when the group is socially healthy.

Jones Crater was a big one, fifty kilometers in diameter, and its rim town was a beautiful new thing of transparent mushroom buildings and water tanks, and stone-faced skyscrapers clustered at the four points of the compass. Most of our farm group had been working up in town for some time, and eventually twenty families working on various ag projects decided to try moving downslope together, establishing a homestead and entering it into one of the ag travel loops. So we asked the regional environmental court for tenant rights to unclaimed land on the ray ridge, some forty kilometers down the south-southwest slope of the rim, and when we got the stewardship permits we moved on down and lived in tents that first winter. We had nothing, really, but the tents were big house tents from an earlier era, for the most part transparent and very pleasant to live in, as we could see so much of the world and its weather. So even though we were short on many things, that winter was so nice that we decided to build diskhouses as our permanent structures, so that we would continue to "live outdoors when indoors."

These diskhouses were based on a design by a Paul Sattelmeier, from Minnesota. They were very simple, functional, and open places to live in, and easy to build. We got on the list for a mobile mold, and when it rolled by we punched in the commands and watched it throw big pottery: round roofs and slightly larger round floors, and then the walls, which were all interior straight segments; in effect the roof rested on a kind of double M made of interior walls, located under one semicircle of the roof only; the other side was the living room, a kind of big semicircular verandah, the roof freestanding over it. The several short walls extended from the central cross-wall into the other half of the house, dividing that semicircle into three bedrooms, two interior bathrooms, and part of a kitchen. The living rooms we faced downslope to give us the long view to the southwest, and the exterior circular "wall" on that side was only a clear tenting drape, which could be left open, which is what we did most of the time, living out in the wind; or else closed if it was cold or rainy. Same with the bedrooms on the upslope side, except their drape walls were white or colored or polarized to make them opaque. But those too were usually left open.

So we threw the parts for sixteen of these diskhouses, and then put them together. If you're willing to do the labor the whole operation is not that expensive, although admittedly we were in hock to our town co-op right to the ears. For the most part the assembly of the diskhouses was straightforward, indeed a great pleasure. Some parts just grew into place after we set the right cultures to work: Our toilets and sinks and bathtubs and tile floors, for instance, were all bioceramic and grew right into their places, essentially as a kind of templated coral. Really lovely to see.

Long before we had even started on the houses, however, we were out laying soil and planting our orchards and vineyards. We grew as much of our own food as we could in truck gardens around the tents, using complete soils trucked in, but our money crop, our contribution to the Jones economy, was to be almonds and wine grapes, both proven growers on that flank of the apron. The wines being made up to that point had a volcanic tang to them that I didn't like, almost a sulfur touch, but that was okay; it left room for improvement. And the almonds were great. We prepped soil and planted three hundred hectares of almonds and five hundred of wine grapes, in broad terraces concentric to the rim far above us, the ag zones broken by ponds and swamps, and all of them widening as they dropped downslope, so that they made a kind of giant quilt, pendant on our little farm which lay at the top of the land in our care. It was our work of art, and we were very devoted to it. I imagine we were like first-generation kibbutzim in many respects. About twenty couples, four of them same-sex; eleven single adults; thirty-odd kids, later fifty-three. Lots of travel by all of us on the local cog rail line up to Jones, and also laterally to other farms on the apron, to socialize and see what other people were doing agriculturally, and in their settlement design. They were all artists too.

I was involved throughout with our enology, and we made a good fumé blanc eventually, but my field work ended up being mostly in the almond orchards, strangely enough. It happened because I got caught up in the nutsedge problem. Early on we found some sedge creeping out of a radial-strip swamp into the vineyards, and I had gotten rid of it by direct removal. So when the almond orchards were infested I was called on to do it again there. But this time it wasn't so easy. Nutsedge is one of several plants I wish they had never introduced to Mars, but it's good in wet sandy areas, so at first people seeded it to help build meadows. It's a very ancient plant, coevolved with dinosaurs, I suspect, making it very hardy; and impervious to most attempts at eradication. In fact I've come to believe it regards such efforts as friendly stimulation, like a massage. But I only found that out the hard way.

I can't tell you how many days I spent out in our orchards weeding nutsedge. We had decided to be an organic farm, no chemical pesticides, so it was a matter of either biological control or hand-to-hand combat. I tried both, so what I was doing was integrated pest management. But ineffective no matter what you called it. For many hours I sat on the low ground at the southern end of the young almond trees, in what was in effect a ragged lawn of purple nutsedge. *Cyperus rotundus*. If it had been yellow nutsedge there would have been people in my group encouraging us to harvest it and eat the nuts. But purple nuts are hard brown gnarled oblong fibrous tubules, white inside and ghastly bitter to the tongue. They lie about half a meter below the ground, connected to the surface blades of grass by thin shoots that break at the slightest tug, and connected to each other underground by wiry rhizomes that also break easily, leaving the nuts behind. At first I thought I was succeeding when I loosened the soil and sifted through it to get all the nuts out of it. It was slow but not unpleasant work, sitting on the dirt in the sun, getting dirt under my fingernails, looking at the friable soil for the dirt clods that were actually living pebbles. The blades above, stacked in triplet tassels, V-shaped in cross section and stiffer than grass blades, I pulled and composted. The nuts I ground up and tossed in the supercooker compost, feeling superstitious. Which turned out to be not inappropriate given what happened.

A careful sifting of soil to a depth of half a meter, throughout the entire region of its growth—and the next spring the precise region I had weeded sprang forth in a thick lawn of young nutsedge. I couldn't believe my eyes. That was when I got serious about my research, and found out about the Sedge Grass Support Group, and learned from them that fragments of the rhizomes only five hundred nanometers long had been observed to regenerate the full plant in a single growing season.

Some other method was called for. And around that time I got to take a break to regroup as well, as our farm began full participation in one of the ag labor rings of the River League, which meant we went out on the road as nomad farm labor for two months of the fall harvests, moving from farm to farm in the ring as the various crops came ready. Other groups passed through our place while we were gone, with Elke and Rachel left behind to supervise their work. I saw nutsedge in many other places around Jones Crater, and began to exchange stories and theories with the people who had tried to combat it. It was a nice way to meet people. I noticed that quite a few of them had become fanatical on the sedge issue without actually conquering their infestation, which struck me as a bad sign. But I got home that 2 November and tried cover-cropping, on the suggestion of someone who had said, "It's a long-term project," in a way that made me think this was not a bad thing to have in one's life. So it was clover in the fall and winter and cowpeas in the spring and summer, always thickly matted over the sedge, which as a result sometimes did not appear for years at a time. But then if I was late planting a new spring cover crop by even a week, a carpet of tasseled green little pagodas would shove through the dying old cover crop, and it was back to square one.

Once when a cowpea crop got beat to the punch I solarized the ground with clear plastic sheets, and recorded temperatures near boiling underneath it. Some IPM folks looked at it and estimated that everything had to have been killed down to twenty centimeters; but others said two; and though the plant matter on the surface was indeed toasted by the end of the summer, the moment I took the plastic off the green carpet came shooting back.

Tilling and drying the soil for four years was my next option. But then someone visiting the farm innocently suggested a new chemical pesticide that had gotten good results for the Namibians to the north.

That provoked a controversy. Some were content to continue pursuing the various fruitless strategies of the organic battle. Others suggested we give up and let the area become a sedge swamp. But because sedge seed-disperses as well as spreading by underground growth of the rhizomes, little patches of it were springing up everywhere downwind of my orchard lawn. And the wind blows in all directions eventually. So leaving it alone was not really acceptable. Meanwhile, eight years of combat had only made the lawn more luxuriant. You could have played croquet on my patch at that point.

So a majority of our group finally talked a small minority into a one-time exception to our organic policy, in order to make an application of some methyl 5-{[(4,6 dimethoxy-2-pyrimidinyl)amino]carbyonylaminosulfonyl}-3-chloro-1-methyl-1-H-pyrazole-4-carboxylate. When we did it we turned it into a kind of Balinese mask dance ceremony, and the people against the idea dressed as demons and cursed us, and we sprayed the stuff and left for an extended work trip. We harvested grapes in riverside vineyards and built stone drywall terracing, and saw parts of Her Desher Vallis, Nirgal Vallis, Uxboi Vallis, Clota Vallis, Ruda Vallis, Arda Vallis, Ladon Vallis, Oltis Vallis, Himera Vallis, and the Samara Valles. All these are little riverine canyons to the immediate southwest of Jones—beautiful country, reminiscent of the Four Corners area of North America, though our neighbors assure us it is also very like parts of central Namibia. Whatever; when we returned home, the land downslope to the southwest now seemed to suggest the beautiful little canyons that we knew broke the plateau even though we could not see them, canyons held now in our minds' eye, sunken meandering gardens floored with streams and cottonwood islands. And the nutsedge was gone. Not all of it, but everything that we had sprayed. And if you catch it early enough new sedges do not have the regenerative ability of an established bed, because the nuts are not yet down there.

So we planted new ground cover under the blossoming almond trees, and life went on, the farm growing more luxuriant all the time. Of course things changed; Elke and Rachel moved to Burroughs, and later Matthew and Jan did too, complaining that among other things it was not an organic farm anymore, which made me feel bad. But the others in their house assured me that pesticide policy was the last thing they had been thinking of when they left; and I was shocked to hear what some of the other things were. Apparently I had been oblivious; and in fact, they all went on to tell me, no one else but me on the farm had considered the nutsedge problem to have been of much importance. What I had thought was a crisis and a knotty problem in invasion biology, they considered a matter of housekeeping, a mere irritant among more important issues, and, more than anything else, the bee in my bonnet.

Of course compared to the big climate shift that came later, this was probably the right way to regard it. But at the time it had mattered. Or I enjoyed it, whatever. Those were the years when everything mattered, really. We had nothing but each other. We were on our own, growing most of our food, making a lot of our tools, even our clothes, with all the kids growing up. We all grew up together. It matters, in a time like that, whether you can make your agriculture work or not.

Then things changed, as they will, and the kids went off to school, people moved; the whole feeling changed. It always happens that way. Now of course it's still a beautiful place to live, but the feeling from those years is hard to recapture, especially given the cold, and the kids gone. I now think that *kibbutz* is a name for a certain time, a time in the life of a settlement, early on, when it is as much an adventure as it is a home. Later you have to reconceptualize it as a different kind of experience, as home ground or something, the whole shape of a life. But I remember the first time we had a big party and invited the neighbors, and fed everybody with only the food we had been able to grow there in our new gardens, there in our new homes. It was a good feeling. It was a good place to live.

What Matters

For a long time Peter Clayborne worked in hydrology. His co-op was called Noachian Aquifer Redistribution, or NAR. He joined because he got interested as an ecologist in the work, and because he was deeply involved at the time with a woman who had been in the co-op since her teens. Her seniority was one of the things that led to problems in their relationship later, though clearly that was only a symptom rather than a cause. Seniority in their co-op created some of the usual advantages in "pay, say, and time away," but the interests of everyone in the organization were substantially the same. Potential members were chosen for invitation by selection committees, and sometimes had to join a waiting list if the co-op was stable in size. Peter had waited for four years before resignations, retirements, and a few accidental deaths opened up a spot. After that he was a member and, like everyone else, working twenty hours a week, voting on all membership policy issues, and receiving an income share and insurances. The pay scale ran the full legal magnitude, based on work time, contributions to efficiency and productivity, and seniority. He started at twenty percent max, like everyone, and found his needs were satisfied. Some years he sank to the minimum recompense, which supported him both while working and in his time off, which was six months every m-year. It was a good life.

But he and his partner slowly drifted apart, and then broke up. It wasn't Peter's idea. After that he took a series of sabbaticals and did various things on them, all away from Argyre and the membership of NAR. He staffed for the duma in Mangala; he lived on a township in the northern sea; he planted orchards on Lunae Planitia. Everywhere he was haunted by the memory of his partner from NAR.

Eventually time passed and had its way with him; not so much a matter of forgetting as of bleaching, or numbing. We look at the past through the wrong end of the telescope, he thought one day; eventually the things we can see in there become simply too small to hurt us.

It was a cold northern spring, orchards budding and blossoming all around him for as far as the eye could see, and all of a sudden he felt free of his past, launched on a new life. He decided to take a tour he had long been contemplating along the south rims of the great Marineris canyons—Ius, Melas, Coprates, and Eos. This famous long walk was to be a mark for him, a celebration of his transition to a new existence. When he finished it he would return to Argyre and NAR, and decide then whether he could continue living and working there or not.

Near the end of this trek, which turned out to be a hard slog through many deep drifts of snow, though the views down into the canyons were superb, of course—he came on a Swiss alpine hut, set right on the rim overlooking Coprates Chasma, at the Dover Gate. Like most Swiss huts it was actually a very extensive stone hotel and restaurant, with a rimside terrace that would seat hundreds, but located all by itself in the wilderness, away from any roads or pistes. Nevertheless on that evening there were a lot of people there—walkers, climbers, fliers—and the terrace café tables were full.

Peter passed through the crowd and went directly to the rail of the flagged terrace, to have a look down. Directly below the hut the great canyon narrowed, and the scar of the old flood marked the whole floor of it, from wall to wall. A gray remnant glacier still lay in the lowest trough of the canyon, all covered with gravel and pocked with potholes and meltponds and fallen seracs. The cliff of the canyon's opposing wall stood massive and stratified, and the stupendous gulf of empty air shimmered and glittered insubstantially in the late-afternoon light, with the hut standing over it isolate and small. Perched on the edge of a world.

In the hut's restaurant it was even more crowded than the terrace, and so Peter went back outside. He was content to wait; the late sun was illuminating clouds passing just over their heads, turning them to swirling masses of pink spun glass. No one noticed or cared about a solitary observer standing at the rail; indeed there were others along it doing the same thing.

Near sunset it began to get cold, but the hikers who passed by there were used to cold, and dressed for it, and all the tables on the terrace remained full. Finally Peter went to the headwaiter to get on a waiting list, and the waiter pointed to one of the two-person tables right on the railing, down near the end of the terrace, occupied by a single man. "Shall I see if he'll share?"

"Sure," Peter said. "If he doesn't mind."

The waiter went and asked the man, then waved Peter over.

"Thanks," Peter said as he approached, and the man nodded as he sat across from him.

"No problem." He appeared to be nursing a beer. Then his meal came, and he gestured at it.

"Please go ahead," Peter said, looking at the day's menu. Stew, bread, salad; he nodded at the passing waiter, pointing at the menu, and ordered also a glass of wine, the local zinfandel.

The man had not been reading anything, and now Peter wasn't either. They looked at clouds tumbling by, the canyon below, and the great shattered wall opposite them, shadows stretching long to the east, emphasizing the depth of every little embayment, the sharpness of every spur.

"What textures," Peter ventured. He had not made conversation for a long time.

"You can see how deep the Brighton Gully really is from here," the man agreed. "That's rare from any other angle."

"Have you climbed it?"

The man nodded. "It's mostly a hike, though. All of it, now, if you take the ladder trail, which most people do."

"I'll bet that's fun."

A squint. "It is if you're with a fun group."

"You've done it often then?"

Swallow. "Guide." Another swallow. "I guide groups in the canyonlands. Treks, climbs, boating."

"Oh I see. How nice."

"It is. And you?"

"Noachian Aquatic Redistribution. A co-op in Argyre. On leave now, but going back."

The man nodded and stuck out a hand, mouth full. Peter took it and shook. "Peter Clayborne."

The man's eyes rounded, and he swallowed. "Roger Clayborne."

"Hey. Nice name. Nice to meet you."

"You too. I don't often meet other Claybornes."

"Me neither."

"Are you related to Ann Clayborne?"

"She's my mom."

"Oh! I didn't know she had kids."

"Just me. Do you know her?"

"No no. Just stories, you know. Not related, I don't think. My folks came on the second wave, from England."

"Oh I see. Well—cousins, no doubt, somewhere back there."

"Sure. From the first Clayborne."

"Some kind of potter."

"Maybe so. Do you spell yours with an i or a y?"

"Y."

"Oh yeah. Me too. I have a friend spells his with an i."

"Not a cousin then."

"Or a French cousin."

"Yeah sure."

"E on the end?"

"Yeah sure."

"Me too."

The waiter dropped off Peter's meal. Peter ate, and as Roger had finished, and was nursing a grappa, Peter asked him about himself.

"I'm a guide," he said with a shrug.

He had gotten into it in his youth, he said, when the planet was raw, and had stayed with it ever since. "I liked showing people my favorite places. Showing them how beautiful it was." That had gotten him into various red groups, though he did not seem to mind the terraforming in the way Peter's mom did. He shrugged when Peter asked. "It makes it safer, having an atmosphere. And water around. Safer in some ways, anyway. Cliffs fall on people. I've tried to keep the canyons free of reservoirs, because they saturate the sidewalls and cause collapses. We had some successes early on. The dam down there at Ganges, keeping the north sea out of the canyons, that was our doing. And the removal of the Noctis Dam."

"I didn't know it was gone."

"Yeah. Anyway that's about all I've done for the red cause. I thought about getting more into it, but . . . I never did. You?"

Peter pushed his stew bowl away, drank some water. "I guess I'm what you'd call a green."

Roger's eyebrows went up, but he made no comment.

"Ann doesn't approve, of course. It's caused problems between us. But I spent my whole childhood indoors. I'll never be outdoors enough."

"The suits didn't suit you."

"No they didn't. Could you stand them?"

Roger shrugged. "I was willing to put up with them. I felt like I was still out there. Although now that I can get my face in the wind, I like that quite a bit. But the primal landscape—it had a quality. . . ." He shook his head to show he was unable to express it. "That's gone now."

"Really? I find it just as wild as ever." Gesturing over the side of the railing, where they could now see sheets of sunlit snow falling from the bottom of one dark cloud.

"Well, wild. It's a tricky word. When I was first guiding, that's when I would have said things were wild. But ever since the air came, and the great lakes, it doesn't seem so wild to me. It's a park. That's what the Burroughs Protocol means, as far as I'm concerned."

"I don't know about that."

"You know—the big land-use thing."

Peter shook his head. "Must have been a while ago."

Roger shook his. "Not so long."

"But Burroughs was flooded, back when . . ."

"Sure. Every spring, like clockwork. But I worry how it's been starting later, and running harder. I think there's something we're not catching that's causing these long cold winters."

"I thought this winter was pretty warm, myself."

Then the members of a band crowded by their table, carrying their instruments and equipment. While they set up their amps and music stands on a little platform at the terrace's railing right by the two Claybornes, a great number of masked people poured onto the terrace, as if the band had led in some kind of parade. Roger stopped their waiter as he rushed by. "What's this?"

"Oh it's Fassnacht, didn't you know? It'll start getting crowded now that the train is in. Everyone will be here tonight, you're lucky you got here early." From one of his vest pockets he pulled two small white domino masks out of a nestled stack and tossed them onto their table. "Enjoy."

Peter pulled the masks apart, gave one to Roger. They put them on and grinned at the odd look that resulted. As the waiter had predicted, the terrace and the whole complex—hotel, restaurant, outbuildings, co-op quarters—were all quickly filling with people. Most of the masks people had on were much more elaborate than Roger's and Peter's. Apparently their wearers were locals of the region, mostly Swiss in the mountaineering and tourist trade; also a lot of Arabs from

Nectaris Fossae, and from roving caravans rolling in for the night. The equinoctial sunset poured light directly up the great gorge of the canyon, illuminating everything horizontally; indeed it appeared that the sun was well below them, the light shining upward. Their terrace the edge of the world; the sky dark, and filled now with twirling flakes of snow, like bits of mica.

The band started to play. Trumpet, clarinet, trombone, piano, bass, drums. They were loud. From Munchen, down to the south in Protva Vallis. Clearly favorites of the local Swiss—a privilege to have them there, you could tell by the enthusiastic response. Hot jazz blaring in the cold dusk.

Peter and Roger ordered a pitcher of dark beer and cheered them on with the rest of the crowd. Some maskers danced, many sat, some stood and wandered from table to table, chatting with seated people or each other. Some groups had their waiters take rounds of grappa up to the band between songs, and happily the band members downed them, until they were saturated, at which point they passed the drinks out to people in the front row; two or three times these medicinal toasts came to Roger and Peter, who drained them in tandem. Without intending to they got a bit drunk. In the frequent "kleines pauses" they continued talking, but the noise of the crowd obscured their hearing, and they often found themselves misunderstanding each other.

Eventually, after a rousing final number ("King of the Zulus," with spectacular trumpeting by "our star, Dieter Lauterbaun!"), the band ended their first set. The two men ordered another round of grappa, which at that point had actually begun to taste good to them, even to become the one true ambrosia. The dusky evening was still chill, but the terrace remained crowded with the chattering crowd of masked celebrants; these were not the kind of people to be driven indoors by a few flakes of snow drifting onto their tabletops. The slight breeze both Claybornes recognized as the feel of basically still air, falling under its own weight over the cliff into the black canyon below.

"I love this."

"Yeah."

"It must be nice, taking people out into these kinds of nights."

"Yeah. If they're nice."

"I suppose that's variable."

"Oh yeah."

"But when they're *really* nice—you know?"

"Ah yeah. Fun."

"So sometimes you . . ."

"Well, you know. Sometimes."

"Sure."

"It's not like teacher and student, or lawyer and client."

"Not a power relationship."

"No. Shouldn't be. I guide them—they can take it or leave it. They hire me. A matter of equals. If something else happens . . ."

"Sure."

"But . . ."

"But what?"

"I have to admit it's not happening as much lately, now I think of it. I don't know why."

They laughed.

"Just chance."

"Or age!"

More laughter at this horrible possibility.

"Yeah—the tourists are getting too old."

"Ah ha ha. Exactly. But . . ."

"But what?"

"Well, the thing is, it's more trouble than it's worth."

"Ah yeah. Getting them to go back home."

"Yeah, sure. Or not getting to go home with them! I mean, either way. . . ."

"Well, that way's worse, clearly."

"Yes it is. I remember the first time it happened. I was young, she was young. . . ."

"It was love."

"It was! I mean really. But what were we supposed to do? She was a student, I was a guide. I couldn't just quit, even if I wanted to. And I didn't. I couldn't leave the land. And she couldn't leave her work either. So . . ."

"That's tough. You hear about that kind of thing a lot. People's work taking them in different directions, what they do—"

"What they are!"

"Right. Keeping them apart even when they, when the feeling between them . . ."

"It's hard." Big sigh. "It was hard. That time it—I don't know. It was hard. Nothing since has really ever felt the same."

Long silence.

"You never saw her again?"

"I did, actually. We ran into each other, and then after that we've stayed in touch, sort of. I see her every few years. It's always the same. She's great, she really is. She even got into canyon guiding herself, for a while there. And I can still see why I felt that way about her, so long ago. And she even seems to feel sort of the same. But, you know. . . ."

"No?"

"Well, one or the other of us is always partnered with someone else! It never fails. She's been single when I've been partnered, and vice versa." A shake of the head. "It keeps happening."

"I know that story."

"Yeah?"

"Yeah. A long time ago. Like yours, sort of, though . . ."

"Someone you met?"

"Someone I grew up with, sort of. In Zygote. You know Jackie Boone?"

"Not really."

"Well, when she was a kid, she thought I was—well, I was it for her." A shrug. "But she was just a kid. Even when she had grown up a bit, I thought she was just a kid. Then one time years later I ran into her when I was—when I had been alone a long time."

Deep nod.

"And she was—grown-up. She'd been living in Sabishii and Dorsa Brevia. She had become one of the great ones. A power. And still interested. So finally I was ready, you know, and we got together, and it was incredible. I was . . . I was in love, sure. But the thing was, she wasn't *really* interested anymore. Not in the same way. It had just been settling old business. Like doing a climb just to show you can, but without the feeling you had when you couldn't do it."

"People do that."

"All the time. So, well, I got over it. She's become, I don't know, kind of strange these days anyway. But I think that if we had ever been in the same place, you know, in the same frame of mind, at the same time. . . ."

"Sure. That's just it with me and Eileen. I think we might have . . ."

"Yeah."

The sodden, somber silence of the what-might-have-been.

"Lost chances."

"Right. The fate of chance."

"Some fate is character."

"Sure. But most fate is *fate*. It's what picks you up and carries you off. Who you meet by accident, what happens—what you feel inside, no matter what you think. And it affects everything. Everything!

Every thing. People argue about politics, and when people write history books they talk about politics, and policy, the *reasons* why people did this or that—but it's always the personal stuff that mattered."

"It's always the stuff they don't write about. The stuff they can't write about. The look in someone's eye."

"Right, the way something catches you. . . ."

"The way it carries you away."

"Like falling in love. Whatever the hell that means."

"That's it, sure. Falling in love, being loved back—"

"Or not."

"Right, or not! And everything changes."

"Everything."

"And no one knows why! And later on, or from anywhere on the outside, they look at your story and they say that story makes no sense."

"When if you only knew—"

"Then it would make sense."

"Yes. Perfect sense."

"It would be the story of the heart, every time."

"A history of the emotions. If you could do it."

"It would be the heart's story."

"Yes."

"Yes."

"Yes."

"Which means . . . when you're trying to decide what to do—in the here and now, you know. . . ."

"Yes."

Another long thoughtful silence. The band came back for its second set, and the two men watched them play, both lost in their own thoughts. Eventually they got up to go into the men's room, and afterward they went back out and wandered the milling crowd, and got separated and did not run into each other again. The band finished its second set, then played a third, and it was nearly sunrise before the crowd finally dispersed, the two men among them. And one of them left determined to act. And the other one didn't.

Coyote Remembers

I followed her everywhere she went, and then she was gone. You don't know what that does to you—loss. Or maybe you do. Sure, everyone does. Who hasn't lost someone they love? It's impossible to avoid. So you know how I felt.

After that it's your friends who save you. Maya. Later on we couldn't sleep together because she was with Michel, but it wasn't like that with her anyway, except the once. She's like a sister, or something better than that, some ex-lover friend, who is for you no matter what, who's there even when she's not. Like when those high-altitude climbers hallucinate companions who aren't there, keeping them company up in the jet stream, the death zone. She's my brother.

And Nirgal. It is so strange to look at him and think that he in his genetic material is half me and half Hiroko. I don't see how that can be or how it might explain anything. Who knows how that works anyway. It could be that genes are the accidental sign of some deeper thing, some morphic resonance or implicate order—but nothing can be said, probably we shouldn't even use those names, because then it's just another level, with the real cause still left below, unexplained. Sax always worried about how much was unexplainable. But we are pattern dust devils in the unexplainable. Flying on an unknowable wind. Hiroko and I collided like two dust devils spinning into each other—that happens—and the resulting dust devil was Nirgal, golden boy that he is. Such a pleasure it is to me to watch him flow through his life, fly through it always high, in good spirits, active, inquisitive, interested, empathic. Lucky.

But only when he was young, before the revolution succeeded. After that—things changed. Maybe it wasn't that simple. He was always looking for something. Hiroko—she's like a big hole in all our lives. The one that got away. And then Jackie was no help either. Let us not mince words here, that woman was a bitch. That was why I liked her, myself. She was tough, and she knew what she wanted. She and Nirgal were actually a lot alike in that sense, it should have worked. But it didn't, and that poor boy wandered the world as lonely as old Coyote himself. And he didn't have Maya—or he did, but for him she replaced Hiroko, not Jackie. Not motherless but partnerless. I felt for him. You see couples who have grown together like two old trees making one plant, trunks intertwined like the double helix itself, and you think, Yes that's the way it's supposed to be. It wouldn't be so lonely then. But there you are. You can't make partners by wanting them.

So it's back to friends, and loneliness. And so I watched Nirgal live his lives like a second self cast loose on the wind. We all live the same stories. Nirgal is like a brother to me.

And Sax is my brother in wonder. In all truth, there isn't a purer soul in the world. He's so innocent that you can't think of him as truly smart. All his intelligence is thrown in one deep hole, and as for the rest he's a newborn babe. The interesting thing is to watch a mind like that try to use its one talent to educate the rest of him. To get along. After his accident—after those fuckers torched his brain I should say—he had to do it all again from scratch too. And that second time he got it right. He got all round. Michel helped—hell, Michel threw him like a vase. And I helped too I think. I took that vase through the kiln, through the fiery furnace. Now he's my brother in arms, the person I love above all—but they all—well you know. There is no above and below in this realm. He is my brother.

As for Michel, I can't speak of it yet. I miss him.

And Hiroko too, God damn her. If she ever reads this, if she really is alive and out there hiding as they all say, which I doubt, may she get the message: God damn you. Come back.

Sax Moments

When Sax was pretending to be Stephen Lindholm, he often asked the lab's computer to display articles from *The Journal of Irreproducible Results*, and though most of the articles were silly, some made him laugh. He was still spluttering one day when he came into Claire and Berkina's lab to describe to them Henry Lewis's "Data Enrichment Method."

"Say you do an experiment to see if sounds can be detected at various decibel levels, and you have your data in a table. Then since you want more data but don't actually want to do more experiments, you assume that if a sound isn't heard at decibel level *a*, it wouldn't be heard at any lower levels either, and so you add the result of test *a* to all the trials at lower decibels."

"Uh-oh."

"Then say you're trying to prove that coin tosses are more likely to turn up heads the higher the altitude you make the toss at—"

"What?"

"That's your hypothesis, and you make your trial and arrange your data in the same kind of table, see here" (he had printed it out) "and it looks a little ambiguous, sure, but you just use the data enrichment method as described with the decibels, so that every time you get heads, you add it to all the tests higher up the stairs, and there you have it—the higher on the stairs you toss the coin, the more heads you get! Very convincing!" And he collapsed on a chair, giggling. "It's exactly how Simons showed that CO_2 levels were going to drop after they got them to two bar."

Claire and Berkina stared at him, nonplussed. Claire said, "Stephen likes the *reductio ad absurdum.*"

"I do," Sax admitted, "I definitely do."

"It's science," Berkina said. "Science in a nutshell."

And they all sat there grinning.

"Nobody can get more out of things, including books, than he already knows."

Sax read that in a book and went out for a walk to think it over.

When he came back he read on. "If one has character one also has one's typical experience, which recurs repeatedly."

Sax found this Nietzsche an interesting writer.

The more Sax studied memory, the more worried he got that there would be anything they could ever do to improve it. During one night's reading early on, the worry turned to cold fear.

He was reviewing the classic Rose papers on memory in chicks whose intermediate medial hyperstriatum ventrales had been burned away before or after training sessions with sweet or bitter pellets of food. Chicks that had been given left-hemisphere IMHV lesions forgot later lessons to avoid a bitter pellet; chicks with right-side lesions remembered. This gave one the impression that it was the left IMHV that was necessary to memory. But if the training was done before the lesions, the chicks needed neither IMHV to recall the lesson. Perhaps, Rose postulated, the memory was actually stored in the lobus parolfactorius, left or right, so that once learned, neither IMHV was needed. Further lesions seemed to confirm this hypothesis, eventually justifying a pathway model, in which lessons are first registered in the left IMHV, then move to the right IMHV, and then move on to both the left and right LPOs. And if this model were correct, then a pretraining right-IMHV lesion, already shown not to be amnestic by itself, would disrupt this flow, and posttraining LPO lesions, otherwise amnestic, would no longer be so because the memory would have been stranded in the left IMHV. And that proved to be the case. It followed, then, that a pretraining right-IMHV lesion, followed by a posttraining left-IMHV lesion, would also produce amnesia, for first the transfer path would be blocked, and then the only repository destroyed.

Except it wasn't so. Right lesion; train chick; recall displayed; left lesion; and the chick still recalled the lesson. The memory had escaped.

Sax left his desk and took a walk down to the corniche to think this over. Also to recover from the stab of fear that had struck him: that they would never understand. Darkness, voices from restaurants, clanking dishes, starlight on the still sea. He couldn't find Maya, she was in none of her usual haunts.

He sat on one of their benches anyway. The mind was a mystery. Memories were nowhere and everywhere: The brain had a tremendous equipotentiality, it was a hugely complex dynamic system, almost anything was possible.

In theory that should be a cause for hope. Surely with such a flexible, versatile system, they could shore up the failing parts, shunt the memories elsewhere. If that was the right way to state it. Very possibly; but in such an immensity, how could they learn (quickly enough) what to do? Didn't the very power of the system place it beyond their comprehension? So that the greatness of the human mind actually added to the great unexplainable, rather than lessened it?

Dark sky, dark sea. Sax got up and walked, clutched the railing of the corniche, teeth clenched as he suddenly thought of Michel. Michel would have welcomed this great unexplainable inside them. He had to learn to consider it as Michel had.

A clenching of all one's muscles did not actually impede or redirect one's thoughts. He groaned and took off again in search of Maya.

Another time, thinking about aspects of this same problem, he went down to the corniche and found Maya in one of her usual haunts, and they went out to a bench to sit and watch the sunset, bags of food in hand, and Sax announced to her, "The thing that makes us specifically human doesn't exist."

"How so?"

"Well, we are just animals, mostly. But we have a consciousness which sets us apart, because we have language and memory."

"Those exist."

"True, but the only reason they work is because of the past. We remember the past, we learn from it, and everything we have learned is in the past. And the past, being past, properly speaking does not exist. Its presence in us is an illusion only. So the thing that makes us human does not exist!"

"I've always maintained that," Maya said. "But not for the same reason."

"Technology is the knack of so arranging the world that we don't have to experience it." Sax read that in one of the feral rhapsodies, and went outdoors for a walk.

Down on the corniche he saw that a front had passed. Across the sky black clouds pulled east. The evening sun broke underneath them, dull silver at the storm's west edge; the air over the city was still and dim, dark air between dark planes of sea and cloud. Looking at reflections of the city across the harbor he noticed that the sea's surface was rippled in some places, flat in others, and the boundaries between the two were delineated with amazing sharpness, though presumably the wind was the same over both. This was puzzling, until it occurred to him that there could be a thin film of oil damping the ripples in the flat patches. Someone's boat engine must be leaking. If he could get a sample from the water, and from everyone's boats, he could probably ascertain which one it was.

In preparation for his sea trip with Ann, Sax did research on the various psychological studies of the personality of the scientist. He discovered that Maslow had divided scientists into cool and warm types, which he characterized as green and red in color—to avoid assigning any unwanted value judgments, he said, which made Sax smile. Green scientists were reductive, lovers of lawful explanation, tough-minded, looking for regularity, explanation, parsimony, simplicity. Red scientists on the other hand were expansive, warm, intuitive, mystical, soft-minded, and in search of peak moments of "suchness understanding."

"Dear me," Sax said. He went out for a walk. Up the alleyways above Paradeplatz a row of red roses was in bloom, and he stopped to inspect the perfect petals of one young rose, nose a centimeter from it. Such velvet dark reds, there against a stucco wall. Okay, he said, here I am. I wonder what makes that red.

Cosmology and particle physics had become a single science before Sax was born, and in all the time since the hope of both sides was for the grand unified theory which would reconcile quantum mechanics and gravity, and even time itself. And yet his whole life physics had been getting more and more complicated, with postulated microdimensions taken as fact, and symmetries of fairly simple but scarily small strings invoked as explanations even though they were many magnitudes of size smaller than could ever be observed—the unobservability was itself mathematically provable. Thus the search for a final unifying theory was, as Lindley noted, a kind of religious quest; or the messianic movement in the religion that the scientific worldview had become. Then he met Bao Shuyo.

. . .

Over a winter in Da Vinci Bao took him through the latest in superstring theory, step by step. The idea of extra microdimensions was straightforward. There were seven extra dimensions but all very small, and arranged in a thing called the "seven sphere." Then to describe a point in our conventional four dimensions one had to add coordinates in all of the extra seven dimensions, and various combinations determined what kind of particle it was, muon, top quark, etc. But these points are just the ends of strings, and the basic quantum-mechanical unit is a vibration in the whole string. Trying to do calculations of these produced many faster-than-light problems unless twenty-six dimensions were invoked, and so they were. But that stage of the theory yielded only bosons and not fermions. A derivative of the twenty-six-dimensional string was invoked which existed in ten dimensions, the other sixteen having become properties of the string itself, and part of the geometry of supersymmetry. But the sixteen string dimensions could be combined in a huge variety of ways, all equally possible, none preferred. Then mathematical considerations had shown that of all the possibilities, only two of them, SO(32) and $E_8 x E_8$, exhibited handedness rather than mirror symmetry. And the universe is right-handed. That only two possibilities remained out of the myriad possibilities was startling. But there matters rested, until this winter, when Bao had shown that $E_8 x E_8$ was the preferred formulation, and that if you pursued the implications and advanced this formulation, you had quantum mechanics, gravity, and time all explained in a single theory, complex but clear, and powerful throughout.

"So beautiful it must be true," Bao concluded.

Sax nodded. "But that beauty is its only proof."

"What do you mean?"

"It is otherwise unconfirmable by experiment. It is the beauty of the mathematics that confirms it."

"As well as matching all physical observations we can make! That's more than just math, Sax. That's everything we've ever seen, all conformable to this single theory!"

"True." He nodded uneasily. It was a good point. And yet. . . . "I think it needs to predict something we have not yet seen, that happens because it and not any other explanation is the right one."

She shook her head, dismayed by his stubbornness.

"Otherwise it's just a myth," he said.

"The Planck realm will never be observable," she said.

"Well. A very beautiful myth. And valuable, believe me I am quite convinced of that. Perhaps we now say we have reached the end of what physics can explain. And so . . ."

"And so?"

"What next?"

Imbibition is the tendency of granular rock to imbibe a fluid under the force of capillary attraction, in the absence of any pressure. Sax became convinced that this was a quality of mind as well. He would say of someone, "She has great imbibition" and people would say, "Ambition?" and he would reply, "No, imbibition." "Inhibition?" "No, imbibition." And because of his stroke people would assume he was just having speech trouble again.

Long walks around Odessa at the end of the day. Aimless, without destination, except perhaps for an evening rendezvous with Maya, down on the corniche. Sauntering through the streets and alleyways. Sax liked Thoreau's explanation for the word *saunter*: from *à la Saint Terre*, describing pilgrims on their way to the Holy Land. There goes a *Saint Terrer*, a saunterer, a Holy Lander. But it was a false etymology, apparently spread from a book called *Country Words*, by S. and E. Ray, 1691. Although since the origins of the word were obscure, it might in fact be the true story.

Sax would have liked to be sure about that, one way or the other. It made the word itself a problem to mull over. But as he sauntered Odessa thinking about it, he did not see how the matter could be investigated any further, the etymologists having been thorough. The past was resistant to research.

Automorphism; idiomorphism. These were qualities Sax found underconsidered in Michel's personality theories. He said to Michel, "We make ourselves."

Altruistic behavior will tend to be chosen when $k>1/r$, where k is the ratio of recipient benefit to altruist's cost, and r is the coefficient of relationship between altruist and recipient, summed for all recipients. In the classical version of the theory r is the proportion of genes in two individuals that are identical because of common descent. But what if common descent is taken to mean the same phylum or order? What if r is not a function of common descent but of common interest? Sax found the social sciences very interesting.

.   .   .

For a time after he had mostly recovered from his stroke, Sax read quite a lot about strokes and brain damage, trying to learn more about what had happened to him. One case, famous in the literature, concerned a brilliant student at the polytechnic in Moscow, wounded in the head during World War Two. This young Russian, Zasetsky by name, had suffered gross trauma to the left parietal-occipital area (like Sax), and could no longer perceive his right visual field, could not add, knew not the order of the seasons, and so on; his symbolic and conceptual faculties had been crippled. But his frontal lobes had remained intact (as had Sax's), leaving him his will, his desires, his sensitivity to experience. And so he had spent the rest of his days struggling to write down an account of his mentation, for the benefit of science, also for something to do; it was his life project, at first titled "The Story of a Terrible Injury," later changed to "I'll Fight On." He wrote every day for twenty-five years.

Sax read this journal with immense feeling for Zasetsky, the sentences sometimes causing a terrible stab to the heart, the perceptions in them were so familiar: "I'm in a kind of fog all the time, like a heavy half-sleep. . . .Whatever I do remember is scattered, broken down into disconnected bits and pieces. That is why I react so abnormally to every word and idea, every attempt to understand the meaning of words. . . . I was killed March 2, 1943, but because of some vital power of my organism, I miraculously remained alive."

That hand on his wrist, how to tell it!

As Ann and Sax were being blown around in the storm, Sax felt an updraft in the thunderhead drawing them up and concluded they had escaped drowning at sea only to be thrown right up out of the sky. The cockpit dome would probably hold even against the vacuum of space, but the cold would kill them. It was too loud to remember anything, but he wanted to remember to say to Ann, We ask Why all our lives and never get past Because. We stop after that word, in disarray. I wish I had spent more time with you.

The Names of the Canals

Laestrygon, Antaeus, Cimmeria, Hyblaeus, Scamander, Pandoraea, Fretum, Hiddekel. Phison, Protonius, Python, Argaeus.

Mostly Greek, Latin, and Hebrew. Some names refer to real features, visible from Earth through early telescopes: the big volcanoes, Hellas and Argyre, the great canyons, the dark land on Syrtis, the shifting polar caps.

Idalius, Heliconius, Oxus, Hydroates.

But the lines. Lines connecting everything. Even at the time illusory lines were known to occur between dark dots in a telescope, a matter of optics and vision. And the minimal width of any line that could be visible on Mars through those telescopes was known to be a hundred kilometers. And yet the names. We want life. We want to live.

Cadmus, Erigone, Hebrus, Ilisus.

So silly. But I too I live in a world I love.

Pyriphlegeton, Memnonia, Eumenides, Ortygia.

I live in a big valley, on its flat floor, the mountains on both sides visible on most days, the smaller range closer to the west, the larger one farther away to the east. To north and south, as far as the eye can see, a valley. A valley about as wide as a Martian canal.

The Soundtrack

Before work every morning, espresso and Steve Howe's "Turbulence." For *Red Mars*, Glass's *Satyagraha*. For *Green*, *Ahknaten*. For *Blue*, *Mishima* and *The Screens*. For Maya, Astor Piazzolla, especially "Tango: Zero Hour." For Ann, Gorecki's Third Symphony, Paul Winter's "Sun Singer," and the Japanese folk song "Sakura." For Sax, Beethoven's late string quartets and piano sonatas. For Nadia, Louis Armstrong 1946–56, also Clifford Brown and Charles Mingus. For Michel, Keith Jarrett's "Köln Concert." For Nirgal, Najma. And always Van Morrison, Pete Townshend, and Yes.

> *Van when I'm happy*
> *Pete when I'm mad*
> *Steve when I'm energetic*
> *Astor when I'm sad*

A Martian Romance

Eileen Monday hauls her backpack off the train's steps and watches the train glide down the piste and around the headland. Out the empty station and she's into the streets of Firewater, north Elysium. It's deserted and dark, a ghost town, everything shut down and boarded up, the residents moved out and moved on. The only signs of life come from the westernmost dock: a small globular cluster of yellow streetlights and lit windows, streaking the ice of the bay between her and it. She walks around the bay on the empty corniche, the sky all purple in the early dusk. Four days until the start of spring, but there will be no spring this year.

She steps into the steamy clangor of the hotel restaurant. Workers in the kitchen are passing full dishes through the broad open window to diners milling around the long tables in the dining room. They're mostly young, either iceboat sailors or the few people left in town. No doubt a few still coming out of the hills, out of habit. A wild-looking bunch. Eileen spots Hans and Arthur; they look like a pair of big puppets, discoursing to the crowd at the end of one table—elderly Pinocchios, eyes lost in wrinkles as they tell their lies and laugh at each other, and at the young behemoths passing around plates and devouring their pasta while still listening to the two. The old as entertainment. Not such a bad way to end up.

It isn't Roger's kind of thing, however, and indeed when Eileen looks around she sees him standing in the corner next to the jukebox, pretending to make selections but actually eating his meal right there.

That's Roger for you. Eileen grins as she makes her way through the crowd to him.

"Hey," he says as he sees her, and gives her a quick hug with one arm.

She leans over and kisses his cheek. "You were right, it's not very hard to find this place."

"No." He glances at her. "I'm glad you decided to come."

"Oh, the work will always be there, I'm happy to get out. Bless you for thinking of it. Is everyone else already here?"

"Yeah, all but Frances and Stephan, who just called and said they'd be here soon. We can leave tomorrow."

"Great. Come sit down with the others, I want some food, and I want to say hi to the others."

Roger wrinkles his nose, gestures at the dense loud crowd. This solitary quality in him has been the cause of some long separations in their relationship, and so now Eileen shoves his arm and says, "Yeah yeah, all these people. Such a crowded place, Elysium."

Roger grins crookedly. "That's why I like it."

"Oh of course. Far from the madding crowd."

"Still the English major I see."

"And you're still the canyon hermit," she says, laughing and pulling him toward the crowd; it is good to see him again, it has been three months. For many years now they have been a steady couple, Roger returning to their rooms in the co-op in Burroughs after every trip away; but his work is still in the backcountry, so they still spend quite a lot of time apart.

Just as they join Hans and Arthur, who are wrapping up their history of the world, Stephan and Frances come in the door, and they hold a cheery reunion over a late dinner. There's a lot of catching up to do; this many members of their Olympus Mons climb haven't been together in a long time. Hours after the other diners have gone upstairs to bed, or off to their homes, the little group of old ones sits at the end of one table talking. A bunch of antique insomniacs, Eileen thinks, none anxious to go to bed and toss and turn through the night. She finds herself the first to stand up and stretch and declare herself off. The others rise on cue, except for Roger and Arthur; they've done a lot of climbing together through the years, and Roger was a notorious insomniac even when young; now he sleeps very poorly indeed. And Arthur will talk for as long as anyone else is willing, or longer. "See you tomorrow," Arthur says to her. "Bright and early for the crossing of the Amazonian Sea!"

. . .

The next morning the iceboat runs over ice that is mostly white, but in some patches clear and transparent right down to the shallow sea floor. Other patches are the color of brick, with the texture of brick, and the boat's runners clatter over little dunes of gravel and dust. If they hit meltponds the boat slows abruptly and shoots great wings of water to the sides. At the other side of these ponds the runners scritch again like ice skates as they accelerate back up to speed. Roger's iceboat is a scooter, he explains to them; not like the spidery skeletal thing that Eileen was expecting, having seen some of that kind down in Chryse—those Roger calls DNs. This is more like an ordinary boat, long, broad, and low, with several parallel runners nailed fore and aft to its hull. "Better over rough ice," Roger explains, "and it floats if you happen to hit water." The sail is like a big bird's wing extended over them, sail and mast all melded together into one object, shifting shape with every gust to catch as much wind as it can.

"What keeps us from tipping over?" Arthur asks, looking over the lee rail at the flashing ice just feet below him.

"Nothing." The deck is at a good cant, and Roger is grinning.

"Nothing?"

"The laws of physics."

"Come on."

"When the boat tips the sail catches less wind, both because it's tilted and because it reads the tilt, and reefs in. Also we have a lot of ballast. And there are weights in the deck that are held magnetically on the windward side. It's like having a heavy crew sitting on the windward rail."

"That's not nothing," Eileen protests. "That's three things."

"True. And we may still tip over. But if we do we can always get out and pull it back upright."

They sit in the cockpit and look up at the sail, or ahead at the ice. The iceboat's navigation steers them away from the rottenest patches, spotted from satellites, and so the automatic pilot changes their course frequently, and they shift around the cockpit when necessary. Floury patches slow them the most, and over those the boat sometimes decelerates pretty quickly, throwing the unprepared forward into the shoulder of the person sitting next to them. Eileen is banged into by Hans and Frances more than once; like her they have never been on iceboats before, and their eyes are round at the speeds it achieves during strong gusts over smooth ice. Hans speculates that the sandy patches mark old pressure ridges, which stood like long stegosaur backs until the winds ablated them entirely away, leaving their load of sand and silt behind on the flattened ice. Roger nods. In truth the whole ocean surface is blowing away on the wind, with whatever sticks up going the fastest; and the ocean is now frozen to the bottom, so that no new pressure ridges are being raised. Soon the whole ocean will be as flat as a tabletop.

This first day out is clear, the royal blue sky crinkling in a gusty west wind. Under the clear dome of the cockpit it's warm, their air at a slightly higher pressure than outside. Sea level is now around three hundred millibars, and lowering year by year, as for a great storm that never quite comes. They skate at speed around the majestic promontory of the Phlegra Peninsula, its great prow topped by a white-pillared Doric temple. Staring up at it Eileen listens to Hans and Frances discuss the odd phenomenon of the Phlegra Montes, seaming the north coast of Elysium like a long ship capsized on the land; unusually straight for a Martian mountain range, as are the Erebus Montes to the west. As if they were not, like all the rest of the mountain ranges on Mars, the remnants of crater rims. Hans argues for their being two concentric rings of a really big impact basin, almost the size of the Big Hit itself but older than the Big Hit, and so mostly obliterated by the later impact, with only Isidis Bay and much of the Utopian and Elysian Seas left to indicate where the basin had been. "Then the ranges could have been somewhat straightened out in the deformation of the Elysium bulge."

Frances shakes her head, as always. Never once has Eileen seen the two of them agree. In this case Frances thinks the ranges may be even older than Hans does, remnants of early-tectonic or prototectonic plate movement. There's a wide body of evidence for this early-tectonic era, she claims, but Hans is shaking his head: "The andesite indicating tectonic action is younger than that. The Phlegras are early Noachian. A pre–Big Hit big hit."

Whatever the explanation, there the fine prow of rock stands, the end of a steep peninsula extending straight north into the ice for four hundred kilometers out of Firewater. A long sea cliff falling into the sea, and the same on the other side. The pilgrimage out the spine to the temple is one of the most famous walks on Mars; Eileen has made it a number of times since Roger first took her on it about forty years ago, sometimes with him, sometimes without. When they first came they looked out on a blue sea purled with whitecaps. Seldom since has it been free of ice.

He too is looking at the point, with an expression that makes

Eileen think he might be remembering that time as well. Certainly he would remember if asked; his incredible memory has still not yet begun to weaken, and with the suite of memory drugs now available, drugs which have helped Eileen to remember quite a bit, it might well be that he will never forget anything his whole life long. Eileen envies that, though she knows he is ambivalent about it. But by now it is one of the things about him that she loves. He remembers everything and yet he has remained stalwart, even chipper, through all the years of the crash. A rock for her to lean on, in her own cycles of despair and mourning. Of course as a red it could be argued he has no reason to mourn. But that wouldn't be true. His attitude was more complex than that, Eileen has seen it; so complex that she does not fully understand it. Some aspect of his strong memory, taking the long view; a determination to make it well; rueful joy in the enduring land; some mix of all these things. She watches him as he stares absorbed at the promontory where he and she once stood together over a living world.

How much he has meant to her through the years has become beyond her ability to express. Sometimes it fills her to overflowing. That they have known each other all their lives; that they have helped each other through hard times; that he got her out into the land in the first place, starting her on the trajectory of her whole life; all these would have made him a crucial figure to her. But everyone has many such figures. And over the years their divergent interests kept splitting them up; they could have lost touch entirely. But at one point Roger came to visit her in Burroughs, and she and her partner of that time had been growing distant for many years, and Roger said, I love you, Eileen. I love you. Remember what it was like on Olympus Mons, when we climbed it? Well now I think the whole world is like that. The escarpment goes on forever. We just keep climbing it until eventually we fall off. And I want to climb it with you. We keep getting together and then going our ways, and it's too chancy, we might not cross paths again. Something might happen. I want more than that. I love you.

And so eventually they set up rooms in her co-op in Burroughs. She continued to work in the Ministry of the Environment, and he continued to guide treks in the backcountry, then to sail on the north sea; but he always came back from his treks and his cruises, and she always came back from her working tours and her vacations away; and they lived together in their rooms when they were both at home, and became a real couple. And through the years without summer, then the little ice age and the crash itself, his steadfast presence has been all that has kept her from despair. She shudders to think what it would have been like to get through those years alone. To work so hard, and then to fail . . . it's been hard. She has seen that he has worried about her. This trip is an expression of that: Look, he said once after she came home in tears over reports of the tropical and temperate extinctions—look, I think you need to get out there and see it. See the world the way it is now, see the ice. It's not so bad. There have been ice ages before. It's not so bad.

And as she had been more and more holing up in Burroughs, unable to face it, she finally was forced to agree that in theory it would be a good thing. Very soon after that he organized this trip. Now she sees that he gathered some of their friends from the Olympus Mons expedition to help entice her to come, perhaps; also, once here, to remind her of that time in their lives. Anyway it's nice to see their faces, flushed and grinning as they fly along.

Skate east! the wind says, and they skitter round Scrabster, the northeastern point of Elysium, then head south over the great plate of white ice inserted into the incurve of the coast. This is the Bay of Arcadia, and the steep rise of land backing the bluffs is called Acadia, for its supposed resemblance to Nova Scotia and the coast of Maine. Dark rock, battered by the dark north sea; sea cliffs of bashed granite, sluiced by big breakers. Now, however, all still and white, with the ice that has powdered down out of the spray and spume flocking and frosting the beach and the cliffs until they look like wedding-cake ramparts. No sign of life in Acadia; no greens anywhere in sight. This is not her Elysium.

Roger takes over the sailing from Arthur, and brings them around a point, and there suddenly is a steep-walled square island ahead, vivid green on top—ah. A township, frozen here near the entrance to a fjord, no doubt in a deep channel. All the townships have become islands in the ice. The greenery on top is protected by a tent which Eileen cannot see in the bright sun. "I'm just dropping by to pick up the rest of our crew," Roger explains. "A couple of young friends of mine are going to join us."

"Which one is this?" Stephan inquires.

"This is the *Altamira*."

Roger sails them around in a sweet curve that ends with them stalled into the wind and skidding to a halt. He retracts the cockpit dome. "I don't intend to go up there, by the way, that's an all-day trip no matter how you do it. My friends should be down here onshore to meet us."

They step down onto the ice, which is mostly a dirty opaque white, cracked and a bit nobbled on the surface, so that it is slippery in some places, but mostly fairly steady underfoot; and Eileen sees that the treacherous spots stand out like windows inlaid in tile. Roger talks into his wristpad, then leads them into the fjord, which on one steep side displays a handsome granite staircase, frost lying like a fluffy carpet on the steps.

Up these stairs Roger climbs, putting his feet in earlier boot prints. Up on the headland over the fjord they have a good view over the ice to the township, which is really very big for a manufactured object, a kilometer on each side, and its deck only just lower than they are. Its square-tented middle glows green like a Renaissance walled garden, the enchanted space of a fairy tale.

There is a little stone shelter or shrine on the headland, and they follow the sidewalk over to it. The wind chills Eileen's hands, toes, nose, and ears. A big white plate, whistling in the wind. Elysium bulks behind them, its two volcanoes just sticking over the high horizon to the west. She holds Roger's hand as they approach. As always, her pleasure in Mars is mixed up with her pleasure in Roger; at the sight of this big cold panorama love sails through her like the wind. Now he is smiling, and she follows his gaze and sees two people through the shelter's open walls. "Here they are."

They round the front of the shrine and the pair notices them. "Hi all," Roger says. "Eileen, this is Freya Ahmet and Jean-Claude Bayer. They're going to be joining us. Freya, Jean-Claude, this is Eileen Monday."

"We have heard of you," Freya says to her with a friendly smile. She and Jean-Claude are both huge; they tower over the old ones.

"That's Hans and Frances behind us, down the path there arguing. Get used to that."

Hans and Frances arrive, then Arthur and Stephan. Introductions are made all around, and they investigate the empty shrine or shelter, and exclaim over the view. The eastern side of the Elysian Massif was a rain shadow before, and now it bulks just as black and empty as ever, looking much as it always has. The huge white plate of the sea, however, and the incongruous square of the *Altamira*; these are new and strange. Eileen has never seen anything like it. Impressive, yes; vast; sublime; but her eye always returns to the little tented greenhouse on the township, tiny stamp of life in a lifeless universe. She wants her world back.

On the way back down the stone stairs she looks at the exposed granite of the fjord's sidewall, and in one crack she sees black crumbly matter. She stops to inspect it.

"Look at this," she says to Roger, scraping away at rime to see more of it. "Is it lichen? Moss? Is it alive? It looks like it might be alive."

Roger sticks his face right down into it, eyes a centimeter away. "Moss, I think. Dead."

Eileen looks away, feeling her stomach sink. "I'm so tired of finding dead plants, dead animals. The last dozen times out I've not seen a single living thing. I mean winterkill is winterkill, but this is ridiculous. The whole world is dying!"

Roger waggles a hand uncertainly, straightens up. He can't really deny it. "I suppose there was never enough sunlight to begin with," he says, glancing up at their bronze button of light, slanting over Elysium. "People wanted it and so they did it anyway. But reality isn't interested in what people want."

Eileen sighs. "No." She pokes again at the black matter. "Are you sure this isn't a lichen? It's black, but it looks like it's still alive somehow."

He inspects some of it between his gloved fingers. Small black fronds, like a kind of tiny seaweed, frayed and falling apart.

"Fringe lichen?" Eileen ventures. "Frond lichen?"

"Moss, I think. Dead moss." He clears away more ice and snow. Black rock, rust rock. Black splotches. It's the same everywhere. "No doubt there are lichens alive, though. And Freya and Jean-Claude say the subnivean environment is quite lively still. Very robust. Protected from the elements."

Life under a permanent blanket of snow. "Uh-huh."

"Hey. Better than nothing, right?"

"Right. But this moss here was exposed."

"Right. And therefore dead."

They start down again. Roger hikes beside her, lost in thought. He smiles: "I'm having a déjà vu. This happened before, right? A long time ago we found some little living thing together, only it was dead. It happened before!"

She shakes her head. "You tell me. You're the memory man."

"But I can't quite get it. It's more like déjà vu. Well, but maybe . . .

maybe on that first trip, when we first met?" He gestures eastward—over the Amazonian Sea, she guesses, to the canyon country east of Olympus. "Some little snails or something."

"But could that be?" Eileen asks. "I thought we met when I was still in college. The terraforming had barely started then, right?"

"True." He frowns. "Well, there was lichen from the start, it was the first thing they propagated."

"But snails?"

He shrugs. "That's what I seem to remember. You don't?"

"No way. Just whatever you've told me since, you know."

"Oh well." He shrugs again, smile gone. "Maybe it was just a déjà vu."

Back in the iceboat's cockpit and cabin, they could be crowded around the kitchen table of a little apartment anywhere. The two newcomers, heads brushing the ceiling even though they are sitting on stools, cook for them. "No, please, that is why we are here," Jean-Claude says with a big grin. "I very much like to be cooking the big meals." Actually they're coming along to meet with some friends on the other side of the Amazonian Sea, all people Roger has worked with often in the last few years, to initiate some research on the western slope of Olympus—glaciology and ecology, respectively.

After these explanations they listen with the rest as Hans and Frances argue about the crash for a while. Frances thinks it was caused by the rapid brightening of the planet's albedo when the north sea was pumped out and froze; this the first knock in a whole series of positively reinforcing events leading in a negative direction, an autocatalytic drop into the death spiral of the full crash. Hans thinks it was the fact that the underground permafrost was never really thawed deeper than a few centimeters, so that the resulting extremely thin skin of the life zone looked much more well established than it really was, and was actually very vulnerable to collapse if attacked by mutant bacteria, as Hans believes it was, the mutations spurred by the heavy incoming UV—

"You don't know that," Frances says. "You radiate those same organisms in the lab, or even expose them in space labs, and you don't get the mutations or the collapses we're seeing on the ground."

"Interaction with ground chemicals," Hans says. "Sometimes I think everything is simply getting salted to death."

Frances shakes her head. "These are different problems, and there's no sign of synergistic effects when they're combined. You're just listing possibilities, Hans, admit it. You're throwing them out there, but no one knows. The etiology is not understood."

That is true; Eileen has been working in Burroughs on the problem for ten years, and she knows Frances is right. The truth is that in planetary ecology, as in most other fields, ultimate causes are very hard to discern. Hans now waggles a hand, which is as close as he will come to conceding a point to Frances. "Well, when you have a list of possibilities as long as this one, you don't have to have synergy among them. Just a simple addition of factors might do it. Everything having its particular effect."

Eileen looks over at the youngsters, their backs to the old ones as they cook. They're debating salt too, but then she sees one put a handful of it in the rice.

In the fragrance of basmati steam they spoon out their meals. Freya and Jean-Claude eat seated on the floor. They listen to the old ones, but don't speak much. Occasionally they lean heads together to talk in private, under the talk at the little table. Eileen sees them kiss.

She smiles. She hasn't been around people this young for a long time. Then through their reflections in the cockpit dome she sees the ice outside, glowing under the stars. It's a disconcerting image. But they are not looking out the window. And even if they were, they are young, and so do not quite believe in death. They are blithe.

Roger sees her looking at the young giants, and shares with her a small smile at them. He is fond of them, she sees. They are his friends. When they say good night and duck down the passageway to their tiny quarters in the bow, he kisses his fingers and pats them on the head as they pass him.

The old ones finish their meal, then sit staring out the window, sipping hot chocolate spiked with peppermint schnapps.

"We can regroup," Hans says, continuing the discussion with Frances. "If we pursued the heavy-industrial methods aggressively, the ocean would melt from below and we'd be back in business."

Frances shakes her head, frowning. "Bombs in the regolith, you mean."

"Bombs *below* the regolith. So that we get the heat, but trap the radiation. That and some of the other methods might do it. A flying lens to focus some of the mirrors' light, heat the surface with focused sunlight. Then bring in some nitrogen from Titan. Direct a few comets to unpopulated areas, or aerobrake them so that they burn up in the atmosphere. That would thicken things up fast. And more halocarbon factories, we let that go too soon."

"It sounds pretty industrial," Frances says.

"Of course it is. Terraforming is an industrial process, at least partly. We forgot that."

"I don't know," Roger says. "Maybe it would be best to keep pursuing the biological methods. Just regroup, you know, and send another wave out there. It's longer, but, you know. Less violence to the landscape."

"Ecopoesis won't work," Hans says. "It doesn't trap enough heat in the biosphere." He gestures outside. "This is as far as ecopoiesis will take you."

"Maybe for now," Roger says.

"Ah yes. You are unconcerned, of course. But I suppose you're happy about the crash anyway, eh? Being such a red?"

"Hey, come on," Roger says. "How could I be happy? I was a sailor."

"But you used to want the terraforming gone."

Roger waves a hand dismissively, glances at Eileen with a shy smile. "That was a long time ago. Besides, the terraforming isn't gone now anyway"—gesturing at the ice—"it's only sleeping."

"See," Arthur pounces, "you do want it gone."

"No I don't, I'm telling you."

"Then why are you so damn happy these days?"

"I'm not happy," Roger says, grinning happily, "I'm just not sad. I don't think the situation calls for sadness."

Arthur rolls his eyes at the others, enlisting them in his teasing. "The world freezes and this is not a reason for sadness. I shudder to think what it would take for you!"

"It would take something sad!"

"But you're *not* a red, no of course not."

"I'm not!" Roger protests, grinning at their laughter, but serious as well. "I was a sailor, I tell you. Look, if the situation were as bad as you all are saying, then Freya and Jean-Claude would be worried too, right? But they're not. Ask them and you'll see."

"They are simply young," Hans says, echoing Eileen's thought. The others nod as well.

"That's right," Roger says. "And it's a short-term problem."

That gives them pause.

After a silence Stephan says, "What about you, Arthur? What would you do?"

"What, me? I have no idea. It's not for me to say, anyway. You know me. I don't like telling people what to do."

They wait in silence, sipping their hot chocolate.

"But you know, if you did just direct a couple of little comets right *into* the ocean . . ."

Old friends, laughing at old friends just for being themselves. Eileen leans in against Roger, feeling better.

Next morning with a whoosh they are off east again, and in a few hours' sailing are out on the ice with no land visible, skating on the gusty wind with runners clattering or schussing or whining or blasting, depending on wind and ice consistencies. The day passes, and it begins to seem like they are on an all-ice world, like Callisto or Europa. As the day ends they slide around into the wind and come to a halt, then get out and drive in some ice screws around the boat and tie it into the center of a web of lines. By sunset they are belayed, and Roger and Eileen go for a walk over the ice.

"A beautiful day's sail, wasn't it?" Roger asks.

"Yes, it was," Eileen says. But she cannot help thinking that they are out walking on the surface of their ocean. "What did you think about what Hans was saying last night, about taking another bash at it?"

"You hear a lot of people talking that way."

"But you?"

"Well, I don't know. I don't like a lot of the methods they talk about. But—" He shrugs. "What I like or don't like doesn't matter."

"Hmm." Underfoot the ice is white, with tiny broken air bubbles marring the surface, like minuscule crater rings. "And you say the youngsters aren't much interested either. But I can't see why not. You'd think they'd want terraforming to be working more than anyone."

"They think they have *lots* of time."

Eileen smiles at this. "They may be right."

"That's true, they may. But not us. I sometimes think we're sad not so much because of the crash as the quick decline." He looks at her, then down at the ice again. "We're two hundred and fifty years old, Eileen."

"Two hundred forty."

"Yeah yeah. But there's no one alive older than two-sixty."

"I know." Eileen remembers a time when a group of old ones were sitting around a big hotel restaurant table, building card houses, as there was no other card game all of them knew; they collaborated on one card house four storeys high, and the structure was getting shaky indeed when someone said, "It's like my longevity treatments." And though they had laughed, no one had the steadiness of hand to set the next card.

"Well. There you have it. If I were twenty I wouldn't worry about the crash either. Whereas for us it's very likely the last Mars we'll know. But, you know. In the end it doesn't matter what kind of Mars you like best. They're all better than nothing." He smiles crookedly at her, puts an arm around her shoulders, and squeezes.

The next morning they wake in a fog, but there is a steady breeze as well, so after breakfast they unmoor and slide east with a light slick sliding sound. Ice dust, pulverized snow, frozen mist—all flash east past them.

Almost immediately after taking off, however, a call comes in on the radiophone. Roger picks up the handset, and Freya's voice comes in. "You left us behind."

"*What?* Shit! What the hell were you doing out of the boat?"

"We were down on the ice, fooling around."

"For Christ's sake, you two." Roger grins despite himself as he shakes his head. "And what, you're done now?"

"None of your business," Jean-Claude calls happily in the background.

"But you're ready to be picked up," Roger says.

"Yes, we are ready."

"Okay, well, shit. Just hold put there. It'll take a while to beat back up to you in this wind."

"That's all right. We have our warm clothes on, and a ground pad. We will wait for you."

"As if you have any choice!" Roger says, and puts the handset down.

He starts sailing in earnest. First he turns across the wind, then tacks up into it, and the boat suddenly shrieks like a banshee. The sail-mast is cupped tight. Roger shakes his head, impressed. You would have to shout to be heard over the wind now, but no one is saying anything; they're letting Roger concentrate on the sailing. The whiteness they are flying through is lit the same everywhere, they see nothing but the ice right under the cockpit, flying by. It is not the purest whiteout Eileen has ever been in, because of the wind and the ice under the lee rail, but it is pretty close; and after a while even the ends of the iceboat, even the ice under the lee rail, disappear into the cloud. They fly, vibrating with their flight, through a roaring white void; a strange kinetic experience, and Eileen finds herself trying to open her eyes farther, as if there might be another kind of sight inside her, waiting for moments like this to come into play.

Nothing doing. They are in a moving whiteout, that's all there is to it. Roger doesn't look pleased. He's staring down at their radar, and the rest of the instrumentation. In the old days pressure ridges would have made this kind of blind sailing very dangerous. Now there is nothing out there to run into.

Suddenly they are shoved forward, the roar gets louder, there is darkness below them. They are skating over a sandy patch. Then out of it and off again, shooting through bright whiteness. "Coming about," Roger says.

Eileen braces herself for the impact of their first tack, but then Roger says, "I'm going to wear about, folks." He brings the tiller in toward his knees and they career off downwind, turn, turn, then catch the wind on their opposite beam, the boat's hull tipping alarmingly to the other side. Booms below as the ballast weight shifts up to the windward rail, and then they are howling as before, but on the opposite tack. The whole operation has been felt and heard rather than seen; Roger even has his eyes closed for a while. Then a moment of relative calm, until the next wearing about. A backward loop at the end of each tack.

Roger points at the radar screen. "There they are, see?"

Arthur peers at the screen. "Sitting down I take it."

Roger shakes his head. "They're still mostly over the horizon. That's their heads."

"You hope."

Roger is looking at the APS screen and frowning. He wears away again. "We'll have to come up on them slow. The radar only sees to the horizon, and even standing up it won't catch them farther than six k away, and we're going about a hundred fifty k an hour. So we'll have to do it by our APS positions."

Arthur whistles. Satellite navigation, to make a rendezvous in a whiteout. . . . "You could always," Arthur begins, then claps his hand over his mouth.

Roger grins at him. "It should be doable."

For a nonsailor like Eileen, it is a bit hard to believe. In fact all the blind vibration and rocking side to side have her feeling a bit dizzy, and Hans and Stephan and Frances look positively queasy. All five of them regard Roger, who looks at the APS screen and shifts the tiller minutely, then all of a sudden draws it in to his knees again. On the radar screen Freya and Jean-Claude appear as two glowing green columns. "Hey you guys," Roger says into the radio handset, "I'm closing on you, I'll come up from downwind, wave your arms and keep an eye out, I'll try to come up on your left side as slow as I can."

He pulls the tiller gently back and forth, watching the screens intently. They come so far up into the wind that the sail-mast spreads into a very taut French curve, and they lose way. Roger glances ahead of the boat, but still nothing there, just the pure white void, and he squints unhappily and tugs the tiller another centimeter closer to him. The sail is feathering now and has lost almost all its curve; it feels to Eileen as if they are barely making headway, and will soon stall and be thrown backward; and still no sign of them.

Then there they are just off the port bow, two angels floating through whiteness toward the still boat—or so for one illusory moment it appears. They leap over the rail onto the foredeck, and Roger uses the last momentum of the iceboat to wear away again, and in a matter of seconds they are flying east with the wind again, the howl greatly reduced.

By that sunset they are merely in a light mist. Next morning it is gone entirely, and the world has returned. The iceboat lies moored in the long shadow of Olympus Mons, hulking over the horizon to the east. A continent of a mountain, stretching as far as they can see to north and south; another world, another life.

They sail in toward the eastern shore of the Amazonian Sea, famous before the crash for its wild coastline. Now it shoots up from the ice white and bare, like a winter fairy tale: Gordii Waterfall, which fell a vertical kilometer off the coastal plateau directly into the sea, is now a great pillared icefall, with a great pile of ice shatter at its foot.

Past this landmark they skate into Lycus Sulci Bay, south of Acheron, where the land rises less precipitously, gentle hills above low sea bluffs, looking down on the ice bay. In the bay they slowly tack against the morning offshore breeze, until they come to rest against a floating dock, now somewhat askew in the press of ice, just off a beach. Roger ties off on this, and they gear up for a hike on the land. Freya and Jean-Claude carry their backpacks with them.

Out of the boat and onto the ice. *Scritch-scritch* over the ice to shore, everything strangely still; then across the frosty beach, and up a trail that leads to the top of the bluff. After that a gentler trail up the vast tilt of the coastal plateau. Here the trailmakers have laid flagstones that run sometimes ten in a row before the next low step up.

In steeper sections it becomes more like a staircase, a great endless staircase, each flag fitted perfectly under the next one. Even rime-crusted as it is, Eileen finds the lapidary work extraordinarily beautiful. The quartzite flags are placed as tightly as Orkney drywall, and their surfaces are a mix of pale yellow and red, silver and gold, all in differing proportions for each flag, and alternating by dominant color as they rise. In short, a work of art.

Eileen follows the trail looking down at these flagstones, up and up, up and up, up some more. Above them the rising slope is white to the distant high horizon, beyond which black Olympus bulks like a massive world of its own.

The sun emerges over the volcano. Light blazes on the snow. As they hike farther up the quartzite trail it enters a forest. Or rather, the skeleton of a forest. Eileen hurries to catch up with Roger, feeling oppressed, even frightened. Freya and Jean-Claude are up ahead, their other companions far behind.

Roger leads her off the trail, through the trees. They are all dead. It was a forest of foxtail pine and bristlecone pine; but the tree line has fallen to sea level at this latitude, and all the big old gnarled trees have perished. After that a sandstorm, or a series of sandstorms, have sandblasted away all the trees' needles, the small branches, and the bark itself, leaving behind only the bleached tree trunks and the biggest lower branches, twisting up like broken arms from writhing bodies. Wind has polished the spiraling grain of the trunks until it gleams in the morning light. Ice packs the cracks into the heartwood.

The trees are well spaced, and they stroll between them, regarding some more closely, then moving on. Scattered here and there are little frozen ponds and tarns. It seems to Eileen like a great sculpture garden or workshop, in which some mighty Rodin has left scattered a thousand trials at a single idea, all beautiful, altogether forming a park of surreal majesty. And yet awful too; she feels it as a kind of stabbing pain in the chest; this is a cemetery. Dead trees flayed by the sandy wind; dead Mars, their hopes flensed by the cold. Red Mars, Mars the god of war, taking back its land with a frigid boreal blast. The sun glares off the icy ground, smeary light glazing the world. The bare wood glows orange.

"Beautiful, isn't it?" Roger says.

Eileen shakes her head, looking down. She is bitterly cold, and the wind whistles through the broken branches and the grain of the wood. "It's dead, Roger."

"What's that?"

" 'The darkness grew apace,' " she mutters, looking away from him. " 'A cold wind began to blow in freshening gusts from the east.' "

"What's that you say?"

"*The Time Machine,*" she explains. "The end of the world. 'It would be hard to convey the stillness of it.' "

"Ah," Roger says, and puts his arm around her shoulders. "Still the English major." He smiles. "All these years pass and we're still just what we always were. You're an English major from the University of Mars."

"Yes." A gust seems to blow through her chest, as if the wind had suddenly struck her from an unexpected quarter. "But it's all over now, don't you see? It's all dead"—she gestures—"everything we tried to do!" A desolate plateau over an ice sea, a forest of dead trees; all their efforts gone to waste.

"Not so," Roger says, and points up the hill. Freya and Jean-Claude are wandering down through the dead forest, stopping to inspect certain trees, running their hands over the icy spiral grain of the wood, moving on to the next magnificent corpse.

Roger calls to them, and they approach together. Roger says under his breath to Eileen, "Now listen, Eileen, listen to what they say. Just watch them and listen."

The youngsters join them, shaking their heads and babbling at the sight of the broken-limbed forest. "It's so beautiful!" Freya says. "So pure!"

"Look," Roger interrupts, "don't you worry everything will all go away, just like this forest here? Mars become unlivable? Don't you believe in the crash?"

Startled, the two stare at him. Freya shakes her head like a dog shedding water. Jean-Claude points west, to the vast sheet of ice sea spread below them. "It never goes backward," he says, halting for words. "You see all that water out there, and the sun in the sky. And Mars, the most beautiful planet in the world."

"But the crash, Jean-Claude. The crash."

"We don't call it that. It is a long winter only. Things are living under the snow, waiting for the next spring."

"There hasn't been a spring in thirty years! You've never seen a spring in your life!"

"Spring is Ls zero, yes? Every year spring comes."

"Colder and colder."

"We will warm things up again."

"But it could take thousands of years!" Roger exclaims, enjoying the act of provocation. He sounds like all the people in Burroughs, Eileen thinks, like Eileen herself when she is feeling the despair of the crash.

"I don't care," Freya says.

"But that means you'll never see any change at all. Even with really long lives you'll never see it."

Jean-Claude shrugs. "It's the work that matters, not the end of work. Why be so focused on the end? All it means is you are over. Better to be in the middle of things, or at the beginning, when all the work remains to be done, and it could turn out any way."

"It could fail," Roger insists. "It could get colder, the atmosphere could freeze out, everything in the world could die like these trees here. Nothing left alive at all."

Freya turns her head away, put off by this. Jean-Claude sees her and for the first time he seems annoyed. They don't quite understand what Roger has been doing, and now they are tired of it. Jean-Claude gestures at the stark landscape: "Say what you like," he says. "Say it will all go crash, say everything alive now will die, say the planet will stay frozen for thousands of years—say the stars will fall from the sky! But there *will be* life on Mars."

If Wang Wei Lived on Mars and Other Poems

If Wang Wei lived on Mars, we'd spend more time outdoors

VISITING

No one on Mars has a home
ceaseless wandering motel to motel
those friends I had all moved along
most will never cross paths again
strange to think each life is only
a few years long
settle down in your habits
same thing every day
food rooms streets friends
you can think it will go on
forever

AFTER A MOVE

One night I half awoke from a dream
And struggled up to go to the bathroom.
Past bookcases to the foot of the bed, left through
The doorway, touch the wall—but it wasn't there.
    Emptiness: timeless moment, dark nowhere,
    The space between the stars—
Ah. A different bedroom
With no wall there, no bookcases—
A straight shot to a different bathroom,
In a different apartment.
I realized where I was and
A whole world slipped away.

CANYON COLOR

In Lazuli Canyon, boating.
Sheet ice over shadowed stream
Crackling under our bow.
Stream grows wide, curves into sunlight:
A deep bend in the ancient channel.
Plumes of frost at every breath.
Endless rise of the red canyon,
Canyon in canyons, no end to them.
Black lines web rust sandstone:
Wind-carved boulder over us.
There, on a wet red beach—
Green moss, green sedge. Green.
Not nature, not culture: just Mars.
Western sky deep violet,
Two evening stars, one white one blue:
Venus, and the Earth.

VASTITAS BOREALIS

The red rock and sand are all under water
that we ourselves pumped out of the ground
drowning what little we knew at the time
of this place as it was in the air
like gas burned off in a welder's fire

The whole world flicking before us like fire
tossing its orange flames into the air
that was not here at the time
we first stepped out on this ground
where everything is writ in water

NIGHT SONG

The baby cries out
I get up to check
He is still asleep
I go back to bed

So many hours
Spent like this
Awake in the night
The family asleep

Wife moves her leg against me
Wind pours in the south window
Rumble of distant night train
Crickets' vibrant electric chorus

Thoughts pulsing up and down
Mind ranging here and there
How many times

DESOLATION

Above the dip of the pass float clouds.
Sunbeams spray the skyline ridge.
White granite, orange granite,
Patches of snow. A lake.
Clustered in rocks,
Trees. Shadows.
The lake ripples its
Chill snow reflections:
Fish, breaking the surface.
Blooming circles on the water,
Why can't the heart grow as fast?

ANOTHER NIGHT SONG

Toss and turn in rumpled sheets
Hot but cold. Small pains
Smolder in the flesh.
Gears of the mind half-engaged:
The years grind jumbled and broken.
Regret, nostalgia, grief-at-nothing,
Grief-at-something, worry at this and that,
Anxiety without cause, confusion,
The past: remember? remember?

Shards of painted glass. Memory
Speaks in a language
You no longer understand.
The future you understand too well.
Pain in the knee, prescient
Sighs from the wife,
From the boys in their room—
With redoubled effort, sleep, sleep!

SIX THOUGHTS ON THE USES OF ART

for Pierre-Paul Durastanti and Yves Frèmion

1. What's in My Pocket

I remember during my year in Boston
I was walking alone at sunset by the Charles
The riverbank all covered with snow
The trees black spikes against the sky
The river's surface a glossy sheen

Cold hand thrust into down jacket pocket
I felt a book I had left behind
Title forgotten just a book any book
But suddenly all I saw was joy

2. In the Finale of Beethoven's Ninth

The passage when each section
of the choir begins to sing
a different song and the orchestra echoes
these parts or adds their own in a
thick fugue during which so many
melodies are being sung at once they can
only be grasped as whole sound it always
occurs to me Beethoven wrote
this music when he was entirely
deaf for him it was all just patterns
on a page he had to imagine the confluence
of voices singing in his mind he had
to be a novelist

3. Reading Emerson's Journal

"Grief runs off us
Like water off a duck"

Ah Waldo Waldo
If only it were so
But it is the verso

Grief seeps in us
Like a blotter takes ink

4. *The Walkman*

Running to *Satyagraha*
I saw a hawk soaring
and every turn every shift of its wings was
sung aloud in the sunny air

5. *Dreams Are Real*

The day passes into a book
For a time we are outside
Time at sea in an open boat

Rogue waves hit from nowhere
Cast into the next reality
Shackleton saw a wave so big

He thought it was a cloud
The boat rolled under and came
Up in a new world later

On South Georgia Island
Sleeping in a cave he leaped
To his feet shouting and hit

His head on the roof of the cave
So hard he almost killed himself
Dreaming of that wave

6. *Seen While Running*

Four birds in the air fighting
     kestrel
       magpie
         crow
           hawk
all involved spinning
   in a brief spat overhead

CROSSING MATHER PASS

At the turning point of my life
I hiked toward Mather Pass.
With every step clouds thickened above
Until the world was roofed in gray.

Thunder rolled from west to east
Like big barrels over a floor
And as I crossed great Upper Basin
It began to snow.

Soon I walked in a white bubble
Slush piled on every rock.
Warm and dry in parka and pants
I felt my life fall away.

I gave it up. Fly away
On the wind, drift into slush,
I'll never go back! I quit!
Each step up was a step away.

A convex shattered slope of stone
Rose into mist. A boulder wall.
The pass on top, unseen. The trail
Swept up without a switchback,

Right to left in a single shot,
The Muir Trail crew's one touch of art.
It cost a life: I passed a plaque
And read the name: my own.

Then I was in the pass.
Flakes blew up one side and
Down the other. In the lee I tried
To eat but started shivering. Go.

With easy strides I clumped down
The white Ss on the northern slope
Until I saw the Palisade Lakes,
Far far below. The sun came out.

White lace on wet gold granite,
A new world, a new life,
A new world I'll make it new!
I passed two hikers setting camp.

Did you come over in that storm?
Yes, I said, I left my life on the other side
And now I'm not afraid.

NIGHT IN THE MOUNTAINS

> *"Or I can say to myself as if I were*
> *A wanderer being asked where he had been*
> *Among the hills: 'There was a range of mountains*
> *Once I loved until I could not breathe.' "*
> —THOMAS HORNSBY FERRIL

1. Camp

Stream falling over rock:
Loud music. Night and a candle.

Halfway through this life:
It doesn't feel so long.

Ridges, cliffs, peaks, cols:
I'll never stop wanting them.

Ponds, meadows, streams, moss:
My knees number them.

Stars outside my tent door:
All my troubles as far away.

2. The Ground

Candleflame, minutes.
Pine needles, months.
Branches, years.
Sand, centuries.
Pebbles, millennia.
The bedrock, eons.
Me and broken sticks.

3. Writing by Starlight

Can't see the words.
Waterfall a rope of sound,
Rushing about, pushed by the wind.
Trees black against the stars.

Dim blank white page.
I write on it and see a
Dim blank white page.
The story of my life!

Juniper, tent, rock, dark.
Wind dying. My heart
At peace. A Friday night.

The Big Dipper sits on the mountain.
My friends lie in their tents.
My back against the white rock,
Star bowl spinning overhead:
Feel the movement and soar away.

Who knows how many stars there are,
All those dim ones filling the black
Until it seems no black is there.
And then you see the Milky Way.
The sky should be pure white with stars,
That's black dust up there blocking the view,
Carbon just like us! All flung together through space
In just this way.

By starlight everything is clear.
Trees are alive. Rocks are sleeping.
Waterfalls, so noisy!
All the rest—
Quiet as my heart.

INVISIBLE OWLS

I remember our night on the ridge
I had seen a nook some years before
Flat sand and shrubs in broken granite
Right on the crest so I thought I could find it
And you were game for anything

We hiked up in late afternoon
Carrying water in our packs
Up in the shadow of the Crystal Range
Up shattered granite all patched with grasses
Until we stepped back into the light

We found the nook and pitched the tent
Between two gnarly junipers
The sun set in the big valley's haze
The light leaked out of the sky
We leaned against rock cooking our supper

And in the last electric blue
The richest color in all the world
We jerked at a flash in the air above
And jerked again as out of the night
Black shapes dove at both our heads

In the dark we could barely see them
Their quick dives made no sound at all
Too big for bats too quiet for hawks
We ducked it seemed at an onslaught of owls
Out hunting in a little pack

A strange disjunction of the senses
Wings baffled to damp their noise
So we heard nothing except the stove
Yet saw the steep black strobe approaches
The braking the sharp glides turning away

Then one came close we sensed the talons
I picked up the stove and held it aloft
A Bluet canister with blue flames burning

Bright in the dark blue expanse of space
Beyond it black wings flitting away

We laughed with just a touch of a shiver
Actually to be considered as food
Above the stars popped out all over
Netted in the Milky Way
And afterimages of blue flame

Then we lay in our blue tent
The moon rose and our air turned blue
A blue still in us
It will always be with us
All the color of the twilight sky

All the time and space we travel
The years pass so many now
Falling asleep owls twirl overhead
I feel the granite under our bodies
We soar in blue without a sound

TENZING

Tenzing did not speak much English
Hungry food tired rest
Paragraphs from a power in the land

Teahouse to teahouse he led us
Across land scored deep
Rivers in mountains no end to them

He arranged our food
He arranged our sleep
He showed us the way

Up the gorge of the Dudh Khosi
Green leaves leeches everything wet
Always within the monsoon clouds

One evening they cleared and there
Above the peaks above the clouds
Another range above the world

We walked up there
Namche Bazaar perched in space
Thyangboche Pengboche Pheriche

Up glacier canyons up their walls
Over ice and rock to Gorak Shep
Dead Crow the last teahouse

Dawn struggle up Kala Pattar
Sit on the peak necks craned up
To look at Everest

Massive slab bright in the sky
Sargarmatha Chomolungma
Mother Goddess of the World

Tenzing pointed at South Col
Fabled last camp littered with gear
Terrible stories corpses

Tenzing had been there four times
Portering up and down Khumbu Icefall
The sidewalk over the white abyss

Where any moment the world could crash
And end it all a place in other words
Like any other place we stand

Beside Tenzing we do not yet know
The world and the icefall are the same
We see it in his face's Himalaya

Gleaming like ice in the sun
Windy he said South Col very windy
He was fifty-four

Later that morning Lisa got sick
He led her down by the hand
Offering tea sips of water

And brought us down to Pheriche
Helped run the teahouse while Lisa recovered
Helped the Sherpani who cooked all day

Led us to the ancient monastery
Showed us the wall of demon masks
Took us to Thyangboche in the rain

Made sure we saw the monks' mandala
Five men in red sitting and laughing
Over a circle of colored sands

Rubbing funnels with sticks
To free trickles of red green yellow blue
Intent then a joke and we three

Sitting with them through a dark rainy day
We sit there still in some inner space
He led us back down into the world

Down to Namche down down to Lukla
The little airstrip hacked into the wall
Of the gorge an outpost of everything

Led us into the Sherpa Co-op at dusk
Everyone in there watching TV
Powered by the Honda generator out back

A video of the Live Aid concert
Everyone stunned at the sight
Of Ozzy Osborne chewing up the stage

Tenzing the man who led us
Who took care of us who taught us
Finished eating and crossed the room

Crouched beside me gestured at the TV
America? he said
No I said no that's England

A REPORT ON THE FIRST RECORDED CASE OF AREOPHAGY

for Terry Bisson

On my forty-third birthday I was nearly done
With Mars the drafts were in a shambles
Beauty in a novel (as in everything) is
An emergent property emerging
Late in the process and before that all
Is chaos and disorder but my hopes
Were high I felt that it was coming
Together I wanted the final push to be
The convergence of everything I wanted
Unreasonable things I had in my possession
Some bits of Mars a gram or two of the SNC
Meteorite that fell on Zagama Nigeria
In October of 1962 after thirteen million years
In space little gray chunks of rock
Mounted in a necklace given to my wife
I unscrewed the casing took out a chunk
Climbed onto my roof at sunset
A clear day crows flying back
From the fields the coastal range dark
To the west gilt clouds above it
The vault still blue the wind fresh
From the delta and there I was
On the roofbeam of my house in the middle of
My life in the open air about to eat a rock
That if not fraudulent a piece of Jersey
Was an actual chunk of the next planet out
It felt odd even in the performance
I have never been able to explain
Myself but can only note that in the
Attempt to imagine Mars I came to see
Earth more clearly than ever before
This beautiful world now alive
With the drama of an everyday sunset
Black birds sailing east in lines
Under my feet my home the sun
Touching the coastal range I put the rock in
My mouth all went on as before

No electric shiver that the sunset itself did not
Provide no speaking in tongues I bit down
It was too hard to break in my mouth
Tongued it side to side tasted no taste
Ran it over my teeth a little rock
Most of it would pass through me
But the stomach's fierce acids would
Surely tear at the surface of the rock
And some few atoms I hoped would stick
As carbon incorporated into my bones
For their seven-year cycle or
For good perhaps and so I sat
Digesting Mars and the view the sun
Ablink through the Berryessa gap
The wind rising each life has its trajectory
Up and down in the shimmer of ordinary moments
Sudden euphoria stab of grief the pattern dustdevil
Funneling down spiraling up in most
Exquisite sensitive dependence
On unknown factors that dusk nothing of the sort
Happened it was a matter of will a
Meditative discipline exerted day after
Day for years to make a world
Transparent in me and my mind at home
And as I swallowed parts of another world
This one wheeled about me like a veritable
California

THE REDS' LAMENT

They never got it right
not any of them not ever
never on Earth by definition
nor hardly ever on Mars itself
the way it was back in the beginning
the way it was before we changed it

The way the sky went red at dawn
the way it felt to wake under the sun
light in the self rock under boot
.38 g even in our dreams
and in our hopes for our children

The way the way always came clear
even in the worst of the gimcrack chaos
Ariadne's thread appearing or not
in the peripheral moment lost
lost then found and walking on
a sidewalk through the shattered land

The way so much of it had to be
inferred through the suits we walked in
cut off from the touch of the world
we watched like pilgrims
in love from afar alight
with fire in the body itself felt
as a world the mind apulse in a living
wire of thought tungsten in
darkness the person as planet
the surface of Mars the inside
of our souls aware each
to each and all to all

The way we knew the way had changed
and never again would remain the same
long enough for us to understand it

The way the place was just there
the way you were just thinking stone there

The way everything we thought we knew
in the sky fell away and left us
standing in the visible world
patterned by wind to a horizon
you could almost touch a little
prince on a little world looking for

The way the stars shone at noon
on the flanks of the big volcanoes
poking through the sky itself
out into space we walked in space
and on the sand at once and knew
we knew we were not at home the way

We always knew we were not
at home we are visitors on this planet
the Dalai Lama said on Earth
we are here a century at most
and during that time we must try
to do something good something useful

The way the Buddha did with our lives
the way on Mars we always knew this
always saw it in the bare face
of the land under us the spur
and gully shapes of our lives
all bare of ornamentation
red rock red dust the bare
mineral here of now
and we the animals standing in it

TWO YEARS

We were brothers in those days you and I
Mom off to work ten hours a day
No child care no friends no family

So off we went on our merry way
To a nearby park walled by city streets
Where Jamaican nannies watched us play

One eye on their charges all stunned by the heat
Kids here and there mom following daughter
Me following you so cautious and neat

Hands gripped as you rose on the teeter-totter
Intent as you stepped on the bouncy bridge
Then tossed your head back burbling laughter

When you reached solid ground and stood on the edge
Looking back at the span you had crossed without falling
Plop on the grass to eat our first lunch

You tease as we eat your laughter upwelling
Pretend to refuse your apple juice
Knock it aside and laugh at its spilling

And laugh again at the flight of a bluejay
Off to used bookstores' dim musty aisles
Retrieving the books you have pulled out and used

To toss on the ground and collect people's smiles
Until I stop you and you throw a fit
And so into the backpack off hiking for miles

Your forehead snug on the back of my neck
Home then to microwave Mom's frozen milk
So that when you wake ravenous for it

I'll have tested the temperature with a lick
And can lay you out in my elbow's nook
And watch you suck to the last *squick squick*

And then you nap again I write my book
And for an hour I am on Mars
Or sitting at my desk lost in thought as I look

Down at the perpetual parade of cars
Your cry wakes us both from this dream
And we're back at it the movement of the stars

No more regular than our routine
Untellable tedium not just the diapers
The spooning of food the screams

But also the weekly pass of the street sweeper
The hours together playing with blocks
I set them up you knock them down nothing neater

And all the time you learning to talk
Glossolalia peppered with names
Simple statements firm orders Let go walk

Telling me to do things a game
That made you laugh also knowing
When things were in different ways the same

Blue truck blue sky your face glowing
With delight as your language grew
Till description became a kind of telling

Power I spit out the sun I sky the blue
Sitting in that living room together
Each in his own world surprised by new

Things spaced out lost to each other
Used to each other like Siamese twins
Confined to the house by steamy weather

Me watching volleyball on ESPN
Listening to Beethoven reading the *Post*
You moving your trucks around babbling when

You felt like it absorbed focused lost
In your own space so fully that watching you
I forgot my many selves collapsed to one and was most

Happy the past is gone David I asked beloved of
God do you remember Bethesda
The way my mother would have

Asked me Do you remember Zion
And David looked at me curiously and said No
Dad not really I know how the house looked but all

That comes from pictures in Mom's albums you know
Yes my first memory is not of Zion but
California the Christmas I was three a brown

Trike put together by my dad next to the tree but
My dad tells me he bought the trike assembled
How can we say what did or did not

Happen David watching you I tremble
You know the world are sophisticated
You say you do not remember

That time and now you know so much of hate
Of anguish of death
Will you ever again be so elated

By the sight of swans swimming under the wharf
Shrieking with laughter as they dove for tossed bread
I hope we are these moments deeper than self

Deeper than memory always connected
Inside each other hoping
This helps hope stave off dread

Brother of mine boy receding
I will try to remember for us
The time when you could be so purely happy

I SAY GOOD-BYE TO MARS

Hiking alone in the Sierra Nevada
I stopped one evening in Dragon Basin
Above treeline by a small stream

Trickling down a flaw in the granite
On the floor of this crack were
Lush little lawns green moss

Furring the banks krummholz bonsai
Clustering over low black falls
Transparent water glossed on top

Standing there I looked
Over the fellfield basin a cupped
Hand of stone catching rocks

Inlaid with a tapestry of plants
Lichen sedge and saxifrage
Tippling green the pebble all bare

Under jagged ridges splintering the sky
Beside the rill I made my camp
Ground cloth foam pad sleeping bag

Pack for a pillow stove at my feet
In the failing light my dinner steaming
To the gurgle of water and the sky

And the stars popping into existence
Over the crest of the range still
Alpenglow pink spiking indigo

The line between the colors pulsing
As they faded to two shades of black the number
Of stars amazing the Milky Way perfectly

Articulating my fall up and into sleep
And was never tired
Dreamed the same dreams

And heard the rockslides rattle and thunder
In the throats of these living mountains
Something woke me I put on my glasses

I lay looking up at stars and the Perseids
Meteors darting across the starry black
Every few heartbeats every direction

Fast slow long short far near
White or some a shade of red some
Seeming to hiss slow down break up

Firing great sparks away to the sides
In their wakes I watched held by granite
Entrained to a meteor shower beyond

Any I had imagined possible the stars
Still fixed in their places lighting
The great shattered granite walls

Of the basin all pale witness
Together to fireworks one
Plowing the air right over the peaks

Fizzing sparks over Fin Dome
One shot down just overhead
Wow I cried and sat up to look

As a great BOOM knocked me into
A dark land sparked by fire
Fires burning My God

I cried oh my God oh my God
Struggling to get out of bag into boots
On my feet out stumbling around a smell

Like autumn leaves burning the past
I took up my water bag and crashed about
Quenching fires that reignited

As I ran to the next oh my God
And ran to the stream and stopped thinking
That here was the action of my life

Putting out fires where there was no wood
Vision crisscrossed with afterimages
Of the final fall green bolts

In every blink of the eye finally
I stood in the dark understanding
There was no need to hurry

I came to a chunk of vivid orange
A stone standing alone on a slab
A meteorite still glowing with heat

I sat down before it
I calmed my breathing
Cross-legged I watched it glow

I put my hand out to it
I could feel its heat some distance
Away the pure color of fire

Films feathering on its surface
Incandescent in the night
Illuminating the glacial polish

Of the slab reflecting in that black
Mirror the night quiet the air still
Slightly smoky the stars again

Fixed in their places the meteor
Shower past its peak the stream
Chuckling as it had all along

Oblivious to the life in the sky
A companion of sorts as I watched
The burning visitation warm

My hands as it filmed over
Darkening in its orange
Brilliance until it was both orange

And black I went to get my sleeping
Bag to drape me in my vigil
Sleep gone again so many nights

Like that but this time justified by
My visitor cooling aglow black flakes
Crusting over growing

Orange darker underneath
The moon rose over the jagged peaks
Bathed the basin in its cool light

Flecked the water in the stream
Dark air holding invisible light
The meteorite now black over orange

Still warm still the center
Of all that basin dark on its slab
Of polished pale granite

In the dawn the rock was purest black
Of course I took it home with me
And put it on the mantelpiece as a

Memento of that night and a mark
Of where we stand in the world but
I will always remember how it felt

The night it shot down out of the sky
And it glowed orange as I sat beside it
And it warmed me like a little sun

Purple Mars

He crawls out of troubled dreams half-stunned and begging for coffee. Out to the family around the kitchen table. Breakfast a succession of Cassatts as painted by Bonnard, or Hogarth.

"Hey I'm going to finish my book today."

"Good."

"David hurry up and get dressed, it's almost time for school."

David looks up from a book. "What?"

"Get *dressed* it's almost *time*. Tim do you want cereal?"

"No."

"Okay." He puts Tim back on a chair in front of cereal. "This okay?"

"No." Shoveling it in.

School time approaches and David begins his daily reenactment of Zeno's paradox, a false conundrum first proposed by Zeno, concerning Achilles and how the closer it came time to go to school the slower Achilles moved and the less he heard from the surrounding world, until he entered an entirely different space-time continuum interacting very weakly with this one. Wondering how Neutrino Boy can ever have become so absentminded, his father reads the coffee cups while grinding the beans for his little morning pitcher of Greek coffee. He used to drink espresso, a coffee drink made by vapor extraction, but recently he has advanced to a muddy Greek coffee he makes himself, savoring the smells as he works. On Mars the thinner atmosphere would not allow him to smell things as well, and so nothing there would taste as good as this morning coffee. In fact it might be a culinary nightmare on Mars, everything tasting like dust, partly because it was dusty. But they would adjust to that if they could.

"Are you ready yet?"

"What?"

He bundles Tim into the bike cart with a bowl of cereal, bikes behind David through the village to school. It is late summer at the 37th latitude north, and flowers spangle the sides of the bike path. Clouds puff like puffy clouds in the sky. "If we were biking to school on Mars it would be easier to pedal but we'd be colder."

"On Venus we'd be colder."

Schoolyard full of kids. "Have a good day at school. Listen to your teacher."

"What?"

He pedals to Tim's day-care, drops him off, then rides quickly home. There he writes a list of things to do, which makes him feel virtuous and helps to organize his inchoate feeling that there is too much to do, which in itself is helpful, which leads him to think that things aren't really as bad as he thought, which gives him the inspiration to turn the list into a paper airplane and shoot it at the trash can. Not that any causation can be deduced from this sequence. But things will work out. Or not.

He decides that before working he will mow his lawn. You have to mow a yard before the grass reaches knee high, especially if you use a push mower, which he does, for reasons ecological, aesthetic, athletic, and psychopathological. His next-door neighbor waves to him and he stops abruptly, stunned by a realization. "On Mars these grass clippings would fly out the mower right over my head! I'd have to pull the basket behind me somehow! But the grass wouldn't be as green."

"You don't think so?" says the neighbor.

Back inside to recover the list and check off mowing. Then he rushes to his desk ready to write. Immense concentration brought to bear instantaneously, or at least as soon as another cup of black mud hits the bloodstream. The first word for the day comes quickly:

"The"

Of course it might not be the right word. He considers it. Time passes in a double helix of eternal no-time, in the blessing that cannot be spoken. He revises, rewrites, restructures. The phrase grows, shrinks, grows, shrinks, changes color. He tries it as free verse, sestina, mathematical equation, glossolalia. Finally he returns to the original formulation, complexifying it with an added nuance:

"The End"

It says what needs to be said; and it's twice as many words as his usual daily output. Time to party.

The printer prints out the typescript of the novel as he rides over and picks up Tim from day-care. Back at home he changes the boy's diaper. The boy's protests and the buzzing printer are counterpoint in the warm summer air. Davis warm summer air; 109 degrees, at least in the antiquated Fahrenheit scale used to accommodate twentieth-century American readers who cannot conceptualize Celsius, not to mention the eminently practical and extremely interesting Kelvin scale, which begins at absolute zero where really one ought to begin. At this moment it is over 300 Kelvin, unless he has miscalculated.

"Boy this is a stinky one."

Which when one considers it is rather amazing: Diapers stink because of volatile gases released from poop, gases made of organic molecules that did not exist in the earlier ages of the cosmos, among the first generation of stars. Thus these smells are only possible after enough stars have exploded to saturate the galaxy with complex atoms; so every molecule of the scent is a sign of the immense age of the universe, and of life's likely omnipresence as a late emergent phenomenon, and taken as such a cosmological mystery, in that it indicates an increase of order in an entropic system, i.e., a miracle. Amazing!

The phone rings, carrying to him in electrons flying through complicated continuous pathways of metal the digitalized voice of his beloved, re-created in his ear by the vibration of small cones of reinforced cardboard.

"Oh hi babe."

"Hi." A quick exchange of information and endearments, ending with, "Remember to put the potatoes in the oven."

"Oh okay. What temperature again?"

"About three-seventy-five."

"That's Fahrenheit?"

"Yes."

"Hey that reminds me, I had an epiphany when I was changing Tim's diaper!"

"Did you. What was it?"

"Um—uh-oh. I forget."

"Good. But don't forget the potatoes."

"I won't."

"I love you."

"And I love you."

When the printer finishes the stack of paper is waist-high. "Three! Three! Three!" says Tim.

"Many threes," he agrees, feeling some alarm at the length of the thing, as well as guilt for the trees chopped down to publish it; but doubt is the peripheral vision of courage's foresight. "A genuine bug crusher all right."

Tim tries to help by pulling out pages and eating them.

"No, wait. Continuity is already abused enough in this, stop that."

"No."

He boxes the typescript in three boxes, fending off the ravenous child. "Here have a cookie."

He gives Tim cookies while addressing and stamping the boxes, exhibiting that ambidextrous bilateral competence so characteristic of contemporary American parents—all boasting hypertrophic corpus callosums, no doubt, could one but see them. "All right, let's walk these down to the mailbox, if we hurry we'll get there before pickup time. I'll have to carry them so you get in the baby backpack, okay?"

"No."

"In the big-boy backpack then. Yes."

Ten minutes of ingenious wrestling gets Tim into the baby backpack and onto his back, a victory on points only as his lip is split and he is now vulnerable to ear boxing.

"Ow stop that."

"No."

Now a squat to pick up the three boxes, and his ears are grabbed rather than boxed as Tim tries to stay in the backpack. A mighty jerk and lift and he is standing, toddler counterbalancing the weight of the boxes cradled against his chest.

"Oof! This would be sixty-two percent easier on Mars! Here, let's see if we can walk. No problem. Oh the door isn't open. Hmm. Here, can you open it Tim? Just twist the knob? Please? Here I'll bend over just a bit more . . . oops. Never mind, I can do it now. Here, let me do it. Let me."

"No."

"Okay, we're up again. We're off. Oh—what about the potatoes in the oven! Will we remember that when we get back?"

"No."

"Yes we will. Tell you what, I'll leave the door open and when we see it we'll say, 'Oh yeah, door open, put potatoes in oven.' Off we go."

Into the street. Winding village lane, flanked by flowers and trees. Terraforming at its finest: flat desert valley, now blooming with plants from all over the planet. All overlooked in the long march to the post-box carrying forty kilos of paper and a writhing toddler.

"Ah. Oh. Ow."

Sweating, trembling, he reaches the postbox and rests his load on top.

"We made it. We're here at last. Can you believe it?"

"No."

The typescript boxes are almost too big to fit through the slot. Push them in. A nearby stick will serve well. Beat them through one by one.

"You should have eaten a few more pages. I know just which ones I should have given you."

"No."

Last one through. Mission accomplished.

He stands there for a moment, sweat overwhelming the evolutionary purpose of his eyebrows and stinging even his spirit's vision. "Let's go home."

"No."

They start back down the lane. The sun is setting at the end of the street, and the clouds in the western sky have turned gold, orange, bronze, violaceous, burgundy, pewter, and a touch of chartreuse. Walk on my friends walk on: Even if posterity laughs at the silly boxed lives we lead in the late twentieth century, even if we deserve to be laughed at, which we do, there are still these moments of freedom we give ourselves, walking down a lane at sunset with a child babbling on one's back. "Oops, we left the door open." Like a Zen master his boy whacks him on the side of the head, and at that moment he experiences an enlightenment or satori: The planet wheels underfoot. The signifier signifies a great significance. And the potatoes are to go in the oven. Happiness makes him light on his feet, very light, so light that he is almost floating, so light that if you tried to quantify this quality, if you could put him on the scale of human feeling and weigh him, his weight (in Terran kilograms) would clock in at exactly 3.14159265358979323846264338327950288419 7 . . .

About the Author

KIM STANLEY ROBINSON is the author of the Nebula and Hugo Award–winning Mars trilogy, *Red Mars*, *Green Mars*, and *Blue Mars*, as well as *Antarctica*, *The Wild Shore*, *The Gold Coast*, *Pacific Edge*, *A Short, Sharp Shock*, and other novels. He lives in Davis, California.